OK s/org

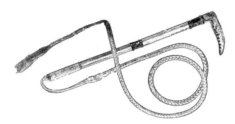

ALSO BY

Jan Neuharth

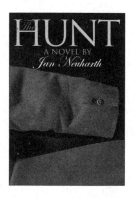

The CHASE

A NOVEL BY
Jan Neuharth

PAPER CHASE FARMS PUBLISHING GROUP
MIDDLEBURG, VIRGINIA

Published by
Paper Chase Farms Publishing Group
a division of Paper Chase Farms, Inc.
Post Office Box 448
Middleburg, Virginia 20118
www.paperchasefarms.com

This novel is a work of fiction. Names, characters, places, organizations, business establishments, events and incidents are either products of the author's imagination or are used fictitiously. Any resemblance to actual events, locales, or persons, living or dead, is entirely coincidental.

Library of Congress Control Number: 2006901088

ISBN-13: 978-0-9729503-2-9
ISBN-10: 0-9729503-2-X

PRINTED IN THE UNITED STATES OF AMERICA

First Edition
Second Printing December 2006
Book design by Judy Walker

For Al and Loretta

*M*any individuals gave generously of their time to assist with the research for this novel. I am indebted to them for sharing their expertise and grateful for their good-natured tolerance of my often ignorant questions. The fault for any errors or inaccuracies lies solely with me. My sincere thanks to Loudoun County Sheriff Steve Simpson; Dr. Nat White, Director of the Marion duPont Scott Equine Medical Center; and Dr. Edward Puccio, Janell Hoffman, RN, Lida Leech, RN, and Alyssa Menzenwerth, RN, from INOVA Loudoun Hospital Center.

My appreciation and respect go to the talented professionals who worked with me on this book: my editors, Jerry Gross, Karen Stedman, and Carol Edwards; photographers, Janet Hitchen and Chris Considine; and my book designer, Judy Walker.

Heartfelt thanks to friends and colleagues who kindly gave their time, support, and advice: Janell Hoffman, Fern Kucinski, Michelle Martinson, Marion Pietruszewski, Del Walters, and Yvonne Weber.

A special thanks to the Alcock family, Marion and Grant Chungo, Eve Fout, and Shelly O'Higgins for the title page photo shoot of the Middleburg Orange County Beagles.

Finally, my deepest gratitude goes to my family: Al and Dan, who selflessly spent more time reading and giving me feedback than their schedules permitted; Loretta, for her behind-the-scenes support and motherly love; Dani and A.J., my greatest fans, whose enthusiasm never wavered, even when my writing interfered with family activities; and Joseph, my real-life hero and expert in all things equestrian, whose contribution, as always, was invaluable.

P R O L O G U E

IN PRISON

Zelda McGraw shifted in the metal chair and crossed her legs, wiggling one foot nervously as she glanced at the clock that hung askew on the gray cinder-block wall. *Why was it taking them so long to bring Zeb out?*

The scrawny guard by the door to the cells had been eyeing her ever since she'd sat down, and Zelda's heart quickened as she stole a glance in his direction. *He was still staring at her. Did he suspect something?*

She twirled a strand of bleached hair around her finger and forced herself to look nonchalantly around the half-full visitation room. The guard by the main door wasn't paying her any mind, and the guard on the far side of the room had his eyes fixed on a beefy red-haired inmate seated near him.

Zelda wiped her palms on her jeans and turned back towards the cell-block door, letting out a rush of air as she saw a guard lead Zeb into the room. As her brother shuffled towards her, Zelda couldn't help noticing his ashen complexion and how loosely the orange-and-white-striped uniform hung on his gaunt frame. It seemed as if he'd lost more hair since the last time she'd been to visit, and she winced at the sight of the straggly graying strands that swept haphazardly from above his left ear across his shiny scalp.

Zeb gave her a nod as he lowered himself into the seat across from her, but neither of them spoke until the guard was out of earshot.

"What took so long?" Zelda asked.

Zeb glared in the direction of the guard who had led him in. "That guard's a fat, lazy ass. He told me he took a cigarette break before he came to get me."

Zelda's eyes darted towards the fat guard, who was leaning against the wall, gabbing with the guard by the cell-block door.

"Are you sure that's it? The guard by the door keeps staring at me. What if they suspect something?" Zelda whispered.

Zeb glanced over his shoulder. "They don't suspect nothing. He probably just thinks you're hot."

Zelda stole a quick look at the scrawny guard and smiled as she stuck her chest out and flung her hair over her shoulder. Sure enough, he smiled back at her and said something to the fat guard.

She heaved a sigh of relief. "I think you're right."

"Of course I'm right." His eyes bore into hers. "So, fill me in."

Zelda leaned towards him. "It won't be long now. I've got good news."

The corners of Zeb's lips twitched. "Tell me."

"Zach got the job."

"Yeah? Has he met Cummings yet?"

"No, but he will."

Zeb nodded his approval, then motioned with his eyes towards the other side of the room. "See the big dude over there?"

Zelda pretended to stretch as she looked over her shoulder.

"You mean the scary-looking guy with all the hair?" she asked, turning back to Zeb.

Zeb nodded. "That's Big Red. He's my ticket out of here. The chick with him is his wife, Gwen. She's going to wait for you outside and give you her phone number. From now on, you give messages to Gwen. She'll tell Big Red when she comes to visit, and he'll tell me. I don't want you coming back here after today."

Zelda frowned at him. "Why can't we keep on with the way we've been doing things?"

"Once shit starts happening to Cummings in a couple of weeks, they'll be watching me like a hawk. I want them to think I haven't had contact with anyone on the outside."

"I don't like it," Zelda said, shaking her head.

He scowled. "Why not?"

"She's not family. I don't even know her. What if she screws up the message? Or rats us out?"

"Gwen ain't going to rat us out, Zelda. She's got a stake in it. Big Red's share goes to her. Besides, Earl's not family, either. And he's doing okay, ain't he?"

Zelda broke into a smile at the mention of Earl's name. "Yeah. Earl's doing just fine."

Zeb narrowed his eyes and hunched forward in his chair. "You and Earl got something going again?"

"That ain't none of your business, Zeb," Zelda replied, feeling a flush creep up her cheeks.

"The hell it ain't!"

Zelda felt the small hairs stand up on the back of her neck, but she glared right back at him, refusing to let him stare her down. After a moment, Zeb waved his hand dismissively and sank back in his chair.

"Hook up with Earl again if you want, Zelda. I don't give a shit. Just don't let it screw up the plan."

"I ain't going to do nothing to screw up our plan, Zeb. Zeke was my brother, too. I want to make Doug Cummings pay just as much as you do."

Zeb shot her a chilling look. "You're wrong about that, Zelda. No one wants Cummings as bad as I do."

CHAPTER

1

Something was driving Chancellor crazy.

Doug Cummings ran his gloved hand down his horse's neck as the big Thoroughbred stomped his foot and snorted, tossing his head wildly from side to side. A swarm of gnats buzzed around Chancellor's ears and Doug batted them away, but the horse continued to prance as they rode down the trail, tugging on the reins and flinging his head low between his front legs.

"Hey, boy, what's bothering you?" Doug said, leaning forward in the saddle to see if he could spot anything on Chancellor's chest.

Chancellor yanked his head to the left, biting at his side, and kicked out with both hind legs. Something sharp stung the back of Doug's neck, and he swatted at it, then ducked as several insects buzzed around his head.

"*Bees,*" Doug yelled over his shoulder, kicking Chancellor into a canter. Chancellor leapt forward and Doug heard the clamor of hooves as horses behind him scrambled to escape the swarm of bees. A low-hanging branch slapped Doug's face, and he raised his arm to shield himself from the dense summer foliage as Chancellor galloped up the trail towards the open field that lay ahead.

As they burst into the clearing, Doug spotted the master of the Middleburg Foxhounds, Richard Evan Clarke, and his group of riders a short distance down the field. Smitty, the huntsman, rode beside Richard. Smitty raised his arm in greeting and Doug cantered Chancellor towards the group.

"Whoa, boy." Doug leaned back and pulled on the reins as he neared Richard.

"I thought you were leading the slow group for the trail ride today, Doug," Richard said with a smile. "You're going at a faster pace than we were."

"Not by design," Doug said breathlessly. "We stirred up a nest of bees."

"Did everyone get by all right?" Smitty asked.

Doug turned in the saddle. "I'm not sure. It just happened. We were down the trail in Snyder's woods."

The men watched as a string of a dozen or so riders cantered into the clearing and rode towards them.

"Is everyone okay?" Doug called.

Wendy Brooks, the hunt secretary, shook her head as she pulled her horse to a stop in front of them. "A couple of Margaret Southwell's students are having a hard time. One little girl got bucked off, but someone retrieved her pony for her, and she got right back on. I think she's fine."

She paused and caught her breath. "Then one of Margaret's adult riders freaked out when the horses started acting up from the bees, and she jumped off and refuses to get back on."

Doug smiled. "I'll bet I know which one it was. The short woman with the dark hair, right?"

Wendy raised an eyebrow. "How'd you know?"

"I thought Margaret might have a problem with her. She was uptight before the trail ride even began."

Smitty chuckled. "I'll bet Margaret's fit to be tied."

Wendy nodded. "That's putting it mildly."

"Where are they?" Doug asked, eyeing the tree line.

"Margaret turned back with her riders and is taking the trail by the creek so they don't have to go through the bees. They're taking it slow, though, because the one lady is on foot."

Doug glanced down at Chancellor. He was lathered with sweat and still breathing hard, but he didn't appear to be having an adverse reaction to the bee stings. "I'll go give them a hand."

"Do you want us to wait for you here?" Richard asked.

Doug shook his head and gathered up his reins. "I'll meet you back at the trailers."

Wendy brought her horse alongside Chancellor. "I'll go with you."

"Great," Doug said, trying to hide his look of surprise. Wendy had pretty much avoided him since Nancy Williams's death the previous fall.

Doug urged Chancellor into a trot. "If we cut through Hunter's Haven Farm, we can meet up with them on the creek trail."

Wendy nodded and they rode in silence until they reached the gate that led to the back pasture at Hunter's Haven. Doug dismounted and opened the gate, pulling Chancellor out of the way so Wendy could walk her horse through first.

Wendy hesitated. "Doug."

"Yes?"

Her round face reddened and she averted her eyes. "I just wanted to say I'm sorry."

He frowned. "For what?"

"For not trusting you." She waved her hand in the air. "For telling that horrible deputy that I feared you had something to do with Nancy's death. And for what I said to that television reporter."

Doug drew in a deep breath. *This was a conversation he'd rather not have right now. Wendy was dredging up memories he had worked hard to forget.*

"You really hurt Nancy when you broke up with her, Doug. I was angry with you for that, and I guess I just wasn't thinking straight."

Doug lowered his gaze and let Chancellor nuzzle his hand. "You weren't the only person who suspected me."

"I know. But we've been friends a long time and I should have known better. I'm truly sorry. And I shouldn't have waited this long to tell you that."

Chancellor nudged his head against Doug's chest, and Doug stroked his horse's face, still slick with sweat from the encounter with the bees. *What should he say? No problem, Wendy. You falsely accused me of murder, but no hard feelings.*

He forced a smile. "Thanks, Wendy. I appreciate it."

She gazed down at him from her horse. "It must have been so hard on you. The murders. Then Samantha being kidnapped. But at least Zeb McGraw is in jail, where he belongs. Thanks to you."

A chill crept up Doug's spine; he pushed McGraw's image from his thoughts. "We'd better get going if we want to find Margaret and her group," he said, gesturing towards the open gate.

Wendy nodded and kicked her horse forward. Doug led Chancellor after her, fastening the chain on the gate, then stepped up on one of the fence boards to climb into the saddle. As Doug gathered the reins, Chancellor tensed and perked his ears, staring towards the tree line at the bottom of the hill. Doug tilted his head and listened.

"Come on. I think they're down there."

Wendy trotted after him down the grassy hillside. As they entered the woods, Doug pulled Chancellor back to a walk.

"Careful. It looks like that downpour we had last week really washed this trail out," he said over his shoulder as he let Chancellor pick his way through the rocks and roots that jutted into the steep trail.

When they reached the creek, Doug stopped for a moment, listening. The musky scent of damp earth and lush undergrowth was heavy, and the muggy air seemed to close in around him.

"Do you think we missed them?" Wendy asked.

Doug brushed a deerfly off Chancellor's neck. "No, they haven't passed by here yet. There aren't any fresh hoofprints."

Wendy turned and looked up the trail.

"Hear them?" Doug said after a moment. "It sounds like they're just around the bend."

The slow sound of hoofbeats grew louder and a few minutes later the group came into sight. Margaret Southwell was in the lead, on a big chestnut horse, and she held the reins of a riderless brown horse. A man, a woman, and two girls rode behind Margaret, and a woman on foot lagged about twenty feet behind them.

When Margaret saw them, she raised her reins in greeting. "I hope you didn't come out here looking for us."

"Sorry about the trouble with the bees," Doug said. "I hope everyone's all right."

Margaret shook her head dismissively, making her gray curls brush across the collar of her navy polo shirt. "Bees are just a fact of life when it comes to summer trail rides. I'm sorry I brought along a student who obviously wasn't up to participating with the group."

Doug detected an uncustomary sharpness in Margaret's deep drawl and he smiled at her. "Don't worry about it. That's one of the reasons we host these trail rides, remember? For inexperienced riders and young horses."

The woman on foot had caught up with them. "I heard what you said, Margaret, and I'm sorry if I'm an embarrassment to you." She paused, gasping for air, and wiped a trickle of sweat off her flushed cheek with her gloved hand. "I told you I was frightened when I first got on the horse. You were the one who insisted that I stick it out and come along on the trail ride."

Margaret pursed her lips. "You said you want to foxhunt this fall, Evelyn. The only way to get ready for hunting is by sitting on a horse."

The woman shot her a look but didn't say anything.

Doug cleared his throat. "I don't believe we've met. I'm Doug Cummings. I was leading your group when we stirred up the bees."

The woman gave him a brief smile. "Hello. I'm Evelyn Jacobs."

"I'm sorry about the bees, Evelyn. It can be a frightening experience when the horses get all riled up like that. I'm glad no one was hurt."

"*Frightening* doesn't begin to describe it. I've never seen Mouse act like that. I've ridden him dozens of times in the ring and he's always been good as gold."

"Well, sometimes the horses get a little more excited in the field than they do in the ring. It's the herd instinct." Doug glanced at the riderless horse next to Margaret. "Mouse seems to have settled down just fine. I'm sure you won't have a problem if you get back on him now."

Evelyn shook her head vehemently. "Not in a million years."

"You're wasting your time, Doug; I've already had this conversation with Evelyn." Margaret's blue eyes flashed beneath the black velvet brim of her hunt cap.

Doug took a deep breath. "Look, Evelyn, it's a pretty long hike back to the trailers on foot, and the forecast is for severe thunderstorms this afternoon. You don't want to be caught out here in bad weather."

Evelyn didn't respond, but she squinted towards the sky, and Doug dismounted and looped Chancellor's reins over his arm.

"Mind if I take Mouse?" he asked, approaching Margaret.

Margaret handed him the reins. "Be my guest."

Doug looped the thong of his hunt whip through the ring on Mouse's bit and looked at Evelyn. "How about if you get back on Mouse and I lead you next to my horse? I'll have hold of Mouse the whole time. Nothing bad will happen. I promise."

Evelyn eyed the whip skeptically. "Can you really control him like that?"

"Absolutely. Come on, I'll give you a leg up."

By the time Doug led the group into the field where the trailers were parked, most of the rest of the riders had already loaded their horses and were mingling around the picnic table.

Richard Evan Clarke met them at the gate. "I was beginning to worry about you. Is everyone all right?"

"We're fine," Doug said.

Richard eyed the makeshift lead Doug had fashioned from the hunt whip. "Would you like me to give you a hand?"

Before Doug could respond, Margaret said, "For God's sake, Evelyn, you can ride back on your own from here to my trailer."

Evelyn smiled at Doug. "I think I'm okay now. Thank you so much for taking care of me."

"No problem." Doug released his hold on the hunt whip's thong and pulled it free from Mouse's bit.

"Margaret, do you need assistance loading the horses?" Richard asked.

She shook her head. "I brought a groom along. He should be waiting at my trailer."

"All right. See you at the picnic."

Margaret turned her horse towards the trailers. "Thank you, Doug. I owe you."

"Nonsense. I was happy to help."

Wendy waved at Richard and Doug as she rode after Margaret. "See you in a few minutes."

"Wendy."

She turned around. "Yes, Doug?"

"Thanks. For what you said earlier."

She smiled. "I'm glad I cleared the air."

Doug waited until she rode off, then dismounted and rolled up his stirrups. "I think I'll just grab a bottle of water and hit the road."

Richard shook his head good-naturedly as they walked towards the food table. "Let me guess. You're going to the office. It's *Saturday*, you know."

Doug smiled. "Actually, the law firm's going to have to cope without me for a day. Anne's baby shower is today. I promised Samantha I'd be home when they return from the shower, so she can show me all the presents."

"Give Anne my best, will you?"

Doug reached into the ice chest for a bottle of water. "Of course."

"Thanks again for leading the nonjumping group today. Will you be at Margaret's Wednesday evening for our board meeting?"

"You bet. See you then."

Doug had parked near the entrance to the field, and as he walked Chancellor past the other horse trailers, he loosed the girth and took note of the welts on his horse's neck and side.

"Those bees really got you, didn't they, buddy?" Doug said, running his hand over Chancellor's neck. "Let's get you home so Billy can give you a cool Vetrolin bath and treat those bites."

He quickly untacked Chancellor and offered him some water, then loaded him on the trailer and climbed into the Range Rover. As he drove the short distance to the road, Doug directed the air vents towards his face and sighed as he felt the welcome blast of cold air.

Doug slowed the rig as he reached Route 7, but traffic was light and he pulled out of the drive onto the divided highway without stopping. As he accelerated up the long hill, he saw the brake warning light illuminate on the dash.

"Damn this car," Doug muttered. He'd had the Range Rover in the shop twice during the last month for false warnings from the onboard computer. He ignored the warning light and continued to step on the accelerator.

The rig crested the hill and Doug eased up on the gas, settling into his cruising speed. The view from the mountain never failed to impress him, and he took a deep breath and let it out slowly as he surveyed the lush countryside down in the valley. Subdivisions hadn't invaded that part of Loudoun County yet, and the landscape was green as far as the eye could see. A peaceful patchwork of dense woods, neatly planted crops, and rolling meadows.

The road began a steep descent and Doug stepped on the brake, turning his attention back to the highway. But the brake pedal offered no resistance, and Doug's pulse quickened as his foot sank to the floorboard.

C H A P T E R
3

*D*oug tightened his grip on the steering wheel as the Range Rover barreled down the hill towards a hairpin curve in the highway. Once again, he pumped the brake pedal, but the brakes failed to engage. Doug lowered his right hand and groped between the bucket seats for the emergency brake lever, peering at the reflection of the horse trailer in the exterior mirror.

"Hold on, Chancellor," he murmured, bracing himself for a jolt as he pressed the brake-release knob and yanked up on the handle.

Nothing happened.

Doug lowered the lever and pulled again.

Still nothing.

Doug slid his right hand under the dash and felt for the trailer's brake control, praying that the trailer brakes would be strong enough to stop the rig. His fingers brushed against the plastic box, and he fumbled for the brake switch, holding the steering wheel tightly as he pressed the button.

Nothing.

Doug jabbed at the button again. Twice. Three times. But the trailer brakes didn't engage.

"Damn it!" He released the button and slammed his fist into the steering wheel. *What the hell was going on?*

Doug's eyes darted towards the shoulder next to him. The narrow asphalt strip gave way to a steep embankment, which fell sharply towards a jagged tree line. He forced his eyes back to the highway. The stretch of road that lay before him snaked to the left through the turn, then straightened out as it began the steep climb up Mount Weather. If he managed to keep the rig on the highway through the hairpin turn, he might have a chance. Doug's palms were sweaty, and he fleetingly spread his fingers and slid them slightly along the leather-covered steering wheel, then wrapped his hands firmly around it again.

"Steady," he murmured as the vehicle's front wheels entered the sharp curve. Doug's muscles strained as he fought to hold the vehicle on course, but momentum overcame him, and the SUV shot sideways through the curve, skidded across the shoulder, and lurched down the hillside.

The vehicle bucked over the rough terrain and Doug was flung into the shoulder harness as a large bump hurled the vehicle into the air; then he slammed against the headrest as the Range Rover dropped back to the ground. For an instant, the descent was so steep, Doug couldn't see the ground in front of him, and, in spite of the air conditioning that was blasting from the vents, he felt sweat pour down his temples and slide down his neck.

Doug drew a deep breath and let it out slowly. "Don't lose it now," he muttered.

The land leveled out, to reveal a rugged rock outcropping directly in front of him, and Doug pulled the steering wheel hard to the left. The right front tire slammed into the rocks, launching the SUV onto its two left wheels, where it teetered precariously, threatening to flip. Doug whipped the steering wheel back to the right, and his breath escaped in a rush as he felt the vehicle steady itself.

The back of the Range Rover jerked to the left, and Doug cast a quick glance in the mirror, feeling his stomach lurch as he saw the trailer sway wildly. Chancellor's throaty whinny pierced the air, and Doug heard the scramble of hooves as his horse struggled to maintain his balance.

"Come on, Chancellor. Hang in there," he urged through clenched teeth.

The rig careened toward a band of trees, and beyond that the terrain dropped sharply. A branch smacked the windshield as Doug managed to maneuver the Range Rover around a massive maple, and the tree line sped towards him in a blur of green. Feathery locust trees. Majestic oaks. Towering poplars. With no room to maneuver between them.

"Oh Jesus," Doug moaned.

The enormous root ball of a fallen oak lay in his path, and Doug swerved the vehicle to the left, just barely managing to avoid it. His right front tire dipped into the void the roots had left, and the sudden jolt twisted the steering wheel out of his grasp. He grabbed the wheel again and steadied it as he stole a glance into the exterior mirror. The horse trailer was wider than the SUV, and he swore as he saw the trailer fender smash into the fallen tree. The impact slammed the trailer to the left and flipped it off the hitch onto its side, sending it skidding down the hill.

A dark blur caught Doug's attention and his eyes darted forward an instant before the Range Rover smashed into a towering walnut tree. It happened in a flash, yet at the same time it seemed slow and surreal, like in a dream. Doug watched the shiny black hood buckle and wrap around the rugged chocolate - brown tree trunk, and heard the nauseating screech of twisting metal. The shoulder harness jerked tightly across his chest, and he felt the punch of the air bag. Then the windshield collapsed towards him, and the last thing Doug heard was Chancellor's guttural scream.

*A*nne Cummings shifted restlessly in the deep chair cushion as she accepted the last unopened baby gift from Samantha's outstretched hand. She appreciated Kendall Waters hosting the baby shower for her, but she was relieved it was almost over. Her back ached and she had a splitting headache. And she wanted to be home by the time Doug returned from the trail ride.

The room was warm despite the air conditioning, and Anne regretted her decision that morning to wear her hair down. She was trying to break the habit of always pulling her hair back in a bun: a style Doug called her "lawyer look." Anne removed the card from the gift and fanned herself lightly with it as she held her blond hair up off the back of her neck.

"Look, Mommy," Samantha said. "See the rattle? I'm going to make sure the baby always plays with this rattle, so she'll learn right from the beginning to love horses."

The gift was wrapped in pink-and-blue-striped paper, with a silver rattle shaped like a horse head secured on top. Anne adjusted the pillow behind her back and untied the ribbon. "Don't forget, honey, we don't know if the baby is a boy or a girl. You might be getting a baby brother."

Samantha frowned. "A sister would be better, but if God gives us a boy, that's okay. As long as he likes horses and he doesn't pull on my pigtails the way Tucker does at play group. Boys can be so mean sometimes."

Kendall sat on the floor next to Samantha. She hugged the little girl and pulled her onto her lap. "I agree with you, Samantha. Some boys can be downright horrid." A wisp of Kendall's shoulder-length sleek brown hair slid over her eye, and she reached up absently and tucked it behind her ear as she gave Samantha a smile.

Anne studied Kendall as she handed the rattle to Samantha. Kendall had recently suffered through a painful divorce, and Anne knew just how horrid her husband, Peter, had been. Kendall had the scars to prove it.

Kendall winked at her and Anne smiled back, relieved to see a twinkle in Kendall's wide brown eyes.

"Come on, Mommy, open it," Samantha said.

Anne unfolded the card. *"To Baby Cummings, with love from the Hortons."*

She carefully removed the wrapping paper and lifted the lid from the box. Anne picked her way through a cushion of tissue until she uncovered a china plate, cup, and bowl, adorned with a colorful rocking horse motif, and a small silver spoon with an elegant *C* engraved on the tiny curved handle.

Anne lifted the china set from the box and held it up. "Deb, it's beautiful. Thank you so much."

She looked at the other eight women seated around the room as she placed the china back in the box. "Thank you all for your lovely gifts. I can't think of a thing we still need for the baby."

"What's your due date, Anne?" Helen Dunning asked.

"August eighteenth. As of today I can officially say I only have three weeks left."

"You're not still working, are you?"

Anne shook her head. "I have another attorney handling my cases. I just stay on top of things."

"Well, I'm relieved to hear that. I cringe to think of you being around that criminal element you represent. Especially in your current condition."

"I've never been threatened by one of my clients, Helen."

"Let's hope it stays that way," Helen said with a shudder. "So, anyway, August eighteenth is the big day. I'll have to mark that on my calendar."

"And that's really lucky, because I won't be in school yet, and I'll be able to be there when the baby is born," Samantha said.

"My goodness, you're already big enough to go to school? What grade are you in, Samantha?"

"I'll be in kindergarten when school starts after summer is over."

"Samantha will be going to school with my daughter, Emma," Deb Horton said. "I think you and Emma will have lots of fun in kindergarten, don't you, Samantha?"

"Uh-huh. And we're also going to have fun at our riding lessons."

"Where do you take lessons?" Helen asked.

"At Fox Run Farm. And next week I'm going to riding camp there, and Kendall is going to be my instructor."

Helen raised an eyebrow. "Really? I didn't know you were going to be teaching camp, Kendall. My niece, Caitlin, is signed up for that camp session."

They were interrupted by the shrill ring of the telephone.

Kendall lifted Samantha from her lap and rose from her spot on the floor. "I'm sorry. I'd better answer that. I'm expecting a call from my blacksmith."

She disappeared into the kitchen and the door swung closed behind her.

Helen looked at Anne. "I had no idea Kendall was teaching summer camp at Fox Run."

Anne nodded. "She worked out a deal with Margaret Southwell to board Wellington at Fox Run for the remainder of the summer in exchange for teaching the riding camp."

"There are a lot of things I'd do to get a stall at Fox Run, but I can't say being a camp counselor is one of them," Helen said, laughing. "That seems a little extreme."

"Kendall didn't exactly have the luxury of choice, Helen."

"You don't mean that she had to do it for *financial* reasons, do you?"

Anne didn't respond.

"*Oh my.* I assumed Kendall took Peter to the cleaners. I guess that explains why she's living here."

Deb frowned. "What do you mean by that, Helen? I think Kendall was lucky to find this cottage to lease. It's the perfect size for her, and this setting in the woods is lovely."

"I agree," Helen replied. "I think it's quite charming. Cozy, actually. It's just not what she was used to, that's all."

"Kendall's very happy here," Anne said. "In fact—"

The kitchen door opened and Kendall burst into the room, holding a cordless phone. "Anne, would you come into the kitchen? I need to talk to you." There was a tremor in her voice, as if she might be about to cry.

Anne imagined that Peter had probably managed to throw yet another legal obstacle at Kendall. She rose from the chair and patted the fluffy chintz cushion, motioning for Samantha to sit down. "Samantha, why don't you make a bouquet with the ribbons from the packages? I'll be right back."

Kendall closed the door behind them and pulled a chair out from the kitchen table. "I think you'd better sit down."

"All right." *What on earth was going on?*

Anne settled into the chair. "What's wrong, Kendall?"

Kendall took a deep breath. "It's Doug. There's been an accident."

C H A P T E R

5

*T*raffic was at a standstill, and Jake Dawson beat his fingers impatiently against the outside of the driver's door in rhythm to the country music that was playing on the radio. The sticky heat was sweltering, but he knew if he turned the air conditioning on, the truck was sure to overheat. He'd have to roll up the window soon, though, because dark thunder boomers loomed overhead, and the wind was gusting strong enough to rock the pickup truck. He batted at a fly that buzzed annoyingly around his ear, and craned his neck to see if there was any movement in the traffic.

Jake knew that there was some kind of wreck up ahead and figured it must be bad, because he'd heard three sets of sirens in the ten minutes he'd been sitting there. A helicopter had approached, but after being tossed around by the wind on several landing attempts, it had flown away without setting down.

Fat raindrops began to splatter the truck, and Jake cranked up the driver's window and turned on the wipers. The blades smeared smashed bugs across the windshield, and he depressed the wiper lever a couple of times to squirt fluid on the mess.

A streak of lightning cut through the sky to his left, followed quickly by a sharp crack of thunder, and then the clouds opened up. Blinding rain beat down on the truck, and even with the wipers on full speed, he could barely see beyond the hood. Not that it mattered. It didn't look like he was going to be driving anywhere anytime soon.

Jake removed his cowboy hat and leaned back against the headrest. The radio station was fading in and out, and he reached over and twirled the knob to turn it off. Lack of sleep was beginning to catch up with him. He sighed wearily and closed his eyes, appreciating the sound of the rain on the roof and the rhythmic swoosh of the windshield wipers.

The loud whoop of a siren blared outside his truck, and Jake sat up and saw the flashing lights of an emergency vehicle pass by slowly on the shoulder to his right. The truck windows had fogged up, and he leaned over and used the heel of his hand to clear an area on the passenger side. A brown sheriff's car glided past him, followed closely by a truck hauling a horse trailer. As the truck and trailer passed by, Jake read the writing on the side of the trailer. *Equine Medical Center Horse Ambulance.*

Jake straightened up in his seat and watched for a moment as the receding taillights of the horse ambulance grew dimmer. After a brief hesitation, he put the truck in gear and nosed it onto the shoulder.

The rain still beat down steadily, but the visibility had improved somewhat, and Jake followed the horse ambulance past a couple of dozen vehicles until it stopped short of where two sheriff's cars and a fire truck blocked the road. An ambulance with its lights and siren on was pulling away, but Jake couldn't see any other vehicles or signs of any kind of accident.

A sheriff's deputy climbed out of his car and walked towards the horse ambulance, but when he saw Jake's truck, he held his hand up and gestured for Jake to back up. Jake rolled down the window and waited for the deputy to approach.

The deputy scowled at him. "What do you think you're doing, following behind an emergency vehicle?"

"Sorry, Deputy, I'm not trying to interfere. I saw the horse ambulance and I followed to offer my help."

The deputy gestured towards Jake's cowboy hat, which lay next to him on the seat. "You work with horses?"

"Yes, sir."

"All right," the deputy said, squinting against the blowing rain. "Leave your vehicle here. I'll let the ambulance driver know you've offered to help."

Jake nodded and rolled up the window. He turned off the ignition, pocketed the keys, and opened the door, jamming his cowboy hat on his head before stepping out into the rain. The horse ambulance's driver had just started up the road, and Jake grabbed the front of his hat and ducked his head to keep the rain from blowing in his eyes as he sloshed through rain puddles to catch up with him. By the time he reached the ambulance driver, his T-shirt and jeans were soaked through to his skin.

He could see that the driver was younger than himself, maybe in his late teens, or early twenties. Definitely too young to be a vet. He was wearing muck boots, a yellow rain slicker, and a Redskins baseball cap.

As Jake drew alongside him, the young man extended his hand. "Hi, I'm Steve. Thanks for offering to help."

"I'm Jake. What happened? I see the rescue vehicles, but I don't see any sign of an accident," he said, shaking Steve's hand.

Steve motioned ahead and to the right. "See the tracks? Some guy was hauling a tagalong. He drove off the road and the trailer flipped off the hitch. There's one horse in it. From the call I got, it sounds like the horse is in pretty bad shape."

"Is a vet here?"

Steve shook his head. "No. Another driver saw the guy go off the road and called nine-one-one from his cell phone. When the rescue squad arrived and found the horse trapped in the trailer, they called the Equine Medical Center. The EMC doesn't usually dispatch the ambulance without a vet referral, but in this case they didn't want to waste time waiting for a local vet to get to the scene."

Jake and Steve followed the tire tracks off the road, and as they started down the embankment, a fireman appeared from over the rise and trudged towards them.

"Hey, guys," the fireman greeted them. "I'm sure glad to see you."

"Where's the horse?" Steve asked.

"He's still trapped in the trailer. You can't see it from here." The fireman gestured for them to follow him down the embankment. They half walked and half slid down the muddy slope until the fireman stopped and pointed. "There it is. Down in the tree line."

Jake looked towards the tree line and groaned. An aluminum two-horse trailer lay on its side, wedged between two trees, at the bottom of a steep drop.

Steve whistled. "Holy shit. How are we ever going to get him out of there?"

The fireman grunted in response and started to descend the slope again. "We can provide manpower to help. But we aren't horse people. You'll have to tell us what to do."

They entered an area that was especially thick with undergrowth. The fireman called out over his shoulder, "Watch your feet. I almost fell flat on my face when I came through here earlier."

Jake grabbed a hanging branch for support and picked his way through the brambles. He climbed over a fallen tree trunk and had just jumped down on the other side when he saw Steve flailing his arms in an effort to keep from falling. Steve's feet were caught in a vine, and Jake reached a hand out and caught him by his arm, just in time to keep him from pitching headfirst into a tree. "Careful. We need you in one piece," Jake said, and reached down to help Steve disentangle his feet from the vine.

Steve let out a deep breath and smiled at Jake. "Thanks, man. I think you're my guardian angel today."

They caught up with the fireman, who gestured towards the trees to his left. "Poor guy driving that sure didn't have a guardian angel watching over him."

Jake followed the fireman's gaze and saw a black Range Rover hugging the trunk of a lofty walnut tree. The roof of the vehicle was cut open, revealing a deflated air bag that hung limply from the steering wheel. Jake shuddered as he imagined what had happened to the driver.

"They use the Jaws of Life to get him out?"

The fireman nodded. "Yup. And it wasn't an easy feat getting it down there, I'll tell you that."

They were approaching the horse trailer, and Jake saw a small group gathered around it. The trailer lay on its left side, and the people door on the right side was open towards the sky. A woman in firefighter gear was crouched on top of the trailer, looking inside.

"The rear doors don't look like they sustained too much damage," Steve said. "Hopefully, they're still operable. Let's take a look inside, and see how bad he is, before we try to open up the rear."

They stopped next to the trailer and looked up at the firefighter.

"What's the horse's condition?" Steve asked.

The firefighter looked down at them. "He's was struggling some before, but now he's quieted down. He seems to have difficulty breathing."

Steve stepped back and studied the trailer. "How'd you get up there?"

"I climbed up on the hitch and then pulled myself up with that tree branch." She gestured towards the front of the trailer.

Steve climbed up the same way and peered through the trailer door. "I can't see much. Anyone have a flashlight?"

The firefighter removed a flashlight from her belt and handed it to Steve, who leaned down and aimed the light into the trailer. Jake heard the horse move inside, followed by a thump as one of the horse's hooves kicked the trailer floor.

"Easy, boy, I'm here to help you," Steve said.

Jake looked up at the sky. The clouds still hung heavy, but the fierce rain had let up, and the electrical storm seemed to have passed through the area.

Steve lifted his head out of the doorway and turned to Jake. "I don't see any obvious critical injuries. He has some abrasions on his head and legs, but they don't look too serious. His breathing is awfully labored, though. Why don't you come up here and take a look at him?"

"Wait, I'll come on down, so there isn't too much weight up here," the firefighter said.

Jake waited for her by the hitch, holding out a hand to help her as she jumped down; then he climbed up to join Steve. As soon as he stuck his head inside the trailer and heard the horse's breathing, Jake knew the horse was in serious distress. The sucking sound he made as he tried to breathe in was unmistakable. It was exactly the way his colt had sounded when he'd impaled himself on a metal stake.

"We've got trouble," Jake said, moving to the side and motioning for Steve to lean into the trailer. "Listen to him. Hear that sucking sound? He must have a chest injury. See how flared his nostrils are? He's struggling for air."

He took the flashlight from Steve. "I'm going to climb inside and get a better look at him."

Jake eased into the trailer and crouched near the horse's head. The scent of horse sweat hung heavy in the enclosed space, and the horse jerked his head back and rolled his eyes at Jake.

"Easy," Jake said softly, extending his hand slowly. He gently stroked the horse's neck with his right hand as he ran his left hand along the animal's chest. The horse laid his head back down. "Good boy."

He waved the beam of the flashlight across the horse. The horse's coat was wet and smooth, and his thick muscles heaved as he labored to breathe. Half a dozen angry welts were scattered across his side and belly, as if the horse had been stung by something. Jake wondered fleetingly whether the horse's breathing difficulties could be the result of an allergic reaction, but he was pretty certain that wasn't it. The sucking sound was a classic indication of a puncture wound.

Jake's fingers probed the front of the horse's chest but felt no sign of a wound. He ran his hand around to the horse's right side. The shoulder felt fine, and the horse's side seemed to be clean.

He looked up at Steve as he slid his hand under the horse's belly. "I don't see any sign of injury. I'm afraid it's on his other side. We might have to pull him out."

Jake was about to give up, when his fingers brushed against something sticky. "Wait, I found something." He pulled the pin that held the breast bar in place and released the bar, so he could lean down closer to the horse. He aimed the flashlight at the area. There it was. On the horse's belly, just behind his right front leg. A puncture wound about the size of a half-dollar.

"I found it. He's got a puncture wound just behind his right front."

Steve leaned farther into the trailer. "Is that why he's breathing so hard?"

Jake nodded. "My colt had a similar injury. What happens is, when he tries to breathe in, his chest cavity fills up with air and that puts pressure on his lungs, so he can't get enough oxygen." Jake lifted the horse's lip and pressed a finger against his gum. "Look how purple his gums are. If he doesn't get help soon, he's not going to make it."

"Can we get him up and into the ambulance?" Steve asked.

Jake frowned. "I doubt it. How far away is the veterinary hospital?"

"About twenty minutes."

"He'll never make it, unless we get this puncture sealed off first."

"Okay, let's do it. Just tell me what you need."

Jake stared at him. "I can't do it, Steve. We need a vet."

Steve shook his head. "We don't have a vet. And we'll never get one here in time. You're his only hope. You've got to try to help him."

Jake rocked back on his heels and tried to recall exactly what Doc Brooks had done when he'd treated his colt.

"What types of supplies do you have in the horse ambulance?"

"I don't have any. I just do transport. No medical treatment."

Jake exhaled slowly. "Okay. We'll have to improvise. I need a plastic tube. There's one by the gas can in the bed of my truck. See if someone out there will climb up and get it. But, in the meantime, look around down here. Maybe there's something in the Range Rover. I also need something to pack around the wound. A rag will do. I noticed another door at the front of the trailer. There must be a dressing room. You might be able to find something in there. I'll also need some kind of tape. If you can't find that, baling twine will work."

"You got it. I'll be right back," Steve said, backing away from the trailer door.

"Steve, wait."

Steve's face reappeared in the doorway.

"I also need a condom."

Steve made a coughing sound. "A what?"

"A condom."

"Are you joking?"

Jake shook his head. "I couldn't be more serious. If you don't have one, ask if anyone else out there does."

Steve hesitated for a second, then reached under his raincoat and pulled out his wallet. He removed a foil-wrapped condom and tossed it down to Jake. "I trust you know what you're doing, but I have a feeling I'm never going to hear the end of this."

Jake couldn't help smiling at Steve. "Go on, now. Get the tube. And hurry."

He set the flashlight down, opened the foil wrap, and unrolled the condom. He used the folding knife that was clipped to his belt to slice the end off the condom, then placed the condom on the center divider of the trailer and turned his attention back to the horse.

The trailer tie must have released during the accident, because one end was snapped to the halter, but the opposite end wasn't hooked to the ring in the trailer. The halter had twisted to the side and was pulling against the horse's left eye, and as Jake lifted the horse's head to adjust the halter, he saw a brass nameplate. He aimed the flashlight at it and read the name engraved in script. *Chancellor.*

"Hey there, Chancellor," Jake said quietly. "You hang in there. We're going to get you fixed up in no time. Just hold on, boy."

Chancellor had some minor scrapes on his nose, and a deep gash above his left eye that needed stitches and would probably leave a scar. Jake let Chancellor's head rest on his lap and stroked him gently, murmuring reassuringly to him, all the while wondering whether the device he was about to rig up would actually work.

*A*nne's hand was already on the door handle of Kendall's Jeep as they pulled up to the curb in front of the emergency room. As soon as the vehicle came to a stop, Anne flung open the door, grabbed her purse, and climbed out of the car.

"I'll see you inside," she called over her shoulder as she slammed the door and headed towards the covered walkway that sheltered the entrance to the emergency room. She rounded the corner and hurried towards a set of double glass doors.

The doors glided open quietly as Anne drew near, and when she entered the reception area, she saw a young woman sitting at a desk immediately to her left. The woman stood up as Anne approached.

"Are you Mrs. Cummings?" she asked.

Anne nodded. "Yes."

"I've been watching for you," the woman said, walking around from behind the desk. "I figured I'd be able to spot you right away, since they told me you're expecting. Your husband was brought in by ambulance a little while ago. If you'll come with me, I'll find someone to fill you in on his condition."

Anne followed her across the crowded waiting room and around the corner. "My name's Jenny," the woman told her as they walked. "I'm a patient advocate."

Jenny stopped before a closed door. "This is the consultation room. You'll have more privacy in here." She opened the door with a key and gestured for Anne to step inside. "Please make yourself comfortable. I'll be right back."

The room was small, just barely large enough to fit a love seat and two chairs, and it was decorated in soothing blue tones, with nondescript pastel artwork on the walls and soft lighting. It was the kind of room you'd take a family member to if the news you were about to deliver was not good, Anne imagined. *A room designed for private grieving.*

Anne hesitated in the doorway and looked at Jenny. "Why did you bring me here?" she asked. "Why can't I see my husband?"

Jenny didn't make eye contact. She patted Anne's arm and tried to ease her gently into the room. "I'm sure they'll take you back there to see him. But I think you'll be more comfortable talking in here first. Please have a seat. I won't be but a minute."

Anne walked through the doorway, but she refused to sit down, as if sitting would somehow validate the need for her to be in the grieving room. She leaned against the wall next to the door and after a moment heard the sound of rapid footsteps in the corridor. She straightened up and turned towards the door. Jenny was approaching, along with an older woman who wore a mint green smock.

"This is the RN who has been caring for your husband," Jenny said.

The nurse extended her hand to Anne. "Nice to meet you, Mrs. Cummings. I'm Beverly Sweeney. Please, have a seat, and I'll give you an update on your husband's condition."

"I'll leave you two alone," Jenny said, her hand on the doorknob. "Is there anything I can bring you? A cup of coffee, perhaps?"

Anne shook her head. "No, thank you. But the friend who drove me here is probably in the waiting room by now. Her name is Kendall Waters. Would you mind letting her know where I am?"

"I'd be happy to," Jenny said, slipping through the door and closing it gently behind her.

Beverly sat on the love seat and patted the cushion next to her. "Please, Mrs. Cummings, sit down."

Anne lowered herself onto the love seat. The baby was kicking hard, and she felt some cramping in her lower abdomen, so she settled back against the cushions and gently rubbed her hands across her belly.

"I'll take you to see your husband in a few minutes," Beverly said, "but first I want to prepare you, so you aren't shocked when you see him. Okay?"

Anne nodded.

"He's been intubated. That means that he has a tube running into his airway, which is connected to a ventilator."

"Doug can't breathe on his own?"

"Right now, the ventilator is doing the work for him."

Anne couldn't come to grips with the thought of Doug hooked up to a machine, unable to breathe on his own.

"You can speak to him," Beverly went on. "In fact, I would encourage it. But he won't be able to respond to you. He's unconscious."

"Unconscious?" Anne fought the impulse to flee the grieving room before Beverly could deliver more bad news. "How bad is it?" she heard herself ask.

Beverly handed her a tissue from a box on the end table. "Your husband's been stabilized; that's the important thing right now. Dr. Adams has been treating him and he'll go over the test results with you. Would you like to go and see him now?"

Anne pressed the tissue against the corners of her eyes and took a deep breath. "Yes, please."

She followed Beverly to a set of wooden double doors and waited while the nurse swiped a card against a sensor on the wall. The doors opened towards them with a clanking sound, and as soon as they passed through the doorway a medicinal hospital odor filled Anne's nose. She shuddered as she was flooded with memories of the last time she'd been at the hospital with Doug. After Zeb McGraw had shot him. But everything had turned out all right then. She had to have faith that it would again.

Beverly led her down a hallway, past several curtained cubicles, and stopped in front of a closed glass door across from the nurses' station. Anne couldn't see into the room through the glass, because a curtain was drawn closed on the other side.

"Your husband's in here," Beverly said, sliding open the door.

C H A P T E R
7

ake felt the trailer rock and heard footsteps on the metal siding above him. A moment later, Steve leaned through the open door.

"I got everything you asked for," he said breathlessly.

"Good work." Jake gently eased Chancellor's head off his lap. "Come on inside. I'm going to need your help with this."

Jake stood up and moved to the side as Steve lowered himself into the trailer, landing deftly beside Jake.

"How's he doing?" Steve asked.

"He's been quiet, but I don't think that's a good thing." Jake took off his cowboy hat and wiped at the sweat on his forehead. The sun was shining again, and the inside of the trailer was beginning to feel like a sauna. "Show me what you found."

Steve jammed his hands into the pockets of his rain slicker and pulled out a roll of duct tape and a flannel polo wrap, which he handed to Jake. "I've got the gas siphon tube right here." He unsnapped his rain slicker, and Jake saw a section of garden hose dangling from around Steve's neck.

"Perfect." Jake squatted down beside Chancellor and used his knife to slice off about a foot of the dark blue polo wrap.

"That's some knife you've got there. Is it a Buck?"

Jake nodded as he picked up the roll of duct tape and began cutting off strips, which he stuck lightly to the center divider post.

"What's the handle made of? Is that elk horn?"

Jake gave him a quick glance. "Stag."

Steve whistled. "I'll bet that cost you a bundle."

"Okay, Steve, I'm going to need your help here." Jake retrieved the

29

condom from the center divider and slipped the opening of the condom over the end of the hose, then fastened it in place with one of the strips of duct tape. "I'm going to insert the hose into the puncture wound, and then I want you to hold it steady while I pack the polo wrap around it and secure it with the tape."

"Do you want to take the center divider out first, so you can get at him better?"

Jake shook his head. "I'd rather keep him confined. He'll be less likely to put up a struggle that way. If you just grab his right front and hold it up, I think I can get at it just fine."

Steve removed his rain slicker and dropped it on the floor, then grasped Chancellor's leg with both hands and pulled it forward and up out of Jake's way. Chancellor tensed and rolled his eyes, and Steve spoke softly to him. "It's okay, boy, we're just trying to help you."

"Pray that this works," Jake said as he probed the puncture wound with his fingers and inched the hose in. Chancellor grunted once as the hose slid in, but he seemed to lack the energy to put up a struggle.

"Okay, it's in. Now hold it right here." Jake shifted out of the way, and Steve tucked Chancellor's leg between his elbow and his side and grabbed the hose with his other hand.

Jake wrapped the strip of flannel around the opening and eased it into the wound to close up the gap around the hose. "There we go. That's as good as it's going to get."

He placed the strips of duct tape around the hose and taped it to Chancellor's side. "Let's hope it does the trick. Keep your fingers crossed."

Chancellor took a labored breath and the condom was sucked tight against the hose, sealing off the end. An instant later he exhaled, and the condom extended, allowing the air to escape in a rush through the hole Jake had cut in the end. Chancellor took another breath. Inhale; the opening closed off. Exhale; the air escaped. Just like clockwork.

"I'll be damned," Jake said, smiling. "It's working."

Steve gave him a high five. "Way to go, man."

Chancellor no longer made a sucking noise when he inhaled, and with each effort his breathing sounded stronger and steadier. They watched the horse breathe for several minutes, and then Jake slipped his thumb under Chancellor's upper lip and lifted it up.

"Look. His gums aren't as purple as they were before. Believe it or not,

I think we're past that hurdle. Let's get him out of the trailer."

"Are we going to pull him out?"

"We'll have to. Hopefully, there are still some folks out there who can give us a hand. I'll handle his front end and make sure this contraption stays in place."

"Gotcha." Steve released his grasp on Chancellor's front leg. "I'll round up some help and get the back doors open. See you in a minute."

Jake found a lead rope hanging from a ring by the door. He unsnapped the trailer tie and hooked the thick rope to Chancellor's halter. He heard voices outside, followed by a harsh squeak as the top rear doors swung outwards, letting sunlight stream into the trailer.

Steve's face appeared in the opening. "We're going to take these doors off the hinges and get them out of the way before we open the ramp."

"Okay."

Jake felt Chancellor's neck muscles tense, and the horse snorted and struggled to see what was happening behind him.

He gently forced Chancellor's head back down. "Easy, boy. Save your energy."

"We've got the doors off," Steve called. "Ready for us to open the ramp?"

"I'm ready whenever you are."

"Okay. I've got a rope here that I'm going to tie around his ankles so we can pull him out. That is, as long as he doesn't try to kick the bejesus out of me in the process. Once I get his legs tied, we'll take the divider out."

Jake shifted his position so that he could still reach the makeshift chest tube, but he was clear of Chancellor's front legs. "Okay," he said, placing a hand on the horse's neck. "I'll try to keep him down and quiet."

The trailer ramp opened with a metallic screech, and Chancellor grunted and struggled to raise his head.

"Easy, boy." Jake increased the pressure on Chancellor's neck, knowing that as long as he kept Chancellor's head down, the horse wouldn't try to get to his feet.

Steve approached the back of the trailer and placed a hand on Chancellor's hind end, then ran it slowly down his legs. "Okay, Jake, I'm going to try to put the rope around his legs now."

"Go ahead. I've got hold of him."

Chancellor snorted and rolled his eyes but didn't put up a struggle, and

Steve quickly wrapped the rope in a figure eight around Chancellor's ankles and pulled it tight.

"Got it." Steve backed away and handed the end of the rope to a man who was standing next to him, then turned to the woman firefighter. "Would you climb up into the tack room and see if you can find some blankets or something I can use to pad the end of the trailer with? The edge is pretty banged up, and I don't want him getting cut when we slide him out."

"Sure thing."

Steve turned his attention back to Jake. "Ready to take the center divider out?"

Jake nodded. "Why don't you unlatch your end first; then I'll release the pin up here and you can lift it out."

"Right." Steve motioned for another man to help him. He pulled the pin to free the butt bar, then grabbed hold of the divider and slid open the latch that held it in place. "Okay, we've got it. Release your end whenever you're ready."

Jake placed his knee on Chancellor's neck and reached for the pin to release the divider. It should have slipped out easily enough, but it was wedged in place and he couldn't get it to budge.

"Damn it." Jake smacked the palm of his hand against the divider in an effort to move the hinge back into alignment.

"Is it stuck?"

"Yeah. Something must have gotten bent during impact. Let me see if I can work it loose. If not, we'll just have to swing the divider out of the way while we slide him out."

Jake fussed with the pin for a minute. "See if you can move your end of the divider to the right, towards the floor of the trailer. It looks like it got bent upwards. Maybe we can force it back down."

The trailer rocked slightly as Steve and the other man tugged on the divider. "Okay, good," Jake said. "Let me try it again."

He wiggled the pin and felt it budge a little. "I can move it now. Try forcing it one more time."

Sweat streamed down Jake's neck, and the combination of heat, exertion, and lack of sleep was starting to make him feel woozy. As the men struggled with the divider, Jake rested his head on his arm and took a deep breath.

"Hey, Jake. You all right?"

Jake straightened up. "Yeah, I'm fine. Let me try it again."

He wiggled it again, as hard as he could, and after working it back and forth several times he finally managed to inch it out.

"Got it!" He removed the pin and slid the divider out from the hinge.

Steve and the other man lifted the divider out of the trailer and set it on the ground.

"Okay, let me just pad the edge here and we're set to go." Steve took an armful of horse blankets from the woman firefighter and stuffed them around the end of the trailer.

Two men took hold of the rope along with Steve, and another man grabbed Chancellor's tail.

"Okay, once we start pulling, we're not stopping until we have him clear of the trailer," Steve said. "Ready? On three. One. Two. Three."

Chancellor probably weighed twelve hundred pounds or more, but the four men heaved backwards and kept going in a steady motion as they slid him out of the trailer. Jake moved with them, keeping Chancellor's head down and holding the chest tube in place. As soon as they had him out of the trailer, Steve swiftly removed the rope from his hind legs.

"He might be a little unsteady on his feet when he gets up," Jake said. "Be prepared to get out of his way."

Jake released his pressure on Chancellor's neck and grabbed the lead rope. "Okay, boy, it's time to get up now."

Chancellor raised his head and looked around, blowing softly.

"Good boy, take your time," Jake murmured.

The horse extended one front leg, then the other, and slowly heaved himself up. He stood awkwardly, with all four legs spread out, and seemed wobbly for a moment. Then he shook, gave a loud snort, lowered his head, and began nosing through the brush for something to graze on.

"All right!" Steve gave high fives to everyone near him. "We did it."

Jake smiled and began to run his hands over Chancellor, down his legs, under his belly, checking to see if there were any other major injuries they had to tend to before transporting him to the hospital. He was pretty scraped up, but, luckily, most of the cuts seemed superficial.

"How's he doing?" Steve asked. "Find anything else we need to worry about?"

Jake shook his head. "Nothing that seems critical. I think we can concentrate on finding a way to get him to the ambulance."

Steve gazed up at the steep, rugged incline. "You think there's any way he can make it up there?"

"It'd be a rough climb even without his chest injury. He's breathing okay for now, but I'd hate to risk exerting him with the climb and have him collapse."

"So what do you suggest?"

Jake took off his cowboy hat and ran his hand through his hair. "I don't know, Steve. I'm not from around here. What happens if we go downhill?"

"I'm not that familiar with this area either, but it looks like these woods go on forever." Steve turned to the rest of the group. "Anyone know if there's a way out of here without going uphill?"

"There's a service road that runs along the creek at the bottom. It's quite a ways down, though," the woman firefighter replied.

"Can I get the horse ambulance down there?"

"Yes," she said, nodding slowly. "The shortest way is to come from the west, off Crooked Run Road, but there's a portion of the service road that goes through the creek bed, and I'm sure the water's pretty high after this storm."

A middle-aged man wearing overalls stepped forward. "Your best bet would be to head east, then come back down Old Schoolhouse Road and connect with the service road that way. You'll avoid the creek crossing by coming from that direction."

"Would you be willing to ride with me and show me the way?"

"Sure, no problem."

Steve turned to Jake. "Will you walk the horse down?"

Jake gave him a tired smile. "You kidding? After all we've been through, I'm not about to desert Chancellor now."

"Thanks, man." Steve turned to the woman firefighter. "Can you walk down with Jake and lead him to the service road?"

"You bet."

"Okay, let's head out. We can keep in touch by cell phone." Steve took the cell phone from the pouch on his belt and glanced at the screen. "The signal's weak, but there's service. Jake, give me your number and I'll program it into my phone."

"You're out of luck there," Jake replied. "I don't believe in those things."

"I have one," the woman firefighter said. She and Steve exchanged cell phone numbers, and then Steve and the man began the climb up the hill.

The woman firefighter looked at Jake and raised her hands. "I'm ready when you are."

"All right. Do you mind walking next to him and holding the chest tube in place?"

"No. Just tell me what to do."

Jake took her hand and placed it on Chancellor's side. "Just keep your hand on it, down here near the base, where the wrap is. The tape might come loose once we start moving, and the last thing we need is for the tube to come out."

8

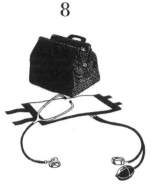

*N*othing Beverly told Anne could have prepared her for what she saw when she entered the trauma room. Anne had expected to find Doug in a small, stark cubicle, like those she had encountered on previous visits to the emergency room. But the area Beverly led her into was large and brightly lit, with glass-fronted cabinets crammed full of medical supplies.

Anne's stomach turned at the antiseptic odor that permeated the room, and she covered her nose with her hand. She could see the outline of Doug's legs under a white blanket on a stretcher in the center of the room, but a nurse stood next to him, fiddling with a machine, and she blocked Anne's view of Doug from the waist up. The nurse stepped back as Anne drew near.

"Oh my God," Anne whispered, clutching the edge of the stretcher for support.

Doug's complexion was pale beneath his tan, and he had a long gash high across his forehead, which was plastered with Steri-Strips, giving it a zippered effect. A tangle of tubes and wires led to the machines that flanked the stretcher, and a tube protruded from Doug's mouth, secured to his handsome face by a mass of white tape.

"Get her a chair," Beverly called as she grasped Anne's shoulders and held her steady. "It's a shock to see him like this, I know. Are you okay?"

Anne nodded as she sank into the chair that was shoved behind her legs.

"How far along are you, honey?"

"I'm due in three weeks."

"Let me get a blood pressure reading on you."

The ventilator made a whooshing sound, and Doug's chest seemed to lift off the stretcher as air was pumped into his lungs. Then the machine emitted

a sigh, and his chest sank back down again. His eyes were closed, and he had
an IV line inserted at the inside of each elbow and another in his right forearm.
A clear tube connected to a canister ran to the right side of his chest and gave
off a soft bubbling sound. Wires ran from his chest to a monitor at the head of
the stretcher, and a half-full bag of yellow liquid hung off the side. Doug's arms
lay motionless on the white blanket and Anne reached for his hand.

"Can he feel my touch?" she asked as Beverly wrapped a blood pressure
cuff around her arm.

"I always encourage family members to talk to loved ones who are in a
coma," Beverly said, squeezing the bulb to inflate the cuff with air. "I can't
tell you for sure exactly what he can hear or feel, but I believe that he will
know you're present. Just talk to your husband. Tell him where he is and what
happened."

Beverly removed the blood pressure device. "One twenty over seventy.
You're fine. Here, let me lower the stretcher so you're level with your husband. Then I'll page Dr. Adams so you can speak with him."

Anne waited until she heard the door slide shut behind the nurses, then
bent down and kissed Doug's hand. "I'm here, Doug. Everything's going to
be all right. You had a car accident, and you're in the hospital, but you're
going to be fine."

She squeezed his hand, hoping for some kind of a response, but it lay
limply between her own. Anne shuddered as the ventilator whooshed, inflat-
ing Doug's lungs with air, then sighed, and his chest deflated again.

Anne heard the sound of the door slide open. She turned, to see Beverly
and a gray-haired man wearing a white coat walk into the room.

"Hello, Mrs. Cummings. I'm Dr. Adams." His voice was deep, with a
hint of a Virginia drawl. "I'd like to bring you up-to-date on your husband's
condition. Would you care to step out into the lounge?"

Anne shook her head. "I don't want to leave my husband. I'd rather talk
in here."

"Very well." He set his clipboard down on the stretcher and pulled a chair
up next to Anne. "Let's start with why your husband is on a ventilator. He has
what's called a pneumothorax. This is a condition in which air gets between
the lung and chest wall and causes the lung tissue to collapse. We've inserted
a chest tube, which will relieve the pressure and drain any fluid."

"How serious is that?"

"Barring any complications, it should heal just fine, and he'll only have a small scar where the chest tube was inserted," Dr. Adams replied. "The only thing we have to watch out for at this time is risk of infection."

"How long will he need to stay on the ventilator?"

"At least until he wakes up. At that time, Dr. Hollins, your husband's pulmonologist, will assess his weaning parameters to determine if he can be extubated."

"When do you think that will be? When will he wake up?"

Dr. Adams cleared his throat. "That's the next thing I want to discuss with you. Your husband has what we call traumatic brain injury, or TBI. It's a closed head injury, meaning there was no penetration of the skull. I've called in a neurologist to consult—"

They were interrupted by a movement in the doorway. A tall African-American man stepped into the room.

"Hello," he said, extending his hand to Anne. "I'm Dr. Martin."

"Dr. Martin is the neurologist I was just starting to tell you about," Dr. Adams said.

Anne reluctantly withdrew her hand from Doug's. "Hello."

Dr. Martin gave her hand a swift, firm squeeze, then turned to Dr. Adams. "Okay. Bring me up to speed on Mr. Cummings's condition."

Dr. Adams picked his clipboard up off the stretcher and flipped through a few pages. "We ran a CAT scan, which was normal and showed no signs of a skull fracture. His GCS is three."

"What does GCS stand for?" Anne asked.

"Glasgow coma score. It's a scoring system we use to quantify consciousness following a head injury. It measures eye, verbal, and motor response."

"Is a GCS of three a good score?"

Dr. Martin hesitated for a moment before responding. "The scores range from three to fifteen, with fifteen being the most favorable response."

"He's at the bottom of the scale?"

"Yes, but that could change at any time, and hopefully it will."

Anne stared at Doug with a renewed sense of alarm. "Can't you do anything to help him regain consciousness?"

"Our job right now is to monitor him closely and support him clinically while we allow Mother Nature to take her course. I've already spoken with ICU and they have a bed available, so we'll move him there as soon as we've run a few more tests. I want to see an MRI and an EEG. In the meantime, we'll keep him on the ventilator and administer fluids and medication to keep down any brain swelling that might occur."

Anne took a deep breath. "What are the odds that Doug won't come out of the coma? Or that when he does, he'll have brain damage?"

Dr. Martin met her gaze. "Mrs. Cummings, I'll do everything in my power to help your husband. But I wouldn't be being honest with you if I didn't tell you I think you should hope for the best and prepare for the worst."

Tears stung Anne's eyes and she looked away. It was the answer she had feared he would give.

Dr. Martin placed a hand on her shoulder. "It's going to take a little while for us to perform the tests and move your husband to ICU, so now would be a good time for you to take a break; maybe get something to eat. Do you have anyone here with you, or someone you'd like to call?"

"I have a friend in the waiting room."

"Would you like me to have someone bring her back here?"

"Yes, please. Her name is Kendall Waters."

"All right. I'll have someone go and get her.

"Thank you," Anne said quietly, turning back to Doug.

endall turned her Jeep into the entrance drive at the Equine Medical Center and paused briefly while the metal gates slid open. She felt a little guilty about leaving Anne at the hospital alone, but when Anne had asked her to drive over to the EMC to check on Chancellor, she had jumped at the chance. She hated hospitals with a passion, and it had taken all her willpower not to lose it in front of Anne when she had seen Doug hooked up to all those machines.

She followed the long driveway around to the unloading area and parked next to the horse ambulance, which stood empty, with its rear doors open and the ramp down. The entrance doors were locked, since it was Saturday, so Kendall rang the after-hours bell and waited for someone to let her in. A few moments passed without a response. She pressed the button again and held it longer.

The door opened towards her almost immediately, and a familiar-looking woman stood in the doorway. "I'm sorry it took so long for me to get here. I was helping with a foal who wasn't being very cooperative. Hey, you're Wellington's owner, aren't you?"

Kendall remembered the woman. She was a veterinary technician who had taken a liking to Wellington when he'd been in for his colic surgery. "Yes, I am. You're Darlene, right? I remember how wonderful you were to Wellington when he was here."

Darlene blushed. "It was my pleasure. He was such sweetheart to take care of. How's he doing?"

"Just great. He's fat and happy."

"Give him a pat for me, will you?"

Kendall smiled. "I sure will. Listen, the reason I'm here is to check up on a horse the ambulance brought in. His name is Chancellor."

"A big bay, right?"

Kendall nodded.

"They just took him into surgery."

"*Surgery?* Do you know what's wrong with him?"

Darlene shook her head. "Sorry, I don't. I was out in 'A' Barn when they were examining him. Do you want to watch the surgery from the observation room?"

"That would be great. Who's doing the surgery? Do you know?"

Darlene moved to one side to allow Kendall to enter. "Dr. Carey."

That was good, Kendall thought. Ned Carey was the most senior surgeon on staff at the EMC.

Darlene said, "If I can find someone who knows more about his condition, I'll send him to the observation room to talk to you."

"Thanks, I'd really appreciate that."

As they walked down the aisle, Kendall sniffed the medicinal scent of Betadine mingled with the pungent garlic odor of DSMO. "I swear, if someone blindfolded me and brought me here, I'd know I was at the EMC because of the smell in the air."

Darlene smiled. "I'm so used to it, I don't even notice it anymore."

They reached the door to the observation room and Kendall paused in front of it. "Thanks for letting me in, Darlene. I'll see you later."

"No problem," Darlene said with a wave. "I'm going to check on that ornery foal again."

Kendall opened the door and saw a man dressed in green surgical scrubs standing with his back towards her. He was looking through the glass window into the operating room, and he glanced over his shoulder at her as she entered the room.

She approached him. "Hi. I'm Kendall Waters. I'm here to check on a horse named Chancellor. I heard he was in the operating room."

The man nodded at her. "Yeah, they wheeled him in a little while ago," he said with a slow drawl.

"Do you know why he's in surgery?"

The man nodded as he turned back towards the window. "He has a chest wound and a punctured lung."

Kendall walked to the window and looked down into the operating room.

She had observed more than her fair share of equine medical procedures, but surgery was never an easy sight for her to see.

Chancellor lay on his back on the operating table in the center of the room, with all four legs up in the air. His hooves were covered with plastic OB sleeves and a massive band of white tape secured an IV line to his neck. A respirator tube protruded from his mouth, and an anesthesiologist sat on a stool near his head, monitoring the equipment. The anesthesiologist said something to Ned Carey and gave him a thumbs-up sign, and Ned lowered the scalpel to Chancellor's chest.

"I can't watch this part," Kendall said, turning away from the window.

The man smiled but didn't shift his gaze away from the surgery. "Are you his owner?"

Kendall shook her head. "No, his owner is in the hospital. His wife asked me if I would come over here and find out how Chancellor is."

The man didn't respond, and Kendall studied him as he stood observing the surgery. She had heard that the EMC had hired a new vet who had just finished his residency at Cornell, and she wondered if that's who he was. His age seemed about right; she guessed he was in his early thirties. He was tall, probably over six feet, and looked lean and fairly muscular, although it was hard to tell because of the baggy scrubs he was wearing. His skin was tanned a golden brown, and his hair was sun-streaked and a bit unruly. He had a rugged air about him, and Kendall noticed he was wearing cowboy boots.

"How is he?" the man asked after a few minutes, turning to half face her. She noticed that his eyes were a very pale blue. And expressionless. Not unfriendly, but not warm, either. "Chancellor's owner. He was the guy driving the rig, right?"

Kendall sighed and ran her hands up her bare arms. "Yes, he was the driver. He's in critical condition. He's hooked up to a million machines and he's in a coma. They were moving him to intensive care when I left."

The man grimaced. "I figured he was in pretty bad shape, from the condition of his vehicle."

"You saw it?"

He nodded. "Yeah."

Then it dawned on Kendall that he was probably the horse ambulance's driver. "Oh, you must be Steve. I've heard great things about you."

"Nope, I'm not. But I agree with all the good things you've heard about Steve. He did a terrific job today."

"Why were you there?"

He hesitated for a moment. "I was just passing by and I stopped to help."

"Are you a vet?"

"No."

"You're just a Good Samaritan?"

His eyes narrowed and he regarded her with a long gaze. "You've got a lot of questions."

There was an edge to his tone, and Kendall flinched, then hated herself for it. *This man wasn't Peter. He wasn't going to hit her.* She took a deep breath and sat down in a chair against the wall, suddenly feeling painfully out of place in her linen dress and pearls.

"I'm just trying to put two and two together," she said. "I don't know any of the details of the accident, and since you're here watching the operation, and you're wearing scrubs, I figured you were a vet. Or a technician, or something."

He glanced down at his clothing. "No, I'm not a vet." His manner was somewhat friendlier. "My clothes were soaked from the rain and a nice young lady offered to put them in the dryer for me. She gave me these to wear while they're drying."

"Well then, that clears that up." Kendall picked up a dog-eared issue of *Practical Horseman* from a side table and began leafing through it.

He turned his back to the window and leaned against the sill, folding his arms across his chest. "Look, I'm sorry I got testy. It's been a long day and I'm exhausted." He ran a hand through his hair and stretched his neck from side to side. "I'm Jake, by the way. What did you say your name was?"

"Kendall."

His eyes lost their iciness and his mouth slid into a slow smile. "Nice to meet you, Kendall."

"Nice to meet you, too." She set the magazine back down. "So will you tell me what happened?"

Jake shifted his weight against the windowsill. "I don't know any details about what caused the accident, but the rig went off the road and down a mountainside. The Range Rover ended up headfirst into a tree, and the trailer came loose and flipped. It ended up on its side farther down the slope. By the time I got there, the ambulance had already taken your friend away. Chancellor was still inside the trailer, and I helped Steve get him out."

"Does Chancellor have any other injuries, besides his chest injury?"

He shook his head. "Nothing that seems serious. He has some cuts and scrapes, but his legs look clean and he is moving remarkably well considering all he went through."

"How serious is his chest injury?"

Jake glanced over his shoulder at the operating room. "It's a pretty dirty wound, so the doc's concerned about the risk of infection. They'll clean it up as much as they can during the surgery. The doc said Chancellor's prospects are good, but he's been through a lot, and he was in a weakened state going into surgery."

"Not to mention the risk of making it through recovery. That's always the scariest part of equine surgery for me. Have you ever watched a horse come out of anesthesia?"

"Yeah, they usually scramble all over the place trying to get up. You think they're going to break a leg. And, unfortunately, sometimes they do. But Chancellor's a smart horse. I think he'll do okay."

"But he's so skittish."

"He's high-strung, that's for sure. But he's not one of those horses who doesn't care if he hurts himself."

Kendall frowned quizzically at him. "You sound like you know Chancellor pretty well for having just met him."

He nodded, giving her another one of his slow smiles. "Yeah, we had quite a bonding experience this afternoon."

She studied him for a moment. "Is that why you're still here?"

Jake shrugged. "I guess so. I figured his owner probably wouldn't be showing up for the surgery, so I decided to stay and make sure he got through the operation all right."

"That's very nice of you."

He didn't respond and turned back towards the window again.

The next few minutes passed in silence, and then Kendall asked, "Are you from around here?"

"Nope. Just passing through."

"Where are you from?"

There was a brief hesitation before he answered. "Oklahoma."

"Really? Based on your accent, I would have pegged you as being from somewhere just south of the Mason-Dixon line."

Jake didn't respond.

"You're a long way from home. Are you in a hurry to be hitting the road again?"

He sighed and slowly turned his head towards her. "Like I said before, you sure do ask a lot of questions."

And you sure don't like to answer them, Kendall thought.

*Z*elda McGraw sat on the bench near the pay phone in front of Kroger's Supermarket. She took a long drag on her cigarette and eyed a blue Camaro that pulled up to the curb.

"Hey there, Zelda," Pinky Barnes said as he stuck his head out the window and revved the engine. "Want to cruise over to Thirsty's with me and have a few cold ones?"

"Beat it, Pinky. I got me a steady man now."

"I don't see him around here nowhere."

"I'm waiting on his phone call right now," Zelda said, pointing towards the pay phone behind her. "He had to leave town on business for a couple of days."

"On business? I had no idea that you'd found yourself a genuine businessman. I'll bet you he don't have no set of wheels like this, now does he?" Pinky revved the engine again.

"Get lost, Pinky. You and me are over and done with."

Pinky laughed and gave her the finger, then floored it, burning rubber as he peeled away from the curb.

"Fuck you," Zelda muttered, staring after him. She was so done with this shitty town and all the redneck assholes who lived in it. Fact was, they could all burn in hell for all she cared. Pretty soon she'd be kissing this town good-bye for good.

Zelda got up and walked over to the phone. The clock on the wall inside Kroger's read twenty minutes past five. Earl was twenty minutes late calling, but that didn't mean that anything had gone wrong. She'd give him another ten minutes; if he didn't call by then, she'd come back at nine o'clock in the morning, just as they had planned.

That's one thing she really liked about Earl, besides how good he was in the sack. He was real smart, and he had understood right from the get-go that they always had to have a backup plan in case things didn't go the way they were supposed to.

Earl was so much smarter than Doug Cummings and his bimbo lawyer wife, they'd never catch on to who he really was. Until it was too late. Of course, it didn't hurt that he was so hot-looking and such a smooth talker.

Zelda looked at the clock again and saw that it was five-thirty, so she moseyed down to the street and stuck her thumb out. It didn't even bother her that she had let Earl take her car to Virginia and she had to thumb a ride home. It was a small price to pay for what she would get in return.

11

*A*nne awoke with a start when the ICU nurse tapped her on the shoulder.

"I'm sorry, Mrs. Cummings, I didn't mean to startle you," the nurse said quietly.

"That's okay," Anne said, rubbing her eyes. "I must have dozed off."

She sat forward in the chair and curled her fingers against Doug's cheek. "Has his condition changed any?"

The nurse shook her head. "No, he's the same."

Anne ran her fingertips lightly over Doug's temple, where a touch of gray crept into his close-cropped dark hair. She spoke quietly to him. "I'm right here, Doug. You're in the hospital and everything's going to be just fine. Kendall went to check on Chancellor. They took him in the horse ambulance to the EMC. She's going to call me as soon as she knows how he's doing."

She was beginning to feel less self-conscious about talking to Doug in front of the nurses. They acted as if it were a natural thing to do and had told her more than once that they believed he could hear her, or at least knew that she was there.

"Mrs. Cummings, there are a couple of sheriff's deputies in the waiting room. They would like to speak with you," the nurse said.

"Sheriff's deputies?"

The nurse nodded. "They want to talk to you about your husband's accident."

"Now? Surely that can wait."

"I already suggested that to them, but they were pretty insistent. They said it won't take long." She smiled sympathetically.

Anne sighed and rose reluctantly. She leaned down and kissed Doug on the top of his head and whispered, "I'll be right back." She turned to the nurse. "Will you come and get me right away if anything changes?"

"Of course I will. By the way, my name is Robin. I just came on shift and I'll be working until eleven tonight. Dr. Martin wrote instructions that you'll be spending the night here, so if there is anything I can do to make it more comfortable for you, please let me know."

"Thank you, Robin."

"Just press the buzzer by the door when you're ready to come back, and I'll let you in."

Anne left Doug's room and headed slowly towards the waiting area. Her lower back was killing her, and she rubbed it with both hands as she walked. She was still wearing the heels she'd put on for the baby shower, and her feet were so swollen, each step was excruciating. She fought the urge to kick off her shoes and go barefoot.

She found the deputies sitting on a couch in the waiting room. One was older, balding and weathered-looking, and he fiddled with a sheriff's hat that rested on his knee; the younger one flipped through an issue of *Sports Illustrated*. They both stood as she approached, and the older man extended his hand.

"Good evening, Mrs. Cummings. I'm Deputy Hodgkins, and this is Deputy Ward," he said, nodding his head towards the younger deputy.

Anne shook both their hands.

"We'd like to talk to you about your husband's accident, Mrs. Cummings. Why don't you have a seat?" Deputy Hodgkins gestured towards an armchair that stood next to the couch.

"Is it really necessary that we have this conversation right now, Deputy?" Anne asked. "As you probably know, my husband is in critical condition, and I really hate to leave him."

He smiled sympathetically. "I can certainly understand that, Mrs. Cummings. I promise we won't take but a few minutes of your time. We have some information about the accident that we really need to discuss with you. Let's sit down, and we'll be as brief as possible."

Anne felt too weary to argue, so she eased herself into the chair. "All right," she said with a sigh.

Both deputies sat back down, and Deputy Hodgkins placed his hat next to him on the couch.

"Mrs. Cummings, there's no easy way to say this, so I guess I'll just get on with it." He cleared his throat. "We have reason to believe that your husband's vehicle was tampered with and that was the cause of his accident."

"What?" Anne couldn't believe that she had heard him right. "What do you mean by *tampered with?*"

"It looks as if someone messed with his brakes," Deputy Hodgkins replied.

"How do you know that?" Anne asked, frowning. "His accident happened just a few hours ago. Have you already inspected his Range Rover?"

He nodded. "Yes, ma'am. One of the witnesses we interviewed told us something that raised our suspicion, so Deputy Ward checked the vehicle out, and, sure enough, he found that the brake line had been cut. We've had the vehicle and the trailer towed to the station, where they will be more thoroughly inspected."

"What did the witness tell you? Did they see Doug's accident?"

The younger deputy sat forward. "I'm the one who spoke with the witness, Mrs. Cummings. He was driving behind your husband and saw your husband's vehicle go off the road. He called nine-one-one from his cell phone."

"He can probably be credited with saving your husband's life," Deputy Hodgkins interjected. "Your husband's vehicle crashed so far down the mountainside that it wasn't visible from the road. Who knows when, or if, someone would have noticed it."

The younger deputy nodded. "Yeah, it was lucky he was there. Anyway, he said that the first thing that caught his attention was how fast your husband was going. They were approaching a sharp curve going down a steep hill on the far side of Mount Weather, and he said he couldn't believe that someone would drive so fast, especially hauling a horse trailer. He said he kept waiting for the driver to slow down, but the trailer brake lights never came on. Then he noticed that some kind of fluid was leaking from your husband's vehicle. He saw it on the highway and said some of it sprayed on his windshield. That's what made us suspect that your husband had some kind of mechanical trouble that caused him to lose control and go off the road."

Anne nodded. "Go on."

"When the vehicle was hauled up to go on the wrecker, I took a look at it and found that there was a good six-inch slit that ran along the brake line. Whoever cut it probably wanted the brake fluid to come out gradually, maybe to make sure your husband was out on the highway before the brakes went out. I also discovered that the emergency brake's cable had been sliced clear through, and the brake line to the horse trailer was all torn up, as if it had been dragging on the highway."

"But who would do such a thing?"

"That's why we wanted to talk to you, Mrs. Cummings," Deputy Hodgkins said. "We were hoping you might be able to shed some light on that."

"I have no idea," she replied.

"No disgruntled employees? Someone who was fired recently, perhaps?"

She shook her head. "No."

"Someone your husband sold a horse to? Or, maybe, someone he didn't buy a horse from?"

Anne frowned as she shook her head again, more vehemently. "No, there's been nothing like that."

Deputy Hodgkins leaned forward and put both elbows on his knees. "Mrs. Cummings, I recall that you and your husband had some trouble a few months back. What was the name of that fella who had it in for your husband?"

Anne stiffened. "Zeb McGraw."

"That's it. Has he gone to trial yet?"

"No. It's set for September." Her voice cracked, and she paused and took a deep breath. "But Zeb McGraw is in jail. He couldn't have tampered with Doug's car today."

The deputy nodded. "Still, I'll make a mention of it. Wouldn't hurt to take a look at who's been visiting McGraw in jail."

"Mrs. Cummings, you're a criminal lawyer, right?" the younger deputy asked.

"Yes."

"Can you think of a client, or a family member of a client, who might have a grudge against you? It happens more than you think, a client seeking retaliation for a case that didn't turn out the way he wanted."

"Yes, I know," Anne said quietly. *That's why Zeb McGraw had come after Doug. Seeking revenge for the way Doug had handled the case for McGraw's brother, Zeke.* "No client comes to mind right now, Deputy."

"Well, just keep it in mind."

She nodded. "Do you think whoever tampered with Doug's car might come here and try to harm him?"

"I wouldn't be too worried about that," Deputy Hodgkins replied. "I think that cutting a brake line is a far cry from coming into a hospital and harming someone. Besides, from what I've seen, it seems like they run a pretty tight ship here. I don't think anyone could get near him."

Anne knew he was right, but, still, a wave of panic washed over her. Doug might be behind secure doors, but what about Samantha? *What if the person who had tampered with Doug's car tried to hurt Samantha?* Anne's heart pounded and she put a hand on her chest and forced herself to slow her breathing.

"Mrs. Cummings, are you all right?" Deputy Hodgkins asked, rising from the couch and placing a hand on her shoulder.

She looked up at him. "What if he goes after our daughter?"

"Where is she?"

"At a friend's house."

"Look, Mrs. Cummings, I don't want you to be unnecessarily alarmed by this incident. I really don't think you need to worry about your daughter right now. For all we know, whoever tampered with your husband's vehicle might not even have known who the car belonged to. Maybe it was a teenage dare, or some kind of gang initiation. And even if they did intend to target your husband, that doesn't mean that they would do anything to your daughter."

Anne let out a deep breath. "I'm sure you're probably right. It's just that after what happened before . . ." Her voice trailed off and she looked away.

"Your concern is certainly understandable, Mrs. Cummings."

"What about you, Mrs. Cummings?" the young deputy asked. "Will you be at home alone tonight?"

"No, I'll be staying here with Doug," Anne replied, rising from her chair.

"That's good," Deputy Hodgkins said, retrieving his hat from the couch. "We'll let you get back to your husband. I hope we didn't cause you too much distress by telling you this, Mrs. Cummings, but we felt that you should know as soon as possible. I don't think you should be overly concerned at this point, but just be on the lookout for anyone or anything suspicious. And if you think of anyone who might hold a grudge against your husband, please give me a call." He pulled out his wallet and handed her a business card.

"Thank you for taking the time to come here and tell me," Anne said, taking the card from him.

Deputy Hodgkins nodded at her. "Yes, ma'am. No problem."

Anne followed them into the hallway and pushed the buzzer to get back into ICU. The baby was kicking incessantly, and she leaned against the wall while she waited for the door to be opened. She rubbed her belly soothingly. "Oh my God, I can't believe this is happening," she whispered.

12

*D*r. Ned Carey pulled off his surgical cap as he entered the observation room, revealing a thick mane of salt-and-pepper hair. He nodded at Jake and took a seat in the chair next to Kendall.

"It's good to see you, Kendall. Are you here because of Chancellor?"

Kendall nodded. "Yes, I just left Anne at the hospital with Doug. She asked me to come over and check on Chancellor."

"How's Doug doing?"

"Not good, I'm afraid. He's in a coma. When I left the hospital, they were moving him to ICU."

"I'm sorry to hear that. Please give my best to Mrs. Cummings."

Jake, who had been lounging against the windowsill with his arms folded across his chest, straightened up and narrowed his eyes at them. "Did you say Cummings?"

Ned looked at him and nodded. "Yes."

"*Doug* Cummings?"

Ned eyed Jake quizzically. "Yes. Doug Cummings."

"He's Chancellor's owner?"

"Yes."

Jake shook his head. "What are the odds of that?" he mumbled under his breath.

"Do you know Doug?" Kendall asked.

Jake opened his mouth as if to respond, then closed it again. "No." He lowered his eyes and looked away. "No, I don't know him."

"You obviously recognized his name."

He nodded, leaning back against the windowsill. "Yeah, you're right.

I recognized his name."

Kendall raised an eyebrow. "If you don't know him, where have you heard his name before?"

Jake shrugged. "I just read an article about him and the name stuck with me."

"Really? What was the article about?"

"I don't remember. It was in some paper I picked up at a truck stop where I had lunch today. I just remember thinking his name sounded like someone who would live around these parts. You know, kind of white-bread and horsey."

Kendall studied him. She didn't believe that explanation for a minute. Something about the fact that Doug was Chancellor's owner had obviously struck a chord with Jake.

Ned broke into her thoughts. "Let me fill you in on Chancellor's condition."

Kendall turned her attention back to the veterinarian. "How's he doing?"

"I'm very pleased with how the surgery went. I was able to patch the hole and reinflate Chancellor's lung. I've inserted a chest tube, which will remain in for a few days, and of course we'll continue to monitor his lungs and heart."

"Does he have a problem with his heart?"

"When he arrived, he had a rapid heartbeat and decreased cardiac output, a condition known as cardiac tamponade. It was caused by a contusion to his heart, which produced fluid retention in the pericardial sac. During surgery, we incised the pericardium and suctioned the blood off, which relieved the pressure on his heart."

Kendall paled as she listened to the veterinarian describe the procedure. "What are his prospects?"

"I'm cautiously optimistic. Pleurisy is my greatest concern at this point. Chancellor's puncture wound was dirty, and although we cleaned it out as much as we could, there is a risk of infection. We'll have him on IV antibiotics, as well as Banamine and Bute."

"What about his recovery time?"

"Sternum wounds generally heal very well. Barring any complications, he should be in the hospital for a week to ten days. When he goes home, he'll be on stall rest for a month; then he'll be able to go on turnout and gradually be put back to work."

"That's amazing, considering what he's been through. I'm sure Doug and Anne would want me to pass on their gratitude. It sounds like Chancellor wouldn't have survived without you."

Ned shook his head and gestured towards Jake. "Don't thank me, Kendall. Chancellor's alive due to Jake's quick thinking and expert horsemanship."

Kendall looked at Jake. "Really? What did you do?"

Jake shrugged off the compliment. "Doc Carey's exaggerating. It was a team effort. I just rigged up a contraption to help Chancellor breathe. Steve's the one who was responsible for getting Chancellor here in time."

"Don't let Jake's modesty fool you, Kendall. The contraption Jake rigged up saved Chancellor's life. Without it, Chancellor wouldn't even have made it to the horse ambulance."

They were interrupted by the sound of the door opening, and Kendall turned, to see a tall, dark-haired young woman enter the room, carrying an armful of clothing and a tan cowboy hat.

"Ah, Elizabeth, my dear, I was wondering where you were," Ned said. "Kendall, do you remember my daughter, Elizabeth?"

Kendall stared at her. "I do, but the last time I saw you, Elizabeth, you were still a kid. When did you get so grown up?"

Elizabeth blushed. "Nice to see you, Mrs. Baxter."

"Waters," Kendall corrected her.

"Pardon me?"

"I'm not Mrs. Baxter any longer. I'm divorced. I go by my maiden name now. Waters."

"Oh, I'm sorry. I didn't know."

"Don't be sorry. It's a good thing."

"Oh, well then, congratulations, I guess."

Elizabeth turned to Jake, extending her arms towards him. "Your clothes are finally dry, and I used a blow dryer on your hat. I hope it's dry enough."

"Thank you, Elizabeth." Jake smiled as he took the clothes from her. "Doc Carey, I think you're going to be busy fighting the boys off this one. Not only is she beautiful but she sure knows the way to a man's heart."

"What, by washing his clothes?" Kendall asked.

Jake grinned. "No. By understanding the affection he has for his cowboy hat."

Kendall looked away without giving him the satisfaction of seeing a reaction. He might have done a good deed and saved Chancellor's life, but she didn't like him very much.

Elizabeth giggled. "It's an *awesome* hat. I want to learn how to ride western and try barrel racing, but *Dad* won't let me." She rolled her eyes at her father.

"Elizabeth, one day when you're rich and famous, you can learn as many riding disciplines as you can afford. But for now, while you're still living under my roof and I'm paying the bills, you're stuck with showing that fancy junior hunter I bought you last fall." Ned gave her long ponytail an affectionate tug.

"Do you show on the circuit, Elizabeth?" Kendall asked.

Elizabeth shook her head. "No, it's too expensive. I showed at Upperville, but I usually just do the local shows. Except Dad lets me enter Warrenton and the Middleburg Classic."

"Maybe I'll see you at some of the shows. I'm just showing at the local shows these days, too."

Elizabeth's mouth hung open. "You're taking Wellington to the *local* shows?"

"For now."

"Oh, I get it. It's because of your divorce, right?"

Kendall felt a flush creep up her cheeks. "Yes, it is."

An uncomfortable silence passed for a moment and Ned cleared his throat. "I'd better go see how Chancellor's doing in recovery. I just wanted to fill you in on how the surgery went."

"Can I observe him in recovery?" Jake asked.

Ned shook his head. "I'm afraid not. I wish I could let you, but it's against the rules."

"I understand," Jake said. "I guess I'll be heading out, then. Any chance Steve's around to give me a lift back to my truck?"

"Oh, that's right. You rode here in the ambulance. Where's your truck?" Ned asked.

"Still on the side of the highway, unless they've towed it away by now."

"Geez, I hope they haven't done that. Why don't you get changed, and I'll have Elizabeth see if she can round up Steve to give you a ride."

"Steve's gone, Dad. I saw him when I went to get Jake's clothes out of the dryer. He said you asked him to wash the horse ambulance so it would look good when it's on display at the Equine Rescue League fund-raiser tomorrow."

Ned hit his palm against his forehead. "Of course, I forgot all about that."

"That's all right," Jake said. "I can hang out here until Steve gets back."

"Nonsense. After all you've done, the least we can do is offer you a ride to your truck."

Elizabeth flashed Jake a smile. "In eight more months, I'd be able to drive you."

"Please, don't remind me," Ned groaned.

"Dad!"

Ned laughed and looked at Kendall.

Oh no. Please don't ask me to give him a ride, Kendall thought, breaking eye contact with the vet.

"Kendall, any chance you'd have time to give Jake a ride?"

13

*K*endall had just driven through the gates of the Equine Medical Center when her cell phone rang. She glanced down at the display and saw that the call was from Anne.

"That's Anne Cummings calling," she said to Jake, pulling the Jeep onto the grassy shoulder and putting it in park.

She flipped the phone open and lifted it to her ear. "Hello."

"Hi, Kendall. It's Anne."

"Anne, how's Doug doing?"

"He's still the same. They've completed all the tests. He's in a room in ICU now," Anne replied in a weary voice.

"What about the tests? Did they show anything?"

"No. His brain activity looks normal, which is good. The doctor says we just have to give him time and hope for the best."

"Everyone's praying for him, Anne. Ned Carey sends his best, by the way."

"How's Chancellor?"

"It looks like he's going to be okay. He just came out of surgery and was still in recovery when I left. But Ned says he's optimistic, barring any complications," Kendall replied.

"How badly was he injured?"

"He had a chest wound and a punctured lung, but Ned was able to repair his lung. His only concern now is the risk of infection. I really think Chancellor's going to be fine, Anne."

"That's great news. I'll tell Doug. The nurses tell me that they believe he can hear what I'm saying to him, so I just keep talking to him, trying to reassure him that everything's going to be all right. I'm sure that if he can hear me, it will help him to know that Chancellor is okay."

"How about you? How are you holding up?"

Anne sighed. "I'm okay, but I'm worried about Samantha. I was hoping you might be able to check on her. Since she's so close to you, I thought it might help her to see you."

"Of course. What do you want me to tell her?"

"As little as possible. I guess just tell her that Doug was in a car accident and hurt his head, and he's in the hospital so the doctor can help him get better."

"All right. Is she going to spend the night at the Hortons', or would you rather have her at home with Nellie? I'm happy to drive her home."

"No, Nellie's out of town. She left yesterday to spend some time with her sister. I spoke with Deb Horton a little while ago, and she's happy to have Samantha stay there as long as necessary."

"I'd also be more than happy to take Samantha to my house, if you think that would be better."

Anne was silent for a moment. "No. I guess she's probably better off being at the Hortons', where she can play with Emma. That might help keep her from worrying. But thanks for offering, Kendall. I may take you up on it later. I guess I just have to take this one day at a time."

"Sure thing. I'll do anything I can to help. I hope you know that."

"I do. Thank you." Kendall heard Anne draw a deep breath. "There's something else I need to tell you."

"What's that?"

"I had a visit from two sheriff's deputies. They think someone tampered with Doug's car and that's why he went off the road."

"*What?*"

"I reacted the same way. They have no leads yet as to who might have done it, or why, but they are pretty confident that it wasn't an accident."

Kendall felt sick to her stomach. "I just can't believe it, Anne. Who would do that?"

"I don't know. But I'm worried that if someone tried to harm Doug, he might try to do something to Samantha. I've already spoken with Deb about it, but I'd appreciate it if when you're there you'd reiterate to Deb the importance of keeping the doors locked and not letting the girls play outside alone."

"Of course."

Neither one of them spoke for a moment; then Kendall broke the silence.

"Anne, I don't want to upset you, but I've got to wonder whether this could have something to do with Zeb McGraw."

Jake made a choking sound, and when Kendall looked at him, he pounded his chest and coughed a couple of times. She frowned and mouthed, "You okay?" He nodded and coughed into his fist once more.

"The deputy asked me the same question," Anne said. "Zeb McGraw obviously has a grudge against Doug. But he's in jail."

Kendall chewed the inside of her lip as she thought it over. "Just because he's in jail doesn't mean he couldn't have set something up. He might have an accomplice."

There was a long pause. "I know."

Anne's voice was strained, and Kendall regretted having said anything. "Look, why don't you get back to Doug, and I'll head on over to the Hortons' to see Samantha. Is there a way I can reach you after I see her?"

"I can't use my cell phone in the hospital. I had to step outside to make this call to you. And there isn't a phone in Doug's room. When I go back in, I can check and see if I can get the phone number for the nurses' station."

"No, don't bother with that now. If there's any need for me to get in touch with you after I see Samantha, I'll figure out a way. Let's just leave it that if you don't hear from me, everything's fine. And if you want to reach me, just call me on my cell. I'll keep it next to the bed, so I'll hear it if you call after I go to sleep. Please, call me whenever you want to. Don't worry about the time."

"Thanks, Kendall."

Kendall snapped her cell phone shut and placed it on the middle console.

"Everything all right?" Jake asked.

She looked at him. "Far from it."

"Anything I can do to help?"

"Actually, there is. Do you mind if I make a stop before taking you to your truck?"

"Sure, I'm in no hurry."

"Great," Kendall said, putting the Jeep in gear.

Jake held on to the dash as she stepped on the accelerator. "Any chance you're going to tell me what's going on?"

"I don't even know where to begin."

"How about at the beginning?" Jake said with a grin, which made Kendall smile in spite of herself.

She sighed. "Anne Cummings just told me that the authorities think Doug's car was tampered with and that's what caused him to go off the road."

"Tampered with? In what way?"

"I don't know. Anne didn't go into detail. But she's worried that someone might try to harm their daughter, Samantha. That's where we're going now. To check on Samantha."

Jake frowned. "That's a pretty big leap, isn't it? From car tampering to harming a child?"

"You wouldn't think that if you knew their history."

"Tell me."

Kendall sighed. "It would take me all night to tell you everything. In a nutshell, a psycho, Zeb McGraw, was stalking Doug last year, and he kidnapped Samantha, killed Samantha's au pair, and shot Doug."

"Is he still on the loose?"

"No, he's in jail, awaiting trial."

"Then it doesn't sound like he's much of a threat. It explains Mrs. Cummings's reaction, though."

"No kidding. I think Anne's holding it together remarkably well. She's eight months pregnant, her husband has a car accident and ends up in a coma, and now she learns that someone intentionally caused his accident. All of that coming on the heels of what happened last year."

"She's *pregnant*?"

Kendall nodded. "In fact, I was having a baby shower for Anne at my house today when we got the call that Doug had been in an accident."

"Oh Jesus!"

"Right. How much more can this family take? That's why Anne wants me to go see Samantha. To make sure she's coping all right."

"Is Samantha their only child?"

"Yes. Well, the baby will be their first biological child. Anne and Doug got married and adopted Samantha after the kidnapping last year."

"Hold on, you lost me there," Jake said. "I thought you said that this McGraw guy kidnapped Samantha because he was stalking Doug Cummings. But now you're saying that Doug Cummings wasn't her father at the time?"

"Right. Samantha's parents both died, and Anne was Samantha's guardian. Since Doug had a relationship with Anne, I guess McGraw figured Anne and Samantha were the closest thing to a family Doug had, so he kidnapped Samantha."

"Who is this McGraw guy?"

"He's a redneck from West Virginia."

Jake smirked and looked out the window.

"What's wrong?" Kendall asked.

"Nothing."

"Then what's the smirk about?"

He turned back towards her. "Oh, just your redneck comment. I guess I probably fall in that category too, being from Oklahoma."

"I didn't mean it that way. I don't have anything against people from West Virginia. Or Oklahoma, either, for that matter."

"If that's an apology, I accept it."

Kendall didn't respond, and they passed the next few moments in silence. Jake lounged in the passenger seat with his legs crossed, his left cowboy boot resting on his right knee. He stared out the window and drummed his fingers on his boot, humming along with the song on the radio. It drove Kendall nuts, but she refrained from saying anything.

Finally, Jake broke the silence. "Why was McGraw after Doug Cummings?"

Kendall reached down and pressed the button to turn the radio off. "Doug's a lawyer, and he represented Zeb McGraw's brother, Zeke, on a drug charge years ago. Zeke ended up in prison, where he committed suicide, and Zeb blamed Doug for it."

"Ah, sweet revenge."

"In his twisted mind, yes."

"When did all this happen?"

"Last fall. November, I think." Kendall thought for a moment. "Yes, it was right around Thanksgiving."

"Sounds like Doug Cummings hasn't had the best of luck, being shot last year and now being in this car accident."

Kendall shrugged. "You could look at it that way. Or, you could say he's an incredibly lucky guy. He survived being shot, got Samantha home safely, and married the woman of his dreams, who's about to give birth to his baby. I only hope his luck will continue and that he'll come out of the coma."

They had reached Gilbert's Corner and Kendall turned right towards Middleburg. She glanced at the clock on the dash. "It's been almost five hours since we got the phone call and Anne left for the hospital. I hope Samantha's been handling it all right."

"Is she still pretty shook up over the kidnapping?"

"Samantha still suffers from anxiety, but she seems to have made great progress since Anne and Doug married and adopted her last spring."

"Last spring?"

"Yes. They combined their wedding and Samantha's adoption in a beautiful ceremony on Easter weekend."

"Easter?" Jake began to count on his fingers. "April, May, June, July, August . . . I thought you said Anne was eight months pregnant."

Kendall glared at him. "Don't sit in judgment of them, Jake. You've never even met them."

"I'm not being judgmental. I was just making an observation."

"It's an observation you don't need to make."

Jake put a hand on her shoulder and gave her a gentle push. "Hey, lighten up."

Kendall sank away from his touch. "I don't need to *lighten up*," she said, pushing the power button on the radio and turning the volume high.

Jake's hand shot out and twirled the knob to lower the volume. "Do you have anger-management problems or something? If I had to guess, I'd bet it has something to do with your ex-husband, and I'm real sorry if you were married to an SOB. But, Jesus Christ, *I* never did anything to you. I was just driving down the highway, minding my own business, when I happened upon Doug Cummings's car accident. And I tried to do a good deed by offering my help. I didn't do it to get any kind of gratitude, and I don't really care if you appreciate what I did for your friend or not. But I'm exhausted, and my patience is really beginning to wear thin here. So, if you don't mind, could you at least make an effort to be civil?"

Kendall didn't give him the satisfaction of responding. She kept her eyes on the road, gripping the wheel so hard, her knuckles turned white.

$\mathcal{K}$endall sat on the sofa in the Hortons' living room with Samantha on her lap.

"When will I be able to see Daddy?" Samantha asked.

"As soon as his head feels better. Right now, he has a big bump right here." Kendall danced her fingertips across Samantha's forehead.

"I banged my head once at preschool and Mrs. Kennedy put ice on it, and after awhile it made it feel lots better. Is Mommy putting ice on Daddy's head?"

"I'll bet she is."

"How did Daddy hurt his head?"

Kendall wasn't sure how much to tell her. "He had a car accident and he bumped his head on the windshield."

Samantha frowned. "But Daddy always wears a seat belt, and that's supposed to protect you in a car accident."

"That's right, Samantha. But he still got a bump on his head."

Samantha fingered Kendall's pearl necklace. "Was Daddy the driver or a passenger?"

"He was driving."

"He always tells me that it's safer in the backseat. That's why he makes me sit there."

Kendall hugged her. "That's because your daddy loves you very much and he wants to make sure you don't get hurt or bump your head if there's a car accident."

Samantha nodded. "Yeah."

"Hey, you know what?" Kendall asked, brushing a strand of hair off

Samantha's face. "You get to have a sleepover here at Emma's tonight."

"How come?"

"Because your mommy is going to stay at the hospital tonight with your daddy so she can help the nurse take care of him."

Samantha's eyes filled with tears. "I want to help take care of him, too."

"I know you do, sweetie. And you'll be a big help when your daddy comes home from the hospital."

"But why can't I help take care of him in the hospital?" Samantha whimpered, burying her face against Kendall's shoulder.

"Because they have rules that kids aren't allowed."

Kendall looked over Samantha's head at Deb and raised her eyebrows.

"Samantha, we are going to have so much fun tonight," Deb said, kneeling down next to them. "What would you think about you and Emma making ice-cream sundaes?"

Samantha turned her head enough to peer down at Deb. "With gummy bears?"

"Of course," Deb said, smiling.

Samantha swiped at her tears with her fist. "I guess that would be okay."

"Great." Deb stood up and held her hand out to Samantha. "Let's go get started."

Samantha looked questioningly at Kendall, who nodded and helped Samantha climb down off her lap. "That sounds delicious, Samantha. I wish I could stay for ice cream."

"Why can't you?" Samantha asked as they walked towards the front door.

Kendall glanced out the window and caught a glimpse of Jake waiting in her Jeep. "See that man out there, sitting in my car?"

Samantha nodded.

"He's waiting for me to give him a ride somewhere."

Samantha looked out the window. "Who is he?"

Kendall hesitated. *How should she explain who Jake was?* "His name is Jake and he's your daddy's friend. And he's friends with Chancellor, too."

"How does he know Chancellor?" Samantha asked.

Oh shit. That was a can of worms she did not want to open.

"Kendall," Samantha said, tugging on Kendall's dress. "How does he know Chancellor?"

Kendall took a deep breath. She knew that Samantha would find out

66

about Chancellor's injuries at some point, so she might as well prepare her for it now.

"When your daddy had the car accident, Chancellor was in the trailer, so he was in the accident, too. Jake helped take care of Chancellor."

"Is Chancellor okay?"

"Chancellor is fine. He got a little bit hurt, but he's at the horse hospital and they're taking good care of him."

Samantha's eyes grew wide with alarm. "Chancellor's in the hospital, too?"

"Yes, sweetie."

"But why is he in the hospital if he's okay?" Her lower lip quivered, as if she were about to cry again.

Kendall knelt down and put her arm around Samantha. "Samantha, I promise you that Chancellor is fine," she said, forcing a reassuring smile.

Samantha didn't return Kendall's smile, but at least she didn't cry. She turned away and stared outside, leaning her forehead against the windowpane. "Is Jake a cowboy?"

Kendall followed her gaze and saw that Jake's cowboy hat rested on the dash in front of him. "Yes, he is."

"I've never met a real cowboy before. Is he nice?"

"Yes." Kendall supposed Samantha probably would think Jake was nice. Elizabeth had certainly seemed smitten with him.

"Why's he sitting in the car?"

"It's such a pretty evening, he wanted to stay outside," Kendall said. The truth was, she hadn't invited him in. Neither of them had spoken a word to each other since his outburst on the drive over.

"Samantha, would you like to go outside and meet him?" Deb asked. "I met him when Kendall arrived."

Samantha turned away from the window and looked at Kendall. "Would that be okay?"

"Sure."

"Can Emma come, too? I don't think she's ever met a real cowboy before, either," Samantha said.

"Of course she can."

"Let me go and get Emma from the playroom," Deb said. "You two go on out. We'll be there in a minute."

Kendall opened the front door and reached for Samantha's hand. "Come on, sweetie. Let's go meet your cowboy."

As they walked towards the Jeep, Jake opened the door and stepped out.

"Jake, I have someone here who'd like to meet you," Kendall said when they reached the vehicle. "Samantha, this is Jake. Jake, this is Samantha."

Jake held out his hand. "It's very nice to meet you, Samantha."

Samantha smiled shyly and put her small hand in his. "It's nice to meet you, too," she said softly.

"I told Samantha that you and Chancellor are friends," Kendall said.

"Oh, boy, are we ever." Jake let go of Samantha's hand and leaned back against the Jeep.

"Kendall told me that Chancellor's in the horse hospital but that he's going to be okay," Samantha said.

Jake glanced at Kendall. "That's right, darling."

The door to the house opened and Deb and Emma walked out. "That's my best friend, Emma," Samantha said. "I'm going to have a sleepover here because my daddy is in the hospital and my mommy is spending the night there with him."

"I heard about that," Jake said.

"Emma, this is Jake," Samantha said when Emma reached them. "He's a real cowboy."

Emma looked down at his boots. "Do you ride bucking broncos?"

Jake smiled. "No. I usually ride a nice quarter horse named Charlie."

"What color is Charlie?"

"He's a bay, just like Chancellor. And he has a big old blaze down his face and four white socks."

"Do you go foxhunting with Charlie?" Emma asked.

"Don't be silly, Emma. Cowboys don't go foxhunting," Samantha said.

"Samantha's right," Jake said. "I don't know the first thing about fox-hunting. Do the two of you foxhunt?"

Both girls giggled. "No, we're still too little," Samantha replied. "But my daddy's going to take me beagling on the leadline next year, when I'm six."

Jake frowned. "Beagling? What's that?"

"That's when you go foxhunting with beagles instead of foxhounds. It's for kids," Samantha explained.

"That sounds like it'll be real fun."

"Girls, I think we've taken up enough of Jake's time," Deb said. "Why don't we head back inside and make those ice cream sundaes?"

"Okay," both girls said in unison.

"It was nice to meet you, Jake," Samantha said. "Thank you for helping make Chancellor feel better."

He nodded at her. "You're welcome, darling. He's a nice horse. I'm glad I got to help him. You tell him hi for me when he gets home, okay?"

"Okay." Samantha turned to Kendall and held her arms out for a hug. "Bye-bye, Kendall. I love you."

"I love you, too, sweetie," Kendall said, giving her a big squeeze. "You have fun with Emma tonight. I'll see you tomorrow."

Kendall turned to Deb. "Thanks, Deb." She leaned close to give her a hug and whispered, "Don't forget about locking the doors."

Deb nodded and held a hand out to each girl. "Come on, girls. The gummy bears are waiting."

Kendall and Jake watched in silence as the girls skipped up the walk to the house.

"Cute kids," Jake said.

"Aren't they? Thanks for being so nice to them. They were thrilled to meet a real cowboy."

He smiled wryly. "Yeah, I guess I kind of stick out like a sore thumb around here."

"You're somewhat of a novelty in hunt country, let's put it that way." Kendall walked around to the driver's door. "I guess we can be on our way."

They both climbed into the Jeep and Kendall put the key in the ignition, but she didn't start the engine. Instead, she took a deep breath and turned to Jake.

"Look—"

"Kendall—"

They both stopped. "Ladies first," Jake said.

She forced herself to look him in the eye. "I was just going to say that I'm sorry if I've seemed inhospitable. I think it's a wonderful thing you did, helping rescue Chancellor."

He gave her a lopsided grin. "Thanks."

"Now, what were you going to say?"

He exhaled loudly. "I was going to say that I'm sorry about what I said about your ex-husband. That was hitting below the belt."

She gave him a curt nod. "Apology accepted."

"And one more thing. I shouldn't have made that remark about when Mrs. Cummings's baby is due."

Kendall was surprised by his admission. Perhaps he wasn't as insensitive as she'd thought. "Anne and Doug are really good people. And they are very much in love. They didn't get married because they *had* to, and it really upset me to hear you imply that. Especially now, with Doug lying in a coma."

She felt Jake watching her as she started the engine and put the Jeep in gear, and when she made eye contact, he smiled. "You're a good friend, sticking up for them like that. I admire your loyalty. And like I said, I'm sorry about the comment. I feel like a jerk for saying it."

At least we agree on one thing, Kendall thought.

*T*he graying light of dawn was just creeping into the hospital room when Anne thought she saw Doug's fingers move. She bolted forward in her chair, her eyes glued to his hand. Had his fingers really moved, or had she imagined it?

She slipped her hand over his and squeezed lightly. "I'm right here, Doug. I'm holding your hand. Can you feel it? Wiggle your fingers if you can hear me."

Anne loosened her grasp on Doug's hand and stared at his fingers. *Please, God, let them move,* she prayed. But Doug's hand lay limply in hers.

She stood up and placed her hand against his cheek. "Doug, please wake up. Our baby needs you. You can't let our baby grow up without ever knowing you. Please, please, try to wake up."

The rhythmic whoosh of the ventilator was the only response, and Anne sank into the chair and closed her eyes.

She awoke with a start to a high-pitched shrieking sound and heard a female voice scream, "He's bucking the vent!"

Anne saw two nurses leaning over Doug's bed. "What's happening?" she asked, struggling to her feet and covering her ears with her hands. She turned her head in the direction of the sound and realized it was coming from the ventilator.

The nurse nearest to Anne held an arm out and motioned for her to stay back. "Mr. Cummings, you're in the hospital, and you have a tube down your airway. The more you fight it, the more uncomfortable it will be," she said in a loud voice. "You must try to calm down."

Anne rushed to the foot of the bed, where she had a clear view of Doug.

His eyes were open and they flashed back and forth wildly as he strained against the nurses' grasp.

"What's happening to him?"

"He's trying to pull the ventilator tube out," the nurse replied. "If he doesn't settle down, we'll give him Diprivan."

"What's that?"

"It's an anesthetic."

Anne slid around the side of the bed so she was closer to Doug. She put her hand on his leg. "Doug, it's okay. Stop fighting. Everything's okay. Just try to relax."

Doug's blue eyes focused on Anne and his struggling stopped.

"There you go. Just take it easy," the nurse said, keeping her hold on his arm while reaching over and silencing the alarm on the ventilator. "I know it's uncomfortable."

Anne touched the nurse's shoulder. "Please, may I stand next to him?"

The nurse spoke to Doug. "Mr. Cummings, if I let go of your arm so your wife can move closer to you, do you promise not to grab at the tube again?"

Doug made a choking noise and tried to lift his hand.

"No, don't try to speak. You won't be able to talk while you're on the ventilator. Just nod your head," the nurse said calmly.

Doug nodded.

"Okay." The nurse let go of his arm and moved aside. "I'm going to call respiratory therapy."

Anne reached for his hand and could have shouted with joy when she felt him squeeze her hand in return. She smiled and leaned close to him. "Doug, you had a car accident and you've been unconscious for a little while."

His eyes were worried and full of questions, and Anne brought his hand up to her mouth and brushed her lips against it, then rested it against her cheek. "Everything's okay. You're going to be just fine."

Anne heard the sound of approaching footsteps. She turned, to see Dr. Martin enter the room.

"I was on the floor and heard that Mr. Cummings is awake," he said, nodding at Anne as he walked around to the opposite side of Doug's bed.

"Respiratory therapy is on the way, Dr. Martin, and we've paged Dr. Hollins," the nurse said.

"Very good."

"The ventilator is bothering him," Anne said. "Can he come off it now?"

"That's what we're going to determine." Dr. Martin placed his hand on Doug's shoulder. "Mr. Cummings, I'm going to ask you to move different parts of your body, okay?"

Doug nodded.

"All right. Let me see you move your right foot. Very good. Now your left foot. Great. And your left hand. Good. And, now, if your wife will let go of your right hand for just a moment, I'd like to see you move it. Wonderful."

He took a penlight out of his jacket pocket and aimed it at each of Doug's eyes. "Excellent."

A woman had arrived while Dr. Martin was examining Doug, and she studied the monitors. The doctor looked expectantly at her.

"Hi, Dr. Martin. I'm Lori from respiratory therapy."

"What's your assessment?"

"Sir, I don't think we need weaning parameters. He's awake, he's pulling big tidal volumes, and his oxygen saturation level is one hundred percent. There's really no need for him to be on the vent."

A nurse entered the room. "Dr. Hollins is on the phone."

"I'll talk to her," Dr. Martin said, walking towards the door.

He returned in a few moments and said to the woman from respiratory therapy, "Dr. Hollins says to go ahead and extubate."

The doctor turned to Anne. "Mrs. Cummings, why don't you and I wait out in the hallway while they extubate your husband. You'll be able to come back in a few minutes."

"Do I have to leave?" Anne asked. "Can't I stay in here, if I keep out of the way?"

Dr. Martin smiled at her. "You're better off waiting outside, Mrs. Cummings. They'll take very good care of him. I promise."

Anne figured she wasn't going to get anywhere arguing with him. She squeezed Doug's hand and kissed him on the forehead. "I'll be back in a minute. I love you."

elda waited next to the pay phone and grabbed the receiver on the first
ring. "Hello?"

"Hi, babe," Earl drawled in his sexy voice.

"Hey. I missed talking to you last night. Is everything okay?" She ran her
hand up and down the metal phone cord as she spoke.

"It is now that I'm talking to you."

Zelda felt a pleasant blush warm her cheeks. "Yeah, I feel the same way.
God, I miss you. I don't know how much longer I can stand it in this hellhole
without you."

"It may be longer than we thought. We've got a problem."

Zelda's heart skipped a beat. "What's wrong?"

"Cummings is in the hospital and he might die."

"*What?*"

"Yeah, and it gets worse," Earl said. "It was Zach's fault."

"What did he do?"

"He cut the brake line on Cummings's car. Cummings was hauling the
horse trailer over Mount Weather and went off the road."

"*Shit.* We told him to get Cummings's attention, not kill him."

"You ain't telling me anything I don't already know, babe."

"Do you really think Cummings might die?"

"I haven't heard how he is today, but last night things didn't look so
good."

"What will we do? That fucks up the whole plan."

"Ain't nothing going to fuck up our plan, Zelda. We just might have to
take a detour."

Zelda thought it over for a moment. "There's still the wife and kid."

He chuckled. "That's what I love about you, babe. You're always thinking."

She flushed with pleasure. "How's Zach doing, other than the fact that he screwed up big-time."

"He's fitting in fine. He says they all act like they like him."

"No problem with his work papers?" Zelda didn't trust Daryl, the guy they'd gotten the fake IDs from.

"Nah. They never took a second look. I told you, Daryl's a pro. Our alibis will hold up."

"What's it like, using a fake name? Do you forget and not answer when folks are talking to you?"

"Nah, it's a piece of cake."

"What about the tags for my car? Did Daryl come through with those?"

"Stop worrying, babe. It's no problem. Besides, I gave your car to Zach."

She frowned. "How are you getting around?"

"I got me a truck. It fits better with my story."

"Don't tell me you went and stole a truck!"

"It's all under control, babe," Earl said coolly. "Look, I've got to go. I'm heading over to make friends at the barn where some of Cummings's buddies ride. I'll find out more about how Cummings is doing, and I'll call you back at noon."

"All right. I miss you," she said. But he had already hung up.

17

*W*ellington sailed over the last fence on the course, and as Kendall turned him into a hunter circle, she heard the sound of someone clapping from the observation area at the opposite end of the indoor arena. As she completed the circle and brought Wellington back to a walk, she turned and saw Jake leaning against the rail. When she'd dropped him off at his truck the night before, she'd invited him to stop by the barn this morning, but she hadn't thought he would take her up on it.

"Hi," she called out, giving Wellington a loose rein and guiding him towards the end of the ring.

"Nice horse," Jake said.

Kendall reached down and patted Wellington on his neck. "Thank you. He's a once-in-a-lifetime horse for me."

She rode over to where Jake stood, and Wellington stretched his long neck and nosed Jake in the chest.

"Hey, buddy." Jake reached up and rubbed Wellington's face. "You're a mighty fancy guy, aren't you?"

"And lucky for me he's also a gentleman. As I'm sure you know, talent and manners don't always go together."

"Yeah, so I've heard," Jake said wryly. He ran his eyes over Wellington. "He's sure put together nice. How big is he; sixteen two, sixteen three?"

She slid down from the saddle and rolled up her stirrups. "He's seventeen hands."

"Really? He doesn't look that big. I guess it's because he takes your leg up nicely. Even though you're petite, you don't look too small on him."

"I'm five foot seven," Kendall said. "And I have a long leg, so I need a tall horse. It wasn't easy to find one that didn't overpower me."

"How long have you had him?"

She flipped the reins over Wellington's head and loosened the girth. "Four years. I got him when he was a six-year-old."

"I heard you talking to Elizabeth about showing him. I'll bet you've got a few trophies with his name on them."

Kendall smiled. "He's earned his fair share of trophies." She opened the gate and led Wellington through. "I'm going to go hose him off. If you want to come with me, I'll show you around."

"Sure, this looks like quite a place," Jake said, following her down the walkway that led to the barn. "Hey, one reason I stopped by is that I wanted to let you know how Chancellor is doing. I went to the Equine Medical Center to see him first thing this morning."

"Oh, how is he? I tried calling earlier, but since it's Sunday, I only got a recording."

"He's doing great. He's still hooked up to IVs, but they fed him a little hay this morning, and he was screaming for more when I got there. Doc Carey wasn't there, but I talked to a nice gal who's been taking care of him, and she told me he's been a trooper."

He paused for a moment and smiled. "She let me go in the stall with Chancellor for a minute, and he nickered when he saw me. It reminded me of that TV show *Fury*."

"I guess you two really did have a bonding experience yesterday."

As they passed the door to the office, Margaret Southwell walked into the barn aisle with a tall, dark-haired man who was on crutches.

"Oh, Kendall, you're just the person I was looking for. I want to introduce you to Stephen Lloyd. He plays polo and he's considering moving to the area. Stephen, this is Kendall Waters."

Stephen smiled and balanced on one crutch while he extended his hand. "As you can imagine, my polo playing is a little limited right now, but I hope to get this cast off in a couple of weeks, and then I'll be back in the saddle again."

"Did you get hurt riding?" Kendall asked, shaking his hand.

"Actually, the riding was fine. It was the fall that did me in," he said with a laugh.

"Stephen's from Aiken, South Carolina," Margaret said.

"Oh, is that right?" Kendall said. "I love Aiken. It's beautiful down there."

"That's what everyone in Aiken says about Middleburg," Stephen said.

Kendall smiled. "Have you been to polo at Great Meadow yet?"

He shook his head. "No, but I'll be there this Friday. I hear there's a tournament going on this week."

"It's a lot of fun. I don't know much about polo, but I enjoy watching."

"I hope to see you there."

Jake had stepped off to the side when they began talking. Margaret was eyeing him curiously. "Kendall, aren't you going to introduce your friend?"

"Oh, sure. I'm sorry. This is Jake. . . ." Kendall realized she didn't know Jake's last name. "He's the one who helped rescue Chancellor yesterday when Doug had his accident."

"So, you're the mysterious Jake." The crow's feet around Margaret's eyes crinkled as she broke into a broad smile. "I've already heard all about you. The talk around town is that you're a real horse whisperer."

Jake removed his cowboy hat. "Hello, ma'am. Jake Dawson. Sounds like someone blew things out of proportion with the horse whisperer talk, but I was happy to help out. Chancellor is an amazing horse, and it's real tragic what happened to Mr. Cummings."

Margaret pursed her lips. "Isn't it, though? Kendall, do you know how Doug is doing today?"

Kendall shook her head and glanced down at the cell phone she had clipped to her belt. "I haven't heard from Anne yet this morning." She checked the phone to make sure she hadn't missed a call.

"Please give her my best when you talk to her, will you? And tell her we're praying for Doug."

"Of course." She patted her horse on the neck. "I'd better get Wellington to the wash stall and hose him off. It was nice to meet you, Stephen."

"The pleasure was all mine."

After they were out of hearing distance, Kendall turned to Jake. "Margaret is the owner here."

"It's sure a nice farm." Jake gestured at the thick oak boards in the aisle and the exterior stone walls in the stalls. "I guess this barn has some history. It looks pretty old."

Kendall nodded. "The farm has been in Margaret's family for several generations. This was the original barn on the property."

"How many horses do they have here?"

"Around fifty, I think."

He whistled. "That's a full-time job, and then some. I hope she has good help."

"Margaret has a pretty decent staff this summer, but they always seem to drop like flies during the winter, once they have to break ice in the water buckets and change the horses' blankets twice a day."

"Yeah, horses are high-maintenance work; there's no denying that."

They rounded the corner and saw a tall, muscular young man mucking out a stall. "Hi, Todd," Kendall said as they passed by.

The young man grinned at her and tossed his blond hair out of his eyes. "Good morning, Miss Waters."

"Todd's a cute kid," Kendall said to Jake. "Margaret just hired him a couple of weeks ago. He doesn't have a whole lot of experience working with horses, but he's reliable and a quick learner, which sometimes is better than experience."

She led Wellington into the wash stall and put the reins over his neck while she unbuckled his bridle and slid it off. Jake reached out and took the bridle from her and handed her a grooming halter.

"Thanks," she said, a little taken aback by his helpfulness.

"No problem. Here, let me help you with the saddle."

Jake moved past her in the narrow wash stall, lifted the saddle flap, and unbuckled the girth. He was so close to her that Kendall could smell his after-shave, and the proximity made her uncomfortable. His arm brushed against her shoulder as he lifted the saddle off Wellington's back, and she stepped to the side.

"Pardon me," he said, sliding past her again as he carried the saddle out of the wash stall and set it on the saddle rack.

Kendall clipped the cross-ties to the grooming halter. As she reached to turn the hose on, she heard the clattering of hooves in the barn aisle.

"Uh-oh," she said, grabbing Wellington by the halter and leaning out into the aisle to see what was happening.

A gray horse galloped towards them, fully tacked, and a girl ran after it, yelling, "Whoa, Cloudy."

Jake stepped into the middle of the aisle, directly in the path of the loose horse, and stretched his arms out to the side. "Whoa, boy, easy," he murmured as the horse neared.

The horse continued towards them at full speed, but Jake didn't flinch, and at the last minute, the horse skidded to a stop on the asphalt surface. The horse's sides were heaving, and it eyed Jake warily.

"It's okay, good boy, just take it easy," Jake said softly, easing his hand out to grasp the dangling reins. "There you go."

The girl reached them and Kendall saw that it was Elizabeth Carey. "Elizabeth, are you all right?" she asked, stepping out of the wash stall.

"Yeah, I'm fine."

"What happened?"

Elizabeth made a face as she brushed some dirt off her breeches. "Cloudy bucked me off. *Again.* He's developed a real bad attitude. Whenever I ask him to do something he doesn't want to do, he tries to dump me. I thought maybe he was getting sour from always being ridden in our small ring at home and a change of scenery might help, so Dad trailered me over here to school him."

"Is your dad here?" Kendall asked.

"No, he had to go to the EMC for a while. He's going to pick me up later." Elizabeth took the reins from Jake. "Thanks for catching him for me. I'm so embarrassed you saw that happen."

"No need to be embarrassed. We all fall off on occasion," Jake said, smiling at her.

Todd had been watching from the nearby stall and he leaned his pitchfork against the stall door and walked over to them. "Anything I can do to help?"

"Yeah, pretend you never saw that, okay?" Elizabeth said.

Kendall laughed. "Elizabeth, this is Todd."

"Hi," Elizabeth said glumly. "I wish we'd met under better circumstances."

"Aw, come on, don't be so hard on yourself," Jake said. "Why don't you get back on and work him some more?"

"That's the problem," Elizabeth said. "I can't ride him through it. I guess Cloudy's figured out that he can avoid work by bucking me off. I'm sure if a professional rode Cloudy a few times, he could straighten him out, but I'm afraid to tell Dad. He paid so much for Cloudy. I don't dare ask him to pay for training."

"Want me to hop on him?" Jake asked.

Elizabeth's eyes widened. "Would you?"

He nodded. "Sure, come on."

"Thank you so much," she said, giving him a big smile. "Miss Waters, do you want to come and watch?"

"You go ahead," Kendall said. "I'll be there after I finish hosing Wellington off."

Kendall watched Jake and Elizabeth walk down the aisle towards the ring, and as she turned back to Wellington, she saw Todd watching them as well.

CHAPTER

18

When Anne was allowed back in Doug's room, he was off the ventilator and had a small oxygen tube running to his nose. He smiled when he saw her, and Anne leaned over and kissed him, then buried her face in his neck. Doug raised his arm and held her close.

They embraced for several minutes, amid the tangle of IV lines, and then Anne pulled back so she could look into his eyes. "I was so worried about you."

Doug frowned. "I drove off the road," he said in a raspy voice.

"Try not to talk, Mr. Cummings," the nurse said. "You need to let your voice box relax."

Doug shot the nurse an annoyed look. "The trailer flipped off the hitch with Chancellor in it."

"Chancellor's okay, Doug. He's at the EMC and he's going to be fine. There's nothing to worry about. You're both going to be just fine."

Doug nodded, but his eyes still darted worriedly as he looked at her. "My brakes went out, Anne. The emergency brake, too. And the trailer brakes."

She nodded and put her fingers on his mouth. "Shhh. Don't strain to talk. I know; something was wrong with your brakes. It wasn't your fault."

"But why would they all go out at once?"

The nurse put her hand on Anne's arm. "Mrs. Cummings, your husband needs to rest now. I must insist that he stop talking, or I'll have to ask you to leave the room."

Anne gave her a quick nod. She knew the nurse was right. Doug was becoming agitated, and it concerned her. "Doug, please don't worry about it now. There are a lot of questions that we'll get the answers to. But right now, you just need to concentrate on getting better. Please, just calm down and try to rest."

Doug glared at the nurse, but he didn't try to speak again, and Anne could see that he was exhausted. "Just sleep now. I'll be right here when you wake up," she said, holding his hand.

Doug's eyes drifted closed and Anne sat down in the chair next to him, her thoughts jumbled with questions about his accident. *Who had tampered with Doug's brakes? And, for God's sake, why? Could it really have anything to do with Zeb McGraw?* A shiver ran down Anne's spine and she gripped Doug's hand tighter. McGraw's trial date was coming up. Was the timing coincidental, or could this somehow be connected to that?

19

$\mathcal{Z}$elda entered the front door of the nursing home, hoping it would be the last time she'd have to suffer through the ordeal.

"How's my mama today?" she asked the woman at the desk when she signed in.

"About the same," the woman replied. "She's sitting out on the veranda."

"Veranda my ass," Zelda muttered. It was nothing more than a rickety old porch. She crossed the lobby, avoiding eye contact with the old people who lounged there. *I ain't never going to end up like this,* she thought. *Sitting in my own shit; not even knowing who I am. I'll kill myself before I let that happen.*

She found her mama in her wheelchair, parked by the railing, staring vacantly off into the parking lot.

"Hey, Mama," Zelda said, squatting down next to her. "How you feeling today?"

The old woman slowly turned her head towards Zelda. "Who are you?"

"It's me, Mama. Zelda."

"I don't know you," her mama said, turning her head back towards the parking lot.

Zelda reached for her mama's hand, shuddering at how bony and wrinkled it was. "Zeb sends his love, Mama. He's doing real good and he wishes he could come and see you."

The old woman didn't respond.

"I've got good news, Mama. I'm back together with Earl Davis. You remember him, don't you, Mama?"

Her mama just stared vacantly at the parking lot.

"You really liked Earl, Mama. You wanted us to get married."

"It's too dang hot out here," her mama said, pulling her hand out of Zelda's grasp. "They just bring me out here and leave me in this heat for hours. I could die of heatstroke sitting out here, and no one would even know about it."

Zelda sighed and looked around the porch to make sure no one was within hearing distance. "I'm going to be going away for a while, Mama. I'm not sure when I'll be able to see you again. But I'll be thinking about you, and I know they'll take real good care of you here. I'll keep paying the bills; don't you worry none."

"I have a boy named Zeke," her mama said, turning her watery blue eyes in Zelda's direction. "But he don't never come see me."

Zelda closed her eyes and sighed. "Zeke's dead, Mama. He died in prison because of that shitty lawyer he had. That's why he don't come see you."

"His name is Zeke," her mama said again, as if Zelda hadn't spoken. "He's a nice boy. Used to take good care of his mama, except he don't come see me no more."

"He's dead, Mama. But you still have Zeb and me. Remember your son Zeb?"

Her mama seemed to perk up at the sound of Zeb's name. "You remember Zeb, don't you, Mama?" Zelda asked. "Your oldest boy, Zeb?"

"Zeb's in jail. My boy Zeb is in jail."

"That's right, Mama." Zelda smiled. "Zeb's in jail. But not for much longer. Zeb is going to be getting out of jail real soon."

Zelda kissed her mama on the cheek and turned towards the door to the lobby.

"Zelda."

She spun around. "Yes, Mama?"

"It's your own fault Earl Davis never married you. You went and let that other boy get you pregnant."

*K*endall flipped her cell phone shut as she opened the door to the observation lounge. Margaret stood by the minibar at the far end of the room and Stephen Lloyd was seated on a couch in front of the cavernous stone fireplace.

"I have great news," Kendall said. "Doug came out of the coma, and it looks like he's going to be fine."

"Oh, thank God," Margaret said.

Stephen Lloyd winced as he eased his leg with the cast onto the coffee table in front of him. "Hey, that's great. I don't even know the man, but the way everyone's been talking about him, he must be some guy. I'm very happy for him and his family."

Margaret held up an ice-filled glass. "I was just getting some iced tea for Stephen and myself. Would you like a glass, Kendall?"

"I'd love one. Thanks."

Margaret poured tea into three mason-jar glasses and placed them on a tray. "Doug will be in the hospital for some time, I suppose. Do you think Samantha will still be coming to riding camp this week?"

"Yes. In fact, I just discussed that with Anne. She thinks it would be best to keep Samantha busy. If Anne stays at the hospital again tonight, I'm going to pick Samantha up and have her spend the night at my house. And even if Anne goes home tonight, I'll bring Samantha to camp tomorrow. I told Anne I'd be happy to bring Samantha to camp all week."

Margaret eyed Stephen's leg as she set the tray on the coffee table and handed a glass to Kendall. "Kendall, that was very kind of you to offer to take Samantha. Let me see if I can't find someone to help you out with the camp.

You have the young group this week, and I'm sure they'll be a handful."

"Wait a minute, I'm confused. I thought you were a boarder," Stephen said, accepting the glass Margaret offered him. "You teach camp here?"

Kendall placed her glass on the counter in front of the observation window and perched on a tall stool. "Yes—"

"I was in a bind and Kendall agreed to help me out," Margaret said, taking a seat on the couch next to Stephen. "She is a boarder here, but my camp counselor quit on me, and since Kendall's an excellent rider and the kids love her, I begged her to fill in. And you've been having fun, haven't you, Kendall?"

Kendall shifted uncomfortably. *Why was Margaret trying to pretend that she wasn't teaching camp in exchange for board?* "Yes, I've really enjoyed teaching the kids."

The door opened and Elizabeth burst into the lounge. "You guys, you would not believe what a different horse I have now! Oh my gosh. Were you watching? After Jake rode Cloudy, I got back on, and he did everything I asked him to. Just like when I bought him, only even better. I'm so excited." She beamed at Jake, who had followed her into the room.

"Whoa, slow down there," he said, grinning broadly and shaking his head. "You're making my head spin."

"I saw you working with him, Jake, and I was quite impressed," Margaret said. "You're firm but patient. I like that."

Jake shrugged off the compliment. "He's a nice horse. He just needed a tune-up, that's all."

Margaret smiled. "Don't be so modest. You're a talented rider. Have you worked much with hunters?"

"No, ma'am."

"What's your background?"

Jake hesitated. "Western. Quarter horses mostly."

"Well, you certainly did a nice job schooling Elizabeth's Thoroughbred."

"I wish you could ride him every day for a week, Jake," Elizabeth said. "Then I'd be sure Cloudy wasn't going to forget. I'm so afraid that I'll get on him at home tomorrow and he'll be back to his old tricks."

"He'll be fine," Jake said. "You underestimate your ability."

Margaret studied Jake thoughtfully. "Are you going to be staying around town for a while?"

"I'm not sure, ma'am. I don't really have any definite plans."

Margaret smiled. "I might just have a solution that helps everyone out."

"What scheme are you cooking up, Margaret?" Kendall asked.

"You know me too well. Kendall, what if Elizabeth helped you out with summer camp this week, in exchange for keeping Cloudy here?"

"Sure, I'd love to have Elizabeth's help."

Margaret looked at Elizabeth. "Elizabeth, what do you think about that arrangement?"

"I'd be happy to help Miss Waters," Elizabeth said. "And I'd love to have Cloudy here for a week. I just have to ask my dad and make sure it's all right. But I'm sure he'll say yes."

"Good," Margaret said. "Now, Jake, how would you feel about staying here for a while and riding some horses for me? I have a few young horses I think you'd be well suited for. You could school my horses and ride Cloudy for Elizabeth. I'll pay your going rate, of course, and I have a cottage you're welcome to stay in while you're here."

Jake's expression was hard to read. He looked serious, as if he were weighing the possibilities, but his mouth also held a faint hint of a smile.

Finally, he tipped his hat and nodded at Margaret. "Mrs. Southwell, you've got yourself a deal."

"Wonderful," she said, clapping her hands together. "Stephen, remember what I was saying earlier about how everyone in this community is so willing to help out when others are in need? This is a perfect example of that."

"Yes, I see what you mean," Stephen said. "It's quite touching. And I love your stable. I hope that when my polo ponies arrive, you'll have room for me to board them here."

Kendall thought she detected a note of sarcasm in Stephen's voice, but she couldn't be certain.

"I'll be happy to put you on the waiting list," Margaret said. "Do you have any idea when they'll ship up here?"

"No, I don't have a firm date yet. I thought I'd leave them in Aiken until I get this cast off and can start riding again. That way, my stable help can keep them exercised."

"Just give me as much notice as possible. We're full up now, but if I have some notice, I might be able to move some of the lesson horses around to make room for you."

"I appreciate that." Stephen glanced at his watch and picked up his crutches. "I need to be heading back to the Red Fox. I have a conference call

I need to make."

"I should go, too," Jake said. "I stayed at a motel in Leesburg last night, and checkout time is noon."

"Can I use the phone to call my dad?" Elizabeth asked.

"Of course, dear. Use the one in the office."

"Do you need help getting to your car?" Jake asked, opening the door for Stephen.

"No, thanks. My truck's parked right outside."

Jake turned to Margaret. "I'll be back in a little while, Mrs. Southwell, and I'll be happy to ride whatever you have for me."

"Thank you, Jake. By the time you return, I'll make sure the air conditioning is on in the cottage and there are clean sheets on the bed."

Jake looked at Kendall. "See you later."

"Bye."

Kendall watched the door close behind Jake and then realized that she hadn't told him the good news about Doug. She jumped up from her chair and rushed to the door. "Jake, wait."

He turned around. "What's the matter?"

"Nothing. I just forgot to tell you that I had a call from Anne a little while ago and Doug's out of the coma. They think he's going to be fine."

He smiled. "Hey, that's great news."

"Yeah, I thought you'd want to know." Suddenly, she felt foolish for running after him. "Well, I'll see you later." She closed the door and walked back to Margaret.

"Have a seat," Margaret said. "If you have a minute, we can go over the list of campers for this week."

"Sure." Kendall sat beside Margaret on the couch. "Margaret, I have a question."

"What is it?"

"Why did you imply to Stephen that I wasn't teaching camp in exchange for free board?"

"I simply wanted him to know you are both of the same social class, that's all."

"What do you mean?"

Margaret patted Kendall's hand. "Men like Stephen Lloyd date their own kind. Not the local riding instructor."

Kendall's eyes widened. "I'm not interested in *dating* Stephen Lloyd."

"Well, perhaps not. But in due time you'll be ready for a relationship. And when that day comes, I want you to find the right kind of man. You're young and beautiful, Kendall. And you deserve to find someone who'll treat you right. I think Stephen seems like a good prospect."

"Why? Because he's rich?"

Margaret smiled. "That doesn't hurt, Kendall. Remember, love alone won't keep shoes on your horse."

Kendall folded her arms across her chest and looked away. *But money alone can't compensate for lack of love.*

*Z*elda was beginning to feel conspicuous hanging out around the pay phone again. Church had just let out, and it seemed like half the town had come to Kroger's to get their groceries. She wandered over to the soda machine and took a long time selecting a drink, all the while keeping her ear tuned to the phone.

The shrill ring of the phone caught her attention. She sprinted over and picked up the receiver.

"Hello?" she said breathlessly.

"We're back in business, babe. Cummings is out of the coma."

Zelda squealed, "Yes!"

"I say we step it up, now that we've got their attention."

"I couldn't agree more. What's next?"

"We'll have to play it by ear. Cummings is still in the hospital, and it sounds like his wife hasn't left his side. The kid's staying at a friend's house. We'll just scope it out and seize whatever opportunity comes our way."

Zelda didn't like his choice of words. "Hey, you've been hanging out with Cummings's snobby friends for a day, and you start talking all fancy like. *Seize whatever opportunity comes our way.*"

Earl laughed. "You ain't jealous, are you, babe?"

"No, I ain't jealous. But I miss you like hell," Zelda said.

"Yeah, me too. Listen, I've got to go. I'll call you back tonight if I can."

"Wait. This ain't working with me hanging around the pay phone. People are starting to look at me funny."

"Damn it, what do you expect me to do about that now, Zelda? I told you in the beginning, we should have got cell phones."

"Yeah, well, I didn't want them to be able to trace our calls or listen to our conversations. That's why I thought using a pay phone was the safest," Zelda replied.

"I tried telling you that you can buy a disposable cell phone, and even if they trace the call, they don't know who the cell phone belongs to. But you wouldn't listen."

Zelda bit back a retort. She could tell by Earl's tone that he was pissed at her. "Hey, let's not fight. You're right. I should have listened to you. But now what do we do? Where am I going to find a cell phone around here? You've got my car, remember?"

Earl sighed. "Can't you catch a ride to Wal-Mart?"

"I guess so."

"All right, babe. Go get yourself a cell phone and I'll get one today, too. I'll call you at the pay phone tomorrow morning at nine and we'll give each other our phone numbers. That'll be the last time you have to wait by the pay phone."

"Okay," Zelda said reluctantly. "But I still don't like it. Are you sure they can't trace our phone calls?"

"I'm hanging up, babe."

"Wait," Zelda said. But he was gone.

*A*nne stifled a yawn as she sat by Samantha's bedside, waiting for her
to fall asleep. It had been a struggle getting Samantha to go to bed,
and Anne had promised she would stay until Samantha was asleep. When
she'd picked Samantha up from the Hortons' that afternoon, Deb told her
Samantha had awakened crying several times during the night. *She hoped
Samantha's night terrors weren't starting again.*

Samantha's eyes drifted shut, her arms clutched around the stuffed pony
that Doug had given her. After a few moments her mouth parted, and the
muscles in her face relaxed. Her breathing settled into a slow, steady rhythm,
and Anne sighed as she rose and tucked the covers around Samantha, then
slipped from the room.

Anne slid beneath the covers of her bed and rolled onto her side,
appreciating the cool, fresh feel of the cotton sheets as she snuggled into the
mattress. She arranged the pregnancy pillow so that it supported her stomach,
and, for the first time in almost thirty-six hours, tried to relax.

At first, she had balked at Doug's suggestion that she go home for the
night. But he'd remained insistent and she had finally given in. The nurses
had promised to call her during the night if there was any change in Doug's
condition.

A cool breeze from the ceiling fan chilled Anne's bare arms, and she
pulled the covers up over her shoulders and wiggled deeper into the plush
mattress. Even though she was bone-tired, it was hard to fall asleep with the
thoughts that kept racing through her head. Now that Doug was out of the
coma, the reality of what had happened was starting to hit home.

She had been determined to wait until Doug was out of the hospital to tell him that someone had tampered with the brakes on the Range Rover, but he'd been so persistent with his questions that she had broken down and told him about the visit from Deputy Hodgkins. Doug hadn't seemed surprised by the news; she guessed he'd already suspected tampering.

"Mommy!" Anne heard Samantha scream from across the hall, and she threw off the covers and eased herself out of the bed.

"I'm coming, honey," she called wearily, pulling on her robe as she hurried towards Samantha's bedroom.

"Mommy, I heard a noise outside my window." Samantha was huddled at the foot of the bed with her knees clutched to her chest, rocking back and forth.

Anne sat down on the bed and wrapped her arms around Samantha. "It's all right. There's nothing outside your window. It's just the wind blowing the tree branches."

"No, it's not," Samantha whispered hoarsely. "I heard it. Somebody's out there."

Anne pulled Samantha close to her and stroked her hair. "Shhh, don't be scared. You must have had a bad dream. I'm right here. There's nothing to be afraid of."

Samantha curled into a ball and buried her face against Anne's belly. "I wish Daddy was here."

"I do, too, sweetie."

She held Samantha and stroked her until she was more relaxed, then gently tried to ease Samantha back under the covers. "Come on. Let's get you back into your bed."

"No!" Samantha clutched at Anne's robe. "I don't want you to leave. I'm scared."

Anne sighed. She knew that Samantha's fear was real and that she should help her confront it, but that would probably mean an hour or more of coaxing to get Samantha back to sleep. She was simply too exhausted to deal with it.

"Okay, Samantha. I know you're frightened. How about, since Daddy isn't here, if you snuggle up with me in my bed? Would that help you feel better?"

Samantha nodded.

Anne stood up and held her hand out to Samantha. "Okay, then. But you have to promise me that you'll go right to sleep."

"I promise."

Anne picked up Samantha's stuffed pony. "Let's not forget Blackie."

Samantha hugged the pony with one arm and slipped her free hand into Anne's. When they reached the door, she cast a quick backward glance towards the window. "I'm sorry I woke you up, Mommy, but I really did hear a noise outside my window."

They climbed into bed and Anne arranged the pregnancy pillow and tucked the covers around Samantha. "There you go; now we're all cozy."

Samantha yawned. "Nite-nite, Mommy. I love you."

"I love you, too, sweetheart," Anne whispered, kissing the top of Samantha's head.

23

nne felt someone tapping her on the shoulder, and she opened her eyes, squinting in the bright sunlight that streamed across the pillow.

"Mommy, wake up. It's time for me to go to riding camp."

"Oh, Samantha, go back to sleep," Anne groaned. "It's not time to get up yet."

"Yes, it is." Samantha lifted the alarm clock from the bedside table. "See, it's eight o'clock. Camp starts at nine, and we haven't even had breakfast yet."

Anne raised her hand and shielded her eyes from the sun. "You're right, Samantha. Just give me a minute to wake up."

Samantha leapt out of bed. "Okay, I'll go get dressed, and then I'll help you make breakfast, since Nellie isn't here."

Anne wearily raised herself into a sitting position and eased her legs over the side of the bed. It hurt to bend her ankles and she stretched her legs as she picked up the phone and punched in the number of the hospital.

The phone was answered on the second ring. "ICU."

"Hello, this is Anne Cummings. I'm calling to see how my husband is doing this morning."

"Hi, Mrs. Cummings. This is Robin. Your husband is doing just great. In fact, they've removed the chest tube and he's ready to be moved out of ICU."

"That's wonderful news. Will you tell him I'll be there shortly?"

"Will do."

Anne hurried to the closet and rifled through the rack of maternity clothes, searching for an outfit that would be comfortable in the air-conditioned hospital, as well as outside in the sticky summer heat. She finally selected a pair of white pants, a sleeveless butter-colored top with a matching sweater, and a pair of white sandals that had a cushioned sole. She dressed quickly in the bathroom, and had just finished applying her makeup when she heard Samantha run down the stairs.

"I'll be right there, Samantha. Don't start without me," she called, running a brush through her hair.

"Okay," Samantha yelled from downstairs.

Anne put on a pair of simple pearl earrings and slid on her wedding ring. Her fingers were swollen and she had to twist the ring to get it past her knuckle, even though Doug had taken it to the jeweler a couple of weeks before to have it resized. She fingered the emerald-cut diamond and thought back to the day Doug had given it to her. He had asked her to marry him as soon as she'd told him she was pregnant, but she had said no, fearful that he was only asking out of a sense of obligation. Then, on the night he gave her the ring, he had gotten down on one knee, in the middle of the dining room at the Inn at Little Washington, and said he wouldn't get up until she said yes.

"Mommy, I'm starving," Samantha yelled up the stairs.

"Coming," Anne called back, giving the ring one final twist.

Anne let Samantha make a peanut butter and jelly sandwich for her camp lunch while she cooked bacon and eggs for their breakfast. She turned on the morning news and kept an eye out for the weather forecast. Just as she put their plates on the table, she saw Kendall's Jeep pull around the house to the back door.

"Uh-oh, Kendall's here, Samantha. You'd better eat in a hurry." Anne waved out the window at Kendall as she unlocked the back door.

"Come on in," she called to Kendall as she rushed to retrieve the bread from the toaster.

She was standing at the counter buttering the toast when she heard Kendall slam the door.

"Oh my God, Anne, what happened?"

Anne turned around and saw Kendall leaning against the door with her hand over her nose.

"What do you mean?"

"The deer. How did it get there?" Kendall motioned towards the back porch.

Anne frowned. "I don't know what you're talking about, Kendall."

Samantha jumped up. "Where's a deer? I want to see it."

Kendall shot a glance at Anne and shook her head.

"No, young lady, you sit right back down and finish your breakfast so you can go to camp," Anne said, steering Samantha back to her chair. "You can watch cartoons while you finish eating." She reached for the remote and tuned the TV to the Disney Channel, turning up the volume.

Anne walked over to Kendall. "What's going on?" she asked quietly.

"There's a dead deer. It's been gutted and its intestines are all over the back porch."

"*What?*" Anne reached for the door.

Kendall grabbed her arm. "Don't go out there, Anne. Believe me, you don't want to see it."

Anne hesitated, her hand on the door handle. "How do you think it got there? Do you think it was shot?"

"I have no idea. I didn't look at it that closely. I suppose it's possible it was shot and wandered up here to die."

"Did you say it was *gutted*?"

Kendall nodded. "Maybe some other animals chewed on it after it was dead."

Anne shuddered. "But it's not deer-hunting season. And, even if it were, no one's allowed to hunt on our property."

24

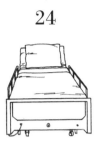

*D*oug had already been moved out of ICU by the time Anne arrived at the hospital, and Robin directed her to his room on the Medical/Surgical floor.

"I know you're going to be surprised by how much progress your husband has made over the last twenty-four hours," Robin said. "He's amazing."

Anne smiled. "Yes, he is."

As she waited for the elevator to take her to the second floor, Anne was haunted once again by the thought of the dead deer. She should have followed Kendall's advice and not gone outside to look, but she'd gone anyway, and now she couldn't get the image out of her mind.

Most disturbing was their farm manager John's certainty that the deer had been deliberately placed on the porch. He said it looked like the doe was roadkill; that it had been moved to the porch once it was already dead, then sliced down the middle and its guts pulled out.

"What kind of person would do such a gruesome thing, Mrs. Cummings?" John had asked. Anne hadn't answered him, but she shivered now as she thought of the obvious answer: the same person who had tampered with Doug's brakes.

Doug was sitting on the edge of the bed when she entered his room. A young nurse stood next to him.

He held his arms out to her. "Look at me. I'm almost as good as new." His voice was still raspy from the ventilator tube.

Anne settled into his embrace. "You look wonderful."

"Mr. Cummings was just getting ready to take a walk," the nurse said. "Would you like to go with him?"

"Of course."

Doug rose slowly to his feet. "If I prove I can walk down the hall without passing out, maybe they'll let me go home."

The nurse smiled. "You're not ready to go home quite yet, Mr. Cummings. But if you keep progressing this well, you'll probably be able to go home in a couple of days."

Anne stepped to the side and held Doug's arm to help steady him as they walked into the hallway.

"How's Samantha doing?" Doug asked.

"She's all right. She misses you."

"God, I miss her, too. Now that I'm out of ICU, she can come and visit. That is, if you think it won't scare her to see me looking like this."

"No. I think it would be good for her to see you. She's at riding camp today, but I'll call Kendall and see if she wouldn't mind bringing her by after camp."

"That sounds great."

Doug was winded, and when they reached the end of the hallway, they paused to rest for a moment before starting back towards his room.

"Did Samantha sleep through the night?"

Anne shook her head. "No, she had a bad dream, and . . ."

Doug frowned at her. "What?"

"She *did* hear something," Anne murmured.

"What are you talking about?"

She shook her head to clear her thoughts. "Nothing. Come on, let's head back to your room."

"It's not *nothing*." Doug reached for the handrail as they started back down the hall. "Tell me what you were thinking about."

Anne lowered her eyes. "Samantha had a bad dream, that's all. And then I let her sleep with me, because I was too tired to stay up with her. I know that's not a good idea, but I was just so exhausted, I did it anyway."

Doug stopped walking. "Anne."

"What?"

"You said Samantha heard something. Tell me what you meant by that."

She had sworn to herself she wouldn't tell Doug about the deer until he was home from the hospital, but now she felt guilty keeping it from him.

When she didn't answer, Doug cupped his hand under her chin and forced her to look at him. "Tell me what's bothering you."

Anne took a deep breath and glanced down the hallway. "Can we go back in your room? I'd rather talk in private."

He nodded and they walked back to his room in silence.

"Okay," Doug said once he was settled in the bed. "Tell me what's going on."

Anne reached for his hand and felt her throat close up. "Someone put a dead deer outside our back door last night."

He narrowed his eyes at her. "How do you know someone *put* it there?"

"Because I had John look at it. He said it looked like roadkill, and that it was definitely dead before it got to our back porch. And that's not all."

"Go on."

Anne closed her eyes for a brief moment, trying to clear the haunting image. "The deer was sliced open and its intestines were strewn around the porch."

"Oh Christ. Did you call the Sheriff's Office?"

"No. I guess I should have. What worries me now is that when Samantha woke up last night, she said she had heard a noise outside her window. Of course, I didn't know anything about the deer at the time, and I just assumed she'd had a bad dream. Now I realize she must have heard whoever was out there with the deer, since her window overlooks that side of the house."

"*Damn it.*" Doug gripped her hand. "I can't believe I let you go home alone last night and didn't even think about getting security for you. You and Samantha were all alone in that house while some psycho was outside spreading deer guts all over our porch."

He threw the sheet back. "I'm going home."

Anne tried to cover him again. "Don't be silly, Doug. You're in no shape to leave the hospital."

"The hell I'm not." Doug pushed her hand away and eased out of bed. "I just need a few days to rest, and I can do that at home just as well as I can here. Better, in fact."

He headed towards the small bathroom. "I need my clothes. Will you call the nurse and ask for them?"

"Oh, Doug, come on, don't be ridiculous. You can't just walk out of the hospital."

"Watch me." He disappeared into the bathroom and closed the door.

25

*K*endall sat in the shade of a willow tree next to the outdoor arena, eating lunch with Elizabeth and the kids. It was an exceptionally humid day and the temperature was forecasted to rise to near one hundred degrees, so she had cut the morning riding session short and let the girls spray themselves with the hose before taking their lunch break.

Jake had just finished riding Margaret's three-year-old horse, Casanova, and he stood in the arena, talking with Margaret and two of her boarders. Kendall couldn't hear what they were saying, but there was a lot of laughter, and the women were flirting shamelessly with Jake.

"He's sure cute, isn't he?" Elizabeth said.

Kendall looked at her. "Who?"

"*Who?* Jake, of course."

"Elizabeth, Jake's almost old enough to be your father."

"I know that. But that doesn't mean I have to stop looking, does it?"

Kendall laughed. "No, I guess not."

"He's such an incredible rider. He makes everything look effortless."

Kendall watched Jake roll up the stirrups and pat Casanova on the neck. She had to admit he did seem to have a way with horses. Casanova could be a handful, but Jake had ridden him beautifully.

Elizabeth smiled dreamily. "I wouldn't mind marrying a cowboy like Jake when I get older. We'd have our own barn. He'd train the horses, and I'd show hunters and teach riding."

"Would that be before or after you go to Harvard Law, as your dad thinks you're going to do?"

Elizabeth groaned. "Please, don't remind me. I was eight when I told

Dad I wanted to be the first female chief justice of the Supreme Court, and even though I'm long over that, he's never forgotten it."

"He just wants what's best for you."

"I know. Ever since Mom died, Dad has been trying so hard to be involved with my life, but sometimes he overdoes it."

"I'm sure it's aggravating at times, but you know he's doing it because he loves you."

"Yeah, I guess. Was it the same way with your father?"

Kendall's smile faded.

"Was your dad like that, too, Miss Waters?"

"That's a tough question for me to answer," Kendall said quietly. "My relationship with my father has changed over the years. When I was your age, we were very close, and I thought I wanted to follow in his footsteps and be an investment banker. We lived in Los Angeles and we often talked about my going east to Princeton undergraduate and then returning to California and getting my MBA at Stanford, just like my father had."

"Did you do that?"

Kendall shook her head. "No. At least not all of it. I did go to Princeton, but then I met Peter and fell in love, and I decided to drop out of school after my junior year and get married."

"Uh-oh. I'll bet that ticked your dad off."

"That's putting it mildly." Kendall took a deep breath. "He basically disowned me."

"No way!"

"Yes. He told me I had to choose between Peter and my family. I think he believed that he could force me to go back to school by giving me an ultimatum. But I was in love and I thought he'd eventually come around, so I went ahead and married Peter, against my father's wishes."

"Did he forgive you?"

"Nope."

"*Still?*"

"Still. And that was over eight years ago."

"Was he happy that you got divorced from Mr. Baxter?"

"He doesn't know. My father and I haven't spoken since the day I eloped."

"Oh my gosh, that is so sad."

"Yes, it is." Kendall forced a smile. "Which is why you should be happy that you have a father who cares so much about you, and you should listen to him."

"I will, Miss Waters. I promise."

"How did we get on such a depressing subject, anyway?" Kendall asked, standing up and brushing the crumbs from her sandwich off her lap. "Let's gather the girls and get them started on their arts and crafts project. And by the way, Elizabeth, please call me Kendall. You make me feel old when you call me Miss Waters."

"Okay." Elizabeth stood and crumpled her lunch bag into a ball, tossing it like a basketball into the trash can by the ring.

"Hey, nice shot," Jake called.

Elizabeth smiled and bowed in his direction. "Thank you."

Jake handed Casanova's reins to Margaret and tipped his hat at the boarders, then ambled in their direction. "You girls looked like you were solving all the problems of the world a little while ago," he said, hopping over the ring railing to join them.

"Yeah, I guess we kinda were," Elizabeth said.

Jake nodded at Kendall. "Hi, Kendall."

"Jake."

"How's camp going?"

"Fine. In fact, we were just getting ready to get back to it." Kendall gestured towards the kids.

"Don't let me hold you up. Try to stay cool." Jake took his hat off and wiped his forehead on his sleeve as he walked towards the barn.

"Oh, Jake, Kendall, wait a minute. I want to ask you something," Margaret called as she opened the gate to the ring and led the horse through.

Jake stopped and turned around.

"Is there any chance the two of you could pick up a horse for me this afternoon?"

Jake shrugged. "Sure."

"I have to take Samantha home after camp," Kendall said. "But I could pick the horse up after that. Where is it?"

"He's at High Meadow. The Worthingtons have generously offered the use of their retired show horse, Patches, for the summer camp. They wanted to trailer him over here for us because he can be a bear to load, but they had to take their van in for service. I told them I'd be sure to send competent horse people so we'd be able to get old Patches loaded on the trailer. That's why I'd

like the two of you to go. And I invited Todd to go along. I thought he'd get
a thrill out of seeing High Meadow."

"Can I go, too?" Elizabeth asked, holding her hands in a praying motion.

"I don't see why not."

Elizabeth jumped up and down. "Thank you, Mrs. Southwell. I've
always wanted to see the stables at High Meadow."

Jake turned to Kendall. "What time do you want to leave?"

"High Meadow is in the same direction as the Cummings's farm, so we
can drop Samantha off at her house on the way. Why don't we plan on
leaving here right after camp ends, say around four o'clock?"

Jake nodded. "That's fine by me. I'm going to hop on Cloudy now, and
then I'd like to go pay a visit to Chancellor. I'll make sure I'm back before
the end of camp, and I'll have the trailer hooked up and ready to go."

"All right. Why don't you give me your cell phone number, just in case
there is a change of plans."

Jake frowned at her. "*What?*"

Kendall gestured towards the cell phone clipped to his belt. "Let me get
your cell phone number, so I can call you if the plans change for any reason."

"Oh, right." Jake took the phone off his belt. "Sorry. I'm still not used to
having a cell phone. I just got this yesterday. It's one of those prepaid deals."

Kendall glanced at the phone. "Oh? Did you leave your cell phone in
Oklahoma?"

"Nah. I never had the need for one before. But I figured if I'm going to
be staying around here for a while, I'd better break down and buy one."

CHAPTER
26

*A*nne put the phone receiver back on the base just as Doug walked into the study.

"That was Kendall on the phone. She's on her way. I warned her about the guard at the gate. Hopefully, Samantha will be so excited that you're home, she won't be too frightened when she sees the guard."

Doug sat on the couch and pulled Anne down next to him, gingerly lifting his arm around Anne's shoulders and drawing her close. "You worry too much. I think Samantha will be just fine."

Anne nuzzled his neck. "Mmm, you smell good. How was your shower?"

"It felt great." He let out a long sigh. "God, it's good to be home."

Anne rested her head on his chest. "It's nice to have you home. Even though you left the hospital as a persona non grata. What did they call it?"

"AMA. Against medical advice."

"Right." She pulled back so she could see his face. Doug had removed the Steri-Strips from the cut on his forehead, and the skin around it looked raw and tender. "I'm going to hold you to your promise to go to the doctor tomorrow."

"I know." There was a note of exasperation in his voice. "Let's not get into that discussion again."

Anne took a deep breath and bit back a reply. "Do you still have a headache?"

"It's not too bad."

She ran her hand over his cheek. "You even shaved."

Doug pulled her close again. "Anne, we've got to talk." He smoothed her hair back and kissed the top of her head.

"About what?"

"About who tampered with my brakes and put the dead deer outside the door." He let out a slow breath. "I know it may sound crazy, but I can't shake the feeling Zeb McGraw is behind this, even though he's in jail. It just smacks of something he'd do."

She nodded. "I agree."

"I've asked Patrick Talbot at Manse Security to hire an investigator to look into it."

"I think that's a good idea."

"I've also hired a bodyguard to accompany you wherever you go. And one for Samantha."

Anne pulled away. "What about you?"

"What do you mean?"

"You hired bodyguards for Samantha and me, but what about you? You almost died in the accident, Doug. *You're not invincible.* You've made all these great plans, but you failed to mention who's going to protect you."

"I'm not trying to play hero, Anne. I'll be careful."

"I don't want you to be *careful.*" Her voice cracked and she took a deep breath. "I want you to be protected."

"All right, don't get upset." Doug slid his hand over hers. "If it will make you feel better, I'll take a guard with me, too."

"Thank you."

Doug smiled and moved his hand to her belly. "How's our baby been handling all this turmoil?"

"Kicking up a storm, as usual."

She heard the sound of tires outside on the gravel drive. "That must be Samantha." She stood and extended her hand to Doug. "Oh, I forgot to tell you. The guy who helped rescue Chancellor is with Kendall. Apparently, they're going to pick up a horse after they drop off Samantha. You probably don't feel up to meeting him now, but I'd like to go out and thank him."

"Nonsense; I may be bruised and battered, but I'm not an invalid. Of course I want to meet him. I spoke with Ned Carey this afternoon, and he told me that Chancellor wouldn't have survived without this guy's help."

They reached the front door just as someone rang the bell, and Doug swung the door open.

"Daddy!" Samantha rushed into Doug's arms.

Doug winced and Anne could tell from his expression that it hurt when she hugged him, but he wrapped his arms around her and picked her up.

He set her down on the hall table. "How's my princess doing?"

"I missed you so much, Daddy." Samantha kept her grip tight around his neck. "You have a big owie on your head. Does it hurt?"

"Nah, I'm a tough guy. You know that."

Anne reached over and gave Samantha a kiss. "How was camp today, sweetie?"

"It was so much fun. Can I tell Mommy and Daddy what I did, Kendall?"

"Of course you can." Kendall had been standing just outside the door, and she stepped inside and gave Doug a light hug. "You look great. I'm so happy you're home."

"Thanks."

"Tell us, Samantha," Anne said. "What did you do in camp today?"

Samantha grinned. "I cantered."

"You're kidding," Doug said.

"Nope. I cantered all by myself."

"Were you scared?"

"Kind of, at first, but then it was really fun."

Doug tousled her hair. "That's my girl."

He turned to Kendall. "Anne told me the guy who rescued Chancellor is with you. I'd love to meet him."

"Oh, that's Jake," Samantha said. "He's really nice and he's a real cowboy."

"Really? Would you introduce me to him?"

"Sure." Samantha hopped down off the table and grabbed Doug's hand. "Come on."

Anne noticed the color had drained from Doug's face. She put her hand on Samantha's arm. "Samantha, why don't we invite Jake inside to meet Daddy? We can offer him something cold to drink, and I'll bet if I look hard enough, I might even be able to find some cookies in the kitchen."

"Okay. Can I help you put the cookies on a plate?"

"Of course."

"I'll go get Jake," Kendall said.

Anne looked at Doug. "And you go sit down."

"Good idea," Doug replied, turning stiffly towards the study.

When Anne and Samantha returned, Doug and Kendall were seated on the couch, and a tall blond man wearing cowboy boots, blue jeans, and a white T-shirt stood by the fireplace, with one foot on the raised stone hearth. He straightened up when they approached.

Anne set the tray on the coffee table and extended her hand. "You must be Jake. It's so good to meet you. Thank you for all you've done to help Chancellor."

"It was my pleasure, ma'am. Chancellor's a real special horse."

"Jake was just telling me he went to see Chancellor this afternoon," Doug said.

"Is Chancellor still in the horse hospital?" Samantha asked.

Jake nodded.

Samantha turned to Doug. "Why didn't Chancellor get to come home when you did, Daddy?"

"Because sometimes it takes longer for horses to get better than it does for people to get better."

"But Chancellor's going to be okay, isn't he?"

"You bet he is, darling," Jake said. "He's doing just fine. In fact, when I was there this afternoon, they let me take him out to graze, and he just about ate all the grass in the pasture."

Samantha giggled and held out the plate of cookies. "Would you like a cookie?"

"Thank you." Jake reached for one. "How'd you know Oreos are my favorite cookie?"

She smiled shyly and raised her shoulders in a shrug. "I didn't know. They were the only cookies we had."

Anne passed out the glasses of lemonade. "Samantha thought lemonade sounded refreshing on such a hot day."

"The perfect choice," Jake said.

Samantha climbed onto the couch between Kendall and Doug. "We were so hot at camp today that Kendall let us squirt each other with the hose. It was really fun."

Kendall smiled at her. "I'm glad you had fun, Samantha. Say, speaking of camp, Jake and I had better hit the road. We're supposed to pick up a horse for Margaret."

"Do you work at Fox Run, Jake?" Doug asked.

Jake shook his head. "Nah, not really. I'm just passing through and I agreed to ride some horses for Mrs. Southwell."

"Well, I'm certainly grateful for what you did for Chancellor. If there's ever anything I can do for you in return, I hope you'll let me know."

Jake shifted uneasily. "There's no need to thank me, Mr. Cummings. I was just in the right place at the right time. I have no doubt you'd have done the same thing under the circumstances."

27

he gates to High Meadow were closed when they arrived, and Kendall pulled to a stop and lowered the driver's window. She pressed a series of numbers on the keypad at the gatepost, and the gates glided open.

"Wow, that's cool," Todd said from the backseat. "How do you know the code to open the gate?"

Kendall looked at Todd in the rearview mirror. "Margaret told it to me."

Todd snorted. "That's great security. What's the point of a code if you give it to everyone?"

Jake cast a glance at the backseat. "I don't think Margaret and Kendall exactly pose a security risk, Todd."

Kendall smiled. "Besides, I don't think they keep the gates closed for security. It's not exactly a high-crime neighborhood. The gates are kept closed mainly to prevent the horses from getting out on the road if they should get loose."

Todd stared out the window. "Mr. Cummings doesn't live in a high-crime neighborhood, but he sure has security guards all over his farm."

"That's different. Doug's had some incidents where people have targeted him and his family. He has every right to be cautious."

They rounded a bend in the drive and a three-story white-columned red-brick house came into view.

Todd whistled. "This place looks like a freaking hotel."

"It's like something out of a movie set," Elizabeth said.

"Wait until you see the stable," Kendall replied. "You'll really flip."

The gravel drive forked as they neared the house and Kendall turned to the left. The road wound around a pond and through a patch of woods, until it finally ended at a courtyard in front of a U-shaped stable. The barn's wooden siding was painted a gleaming white, contrasting with shutters and trim in a forest green. Each interior arm of the U had a dozen Dutch doors, the tops of which were fastened open, and the heads of several refined-looking horses poked out and studied them curiously. In the center of the U, four more Dutch doors flanked a high brick-lined archway, which led into the stable aisle. The high-pitched roof was covered with slate shingles, and a cupola topped the center peak, sporting a weathervane in the image of a jumping horse.

Elizabeth's mouth hung open as she stared out the window at the stable. "Oh my gosh."

Kendall pulled the rig to a stop in the courtyard. "Told you you'd like it."

"Is this big barn just for their private horses?" Todd asked.

Kendall nodded. "For now it is. The Worthingtons planned the barn with the thought that one of their daughters might want to start a training stable someday, so they designed it with enough stalls to accommodate a commercial operation."

"Must be tough," Todd muttered. "Having parents who hand you everything on a silver platter."

"There's no question the Worthington girls have certain advantages, but I don't think it's fair to hold it against them, Todd. They can't help it that they were born into wealth," Kendall said.

"Yeah, and I can't help it that I was born into poverty." Todd got out of the truck and slammed the door.

Kendall turned off the engine. "I think I hit a sore spot with Todd."

"It's a little hard to stomach seeing other folks live like this when you work your butt off mucking stalls all day," Jake said, opening his door. "I'll go talk to him."

Kendall watched out the window as Jake walked up to Todd and put his hand on his shoulder.

"I feel sorry for Todd," Elizabeth said.

"Why?"

"He doesn't have a father, and he had to drop out of school to work to help support his mom. He told me when we were sitting in the truck waiting for you."

"Did his father die when he was a baby?"

Elizabeth shook her head. "No, his dad was never married to his mom. She refuses to talk about it, but Todd thinks it was just a one-night stand."

"Poor kid. How old is he?"

"I'm not sure. I guess he must be sixteen, because he already has his driver's license."

Todd had a sullen expression on his face as he and Jake walked towards the courtyard entrance. Jake was talking, and Todd stopped and leaned against a brick pillar, his arms folded across his chest.

Kendall pulled on the door handle. "Come on. Let's go on into the barn. They can follow us when they're finished talking."

Elizabeth climbed out of the truck after her. "He's cute, don't you think?" she asked, glancing towards Jake and Todd.

Kendall sighed. "*Elizabeth.*"

"What?"

"Didn't we already have this conversation once today?"

"What conversation?"

"About how cute you think Jake is."

"Oh, yeah, but I wasn't talking about Jake just now. I meant Todd. I think he's *really* cute."

Kendall smiled at her. "Elizabeth, I'm beginning to think that you find every male you see attractive."

Elizabeth stuck her bottom lip out in an exaggerated pout. "That's not true." She looked over at the guys again. "I think they kind of look alike. Maybe that's why I think they're both cute."

"They do both have that cowboy look."

"Yeah, but I don't think that's it," Elizabeth said. "Maybe it's their eyes. I love blue eyes on guys, don't you?"

Kendall laughed. "You have a one-track mind. Come on, let's go find Susie. She's the Worthingtons' stable manager."

They walked through the brick archway and saw a balding, elderly man leading a brown-and-white paint horse up the aisle towards them.

"Hello, you must be Kendall," he said. "I'm Albert. I heard you drive in, so I went ahead and got Patches out of his stall. The girls went with Susie to pick up the van, and Mrs. Worthington had to run to the vet with her Jack Russell. As usual, he was where he wasn't supposed to be and got stepped on."

"Oh no, is he going to be all right?" Kendall asked.

"I suspect he is. But he was favoring his paw, and Mrs. Worthington wanted to make sure nothing was broken."

"I guess he'll stay away from horses' hooves from now on," Elizabeth said.

"Nah, he'll never learn. He's been stepped on before and probably will be again. You know how Jack Russells are. Shall we see if we can get old Mr. Patches on the trailer?"

Kendall nodded. "We brought reinforcements, just in case. They're outside."

Elizabeth walked alongside Albert and patted the horse on the neck. "Patches is so adorable. I know the kids in camp are going to love him."

"He's a good old soul," Albert said. "The only quirk he has is getting on horse trailers. He's not as bad about vans."

Kendall lowered the ramp to the trailer. "Will he be better if you lead him on, or do you want me to?"

"I'll let you do the honors." Albert handed the lead rope to her. "Tractors are my specialty, not horses."

Kendall took the rope from him. "Okay, Elizabeth, be ready to fasten the butt bar as soon as I get him in there."

Patches stood quietly, with his head hung low. "He sure doesn't look like he'd put up a fuss," Elizabeth said.

"I hope you're right." Kendall pulled on the lead rope and walked purposefully towards the ramp.

Patches followed placidly until his front feet touched the edge of the ramp, then shot backwards, pulling Kendall along with him. She managed to hang on for a few steps, but when her boots hit the gravel drive, she slipped and fell to the ground. Patches continued to run backwards, and, rather than be dragged, Kendall let go of the lead. The horse trotted over to a patch of grass and began grazing.

"Whoa, take it easy, fella." Jake appeared from the other side of the trailer. He approached Patches slowly and grabbed hold of the lead rope.

"You all right?" he asked, turning to Kendall.

"Yeah." She rolled to a sitting position and looked at the holes in both knees of her breeches. "Guess I won't be showing in these anymore."

Elizabeth squatted down next to her. "Ooh, Kendall, you really skinned your knees."

Kendall's knees stung like crazy, but she wasn't about to show it. "It's no big deal."

Jake led Patches over to her and held out his hand. "You sure you're okay?"

She forced a smile. "The only thing wounded is my pride."

"We have a first-aid kit in the tack room," Albert said. "I'll go get it."

"No. I'm fine." Kendall let Jake pull her to her feet. "Let's concentrate on getting Patches loaded."

"Mind if I take a stab at it?" Jake asked.

"Be my guest."

Jake rubbed Patches's face. "Hey, buddy, you going to cooperate?" he asked softly, looking him in the eye.

Patches butted his face against Jake's hand, and Jake scratched between the horse's eyes, then slid his hand up between Patches's ears and rubbed his forelock. "Okay, old man, let's do this the easy way. Just follow me."

He looked at Elizabeth. "You mind closing the butt bar, darling?"

"Sure."

"All right."

Jake clucked once, then turned his back on Patches and strode towards the trailer, leading the horse close behind him. Kendall waited for Patches to bolt backwards, but the horse followed Jake up the ramp and into the trailer.

Albert chuckled. "Well I'll be damned."

"Way to go, Jake," Elizabeth said as she fastened the butt bar in place.

Jake hooked the trailer tie to Patches's halter, then reached into his pocket and pulled out a sugar cube. He rubbed Patches on the face while the horse chewed the treat.

"I must admit, Jake, I'm impressed," Kendall said as he exited the trailer through the front door.

Jake shrugged. "It was nothing. He's a smart old horse, just like Mrs. Southwell said. He knew what was coming next if he didn't cooperate."

The sound of an engine caught their attention and Kendall saw the Worthingtons' horse van kicking up a cloud of dust as it roared down the drive. A blond girl with a ponytail waved out the passenger window as the gleaming silver-and-green van passed them before disappearing behind the barn.

"How many horses does that van hold?" Todd asked.

"Twelve. Plus it has living quarters up front," Kendall replied. "Want to go see it?"

"Could I?"

Kendall turned to Albert. "Is it all right if we take a peek?"

"I don't see why not. Just try to look past the chaos. They're getting ready to leave for the Hamptons tomorrow and things are probably in an uproar."

"Are you going along to the Hamptons?" Kendall asked.

He shook his head and grinned. "No, ma'am. This is my vacation time at home. The Worthingtons take the horses to the Hamptons every August, and I get this whole place to myself. No people, no horses, just me and my tractors."

"You take care of this big farm all by yourself for a whole month?" Jake asked.

"There's a landscaping crew comes in once a week to mow around the house, weed the gardens, that kind of thing. I just use the bush hog to mow the fields."

Jake smiled. "Doesn't sound like much of a vacation to me."

"Nah, it's all right. The Worthingtons give the staff the month off, but I prefer to stay here and putter around. My wife passed away three years ago, and we never had any children, so I don't have anyplace to go. I'm better off keeping busy." He gestured towards the barn. "You seem to know your way around here, Kendall. Feel free to show them the van and look around as much as you like. I'm going to get back at it."

"Thanks, Albert."

Kendall headed towards the barn. "Let's take a quick tour of the stable and then I'll take you around back and show you the van. They have a huge climate-controlled garage just to store the van. I've never seen anything quite like it. And wait until you see the gigantic pigeon roost they have at the back of the garage."

Elizabeth gazed wide-eyed as they walked through the archway. "This is my dream barn. I don't really care what kind of house I live in when I grow up, but I'd give anything to have a barn like this someday. And I know I'd be just like Albert. I'd never want to leave, even for vacation."

Kendall smiled wistfully at Elizabeth. She'd had similar dreams when she was Elizabeth's age, but she knew now that fancy stables and big houses had nothing to do with happiness. Quite the contrary. In the end, her home with Peter had been a prison.

28

elda caught the bartender's attention and held her beer bottle up. "I'll have another one, Sissy."

"Sure thing, Zelda."

The door to Thirsty's opened, and Zelda glanced over to see who'd come in. Not that she cared, really. The only man she'd want to see walk through the door was a hundred miles away. She saw a guy wearing jeans and a polo shirt standing just inside the door, checking the place out. He ran his eyes over the place, real slow, like he was looking for someone, and when he spotted Zelda sitting at the counter, he ambled over in her direction.

Sissy set a cold bottle of Iron City on the counter and leaned over the bar. "I think you may have yourself some company, Zelda."

Zelda took a long swig of her beer, and ignored the man as he climbed up on the stool next to her.

The man pointed his thumb towards Zelda's beer. "I'll have the same thing she's having."

"Coming right up." Sissy placed a napkin on the bar in front of him.

The man twisted in his stool and fiddled with the paper napkin.

Sissy set the beer down on the bar. "You need a glass with that?"

He shook his head. "Nah, I'm good."

"All right. Enjoy." Sissy winked at Zelda as she walked away.

The man lifted the bottle and tilted it towards Zelda. "Cheers."

Zelda leaned her elbow on the bar and glanced sideways at the man. "Cheers."

"Ahh, that's nice and cold." The man set the bottle on the bar. "It was sure a scorcher out there today."

Zelda nodded. "Yeah, it's summer. What else is new?"

He smiled. "I'm Joe, by the way."

She ran her eyes over him. His jeans were faded in an expensive-looking way, and his polo shirt had a fancy little horse on the chest. Her eyes trailed down to his shoes: leather loafers with a tassel. "Joe, huh? What's your last name, Smith?"

Joe laughed. "You got it."

Zelda had to give him credit for not denying the fake name. She'd met a dozen *Joe Smiths* at Thirsty's over the years. Mostly traveling salesmen from Ohio, or Pennsylvania. Afraid to give their real name because they had a wife and kids back home.

"Wherever you're from, it's obviously not from around these parts."

He shifted closer. "No, I'm just traveling through. It's a nice area."

Zelda took a swig of her beer. "It's a run-down piece of shit town."

"I'll take your word for it," Joe said, grinning broadly. "Do you live around here?"

"Unfortunately."

"I didn't catch your name."

"Zelda."

"It's very nice to meet you, Zelda." He pointed to her bottle. "Can I buy you another one?"

Zelda thought about it for a minute. She was already on her third, and the room was starting to spin a little.

"Sure." She drained the bottle. What the hell difference did it make? She didn't have anything else to do.

Joe waved at Sissy. "Would you bring Zelda another cold one, please?"

"You bet." Sissy grabbed Zelda's empty bottle.

He twisted his stool to face her. "So, what's a pretty girl like you doing sitting all alone at the bar like this?"

"I ain't waiting for Prince Charming, if that's what you think."

Joe dangled his arm around the back of her bar stool. "That's good to hear, Zelda, because I'm no Prince Charming."

He took a sip of his beer, then set it back on the counter next to her bottle. "Hey, I think your cell phone's ringing." He pointed towards her cell phone.

Zelda grabbed the phone off the bar. "Hello?"

"Hey, babe, this is the third time I've called you. Why didn't you answer before?"

She turned her stool so her back was to Joe. "Hey. I guess I didn't hear it ring. I'm still not used to this thing."

The phone was silent for a moment, then Earl said, "Yeah, all right. But I want to be able to get you on the phone when I need to talk to you, so put it on vibrate or something, okay?"

Zelda smiled and lowered her voice. "If you stay away too much longer, I'm going to have to put it on vibrate and use it for something else."

Earl's deep laugh rumbled through the phone. "Babe, that sounds like something we should try together."

"I miss you so much."

"Yeah, I miss you, too. Where the hell are you, anyway?"

"I'm sitting in Thirsty's having a cold one and shooting the shit with Sissy."

"Can she hear you?"

"Nah, she's way down at the other end of the bar." She glanced over her shoulder at Joe as she slid off the bar stool. "But I'm going to walk outside, where no one else can hear me."

"All right. We've had some developments."

"Good or bad?" she asked as she pushed open the door.

"Good."

"Tell me."

"I've got the perfect place."

"For the hideout?"

"Yup."

"What's it like?"

"You'll find out when you see it. Just trust me; it couldn't be any better."

"You know I trust you." Zelda leaned against the hood of a pickup truck. "What else is going on? Any news about Cummings?"

"He's home."

"*What?*"

"Yup, came home this afternoon. He's still a weak puppy, but he checked himself out of the hospital."

"So what are you going to do?"

"Nothing tonight. He's got more guards at his place than they have at Fort Knox."

"You ain't going to let up on him, are you? If this is going to work, you've got to keep the pressure on. Let him know we mean business."

"Relax, I've got things under control. The pressure is on. The reason Cummings came home from the hospital is because he was freaked out about the deer."

Zelda smiled. "Really? How do you know that?"

"The riding camp instructor. Turns out, she's even better friends with Cummings's wife than we thought she was."

"Are you making friends with her?"

"I'm working on it."

"Tell me about her."

"I already told you, she's friends with Doug and Anne Cummings and she teaches the riding camp that Cummings's kid goes to."

"What does she look like?"

"Aw, come on, Zelda. What does it matter what she looks like?"

She didn't answer. He knew why it mattered.

Earl sighed loudly. "Don't worry, babe, she doesn't float my boat. She's a scrawny thing, with no boobs, and a snobby attitude."

A car pulled into the parking space next to her, country music blaring from the stereo, and Zelda walked farther down the parking lot. "Good, because I think you should get to know her better. It sounds like she might be able to give us valuable information."

"Yeah, I already figured that. She's key. Look, I've got to go. I'll call you soon. Just hang in there, babe. This thing is going to come off just like we planned."

"All right. Dream about me tonight."

Zelda lit a cigarette, no longer interested in going back inside and sharing a couple of cold ones with Joe. The passenger door to the car with the country music opened, and two guys got out and slammed the door.

"Hang loose, Larry. We'll catch you later," one of the guys said, leaning down and looking at the driver through the open window.

The driver shifted in his seat to look backwards, and Zelda saw the taillights brighten as he put the car in reverse. She hurried over to the car and pounded on the hood just as the car was starting to roll out of the parking space.

The driver slammed on the brakes and glared at her. "Hey, what's with you, banging on my car?"

Zelda walked to the passenger door and leaned on the open window, making sure to bend low so he could see her cleavage. "Sorry, I was just trying to get your attention. I saw you was leaving, and I was wondering if you might be able to give me a ride."

He eyed her chest. "Where are you going to?"

"Just down the road a bit. I promise, it won't take you but a couple of minutes out of your way."

He reached over and flipped the door handle. "Hop in."

29

No matter how Kendall looked at it, the numbers just didn't add up. Even though she was working off Wellington's boarding fee, her monthly expenses for his shoeing and medical costs were at least two hundred dollars. Plus, even if she just showed on the local circuit, she'd have to shell out another couple hundred a month in entry fees and trailering. Rent for the cottage was twelve hundred a month, and she had to pay utilities, car insurance, gas. . . . The list went on and on.

She read the letter from the health insurance provider again. There was a thirty-day grace period where she was still covered under Peter's policy; after that, she had to apply for individual coverage, which could cost her up to five hundred dollars a month.

Kendall picked up her checkbook and thumbed through the register until she found her balance. Twenty-two hundred forty-eight dollars. At the rate she was going, that would barely last her a month. She never should have splurged the way she had on Anne's baby shower.

"Shit." She dropped the checkbook on the kitchen table and rested her head on her arms. *What was she going to do?*

Maybe her attorney had been right when he'd advised her to fight for alimony. But she hadn't wanted Peter's money. She'd just wanted out of the marriage. The only marital property she'd demanded was Wellington. And she'd had to fight Peter tooth and nail to get him.

A wave of panic washed over her. *How was she going to make ends meet?* Certainly not by working eight hours a day teaching camp at Fox Run just to pay for Wellington's board. But she didn't have a career to fall back on; she'd never even graduated from college. She had no assets to speak of, except for Wellington. And selling him was out of the question. Wellington was the closest thing to family she had.

The shrill ring of the phone made Kendall jump, and she lifted her head and pushed her hair out of her face as she reached for the handset. She glanced at the caller-ID display. *Wireless caller.* That hardly narrowed it down.

She picked up the phone. "Hello."

"Hi, Kendall, this is Stephen Lloyd. We met yesterday at Fox Run."

"Yes, I remember."

"Margaret gave me your phone number; I hope that's all right."

"Of course, no problem."

"Listen, I was wondering if I could take you to dinner."

Kendall glanced down at the tank top and running shorts she'd donned after her shower. "Tonight?"

Stephen chuckled. "Sure, I'm game if you're available. But I had planned on giving you a little more notice than that. I was calling about tomorrow night."

When she didn't respond, he said, "I was thinking of trying that pub in Upperville. Hunter's Head. I've heard great things about it."

"Um, let me check my calendar." *What should she do?* She didn't want to go on a date with Stephen, or anyone else for that matter.

She flipped through the pages of the calendar, making sure he could hear her. "Oh, darn, we have a field trip tomorrow after camp. I'm taking the kids to walk the beagles."

"That sounds like fun. What time will you get back?"

"Not until late. Probably seven o'clock, maybe later."

"I don't mind eating late. How about if I pick you up at eight?"

Kendall took a deep breath. "Stephen, I really appreciate the invitation, but I'm recently divorced and I'm not dating yet."

There was a moment's silence. "I see. I'm sorry if I offended you by asking. Margaret gave me a different impression."

"No offense taken. I think Margaret is trying to play matchmaker for me, but I'm not ready for that yet."

"I understand. I've been there myself. Listen, how about if we grab a bite to eat at the pub tomorrow anyway? Just as friends. Don't get me wrong, but this is a hard community to break into. I think I've eaten alone at every restaurant in Middleburg, and I'm starting to get a complex."

Kendall smiled. "I know what you mean. I hate to eat alone in a restaurant."

"Does that mean you'll join me?"

She hesitated. What could it hurt? He seemed like a nice-enough guy, and she could certainly relate to his loneliness.

"Sure, why not? I'll meet you there."

"Terrific. I'll see you around eight."

Kendall put the receiver back on the cradle. *I hope I won't live to regret that decision,* she thought. She rose and gathered the pile of bills and shoved them in a kitchen drawer, then opened the refrigerator door, wondering what she should eat for dinner. The shelves were bare except for a chunk of cheese, some grapes, a carton of coffee creamer, and an open bottle of Chardonnay. She regretted telling the ladies at the shower that they should take the leftover food home to their kids.

"Looks like the usual for dinner again tonight," she muttered, grabbing the grapes and cheese and placing them on the counter. As she reached into the cupboard for a plate, she heard the doorbell ring. Frowning, she glanced out the window and saw Jake's truck parked in the drive. *What in the world was he doing here?*

She opened the front door and caught her breath as she saw Jake with a bag of groceries in his arms.

"Jake, what are you doing here?" She swung the screen door outwards and held it open.

"I had a hankering for a steak dinner, and, on a whim, I thought I'd stop by and see if you'd like to join me." He nodded towards the bag in his arms. "That is, if you haven't already eaten."

Kendall was dumbfounded. She and Jake had made their peace, but he was the last person she'd expect to show up at her door with dinner. "Sure, come on in. I was just getting ready to make dinner myself. How'd you know where I live, anyway?"

"Mrs. Southwell told me."

Kendall fought a smile. First, the dinner invitation from Stephen, and now this. It wasn't hard to imagine what Margaret was up to.

Jake followed her into the kitchen and set the bag of groceries on the counter. "Do you have a charcoal grill?"

She shook her head. "Sorry."

"That's all right." He took a package of two large steaks and a bottle of

Worcestershire sauce out of the bag. "Let me marinate these, and then I'll gather some wood and get a fire going outside. Mind if I use the rack from your oven?"

"You're going to cook the steaks outside over a wood fire?"

"Why not? It's just like a campfire." Jake opened the package of meat. "Do you have a plate I can use to marinate these on?"

"Sure." She took a platter out of the cupboard and handed it to him.

"Thanks." He glanced down at her running shorts as he took the platter from her. "Did you go running in this heat?"

"No. It's so darned hot in here, I took a shower and put on the coolest clothes I could find." Kendall folded her arms across her chest, suddenly self-conscious about her appearance. "I wasn't expecting company."

"It's hot in here all right. It must be tough sleeping at night without air conditioning."

"I have it. I just try not to use it unless the heat gets unbearable. It really runs up the electrical bill."

"Yeah, I'm lucky I don't have to worry about that at Mrs. Southwell's." He doused the steaks with Worcestershire sauce and flipped them over. "There, that ought to do it."

He reached into the grocery bag and lifted out a six-pack of Budweiser. "Would you like a cold beer?"

Kendall wrinkled her nose. "No thanks; I'm not much of a beer drinker. I'll pour myself a glass of wine."

"Why doesn't that surprise me?" he said, helping himself to a bottle.

"What does that mean?"

Jake shrugged. "Nothing. Just that, now that I think about it, I should have known you wouldn't be a beer-drinking kind of gal."

"Why?"

He smiled, but his eyes held a hint of resentment. "You come from a different world, where you eat at fancy restaurants and drink expensive wine."

"That's not true, Jake," she said, her hands on her hips. "I don't abstain from drinking beer because I'm a snob. I just don't like the way it tastes."

Jake held his hands up in the shape of a *T*. "Okay, time out. Let's not get into a fight about it. I don't care if you don't like beer, Kendall. I don't like wine. Let's call it even, okay?"

"Fine." Kendall opened the refrigerator and took out the bottle of Chardonnay. She wished she'd refused Jake's offer to cook dinner. What she really wanted to do was unwind with a glass of wine and some cheese and crackers, and then crash for the night.

She followed Jake outside and helped gather wood for the fire. "Where do you want to eat? It might be cooler out here than inside."

"Outside sounds good to me. There's a nice breeze stirring."

Kendall set the table on the patio and microwaved the potatoes that Jake had brought. Then she wrapped the potatoes in foil and took them out to the fire.

"The steaks smell good," she said, handing the potatoes to him.

"It's not Oklahoma beef, but they look pretty good." He placed the potatoes in the fire and sat down on the bench next to her. "It'll just be a couple more minutes."

Neither of them spoke for a few minutes; then Jake pointed his beer bottle towards her legs. "You scraped your knees pretty good today."

"It's not my knees I'm worried about. They'll heal. It's the brand-new pair of breeches I ruined that really hurts."

Jake smiled and nodded. "They looked like they cost a pretty penny."

Kendall just nodded and they lapsed back into silence.

After a moment, Jake reached out and ran his fingers over the scar on Kendall's shoulder. "You get that from a riding accident?"

Kendall recoiled from his touch. "No," she said, offering no further explanation.

Jake raised his beer bottle to his lips. "What happened?"

She didn't respond.

"That bad, huh?"

"Worse."

"Tell me about it."

She shook her head. "I don't want to talk about it."

"Suit yourself."

He rose and cut into the steaks with a knife. "They look good. I guess we can eat now."

Kendall held the plates while Jake served the steaks and potatoes, then set the plates down on the patio table. "Do you need another beer or anything else to drink?"

"No, I'm good," Jake said, holding her chair out for her.

"Thank you." Kendall sat down and let him help slide her chair in. She waited until he was seated, then cut into her steak.

"This is delicious."

"Yeah, it's not too bad."

They ate in silence for a few moments, then Jake said, "Is it from your ex-husband?"

"What?"

"The scar on your shoulder. Is it from your ex-husband?"

She paused with her knife and fork in midair. "I told you before that I don't want to talk about it."

Jake ate another forkful of steak. "My father did the same thing to my mother."

"I don't know what you're talking about."

Jake acted as if she hadn't spoken. "He used to get drunk and take it out on her. When I was a little kid, I used to try to make him stop. But then I figured out that made it even worse, so I used to hide under the covers in my room and pretend I didn't hear what was going on."

"Jake—"

He held his hand up to stop her. "Then one day, on my sixteenth birthday, they got in a fight because of me. He beat her up real bad. I stayed awake all night, planning a way to take her away from him. Because I knew that was the only way to save her."

He stopped talking and concentrated on pulling the foil off his potato, seasoning it with butter and salt and pepper.

"Did you?" Kendall asked when he didn't continue.

"Save her? Yup. I scrounged up all the money I could find and bought bus tickets for my mother and myself to the farthest place I could afford. We were gone by the time he got home."

"Did he come after you?"

"I don't know. He didn't find us if he did come looking, but I've spent the better part of the last sixteen years watching over my shoulder."

"Are you still?"

Jake toyed with the food on his plate. "No, my mother just passed away, so there's no more need."

"I'm sorry."

"Thanks."

Kendall studied him. "You said the fight they had on your sixteenth birthday was because of you. I hope you don't blame yourself for what happened to your mother."

He sighed. "Aw, I don't know. I guess I do, in a way."

"What happened?"

He placed his knife and fork on his plate and leaned back in his chair. "Like I said, it was my sixteenth birthday. My dad was drunk, as usual, and he started in on me at dinner. He asked if I was a man yet; whether I'd ever had sex."

Kendall glanced away.

"When I told him I hadn't, he got mad and called me a faggot. He told me he wasn't going to let his flesh and blood embarrass him, and he hauled me into the car and took me down to the local bar." Jake paused and gazed off in the distance.

"But it was a slow night and there weren't any girls there," he continued, shaking his head as if to clear his thoughts. "Just a couple of drunks playing pool. Boy, was my father mad. He made me sit at the bar with him while he had a couple shots of whiskey, getting madder by the minute. Then this woman walked in. *A hooker.* And my father's mood shifted. He told me to wait out in his truck, and about five minutes later the woman came out without him, dangling the keys as she climbed in the cab. She had a big smile on her face, and she told me she was taking me somewhere to give me my birthday present."

He paused and took a long swallow of his beer. "It was some birthday present all right. She drove down to the river and pulled off the road into the woods. Then she taught me about sex in the front seat of my father's Ford."

Kendall felt a warm blush creep up her cheeks. *Why was Jake telling her this?*

Jake shrugged. "Anyway, that's what my parents had a fight about. My mother didn't stand up to my father very often, but that night she summoned up the courage to confront him. Trying to protect me from his evil ways."

Kendall didn't know how to respond, so she just sat quietly across from him, and their silence was filled with the sound of tree frogs and crickets.

"I'm sorry. I don't know why I told you that," Jake said after awhile.

"Don't be sorry. Sometimes it helps to talk about things."

He nodded. "Yeah, it does sometimes."

30

"Come on, kids, the bus is here," Kendall said, motioning for Elizabeth and the campers to follow her. "Who needs to go to the bathroom before we get on the bus?"

She heard a chorus of "I do" and saw several hands shoot up in the air.

"Okay, let's line up out here in the aisle, and three of you can go in at a time." She stopped in front of the door to the girls' bathroom.

"I'll go in and help them," Elizabeth said, herding the first three girls into the bathroom.

The door to the office opened and Margaret leaned out. "The bus is here, Kendall."

"I know. We're just making one last potty stop."

"All right. By the way, do you mind if Todd tags along on the field trip?"

"No, of course not."

"Great! I think he'll enjoy it. Let me find him and tell him you're about ready to go," Margaret said, closing the door.

Elizabeth came out of the bathroom with the first group of girls. "Okay, next three."

Kendall gave her a smile. "Margaret just asked if Todd could come along on the field trip."

"What did you tell her?" Elizabeth crossed her fingers and held her hand next to her heart.

"I said yes."

"Thank you." Elizabeth beamed as she opened the bathroom door. "Come on girls, let's hurry up."

Samantha was one of the girls who had already visited the bathroom.

"Kendall, I'm thirsty. Can I go in the office and get a drink of water?"

"Yes, you may. Wait for me in there. We'll be there in a minute."

"Can Emma come with me?"

"Sure."

The girls took off for the office and Kendall leaned against the wall and stifled a yawn. She hadn't slept well last night. The heat had been unbearable, and even though she'd gotten up around midnight and turned on the air conditioning, she'd still tossed and turned most of the night, unable to get her mind off what Jake had told her about his mother.

"Okay, we're all ready," Elizabeth said, coming out of the bathroom with the last group. "Let's go see those cute little beagles."

"Samantha and Emma are waiting for us in the office. I'll go get them and meet you at the bus."

Kendall opened the office door and saw Jake spinning around in a circle with Samantha and Emma, each holding on to one of his hands.

Samantha giggled. "Whee, I'm getting dizzy."

"Me, too," Emma squealed.

Jake looked at Kendall and smiled as he swung the girls around one more time before dropping them on the couch. "Okay, that's enough. I'm getting dizzy, too."

Kendall laughed. "Come on, girls. That looks like fun, but we'd better hurry, or we'll be late for the field trip."

"Where you going?" Jake asked.

"We're going to walk the beagles."

"Are you dog-sitting for someone?"

She smiled. "No. We're going to exercise the hunting beagles."

"Oh, yeah, I remember Samantha saying something about that. It's a foxhunt for kids, where they hunt with beagles instead of foxhounds, right?"

Kendall nodded. "It's geared towards teaching children about foxhunting."

"Sounds like a fun field trip."

"It is really fun," Emma said. "We get to ride on a bus and everything."

"Do you want to come along, Jake?" Samantha asked. "They allow grown-ups to come as long as they are with a kid. My daddy's going to be there."

Jake glanced at Kendall.

"Why don't you come along? Todd's coming, too," she said.

"Sure, why not?"

"Yay!" Samantha jumped up off the couch. "Let's hurry. We might miss the bus."

"Okay, all aboard," Kendall said, opening the door that led outside. The guard Doug had hired to look after Samantha was already in his car, parked behind the waiting bus.

"What's the Greenfield Academy?" Jake asked, pointing towards the lettering on the side of the bus.

"It's a local private school. Since they're not in session during the summer, they let Margaret use the bus for the horse camp's field trips."

Jake raised his eyebrows. "That's a good deal. Do they provide the driver?"

Kendall nodded. "Mrs. Parker. She's wonderful."

Samantha and Emma skipped ahead, and by the time Kendall and Jake climbed aboard the bus, the girls had filled the last two of the six rows of seats. Elizabeth and Todd were seated next to each other, one row ahead of the girls.

"Let's count heads," Kendall said, tapping each girl on the head as she counted to eight. "Everyone needs to have a partner when we get to the kennels, so I want each of you to pair up with who you're sitting next to on the bus. We went over the bus rules at lunch, so I know I can count on you to behave. If you're really good today, that means that Mrs. Parker will come back again and drive us when we go to see the horses swim later this week. Okay?"

"Okay," the girls cheered.

Kendall gave a thumbs-up to Mrs. Parker and sat down across the aisle from Elizabeth and Todd. Jake hesitated for a second, then chose the seat ahead of her, sitting sideways, with his long legs stretched out into the aisle.

"Did I hear you say that you take your horses swimming?" he asked, turning to face her as the bus lurched forward.

She nodded. "There's a swim center near the training track. It's a wonderful way to condition your horse, or to provide therapy after an injury."

"Sounds interesting. I'd like to see that."

"You can come along on Thursday, if you want."

"I might just do that. Do you go on two camp field trips every week?"

"Actually, we go on three. We walk the beagles and see the horses swim, and then we end up the week of camp on Saturday by going to the Land of Little Horses, in Gettysburg, Pennsylvania."

Jake arched an eyebrow. "Really? That's quite a trip."

"It's about an hour-and-a-half drive. But the kids really enjoy it, and it's a fun way to wrap up the week."

"Do you ride on the bus when you go up there?"

"Yes, so it's a relatively easy trip for me."

Jake nodded and turned away, staring thoughtfully out the window.

31

$\mathcal{D}$oug pulled the Porsche into the drive to the kennels and parked in the shade of an oak tree. The camp bus was next to the barn, along with a dozen or so other vehicles, but he didn't see the kids anywhere.

He turned to Mike, the bodyguard who had accompanied him. "They must still be out with the beagles. I'm going to get out and stretch my legs." Doug popped open the rear of the sunroof, so the car wouldn't be so hot when they returned, then opened the door and eased out of the driver's seat. He heard the melancholy cry of the beagles coming from the pasture to the south. "There they are. If we walk to the top of that knoll, we should be able to see them come in."

Doug's chest was still sore and he climbed the hill slowly. He glanced sideways at Mike. "You go on ahead. I'll come at my own pace."

Mike hesitated. "Mr. Cummings, it's my job to protect you, sir."

Doug sighed. "I'm perfectly safe here, Mike. I just brought you along to keep my wife happy."

"Yes, sir," Mike said, continuing to match his stride to Doug's.

They reached the crest of the hill just in time to see the beagle pack emerge from behind a grove of trees, along with a group of a couple dozen kids and a handful of adults. The beagles loped lazily towards home, their long ears flopping and their sterns at half-staff. Some of the kids ran to keep up with the beagles, while others lagged behind doing cartwheels and summersaults in the high grass.

As the group grew nearer, Samantha spotted Doug and scampered up the hill. "Daddy, you're here." She rushed towards him with outstretched arms.

Doug knelt on one knee and caught her in his arms as she flung herself at him. "I told you I'd be here waiting for you when you got back, didn't I?"

"Uh-huh." She looped her hands around his neck and leaned back so she could see his face. "We had so much fun walking the beagles, Daddy. We took them swimming in the pond, and Mrs. Strump let me walk down in the creek with them. If you feel better by next time, you have to come with us."

"Wow, that sounds like fun; I'll take you up on that. I see there are some other kids here, too, besides the camp kids. Did you make any new friends?"

"I guess." Samantha released her grip around his neck. "Come on, we're going to feed the beagles now, and then we get to see the puppies."

Doug grimaced as he rose to his feet. "All right, you go on in with the other kids, and I'll be there in a minute."

Samantha frowned at him. "Are you okay, Daddy?"

He ruffled her hair. "I'm perfectly fine, princess. Go on, now. You don't want to miss anything."

"I want to stay with you." Samantha grabbed his hand and buried her face against his thigh.

"Okay then, let's hurry." Doug gently pried Samantha loose from his leg and started down the hill. "If beagles are anything like foxhounds, they eat pretty fast."

"Some of them eat slower than others, so they put them in a different pen. That way, the faster eaters don't steal all the food from the slower eaters. That's what Kendall told us."

"Is that right? That's pretty smart."

"Yup." She reached down to pick a yellow wildflower. "Look, I found a pretty little flower. We can take it home to Mommy."

"That's a great idea."

The beagles were out in their pens by the time they reached the kennel, and Kendall opened the gate to the turnout enclosure for them.

"Come on, Samantha, I reserved a very special group of beagles for you to feed," Kendall said, holding out her hand.

Samantha looked up at Doug.

"Go on," he said. "I'll be right here watching."

Jake was leaning against a shade tree in the center of the enclosure. Doug walked over to him.

"Good to see you, Jake."

Jake shook his hand. "Nice to see you, Mr. Cummings. I was surprised when Samantha told me you were going to be here. You must be feeling better."

"I'm doing all right. Nothing time won't heal."

"How's Chancellor doing? I didn't have time to go see him today."

"He's terrific. Ned said he may be able to come home by the weekend."

"That's good news."

Samantha came out of the nearby kennel lugging a red bucket. "Daddy, watch me. I get to feed Sailor and Rocky. They're my two favorites."

"Okay, Sam. I'm watching." Doug smiled at the sight of her hauling the bucket across the yard.

Elizabeth unlatched the gate to the pen closest to them and led four girls out. "Hey, Jake, have you seen Todd?"

Jake shook his head. "Not for a while. You need help with something, darling?"

"No, but we're getting ready to visit the puppies, and I thought he'd like to see them."

"Maybe Mother Nature called. I'll keep my eye out for him and send him in your direction when I see him."

Elizabeth flashed him a bright smile. "Thanks."

"Come on, Daddy. I'm done feeding." Samantha opened the gate to the pen she was in and dragged the empty bucket towards him. "We get to go see the puppies now."

"Can I help you carry that bucket?"

"No, it's okay. It's not heavy."

"How many puppies do we get to see? Do you know?"

"I'm not sure, but Kendall said there are enough for each of us to hold one."

The puppies were in a separate pen on the other side of the kennel, and as Doug followed Samantha around to the far side of the building, he noticed Mike and Samantha's guard, Ben, shift their position in the parking lot so they could maintain visual contact.

Deena Strump, the huntsman for the beagle pack, was in the puppy pen with the kids, and she hurried over to Doug and Samantha as soon as they entered.

"Doug, it's good to see you. I heard you had a terrible accident."

He glanced at Samantha. "I'm fine. I just got a few scratches."

She frowned. "That's more than a scratch you have on your forehead. But, never mind, you're here and it's great to see you. Samantha did a very good job walking the beagles today."

"It was so much fun," Samantha said.

Deena smiled. "I'm glad you enjoyed it. Would you like to hold a puppy?"

Samantha nodded.

Deena looked around the pen at the group of squirming puppies. "Hmm, let me see. I have a very special puppy that I'd like you to meet. Ah, there he is."

She picked up a beagle that looked larger than the rest and placed him in Samantha's arms. "This is Rascal."

"Hi, Rascal," Samantha whispered, petting the puppy gently on the head.

"Do you know why Rascal is so special?"

"Because his ears are so soft?"

Deena laughed. "That they are, but that's not the reason. He's special because he's bigger than the rest of the litter. The thing of it is, he won't hunt well with the rest of the pack because his legs are longer, and he'll run faster than the rest of them. So he won't be having a job as a hunting beagle. He gets to be adopted by a family as their pet."

"Have you found a family to adopt him?"

Deena grinned mischievously at Doug. "I'm still working on that."

Doug smiled and shook his head. "Nice try. The last thing we need right now is a puppy. I'm sure a new baby will keep us plenty busy."

"Ah, but if you adopt Rascal, he and the baby could grow up together," Deena said, winking at Samantha.

"That's a great idea, Daddy."

Doug glared good-naturedly at Deena. "Samantha, Mrs. Strump is just teasing. She knows that puppies require lots of work, and Mommy and I aren't going to have time to do that once the baby is born."

"But I could help."

Deena nodded. "That's a very good point, Samantha. Helping take care of animals is a good way for children to learn responsibility."

Samantha gazed solemnly at Doug. "Please, Daddy? Rascal must be so scared about what will happen if no one wants to adopt him."

Doug reached down and scratched the puppy behind the ears. "Sam, I don't think the puppy really knows that Mrs. Strump is looking for someone to adopt him."

"Yes he does, Daddy. He didn't look very happy before, and now look at him." Samantha looked down at Rascal, who had fallen fast asleep in her arms.

"I must say, he sure does look quite content in your arms, Samantha," Deena said.

"See, Daddy? I think God wants me to adopt Rascal, just like he wanted you and Mommy to adopt me."

Doug swallowed the lump that formed in his throat and knelt down next to Samantha. "You really like Rascal, don't you, princess?"

"I love him."

"And I can see that he loves you, too."

Samantha hugged the puppy tighter and kissed him on the head.

Doug smiled at her. "What do you think Mommy will say when we come home with Rascal?"

"*You mean I can keep him?*"

He nodded and Samantha broke into a wide grin. "Thank you, Daddy."

Doug stood up. "All right then, we'd better get this show on the road. We're going to have to stop at Safeway and get some puppy food on the way home."

"And a collar and name tag, too," Samantha said. "That way, he'll know that we adopted him."

"I have a collar here that you can have," Deena said. "Come with me and I'll put it on him and make the adoption official."

"Is that okay, Daddy?"

"Sure. You go with Mrs. Strump. I'll let Kendall know that you'll be riding home with me and not on the camp bus."

By the time he'd finished speaking with Kendall, Samantha had already reached the car.

"Daddy!" she yelled from across the parking lot. "Can I use the lead rope in your car to see if Rascal knows how to walk on a leash?"

"I don't have a lead rope, Sam," he called. "We'll buy him a leash at the store."

"Yes you do, Daddy. There's one on the seat." Samantha balanced the puppy in one arm and opened the passenger door. She reached towards the seat, then let out a shriek and stumbled backwards. "Daddy! *Help.*"

Doug ignored the pain that shot through his side as he ran towards the car. "Sam, what's the matter?"

Mike and Ben sprinted past him, and by the time Doug reached the car, Ben had grabbed Samantha and pulled her to the side; Mike stood by the open door, his gun drawn.

"What the hell is going on?" Doug gasped when he reached Mike's side.

"There's a snake in the car, sir," Mike replied, motioning with his gun towards the passenger seat.

Doug looked inside and saw a black snake curled up on the seat. He reached up and snapped the end of a branch off the oak tree, slowly lowering it towards the snake. "Put your gun away," he said, giving Mike a sideways glance.

"Daddy, don't!" Samantha screamed. "It might bite you."

"It's not poisonous, Samantha." Doug used the branch to pin the snake's head to the seat, then grabbed the writhing snake just behind the head and lifted it out of the car.

Samantha struggled to get out of Ben's grasp. "Watch out, Daddy. It's hissing at you."

"Sam, it's all right. It's not going to hurt me." Doug carried the snake to the edge of the nearby woods and released it.

Ben let go of Samantha and she ran to Doug, tears streaming down her face. "Are you okay, Daddy?"

"I'm fine." He knelt and wrapped his arms around her.

Samantha buried her face against his shoulder, still clutching Rascal to her chest. "I thought it was going to kill you."

"Oh, come on, Sam. I'm bigger and stronger than any old snake. Besides, black snakes are our friends."

"But it hissed at you and looked like it wanted to bite you."

"It was just scared." Doug eased her away from him. "Hey, let's not squish Rascal. How did he react to seeing the snake?"

Samantha stroked the puppy's head. "I think he tried to protect me. I thought the snake was a lead rope, and I was about to pick it up to use it as a leash for Rascal, but when Rascal saw it was a snake, he squirmed a lot and tried to jump out of my arms. I held him tight, though, so the snake wouldn't hurt him."

Doug smiled at her. "That's my girl."

He rose and put his arm around Samantha's shoulder, steering her back to the car. "Come on, let's take Rascal home so he can meet Mommy."

Samantha sniffled. "But I'm scared. What if there's another snake in the car?"

"There aren't any more snakes in the car, Sam."

"But how do you know?"

"Because snakes usually don't get in cars. That was just a fluke."

"What's a fluke?"

"That means it hardly ever happens."

"But it *could* happen again."

Doug sighed. "How about if I check under the seats and make sure there are no more snakes? Will you feel safe getting in the car then?"

Samantha nodded.

"Okay." Doug stifled a groan as he stooped so he could see under the passenger seat.

"How did the snake get in the car anyway, Daddy?"

Good question, Doug thought. "I don't know, Sam. I left the sunroof open. Maybe it crawled in that way."

$\mathscr{A}$nne tucked Samantha in bed and went back downstairs to the study, where Doug and Patrick Talbot, the head of Manse Security, were talking.

Doug motioned for her to sit next to him on the couch. "Did Samantha go to sleep all right?"

"She's out like a light, with the puppy by her side."

Doug smiled. "See? It's a good thing we had Rascal to distract her from the snake experience."

"We'll talk about Rascal later," Anne said, settling close to him and reaching for his hand. "Patrick, do you mind filling me in on what you've reported to Doug?"

"Of course not," Patrick said, adjusting his wire-framed glasses. "I was just telling Doug that we've been investigating Zeb McGraw's family to see whether he might possibly be working through one of them to arrange these incidents. His mother is in a nursing home back in West Virginia, and hasn't visited Zeb in jail since his arrest, but his sister, Zelda, has visited on occasion."

He consulted his notes. "Let's see, the last time she visited McGraw in jail was about a month ago. Zelda is thirty-seven years old, lives in West Virginia, isn't married, and has no current place of employment. She has one child, a fifteen-year-old boy named Zachary, who dropped out of high school last spring. No one that our man spoke with recalls seeing the boy around recently, and Zelda told some folks around town that Zachary ran away this summer."

"Did your investigator speak with Zelda?"

"Yes. He struck up a conversation with her in a bar, posing as a traveling salesman. He was making progress, when she received a phone call on her cell and left the bar to carry on the conversation. Unfortunately, she never returned."

"Any other family?"

"No, that's it for immediate family. There are a handful of blood relations who live in West Virginia, but it doesn't appear as if they have been in contact with Zeb McGraw or his family for several years."

"What about close friends?" Doug asked. "Or a fellow inmate who has been released?"

"We're checking that out. Friends are obviously harder to track down than family, but we're working on it. McGraw hasn't had any visitors other than Zelda."

Patrick placed his notepad down. "That brings you up to speed on where we stand with McGraw so far. I'm hoping the incident this afternoon with the snake may give us a lead."

"How so?" Anne asked.

"We'll interview everyone who was at the kennels during the field trip today. Hopefully, someone saw something that will help us piece this puzzle together, even though he or she may not realize the significance of it."

"What are the odds that the snake got in Doug's car on its own?"

"I'd say slim to none." He looked at Doug. "What do you think?"

Doug shrugged. "It's possible that it crawled in through the sunroof, but I think it's unlikely. But if someone put it there deliberately, I have a hard time understanding what he thought he'd gain by that. What's the point? Black snakes are harmless."

Patrick nodded. "Sure, but he didn't know you weren't afraid of snakes. More and more, I think he is playing mind games with you, not necessarily trying to harm you physically. Look at what he did with the deer. Anne wasn't in any physical danger from that, but it was sure unpleasant for her to have to see it. And it also made her realize how vulnerable she is in her own home. I think the black snake incident was designed to make the same statement. *He can reach you wherever you go.* And even though you weren't afraid of the snake, it sure sounds like Samantha was. Perhaps that was his intention."

"But Doug's car accident doesn't fit with that line of thinking," Anne said. "He almost died."

"You're right, but maybe he didn't intend for it to go that far. Perhaps he only meant to scare Doug."

"If these events are designed to terrorize us rather than harm us physically, that brings us right back to McGraw again," Doug said.

"Yes, you're right. He seemed to enjoy playing a cat and mouse game with you," Patrick said. "But, of course, he doesn't have exclusive rights to that type of behavior. Anyone who feels they were wronged by you might play that kind of game. We also shouldn't rule out the possibility of a copycat, with all the media coverage there was about the McGraw case."

Patrick stood. "I'll call and report the snake incident to the Sheriff's Office first thing tomorrow, and the episode with the deer as well. I don't expect them to give it much attention, but I want it in their files. I'll arrange a convenient time for them to come here to take your statements."

"Fine."

The phone rang. "I'll get it," Anne said, struggling to her feet.

Patrick raised his hand. "I'll let myself out. You folks have a nice evening."

Anne picked up the receiver on Doug's desk. "Hello."

"Hi, Anne. It's Kendall."

"Kendall, hi." Anne sat down in Doug's desk chair.

"I'm calling to see how Samantha is after her encounter with the snake today."

"She seems fine. She's fast asleep. I think with the excitement of bringing the puppy home, she's forgotten all about the snake."

"What do you think about the puppy? He's awfully cute, isn't he?"

"All puppies are cute."

Kendall laughed. "That's true."

Anne heard static on the line. "It sounds like you're on your cell. You're not coming home from the barn this late, are you?"

"No, I'm driving home from Upperville. I had a dinner date."

"Who with?"

"His name is Stephen Lloyd. He's a polo player from Aiken who's moving up here, or thinking about it anyway."

"A polo player? Sounds interesting. Do you like him?"

"Yes and no. He's a nice guy and fun to be around. I enjoyed the evening, but I don't *like him* like him."

"Well, at least you went out and had a nice evening."

"Yeah, I guess. After dinner he asked me to go to the polo match with him at Great Meadow on Friday night. I said yes, but now I feel like that might be leading him on."

"Oh, Kendall, go ahead and go. Polo at Great Meadow is fun, and, who knows, your feelings towards him may change over time."

"Maybe, but I don't think so."

The cell phone rang just as Zelda stepped out of the shower, and she snatched it off the bathroom sink.

"Hello," she said, reaching for a towel.

"Are you sitting down?" Earl asked.

"No, I just got out of the shower. I'm standing here naked, dripping all over the floor."

"Babe, that's an image I'll carry with me the rest of the night."

She smiled as she wrapped the towel around her. "Why'd you want to know if I was sitting down?"

"How's this Saturday sound to you?"

"Are you serious?" she shouted into the phone.

"Dead serious. Everything's falling into place. The only wrinkle is that Cummings got so scared, he hired bodyguards."

"For the kid?"

"Yeah, and for him and the wife."

"Damn it! Does the guard go to camp with her?"

"Yeah, but we'll figure out a way around him. They went on a field trip today, and Zach managed to put a snake in Cummings's car, even with two bodyguards there."

"Did Cummings freak at the snake?"

"Not too bad, but the kid did, so it was worth it. Anyway, don't worry about the guard. He ain't going to screw up our plan. By this time next week, we should be a million miles away from here."

"And a million dollars richer."

Earl laughed. "Ain't that just like you, to see the financial side of things."

"It's not just the money." Zelda flipped down the toilet lid and sat down. "It's what the money will buy. It's my ticket out of this hellhole."

"I know, babe. You're only there a few more days. Zach will pick you up Friday night after he gets off work."

"*Zach's* picking me up? I thought *you'd* come get me."

"Sorry, babe, no can do. I have business to take care of Friday night. I'll see you and Zach at the motel."

Samantha opened the door and struggled out of the car with Rascal clutched in her arms. "Come on, Rascal. I'm going to teach you how to fetch."

Doug closed the driver's door and smiled as he watched her set the puppy on the lawn and pick up a stick from beneath a dogwood tree. "I'm going inside, Sam."

"Okay, Daddy."

As he climbed the stairs to the back porch, he saw Anne wave at him through the kitchen window. "It looks like Mommy is making dinner. Come inside in a few minutes."

Anne had the door open by the time he reached it. "How was camp?" She stretched up to kiss him.

"Great. I got there in time to see Sam jump her first cross rail."

"How'd she do?"

Doug grinned. "She's a natural." He sniffed as he entered the kitchen. "What smells so good?"

"I put a quiche in the oven for dinner."

"Will you save some for me? We'll probably just have cold sandwiches at the meeting."

Anne frowned. "What meeting?"

"I have a Middleburg Foxhounds board meeting tonight. Remember?" He opened the refrigerator door and grabbed a bottle of water.

She let out a little laugh. "You're not serious."

He twisted off the cap and took a long drink. "Why wouldn't I be serious?"

Anne stared at him. "You should be home recuperating, Doug. No one expects you to be at the meeting tonight."

Doug set the water bottle on the table. "Maybe not, but there are some territory issues that will be addressed, and I told Richard I'd be at the meeting. I'd like to put in an appearance at least."

Her expression tightened. "I'm sure Richard would understand your absence, given what you've been through."

"You're probably right, but I want to be there. The Hunt is important to me."

"So I see." She turned away.

"Come on, Anne. I didn't mean that the way it sounded." He grabbed for her hand.

She shook her hand free and walked to the window.

"*Anne.*"

She kept her back to him.

Damn it. Doug took a deep breath, then crossed the room and slipped his arms around her. "Hey, let's not fight."

Anne tilted her head back against his chest. "I just think you're pushing yourself too hard."

He tightened his embrace. "I'm fine. You were there when I saw Dr. Hollins today. You heard her say my lung is healing beautifully."

"I also heard her tell you to continue to take it easy."

"I am taking it easy."

She shook her head. "Okay."

Doug brushed Anne's hair aside and kissed the back of her neck. "I won't be gone long."

CHAPTER

35

*D*oug downshifted through a turn, then floored it along the straightaway of the gravel road. He caught a glimpse of the bodyguard's car in the mirror and felt a twinge of satisfaction as he saw the image disappear in the cloud of dust kicked up by the Porsche. He felt foolish having Mike follow him to the meeting at Margaret's, but he knew Anne would have been furious if he'd left the bodyguard behind.

The gravel road dead-ended at Route 50, and Doug merged into the heavy stream of west-bound commuters. Traffic crawled at a snail's pace. He drummed his fingers impatiently on the gearshift knob as he crept towards the entrance to Fox Run Farm. Several horses and riders were in the outdoor arena, and Doug saw Kendall standing in the center of the ring. He gave a quick blast on the horn and waved at her as he passed through the front gate. Doug followed the drive as it wound around the barn, then slowed to cross the metal pipes of a cattle guard as he took the turn between black-fenced pastures towards the back of the property.

Margaret's house was situated at the rear of Fox Run, secluded halfway up a hill, beyond the gnarly trees of an abandoned apple orchard. More than once, Doug had expressed his concern about Margaret living alone in such an isolated setting, but she had waved off his worries. Margaret insisted the location was ideal for her. It was far enough away from the stable to ensure her privacy, yet it had an eagle's-eye view of the paddocks and the back of the barn, so she could keep tabs on things.

Doug saw Richard's Lexus and Smitty's truck parked in the drive. He pulled to a stop behind the other vehicles, next to a row of mature boxwoods so voluminous, they almost obscured the brick walkway to the front door.

"Would you like me to patrol outside, sir, or accompany you inside?" Mike asked when they got out of their cars.

Doug motioned for Mike to follow him to the house. "Relax, Mike. I'm perfectly safe here. Consider yourself off duty. You can make yourself at home inside, where it's air conditioned."

Mike frowned. "Pardon me, sir, but that's what you said at the beagle kennels. Yesterday. When the snake was put in your car. I almost lost my job over that incident."

Doug leveled a glance at Mike as he stepped between the boxwoods. "It's safe here, Mike."

There was a flicker of annoyance in Mike's eyes, but he didn't argue. "Yes, sir."

Mike followed him up the narrow walk and stood off to the side of the front stoop while Doug grasped the brass fox-shaped door knocker and rapped a couple of times. When no one answered, Doug pushed open the heavy wooden door and walked inside. "Anyone home?"

Margaret stepped into the hall from the room on the left. "*Doug?* I don't believe it. What on earth are you doing here?"

Doug smiled and leaned down to kiss her cheek. "I'm on the board, remember?"

"I'm well aware of that, but I sure didn't expect to see you here." She gave him a hug, then held him at arm's length, frowning as she studied his face. "That's quite a gash you have on your forehead. Are you sure you should be out and about so soon?"

Doug sighed. "You sound just like Anne." He took a step backwards towards the open door and motioned for Mike to come inside.

"Margaret, this is Mike. Would you have a cool place where he can hang out during the meeting?" He offered no explanation as to who Mike was, and, although Margaret gave the bodyguard a good once-over, she didn't ask.

"Of course," she replied. "Richard and Smitty are in the library. Why don't you join them, Doug. I'll show Mike to the back room."

"Thanks, Margaret." Doug waited for Margaret and Mike to start down the hall before he stepped into the room.

"Doug, what an unexpected pleasure," Richard said, striding across the room to greet him. "I spoke with Anne earlier today. She didn't mention a thing about you attending the meeting tonight."

Doug shook Richard's hand. "It was a last-minute decision."

"Look who's here!" Smitty said, raising his glass. "You look like death warmed over, my friend."

Doug smiled. "Thanks."

Smitty grabbed Doug's hand in his and laughed heartily. "It's good to see you. Come on, have a seat. Margaret has drinks set up in the other room. Can I get you something?"

"Not right now. Thanks, Smitty." Doug eased into a wing chair by the front window.

He heard a knock on the front door and a few minutes later Margaret ushered Wendy Brooks into the library.

Wendy's eyes widened when she saw him. "Doug, it's so good to see you."

He started to rise, but Wendy waved her hand at him. "Don't get up." She leaned down and kissed his cheek. "How are you feeling?"

"I'm good." He gestured towards the chair next to him. "Have a seat."

Wendy sat down and Margaret settled near Doug on the window seat, shoving aside several magazines, which were scattered across the needlepoint cushion. "Well, Richard, shall we get down to business? I know not everyone is here yet, but I don't imagine Doug is interested in having this meeting drag on all night. Let's address the issue that's on everyone's mind. *Territory.* Then we can break and have a bite to eat."

"Fine." Richard took a seat on the sofa. "Let me start with a bit of good news. You all know I received a letter a couple of weeks ago from the farm manager at Rolling Acres, informing us that the Middleburg Foxhounds are no longer welcome to ride across the farm because of the incident last season when the yearlings got all riled up. Well, I finally got Harry Adams on the phone at his summer home in Nag's Head, and he was astonished to hear that his manager had written such a letter. Harry couldn't have been more apologetic and said we have carte blanche to hunt through Rolling Acres whenever we want. I promised him we'd make sure his manager has ample notice when we hunt that territory, so he can put the horses up."

Margaret grunted. "I knew that letter had been sent without Harry's approval. Harry has been a loyal supporter of the Middleburg Foxhounds for too many years to shut down our territory like that."

Richard nodded. "And I'm sure Harry's high regard for you played a part in his gracious response, Margaret. He made a point of asking me to pass along his greetings to you, by the way."

She shrugged off the compliment. "I guess all those hours I spent visiting landowners with Daddy when he was master are still good for something."

"Speaking of landowner relations, Doug's been doing some good in that regard as well." Richard turned towards him. "Tell them how you charmed Lilibet Parsons into letting us hunt across Hickory Vale."

A movement outside the window caught Doug's eye, and he looked towards the door, expecting to be interrupted by a knock. The front hall remained quiet, however, and he turned his attention back to the conversation. "I didn't charm anyone. It's just fortuitous that Samantha is in the same ballet class as Lilibet's daughter. We got to talking after one of the recitals about life in the hunt country and how much nicer it is to raise a family here than in the congested suburb of Dallas where Lilibet used to live. I simply pointed out that as long as there is foxhunting in this area, people will fight to maintain open space. But if large tracts of land are closed to the hunts, the foxhunters will be forced to move farther west and subdivisions will inevitably take over."

"She called me the next day to say she'd changed her mind and we are welcome to hunt across Hickory Vale," Richard said with a smile.

"But I thought she was dead set against the notion of a fox getting killed," Wendy said.

Doug nodded. "She is. But we had a long talk about the sport of foxhunting, and when I explained to Lilibet that in America the emphasis is on chasing the fox, not killing it, I guess she saw things in a different light."

Margaret squared her shoulders. "Well, thank God we dodged a bullet with Harry Adams, and Doug got permission for us to hunt Hickory Vale, because the situation that's brewing next door is a nightmare."

"Which brings us to the bad news," Richard said with a sigh. "I received word yesterday that Mulvaney Farm is off-limits to riders."

Smitty frowned. "With the Callahan subdivision going up on the other side of Fox Run, that means you're landlocked Margaret."

"That's right," Margaret replied, her mouth set in a firm line. "When my granddaddy settled here, I'll bet he never could have envisioned Fox Run being all hemmed in like this."

"It's disheartening, isn't it?" Richard said.

"Thank God you have almost five hundred acres of your own, Margaret. That's still plenty of land for you to hold your horse shows and hunter trials, no matter what happens around you," Doug said.

"I'm not worried about Fox Run. I'll be all right. But we all know five hundred acres isn't enough land for a decent day of foxhunting. We'd end up running around in circles. If we can't ride through Mulvaney Farm, Fox Run is useless as a hunt fixture. And that will put an end to the tradition of having opening meet here."

No one spoke for several minutes; then Doug asked, "Why the sudden move? The sale is contingent on subdivision approval and that application will be tied up in red tape for some time. It will be months, at best, before any work could begin on the property."

"You're right, Doug," Richard said. "There is no immediate need to close off the land, but the lawyer for the purchaser apparently decided it was a liability to have riders crossing the property, so they've padlocked all the gates and posted the farm with No Trespassing signs."

"Are we still in the dark as to who the purchaser is?"

Richard nodded. "Yes. And Percy Fletcher says he's obligated under the sales contract to maintain confidentiality."

Margaret snorted. "Percy just sees big dollar signs, that's all. I've tried talking some sense into him, but he won't give me the time of day."

"Aren't Percy and your son good friends?" Wendy asked. "Maybe Manning could talk to him."

Margaret shook her head. "Manning and Percy parted ways after that debacle they had with their racing stable at Charles Town. Each one wanted to blame the other, rather than own up to their shortcomings. I don't think Manning has spoken a word to Percy in fifteen years."

"Well then, that's a dead end," Richard said. "Doug, do you think it would be worthwhile to talk to the purchaser's attorney and try to alleviate his liability concerns?"

Doug shrugged. "I don't know if it will do any good, but I'm happy to give it a try."

"Great. I think that's our best course of action for now."

Smitty grinned. "Don't underestimate your powers of persuasion, Doug. After all, you were able to turn Miss Lilibet around."

Laughter rippled through the room and Margaret stood. "I think this would be a good time for us to break for a bite to eat. That will give the others time to arrive before we discuss the trail-clearing schedule."

Doug glanced outside and saw that dusk had set in. He rose but hung back with Margaret while the others headed towards the dining room. "If there aren't any other urgent items on the agenda, I think I'll slip out and head home."

"Of course, Doug." Margaret walked with him to the front door. "You go on out to your car. I'll tell your friend Mike you're ready to depart."

"Thanks."

Doug eased outside and waited beside his car, enjoying the peaceful chorus of crickets and the flickering of lightning bugs. Margaret emerged from between the boxwoods a few moments later, with Mike in tow. Mike started to follow her towards the Porsche, but Doug waved him off. "Go ahead and get in your car, Mike. I'll just be a minute."

"Yes, sir."

Margaret studied Mike as he walked to his car. "Is he what I think he is?"

Doug sighed and folded his arms, leaning against the side of the Porsche. "A bodyguard? Yeah. Anne's worried about me."

"And rightfully so."

He nodded. "I know. That's why I brought Mike along. I just can't stand it when he acts like my shadow."

Margaret smiled. "How's Anne holding up?"

"She's okay."

She patted his arm. "You better get home to her."

"Good idea." He opened the driver's door and was halfway into the seat when Margaret grabbed his shoulder.

"Doug! Who drew that on your window?"

He frowned as he backed out of the car. "Drew what?"

She pointed towards the outside of the rear window. Despite the fading evening light, Doug could see a fresh drawing in the dust-covered glass.

Margaret let out a rush of air. "My God, Doug. It looks like a skull and crossbones."

"Thanks." Kendall drank greedily from the bottle of water Jake offered. "What are you doing here so late?"

Jake folded his arms across his chest and leaned lazily against the rail beside the outdoor arena. "I was passing by on my way to my cottage and saw you teaching, so I thought I'd stop and watch the lesson for a while."

She lifted the ice-cold bottle to her temple. "I can't believe it's still this hot at nine o'clock at night."

He smiled. "You've had a long day."

"No kidding." She perched on the rail next to him. "I don't know what I was thinking when I told Margaret I'd teach these lessons tonight, after a long day of camp." Actually, Kendall knew exactly why she'd agreed to it. *She needed the money.*

"You're a good instructor. I enjoyed watching the lesson."

Kendall shrugged dismissively. "You know what they say: Those who can, do; those who can't, teach."

Jake shook his head. "Not in your case. I've seen you ride. You do both well."

She felt her cheeks burn. "Thanks."

"Hey, want to go grab a bite to eat somewhere?"

"*God no.* I'm all dusty and sweaty. I wouldn't dare go into town looking like this. I'm going to go home, take a shower, and collapse in bed."

"You need to eat, don't you?"

"I'll grab something at home."

"Sure. I saw how well your refrigerator was stocked the other night."

She laughed. "Guilty. I survive on wine and cheese."

He smiled at her. "Come on. You deserve a real meal after a day like today. Let me take you out to dinner."

Kendall hesitated. Dinner did sound appealing.

Jake took the empty water bottle from her hand and tossed it in the trash can. "You choose the place. I promise we won't be out late."

She felt her resolve weaken. "Actually, I'd kill for fried chicken from the Coach Stop."

"You're on."

Kendall hopped down from the rail. "Let me just go freshen up. How about if we meet in the parking lot in five minutes?"

He nodded. "See you there."

Kendall grabbed her purse from her car and hurried to the women's rest room. After using a wet paper towel to remove as much dust from her face as she could manage, she applied lipstick and blush, then shook loose her ponytail, which was tangled and limp from the dust in the ring. Brushing helped some, but her hair still looked flat and dull. What she really needed was a haircut and highlights, but she sure couldn't afford to plunk down two hundred dollars at the hairdresser's right now.

"I guess that's as good as it's going to get," she muttered, shoving her makeup into her purse.

Jake was waiting by his truck in the parking lot, and when she approached, he opened the passenger door for her.

"I think I'll drive my own car, so I can head right home from the restaurant," Kendall said.

Jake closed the door. "Suit yourself. I'll follow you." He didn't make eye contact, but as he passed by her, Kendall saw a flicker of annoyance in his eyes.

Darkness had blanketed Middleburg by the time Kendall parked at a meter in front of the Coach Stop, and she was struck by the serenity of the village at night: Old-fashioned streetlamps cast a soft glow over the redbrick sidewalks and illuminated the hand-painted signs that hung above darkened storefronts.

Jake pulled up to the meter behind her. "I hope the kitchen's still open," he said as he stepped out of his truck. "I didn't realize things shut down so early in Middleburg."

"We should be okay. The Coach Stop usually stays open until ten o'clock."

At least half the tables in the restaurant were filled, and as they stood by the front door, waiting to be seated, Kendall was painfully aware of her appearance. Maybe coming there hadn't been such a good idea after all.

A waitress walked by with a large tray of food. "You can sit anywhere you'd like."

Kendall looked at the nearby corner booth. "Is this okay?"

Jake nodded and motioned for her to go first. "Sure."

Kendall slid three-quarters of the way around the circular bench, allowing for plenty of distance between Jake and her.

"Can I get you something to drink?" the waitress asked, placing cocktail napkins in front of them and handing them each a menu. "We're going to be closing the kitchen soon, so I'll need to take your orders in a couple of minutes."

Jake looked at Kendall. "Would you like a glass of wine?"

"I'd love one. Chardonnay, please."

"And I'll have a Budweiser," Jake said.

"Coming right up," the waitress said, hurrying off.

"Kendall, is that you?"

Kendall turned around and saw Helen Dunning sitting in the booth next to them. Helen was dressed in a black silk suit with a crisp white linen blouse, and her hair was expertly coiffed in a French twist. "Helen, hi."

"That was a lovely shower you hosted for Anne the other day. It's just too bad it had to end the way it did. How is Doug doing? Do you know? I heard he was out of the hospital."

"Doug's doing very well, considering what he went through."

"Oh, that's so good to hear." Helen smiled at Jake. "Hello, I'm Helen Dunning."

Jake nodded at her. "Nice to meet you, ma'am. I'm Jake Dawson."

"Have you been at a show today, Kendall?" Helen asked.

"No, I've been teaching at Fox Run."

"Oh, yes, that's right. You have my niece, Caitlin, in your camp session this week. I'll bet teaching camp is quite an experience."

"It is, Helen. I'm really enjoying working with the children."

"And you're a saint to do it. I'll bet when you and Peter went through all those fertility treatments to try to conceive a child, you never dreamed you'd have a whole group of children demanding your attention."

Kendall opened her menu. "You're right, Helen. I didn't."

Helen stood up. "Well, you look great. Very outdoorsy. Are you growing your hair out?"

Kendall kept her eyes on the menu. "I'm thinking about it."

Helen turned to Jake. "It was very nice to meet you."

Jake stood. "Nice to meet you, too, Mrs. Dunning."

The waitress set their drinks on the table and took out a pad and pen. "Ready to order?"

Jake looked at Kendall.

"I'll have the fried chicken," Kendall said.

"You want french fries with that, or whipped potatoes?"

"Fries, please."

"You also get one other side. Our vegetable of the day is broccoli. We also have macaroni and cheese or fried apples. All the side dishes are listed in the menu."

"I'll have the fried apples." Kendall handed her menu to the waitress and looked at Jake. "Might as well make the whole meal fried. It goes with my outdoorsy look."

Jake smiled at the waitress and closed his menu. "I'll have what she's having."

Kendall lifted her wineglass. "Cheers," she said, talking a long swallow.

Jake left his bottle on the table. "Is something bothering you?"

"I'm fine." She took another sip of wine. "Just sitting here feeling *outdoorsy*."

"Aw, come on. I can't believe you'd let that get to you."

Kendall felt anger bubble in her chest. "Of course you can't. You don't know Helen Dunning. By this time tomorrow, she'll have found out who you are, and she'll tell everyone she saw me having dinner at the Coach Stop with *that cowboy from Fox Run*. And she'll be sure to mention that I was dirty, and bedraggled, and badly in need of a haircut."

Jake studied her thoughtfully while he took a swig of his beer. "What bothers you more, that she'll tell people you were having dinner with me or that remark about your hair?"

Kendall hesitated. *Was she embarrassed to be seen dining with Jake?* No doubt, Helen would just assume it was a date. And tongues would start wagging, comparing Jake to Peter. Gossiping about how she'd *lowered her standards* from a CEO to a cowboy. That was sure to send her tumbling down the social ladder in a hurry. The funny thing was, she didn't really care.

"I just don't like to be the subject of gossip," she said finally.

"Fair enough. No one likes to be gossiped about."

The waitress arrived with their meals, and Kendall looked distastefully at the plateful of food in front of her. She'd lost her appetite.

Jake picked up a drumstick and bit into it. "This is great fried chicken."

Kendall nodded, nibbling on a french fry.

"By the way," Jake said, pausing to wipe his mouth on the napkin. "I like your hair. I thought Mrs. Dunning's hairdo looked kind of like a poodle."

Kendall couldn't resist a smile. "Thank you."

"Aren't you going to eat your chicken?" he asked, gesturing towards her full plate.

"I'm just not very hungry anymore. I'll have them wrap it up for me."

He shrugged. "Suit yourself, but it's probably better warm."

Kendall peeled off a small bite of chicken and pushed the rest of the food around on her plate.

"Forgive me if I'm sticking my nose in where it doesn't belong, but I thought that was a low blow for Mrs. Dunning to say what she did about you trying to get pregnant."

"Helen is an expert at low blows."

He chewed thoughtfully for a few moments. "It's tough, going through fertility treatment, isn't it?"

Kendall looked at him in surprise. "Have you gone through it?"

Jake shook his head. "No, not me. Some friends of mine went through it, though, and it almost cost them their marriage."

"It can be very emotionally draining."

"I take it you weren't able to get pregnant?"

"No, I wasn't." She picked up her wineglass and leaned back against the booth.

"I'm sorry."

"Don't be. The reason I wasn't able to get pregnant had nothing to do with the fertility treatment."

Jake frowned. "What do you mean?"

"I mean that there was nothing God or the doctor could do to help me conceive a child with Peter. My husband had a vasectomy before we got married, a small detail that he failed to tell me about."

Jake snorted. "You've got to be kidding."

Kendall looked away. "I wish I were."

"Why didn't the doctor catch that during the fertility treatment?"

"Peter didn't participate in the treatment. He had two children from a previous marriage, so he maintained that he couldn't possibly be the source of the problem. He insisted that if I wanted a child, I was the one who should undergo fertility treatment. I went along with that, assuming that, as he said, he was perfectly capable of fathering a child."

"Which he knew all along he wasn't," Jake said.

Kendall nodded.

Jake shook his head. "No wonder you have no faith in the male species."

She drained her wineglass and attempted a smile. "My therapist tells me it's part of the normal healing process for me to hold all men accountable for Peter's sins."

"Just don't let it make you bitter, Kendall. Hate can eat away at you like a cancer. Trust me, I know."

"Are you talking about the way you feel about your father?"

Jake gazed steadily at her for a moment. "Yeah."

nne watched in fascination as the chestnut Thoroughbred was led down the ramp and into the swimming pool. The pungent smell of chlorine had turned her stomach when they'd first entered the pool area, but she'd grown used to the odor and her stomach had settled down.

"Look, Mommy, he's doing the doggie paddle."

"He sure is." Anne pulled Samantha a step backwards to allow the horse's handler plenty of room to pass in front of them. She sensed a movement next to her, and out of the corner of her eye she saw Ben, their bodyguard, shift closer to Samantha.

"This horse isn't very fit, so I am only going to take him around the pool a couple of times," the handler explained. "That may not seem like much to you, but horses aren't really built to swim efficiently, because of their large bodies and little legs. It can be very tiring for them."

"What's the reason he's swimming?" Jake asked.

"This horse is a racehorse and he has a tendon injury. By taking him swimming, his trainer is able to keep him physically fit without straining the tendon. When the tendon has healed, he will be able to be put back to work much more quickly."

The handler led the horse down the far side of the pool. "Okay, I'm coming around again."

A few of the campers had inched towards the edge of the pool, and Kendall backed them away. "Come on, kids, let's stay together."

"I'm hot, Mommy," Samantha said, pulling on Anne's blouse. "I wish I could go swimming."

"Not in this pool, I hope."

"Eew, no." Samantha wrinkled her nose. "It probably has horse poop in it."

Jake, who was standing nearby, turned and winked at her. "How's that new puppy of yours doing, Samantha?"

"He's doing great. Last night, Rascal slept in my room all night long. He only had two accidents."

Anne fought back a smile. "Tell Jake what else Rascal did."

"Oh, yeah. Rascal was in the kitchen this morning, and we weren't really watching him because we were eating breakfast, and he chewed Daddy's riding boots."

"Uh-oh. Did your daddy get mad?"

Samantha nodded. "A little bit. But then Mommy told him he had to sleep in his own bed."

Anne laughed. "What I said was, 'Daddy made his own bed; now he has to sleep in it.'"

"I hope you weren't too hard on Mr. Cummings for taking the puppy home," Jake said with a smile.

"No, I took pity on him because of his injuries and let him off pretty easy."

"I'm glad to hear that." Jake looked around. "I thought I might see him here today. Is he feeling all right?"

"Doug's fine. In fact, I almost think he's feeling too good. He's at his office in Washington right now."

"You're kidding."

She shook her head. "No. Doug woke up this morning rearing to go to the office. I tried to talk some sense into him, but that fell upon deaf ears. Then I realized it was probably doing him more harm to sit around at home, fretting about work, than it would to go to the office for a few hours."

"Okay, kids, the horse is going to come out of the pool now," Kendall said. "Let's all back up and stay clear of the ramp."

Anne reached for Samantha's hand and held it until the handler led the horse out of the pool and over to the hosing-off area.

"The horses get hosed down before and after they swim," the handler explained, reaching for the hose that hung from the ceiling.

"What did you think, kids, was it fun to see a horse swim?" Kendall asked.

A chorus of "yes" came from the cluster of girls.

Kendall smiled at the handler. "Thank you so much for letting us visit the swim center."

"No problem. Anytime."

"Come on girls." Kendall motioned towards the door. "Let's go outside and I'll show you that clover patch I was telling you about. Maybe Elizabeth will teach you all how to make clover wreaths to hang on the school horses' stalls."

Samantha looked at Anne. "Can I go with them, Mommy?"

"Of course you can. I'll be there in a minute."

Samantha caught up with the other campers, with Ben following close behind.

Anne stopped to thank the horse handler, and as she turned for the door, she saw that Jake had hung back and was waiting for her.

Jake held the door open for her. "Mr. Cummings told me that Chancellor might come home this weekend. If you need help transporting him, please let me know. I'd be happy to lend a hand."

"Thanks, Jake. That's very kind of you. I'll be sure to tell Doug."

When they emerged from the swimming pool building, Anne saw Elizabeth and Kendall sitting with the girls in a grassy area under the shade of a maple tree.

"They look like they've found themselves a cool spot," Jake said.

Elizabeth looked at them and waved.

Jake waved back. "Poor girl, she's a little down in the dumps today."

"Why?"

"Todd didn't get to come along on the field trip."

"Who's Todd?"

"He's a kid who works at Fox Run. He and Elizabeth have taken to spending a lot of time together. Mrs. Southwell told Todd he had to stay behind today because they're short-staffed in the barn, but, in truth, I think she may have picked up on the vibes between Todd and Elizabeth, and she's trying to separate them."

Anne raised an eyebrow. "I wonder if Elizabeth's father knows about Todd."

"I don't know. But it seems like Elizabeth and Doc Carey are real close, just like with your daughter and your husband."

Anne smiled. "I can only imagine how Doug will handle it when Samantha is old enough to date." She watched Samantha, who lay belly-down on the ground next to Kendall, intently combing through the grass. "I wonder what she's looking for."

Kendall glanced over towards where she and Jake were standing and rose to join them.

"What's Samantha doing?" Anne asked.

"They're collecting cloverleafs to make wreaths, and Samantha, bless her heart, is determined to find a four-leaf clover to give to Doug so he won't get hurt again."

Tears welled up in Anne's eyes. *What a burden Samantha must be carrying.* Outwardly, Samantha seemed to be handling Doug's accident all right. But it was obviously weighing heavily on her mind.

Kendall put her arm around Anne's shoulders. "Are you okay?"

Anne nodded.

"You look tired." Kendall gave her shoulder a squeeze. "Why don't you go home and get some rest, and I'll take Samantha home after camp today."

Anne hesitated. "A nap does sound good. Are you sure you don't mind?"

"Of course not; I'm more than happy to do it."

"Can I talk you into staying for dinner?"

"I'd love to, Anne, but I really have to ride Wellington this evening. I've been ignoring him all week."

"I have time this afternoon to exercise Wellington for you, if you want me to," Jake said.

Kendall shook her head. "Thanks for the offer, Jake, but I really should ride him. Besides, Anne, the last thing you need is to wear yourself out cooking dinner."

"It's no problem. I'll stop in town on my way home and pick something up. We'd love to have you. It will just be a relaxed family dinner."

Kendall smiled. "Okay, if you're sure it's no bother, I'd love to."

"Wonderful."

Jake shifted towards the grassy area where the kids were sitting. "Nice to see you, Mrs. Cummings. Don't forget to pass along my offer to help with Chancellor."

"I will, Jake. Thank you."

"Let me know if you change your mind about having me ride Wellington for you, Kendall," Jake said over his shoulder as he walked off. "I promise I won't cowboy him, if that's what you're afraid of. I'll let him hack around like a nice quiet hunter."

Kendall shook her head. "That's not it at all. I trust you."

Jake turned around. "Wait, say that again."

"What?"

"What you just said."

"*I trust you?*"

Jake grinned. "That's progress."

Kendall blushed and made a face at him. "Never mind, I take it back."

Anne smiled as she caught the look that passed between them. "Why don't you join us for dinner, too, Jake?" she asked.

Jake glanced at Kendall before answering. "Thank you, ma'am, I'd like that very much."

Kendall declined Samantha's offer to go along while she and Doug gave Jake a tour of the barn.

"Thanks, sweetie, but I think I'll stay here and help your mommy with dinner."

"Okay. Come on, Daddy; come on, Jake."

"Hold on, Sam." Doug opened the refrigerator and grabbed two bottles of beer. "Jake and I need a cold drink to take along."

Jake grinned as he accepted the bottle from Doug. "You're a man after my own heart."

"Why don't you take Rascal with you?" Anne suggested as Doug headed for the door. "It's been awhile since he's been outside."

"Good idea, Mommy."

"Actually, Sam, I don't think the barn is the best place for a pup—"

Doug stopped when he caught the look Anne gave him. "On second thought, that's a great idea. Come on, Rascal." He knelt down to retrieve the puppy from its crate.

Anne smiled at Kendall and continued to stir the batter for the corn muffins.

Doug handed Rascal to Samantha and walked over to kiss Anne. "Bye, honey, we won't be long."

"Take your time. I'm not serving anything that's complicated, so dinner will keep until you get back."

"Rascal, no!" Samantha shouted.

Doug turned around. "What's the matter?"

Samantha pointed to the hunt whip hanging from an iron horseshoe-shaped hook on the wall by the door. "Rascal was chewing on your hunt whip."

Doug lifted the whip off the hook and ran his hand over the brown leather handle. "What part was he chewing?"

"The end. *Uh-oh, Daddy, look.* It's all chewed up."

"It was already like that, Sam," Doug said, fingering the frayed cord at the end of the long leather thong. "That's called the popper. It's what makes the noise when I crack the whip."

"That's sure a nice-looking whip," Jake said.

"Thanks." Doug held it out for Jake to see.

Samantha stood on her tiptoes and peered over Doug's arm. "It's a really special whip because Daddy's daddy gave it to him. See the writing on it?"

Jake peered at the engraved silver band below the horn handle. "*Good sport. Good friends. Well done.*" He smiled at Doug. "That's nice."

Doug nodded thoughtfully. "My father gave it to me when I was awarded my colors."

"Awarded your colors? What does that mean?"

"It's an honor bestowed by the master upon a member of the hunt, in recognition of the contributions that member has made to the hunt." Doug hung the whip back on the hook.

"Contributions? You mean like money?" Jake asked.

Doug smiled. "Sometimes. But generally colors are awarded for good sportsmanship and hard work: clearing trails, hosting hunt breakfasts, walking hounds, things like that. You have to hunt regularly and be well turned out. And not make too many faux pas—like showing up late at the meet or hunting on a horse that kicks hounds."

"Interesting. Do you get a ribbon or a trophy or something?"

Doug shook his head. "You get to wear buttons on your hunting coat with your hunt's insignia on them and display the colors of the hunt on your coat collar. Each hunt has its own designated colors. Members of my hunt, the Middleburg Foxhounds, wear robin's egg blue collars with navy piping."

"And, more importantly, when men earn their colors, they're allowed to wear a red coat," Kendall said.

Jake raised an eyebrow. "Not the ladies?"

Kendall smiled. "Doesn't seem fair, does it? Ladies can only wear scarlet if they are a master or hunt staff."

"It sure sounds like foxhunting has a lot of rules," Jake said.

"It's steeped in tradition, that's for sure," Doug agreed, opening the door. "Come on; if we're going to give you a tour of the barn before dinner, we'd better get going."

Kendall joined Anne at the window and watched Doug and Jake stroll side by side down the drive towards the barn, while Samantha ran ahead with Rascal. Doug must have said something funny, because Jake threw back his head and laughed.

"Doug and Jake appear to be hitting it off," Kendall said.

Anne nodded, keeping her eyes on Doug. "I'm glad. Maybe this evening will help Doug relax. He's trying to hide it from me, but I can tell he's wound pretty tight."

"What about you? You must be stressed-out beyond belief after what you've been through."

Anne glanced wearily at Kendall. "I just feel like there's a huge cloud of dread hanging over us, and I'm so on edge waiting for the other shoe to drop."

Kendall nodded sympathetically. "I don't blame you. But Doug's hired guards now. Doesn't that make you feel safer?"

Anne sighed. "Safer, but never safe. Never completely safe."

Kendall put her arm around Anne and they watched in silence until Doug and Jake disappeared around the bend in the drive.

Anne picked up the bowl of corn bread batter. "I'd better get these muffins in the oven."

Kendall helped Anne prepare the salad and had just finished setting the table when Doug, Jake, and Samantha returned.

"Perfect timing," Anne said, setting a platter in the center of the round walnut table. "I hope you like crab cakes, Jake."

"I can't say as I've ever had them, Mrs. Cummings, but they sure look good. We don't eat a lot of seafood in Oklahoma."

Anne smiled at him. "I can see why, with all that good Oklahoma beef."

"Mommy, I don't like crab cakes," Samantha said, wrinkling her nose.

"I know that, and that's why I made you a tuna sandwich."

Samantha pulled out her chair. "Yummy!"

"Wait a minute, young lady. Didn't you forget something?" Anne asked, steering Samantha towards the sink.

"Oh, Mommy, do I have to? I'm *starving,* and my hands aren't even dirty."

"Here, let me help," Kendall said, turning the water on for Samantha. She squirted liquid soap on Samantha's hands. "They're not dirty, huh? Weren't you just down at the barn?"

Samantha squeezed the soap foam between her fingers to make bubbles. "Yes, but that's horse dirt. That's different from *dirt* dirt."

"Speaking of going down to the barn, didn't you have a four-legged friend with you when you left here?" Anne asked, raising an eyebrow at Doug.

"Rascal was really tired from running down to the barn, and he fell asleep in Chancellor's stall," Samantha said. "You should have seen him, Mommy; he was all curled up in the hay and he looked so cute. Daddy said we could let Rascal sleep there while we eat dinner, and then he'll go back to the barn and get him."

Doug put his arms around Anne. "And don't forget to tell Mommy that I also said it would be nice for her, so she won't have to listen to Rascal whining to get out of his crate while we're eating dinner."

Kendall felt a stab of loneliness as she watched Anne smile at Doug and kiss him, and as she looked away to grab a paper towel for Samantha, she noticed Jake studying Doug and Anne as well.

"Come on, Kendall, I want you and Jake to sit next to me, okay?" Samantha grabbed Kendall's hand and pulled her towards the table.

Kendall looked away from Jake. "Sure, Samantha, I'd love to."

Samantha patted the chair to her left. "Come on, Jake, you sit right here."

"All right." Jake pushed Samantha's chair in and held the chair to her right out for Kendall.

"Thanks," Kendall said, sitting down.

"Can I say the prayer?" Samantha asked.

Anne nodded.

"Okay." Samantha reached her hands out to Kendall and Jake. "Dear God, thank you for my mommy and daddy, and for my new baby sister or brother, and for Kendall, and for my new friend Jake. And thank you so much, God, for Rascal. And please take good care of my mommy and daddy in heaven. And help Chancellor get all better soon so he can come home. Amen. Oh, and, dear God, please help take care of my daddy so he doesn't get hurt again. Amen."

Doug kept his hands folded in prayer. "And please take good care of Samantha in riding camp tomorrow, and let her have a safe field trip to the little horse land on Saturday."

Samantha giggled. "It's called the *Land of Little Horses,* Daddy."

Doug winked at her. "I'm sure God knows what I meant."

Anne smiled and picked up her fork. "Enjoy your meal."

Jake took a small bite of a crab cake and chewed hesitantly, then took a larger forkful. "The crab cakes are delicious, Mrs. Cummings."

"Thank you, Jake. But I can't claim any credit; I picked them up at Market Salamander in Middleburg on my way home this afternoon."

They were interrupted by a high-pitched tone from the security panel, and Doug pushed his chair back and placed his napkin on the table.

"Excuse me," he said, rising. "That sounds like a trouble alert from the alarm system."

A series of red and yellow lights flickered across the alarm display next to the back door. Doug flipped open the panel and studied the zone chart.

He frowned. "That's the fire alarm indicator for the barn. I'd better go down and make sure everything's all right."

Anne rose from the table and looked out the window. "Doug, I see smoke rising through the trees!"

Jake jumped up from the table so quickly, he knocked his chair over, and Kendall followed him towards the door. The phone rang just as Doug yanked the door open, and they could hear the whooping of the fire alarm resounding from the barn.

"That's probably the alarm company," Doug shouted. "Tell them to send the fire department."

Samantha ran over to Doug. "Daddy, I'm scared."

Doug pried her hands off his leg and handed her to Anne. "It's okay, Sam. The fire's just in the barn. You're safe here in the house with Mommy. And all the horses are out in the pasture for the night, so you don't have to worry about them."

"*But, Daddy, Rascal's in the barn.*"

"Damn it!" Doug shouted, dashing out the door.

"Doug, wait," Anne yelled, but he ignored her.

Jake started after him and Anne grabbed him by his arm. "Don't let Doug go in the barn, Jake. *Please, promise me.*"

He nodded grimly at her. "I promise."

39

Kendall kept pace with Doug while Jake sprinted on ahead. She glanced sideways at Doug, who was wheezing and holding his side as he ran.

"Doug, please slow down. You're going to end up back in the hospital if you don't watch out. Jake's probably there by now; he'll get Rascal out of the barn."

"If anything happens to that puppy, Samantha will be devastated."

"I know, but she'll be even more devastated if something happens to you."

They ran down the hill in silence until they rounded the final bend in the drive and the barn came into view.

"Jesus Christ," Doug gasped.

The center ridge of the roof was engulfed in flames, and smoke poured out of the front hayloft door.

"Oh God, it looks like a hayloft fire. How much hay is up there?"

"It's almost full. They just delivered a load of hay last week."

Kendall knew there probably wasn't much time left before the entire hayloft would be ablaze. "I don't see Jake," she said, shouting to be heard above the alarm siren.

Doug picked up speed. "I don't, either."

"Wait." Kendall grabbed Doug's arm and pointed towards the back of the barn. "There he is."

They ran the remainder of the way down the hill and reached the courtyard in front of the barn as Jake did.

"I just checked the back of the barn. The fire's much worse back there," Jake shouted. "A portion of the hayloft has collapsed into the aisle. The only way to get to the puppy is to enter the barn from the front."

Kendall squinted against the blowing smoke and ashes and tried to see into the barn. The aisle was so full of smoke, it was impossible to tell how far the fire had spread.

"What about going directly into the stall?" Kendall asked. "Can you get in through the window?"

Doug shook his head, breathing heavily. "No, the grille is fastened to the inside of the stall. I don't think we could knock it loose from the outside."

Jake unbuttoned his shirt and took it off. "I'm going in. I remember Rascal's in a stall on the left. How far down is it?" He dipped his shirt in the nearby water trough and put it back on.

Doug eyed the barn. "I can't ask you to do that, Jake. It's too risky."

"You didn't ask me; I volunteered," Jake said, pulling a bandanna out of his back pocket and wetting it in the trough. "We can't just stand here and watch your daughter's puppy fry, Mr. Cummings. And, no offense, sir, but you're in no condition to go in there." Jake held the bandanna to his nose, poised to move.

Kendall watched Doug anxiously, wondering what he'd say. Doug's eyes flicked from Jake to the barn and back, as if weighing the risk.

"We're running out of time, sir," Jake shouted.

Doug gave a curt nod and put his hand on Jake's back. "It's in the middle, the fourth stall on the left. The other stall doors will all be open, so you'll know you've reached the right stall when you find the closed door."

Jake nodded and ducked his head as he dashed towards the smoke-filled aisle.

Kendall grabbed Doug's arm. "Please, God, let him make it back out alive."

Doug put his arm around her and they huddled in silence, watching and waiting. Kendall imagined Jake's movements, picturing where he might be each moment. He'd had plenty of time to reach the stall, assuming the fire hadn't spread that far. She figured he should have the puppy by now, and be on his way back out.

Kendall gasped as a burst of flames shot through the hayloft door, and the front portion of the roof collapsed into the hayloft. *Where is Jake?* He's running out of time."

"Watch out!" Doug pulled Kendall backwards as the hayloft crashed into the barn aisle, showering them with sparks.

Kendall turned her face away from the blast of heat. The collapse of the roof must have taken out the alarm system, because the deafening siren stopped, and the crackling of the fire was sickeningly audible.

"Come on." Doug grabbed her hand and pulled her away from the blaze.

Kendall stumbled after Doug. "Where are we going? We can't leave Jake behind."

Doug tore around the corner of the barn and stopped beside a stall window. "Jake, are you in there?"

Jake's face appeared in the opening. "Yeah, I'm here."

Kendall collapsed against the side of the barn. "Oh, thank God."

"I'm trapped in the stall," Jake said, coughing behind his bandanna. "The entire aisle is in flames."

He reached one hand through the bars and held out the puppy. "Here, take Rascal."

Doug took the puppy and dropped him into Kendall's hands. "Let me see if I can find anything you can use to pry the grille off. I'll be right back."

Kendall clutched Rascal to her chest and peered through the bars. Sweat streamed down Jake's face and he was grimy with soot, but other than that, he appeared to be unharmed. "Are you all right?"

Jake nodded, but Kendall saw fear in his eyes. She reached her hand through the grille. "Here, hold my hand."

Kendall felt his hand cover hers, and she squeezed tightly. "Doug will be right back. He'll find something to get you out of there."

A burning timber landed a few feet from Jake, and he swore under his breath and tried to pull his hand away. "I think you'd better go, Kendall."

"No." She gripped his hand tighter. "I'm not leaving you here all alone."

Jake was seized by a coughing fit, and when he was able to catch his breath, he wiped his face and neck with his bandanna. "It's hotter than hell in here."

Kendall sensed a movement behind her and she turned and saw Doug lugging a metal rod, which looked to be a good six feet long. "Doug's back, Jake. He found something." She released his hand and stepped to the side.

Doug heaved the rod up to the edge of the window and slid it towards Jake. "I found a digging iron. Careful, it's heavy."

Kendall heard a thump inside the stall and Jake's face disappeared from the opening.

"Damn it!"

"Are you all right?" Doug asked.

"A burning rafter almost landed on top of me." Jake's voice was muffled and farther away.

"Can you get back to the window?"

"Yeah, hold on. I'm using the digging iron to move the rafter." He didn't speak for a long moment. "There, got it. All right, I'm trying to get the iron under the edge of the grille."

Kendall heard a loud grunt, followed by the sound of tearing wood. "It's loose on the bottom, but I can't get the iron under the lip at the top."

Doug gripped the grille with both hands. "I'll push, and you pull. On three, ready? One. Two. Three."

Doug groaned as he pushed against the grille. "We almost got it, Jake. Let's go again. Ready?" His breath came in short bursts. Kendall could see sweat bead on his forehead.

"One. Two." Doug threw his weight against the bars. "Three."

The grille disappeared into the stall. Doug sank to his knees as Jake's head and shoulders appeared through the opening. Jake slid headfirst out the window and dropped to the ground beside Doug.

Kendall started towards them but jumped back as a piece of burning roof fell at her foot. "Watch out," she shouted as more flaming debris tumbled down.

Jake scrambled to his feet and helped Doug up. "We've got to get away from here before the whole barn comes down." He held his arm out to Kendall. "Come on."

The three of them half ran, half stumbled to the drive in front of the barn just as a car sped towards them and skidded to a stop on the gravel.

"Now they get here," Doug muttered, shaking his head.

A security guard jumped out of the car. "Mr. Cummings, are you all right, sir?"

Doug eyed him grimly. "Yeah, but we sure could have used your help ten minutes ago."

"I'm sorry, sir. I was patrolling the grounds and was up front by the road. I wasn't aware there was a problem until I returned to the house a few moments ago."

"Listen." Kendall cocked her head in the direction of the road. "The fire truck is almost here."

Doug stood huffing, hands on his hips, gazing at the burning shell of the barn. "There isn't anything left to salvage. With all that hay in there, the barn went up like a tinderbox."

Kendall shuddered as she pictured Jake inside the inferno, just moments before, and she buried her face against Rascal's soft coat.

She felt a hand on her back and heard Jake's voice, husky from the smoke. "Are you all right?"

Kendall raised her eyes to his, and Jake gently pushed a stray lock of hair back from her face. "You okay?"

She nodded.

Doug turned to face them. "Let's go up to the house. There's nothing we can do to help here."

"I'll drive you up, Mr. Cummings, and then I'll come back down to talk to the fire department," the security guard said, opening the rear door.

Jake and Doug waited for Kendall to climb into the car first, and when they were all settled in the backseat, she held Rascal out to Doug. "Here you go."

Doug pushed her hand towards Jake. "You risked your life to save Rascal, Jake. You should give Sam the puppy."

Jake shook his head. "No way. You would have done the same thing I did if you'd been able to. Samantha's your little girl, and I'm sure she's going to be looking for the puppy in your arms when we walk through that door."

Doug regarded Jake thoughtfully for a moment, then reached for the puppy. "I owe you twice now, Jake."

40

*A*nne walked Kendall and Jake to the door while Doug finished giving his statement to the sheriff's deputy. Jake had made an effort to wash off his face and Doug had lent him a clean shirt to wear, but his jeans were covered with soot—a haunting reminder of the close call he'd had.

"Are you sure you don't want to take some dinner home with you?" Anne asked.

Kendall shook her head. "I can't even stand the thought of food right now."

Anne looked questioningly at Jake. "How about you?"

"I'm afraid I don't have much of an appetite, either, ma'am."

Anne gave Kendall a hug. "I hate the thought of you going home alone after what you've been through. The offer still stands for you to stay here tonight."

"Thanks, but I really want to take a long shower and curl up in my own bed. I'll be fine."

"I'll follow Kendall to make sure she gets home okay," Jake said.

Kendall paused with her hand on the doorknob. "You don't have to do that."

"I know, but I want to."

Kendall didn't say anything, and Anne smiled at Jake and mouthed, "Thank you."

She closed the door behind them and returned to the kitchen. Doug was still sitting at the table with Patrick Talbot, but the deputy was on his feet, putting his notepad away.

"As I said before, it's too dark tonight to conduct an investigation, but we'll have the arson team out first thing in the morning. In the meantime, you good people try to get some rest."

The deputy tipped his hat at Anne. "I'll let myself out, Mrs. Cummings."

Anne stood behind Doug and rubbed his shoulders for a moment before sitting in the chair next to him. "You look awfully pensive, Patrick," she said as she poured them each a cup of tea.

Patrick adjusted his glasses. "Well, I think I'm starting to see a pattern emerge among these incidents."

"Oh?"

He nodded. "Assuming for the sake of argument that the fire tonight was deliberately set, I can think of someone who had the opportunity to start it. An individual who was also present during some of the other incidents."

"Who's that?"

Patrick regarded her for a moment. "Jake Dawson."

"*What?*"

"Patrick, that's absurd," Doug said. "Jake just risked his life by running into the burning barn to save Samantha's puppy."

Patrick held his hand out to quiet them. "I know, it may sound crazy, but just hear me out. We have the entrance to the farm guarded, and our roving patrol had been by the barn just moments after you left to come back up to the house. There's no conceivable way in my mind that someone could have come onto the property, made his way down to the barn, set the fire, and left again without being seen by one of our guards."

Doug raised an eyebrow. "We were down there for a good ten minutes after the fire started before one of your men showed up. It seems to me *that* was a pretty big time gap."

Patrick nodded. "Fair enough. But whoever set the fire would have had to make his way past the guards and down to the barn and back."

Doug shook his head. "Not necessarily. He could have come through the woods."

"True. But that's pretty rough going on foot. I think we need to consider Jake as a possible suspect. You stated that when you were showing him around the barn, he asked to see the hayloft, and you didn't accompany him up there because it was uncomfortable for you to climb the ladder with your broken ribs; something, by the way, I think he could have counted on. He was in the hayloft alone. Within a matter of minutes a fire broke out. That's a pretty unlikely coincidence in my opinion."

Anne's mouth tightened. "If Jake set fire to the barn, why would he risk his life by going back inside?"

Patrick shrugged. "Perhaps it was part of the plan all along. Maybe he thought if he rescued Samantha's puppy, he could ingratiate himself with you. He probably didn't bargain on getting trapped inside the barn."

"And I suppose you think he saved Chancellor for the same reason."

"I think it's quite possible."

Anne looked at Doug. "You're not buying this, are you?"

Before he could answer, Patrick broke in. "Look, I'm not saying that Jake Dawson did all these things, but I think we should check him out. It bothers me that Jake showed up out of nowhere at the scene of Doug's accident, and he was here tonight, with ample opportunity to start the fire. Jake was also at the beagle kennels when the snake appeared in Doug's car. And what about last night? He lives at Fox Run and could easily have slipped up to Mrs. Southwell's house and drawn the skull and crossbones on the car window."

Skull and crossbones on the car window? Anne stared at Doug. "What's Patrick talking about?"

Doug exhaled loudly and looked down, running his hand through his hair. "I didn't tell you about it because I didn't want to upset you."

"Tell me now." She struggled to keep her voice steady.

He lifted his eyes to hers. "Someone drew a skull and crossbones in the dust on the back window of the Porsche while I was at the meeting at Margaret's."

"Didn't you have a bodyguard with you?"

Doug nodded. "Mike was inside with me."

Anne clenched her arms across her chest, uncertain whether the trembling in her hands was triggered by fear or anger.

$\mathcal{J}$ake pulled his truck to a stop behind Kendall's Jeep and turned off the engine. "It's awfully dark," he said, walking over to her and gesturing towards the house. "Let me walk you inside so you can turn some lights on."

"Thanks." Kendall searched through her purse for her house keys. "I love the solitude of living out here, but it can get a little spooky in the dark. I normally leave lights on when I go out at night, but I thought I'd be home early."

Jake followed her inside and waited by the door while she turned lights on in the living room and kitchen.

"There, that's better." She walked back to where he stood. "Thanks for going to the trouble of following me home. You're probably dying to take a shower and collapse in bed."

"Don't worry about it." He ran a hand through his tousled hair. "A shower sounds good, but I think if I went to bed right now I'd be counting sheep."

Kendall nodded. "I know what you mean."

"Well, take care. I'll probably see you tomorrow."

"Good night."

Jake was halfway to his car when she called out to him. "Jake."

He turned around. "What?"

She hesitated. "Would you like to have a drink before you go? I still have some of the beer you brought over the other night."

Jake narrowed his eyes and studied her for a moment. "Sure, I'd like that," he said, heading back towards her.

Kendall stepped aside to let him enter. "I'll get the drinks. Why don't you go in the living room? I'm going to turn on the air conditioning. That room usually cools off first."

She flipped the switch on the thermostat in the hall before grabbing a bottle of beer for Jake and pouring a large glass of wine for herself. When she entered the living room, Jake was standing by the bookcase with a picture frame in his hand.

"This is a nice shot of you and Wellington. Where was it taken?"

Kendall handed him the bottle of beer and looked at the framed photograph. "That was at Upperville. It's one of my favorite photos because that was the first big show where we were champion."

"The first of many championships, I gather, from all the trophies you have on these shelves." Jake made a sweeping gesture with his hand.

She nodded. "Yes, thanks to Wellington. Unless I do something to screw him up, he's always in the ribbons."

Jake put the photo frame back on the shelf and held his beer bottle up. "Cheers."

"Cheers." Kendall lifted her glass and took a seat on the sofa.

Jake took a long drink of his beer as he scanned the trophies. "This one's nice," he said, lifting the champagne cooler she'd won at Devon. He whistled. "That's heavy. Guess it's real silver, huh?"

Kendall smiled. "I imagine so."

"Which is your favorite trophy?"

"Probably the one you have in your hand."

"Yeah? Tell me about it." Jake carried the trophy to the sofa and sat down next to her.

"There's not much to tell. Wellington put in brilliant rounds over fences and won the hack, and we were champion."

"Why's it your favorite?"

Kendall closed her eyes for a second, remembering the day. "You really want to know?"

"Yeah."

"Because Peter wasn't there and I could talk to people and just hang out and have fun at the show."

"You couldn't talk to people when your husband was there?"

She shook her head. "Not men."

"Did he get jealous?"

Kendall gave a little laugh. "That's putting it mildly."

Jake set the trophy on the sofa between them and took another drink of his beer. "Did he get physical with you?"

Kendall swallowed against the sudden tightness in her throat and nodded. "Is that how you got the scar on your shoulder?"

"Among others," she said, savoring a long swallow of wine. She knew she was drinking way too fast, but the wine was numbing her and she needed that.

"What finally gave you the courage to leave him?"

Kendall leaned back against the deep cushions and gazed down, fingering the ornate scrolling on the top of the trophy. "One day, I was down at the barn, talking to the blacksmith about Wellington's shoeing, and Peter made a midday surprise trip home to check up on me. He dragged me out of the barn by my hair and told me he'd see to it that Wellington had an *accident* if he ever caught me alone with another man again."

"So you left him in order to protect your horse."

Kendall nodded and drained her wineglass. "Tells you a lot about my self-esteem, doesn't it?"

Jake took her empty wineglass from her and set it on the coffee table, along with the trophy. "What it tells me," he said, placing his hand on her shoulder, "is that you're living with a lot of painful memories, and it's no surprise that you don't trust men."

Jake ran his hand lightly down her arm, and Kendall felt a pleasing shiver run through her. She eased towards him and he cupped his hand under her chin, gently forcing her to look at him.

"I won't hurt you, Kendall. I promise."

As Jake lowered his lips towards hers, Kendall closed her eyes and slid her arms around his neck.

*K*endall awoke the next morning with her head on Jake's chest, and she drew a deep breath, trying to capture the moment in her memory. They had showered the night before, but Jake still smelled faintly of smoke, mixed with the scent of sex, and the soothing aroma of her lavender soap.

Kendall nestled closer to him and he stirred and mumbled something unintelligible as he wrapped his arms tighter around her and settled back into a pattern of deep, rhythmic breathing. She raised her head ever so slightly to get a glimpse of the clock on the nightstand.

She glanced sleepily at the numbers and then blinked and looked again. *Eight-thirty!* Riding camp started at nine. Kendall raised herself on her elbow and shook Jake.

"Jake, wake up. It's eight-thirty."

Jake opened his eyes, squinting lazily at her. "Good morning," he said in a husky voice, pulling her towards him for a kiss.

Kendall planted a perfunctory kiss on his lips and sat up, clasping the sheet to her chest. "We've got to get up, Jake. It's eight-thirty. I've got to be at camp in half an hour."

Jake pulled her towards him by the sheet she was clutching, a sensuous smile playing on his face. "Not so fast. You have to pay a toll before you can get out of bed."

Her protest was smothered by his kiss, and Kendall gave in to his embrace. After a moment, she forced herself to pull away. "I've got to go."

Kendall wrapped herself in the sheet and hurried towards the bathroom, stopping long enough to grab lingerie, a pair of breeches, and a polo shirt from the closet. When she emerged from the bathroom ten minutes later, her bed was empty and the tangled bedding was the only hint of the intimacy she and Jake had shared.

She smelled the aroma of freshly brewed coffee and found Jake in the kitchen, standing next to the gurgling coffeemaker. He was barefoot and wore his soot-covered jeans from the night before and Doug's blue dress shirt, which was unbuttoned, revealing his tanned, muscular chest.

Jake gave her a lopsided grin. "I wanted to make breakfast for you, but your refrigerator's pretty bare. Coffee was about all that I could find."

"That's okay. I'm not a big breakfast eater."

Kendall crossed her arms and looked away, unsure what else to say. Last night, in the safety of the dark, she'd felt so close to Jake. But now, with the bright morning sunlight streaming through the kitchen window, she didn't know how to act towards him. She wasn't going to fool herself by pretending that last night was the beginning of anything serious between them. Jake was just passing through town. Before long he'd undoubtedly move on and befriend another lonely woman.

Jake crossed the room and handed her a steaming mug of coffee. "I saw creamer in the fridge. I assume you use that," he said, pulling open the refrigerator door and taking out the carton of creamer. He pinched open the top of the carton, sniffed it, then made a face and waved it under her nose. "I think this is past its prime."

She raised the mug to her mouth. "I'll just drink it black."

He watched her drink her coffee and smiled at her. "You look like a schoolgirl with your hair all wet and in a ponytail like that."

Kendall smiled tightly and took another sip of her coffee.

Jake regarded her thoughtfully for a moment, then took the mug from her hands and placed it on the counter. "You're not going to go and get all remorseful on me, are you?" he asked, wrapping his arms around her waist and pulling her to him.

He kissed her on the forehead, letting his lips linger, and she caught her breath and closed her eyes.

"I'm just a little overwhelmed right now."

Jake smiled. "That's okay. Last night was pretty overwhelming for me, too."

Kendall slipped her arms around him and buried her face against his chest. "I've got to go."

He kissed the top of her head. "I know. Can I see you tonight?

She remembered her date with Stephen Lloyd to go to the polo match, and frowned. "I can't. I made plans to get together with a friend tonight."

Jake didn't say anything for a moment. "Tomorrow, then?" The warmth was gone from his tone.

Kendall nodded. "I have the field trip all day, but I don't have any plans tomorrow evening."

He released her from his embrace. "Great. It's a date."

43

$\mathcal{A}$nne was catching up on a week's worth of paperwork when Doug returned from taking Samantha to camp. She scribbled a quick note to Trish Fitzsimmons, the attorney handling her cases while she was on maternity leave, and closed the file folder.

"I'm in the study," she called to Doug, rising to meet him as she heard his footsteps in the hallway. "What took you so long?"

Doug held her hand and walked to the couch, drawing her down next to him. "I stopped by the barn, or I guess I should say the remnants of the barn, to talk to the arson investigator."

"Is there anything left to salvage?"

He shook his head grimly. "Not a thing."

"But the horses are all okay?"

"Yeah, Billy and I checked them all over carefully. Thank God they were turned out in the pasture for the night. They're all pretty spooked from the fire, though. Huntley won't stop walking the fence."

"You've had a dozen calls already this morning with offers to put the horses up. The messages are on your desk."

"I've also had several calls on my cell. Richard's going to pick Huntley up this morning and board him at the Hunt kennels. A staff member will ride him when they exercise hounds, so he'll be fit and ready to go when hunt season starts. Richard also offered to keep Chancellor at his barn when he's discharged from the EMC."

"That sounds like a great solution. Are you going to take him up on his offer?"

Doug nodded. "And Billy is going to help out at Richard's as long as Chancellor is there."

"What about Junior and Miss Molly, and the weanlings?"

"Bob Newington called from Rock Hill Stud and he has room for all of them. He's sending his manager over with the van to pick them up this morning."

"That's certainly a relief to have found places for them so quickly."

Doug sighed wearily. "Yeah, that's one less thing to worry about." He hunched forward with his elbows on his knees and his hands knitted together in a fist.

Anne could see his jaw muscle tense as he clenched his teeth, and she reached out and rubbed his back. "Are you all right?"

He closed his eyes for a minute, then turned his head towards her. "They discovered the cause of the fire."

She could tell by Doug's expression it was bad news. "What caused it?"

"Someone shot a flare into the barn."

"*A flare?*"

Doug sat back and rested his arm along the couch cushion. "Yeah. They most likely shot it in through the back hayloft door."

"What distance can you shoot a flare from?"

He shrugged. "A couple hundred feet, maybe."

"*A couple hundred feet?* How could someone get that close with the guards around?"

"He must have come through the back of the property. He probably watched from the woods and waited until the guard patrol left the barn area, then crossed the pasture, shot the flare, and departed the same way he came."

Anne took a deep breath and rubbed her hands over her belly. "So what's to prevent someone from doing the same thing with a real gun, instead of a flare gun?"

"Until today, apparently nothing."

"Until today?" Her voice rose in pitch. "What's to prevent them from doing it now?"

"Patrick has increased the number of guards, and they're patrolling the entire perimeter of the property, not just the road frontage."

"Will that be enough protection?"

Doug lifted his hand in a questioning gesture. "Hopefully."

"'Hopefully'?" She studied him. "Are you sure you want to continue using Manse Security?"

He rocked his head back and forth in a yes/no kind of gesture. "I think so. They're considered the best, and Patrick's always done great work for me, but I don't think the protection he's provided so far has measured up. He should have guarded the rear access to the farm from the beginning. And it really pisses me off that it took so long for a guard to respond last night once the fire alarm went off. Jake was trapped in the barn and almost died. It would have been nice to have had some help down there."

"I hope Jake's been cleared of any suspicion in the fire, now that they know it was started by a flare."

Doug nodded. "He has. I just saw Patrick down at the barn, and when he learned the cause of the fire, he acknowledged that Jake couldn't have been responsible."

Anne slid her arm across Doug's chest and rested her head on his shoulder. "I worry that Patrick doesn't really buy into the notion that McGraw might be behind these incidents, Doug. I think that's why he's grasping at straws, trying to point the finger at someone like Jake. But this whole scenario reminds me of McGraw. The dead deer. The snake. Sneaking around in the woods." She paused. *"The drawing on your car."*

Doug tensed. "I'm sorry I didn't tell you about the car." His tone didn't invite discussion.

She swallowed hard and nodded against his shoulder.

A heavy silence settled over them and Doug stroked her shoulder and the back of her neck. "I agree with you that this stinks of McGraw," he said after a few moments.

Anne fingered a button on the front of his shirt. "Have Patrick's investigators come up with anything else about the McGraw family?"

"Not really. They spent a couple of days tailing Zelda McGraw, but Patrick thinks that's a dead end. She lives alone and apparently doesn't do much except hang out at a local bar. She doesn't even have a car, just hitches rides. They interviewed Mrs. McGraw in the nursing home, but she wasn't much help. Patrick said she's pretty out of it. The only piece of information of any interest they gleaned from her was that Zelda has a boyfriend. She apparently mumbled something that implied he was a friend of Zeb McGraw, but they couldn't get her to repeat it. Anyway, the investigators haven't seen Zelda with a man or any sign of a man around Zelda's trailer, so they think the mother was either confused or that was old news and the guy's out of the picture now."

"Are they still keeping track of who visits McGraw in jail?"

Doug nodded. "He hasn't had any visitors since Zelda's visit about a month ago."

Anne mulled over what Doug had told her. "What if Mrs. McGraw did know what she was talking about? Maybe Zelda is in cahoots with a friend of McGraw, and he's the one doing these things."

"I asked Patrick this morning whether they'd had any luck with their investigation of McGraw's friends, as well as anyone who may have served time with McGraw, and he said so far they haven't come up with anything significant."

Neither of them spoke for a moment, then Anne shifted away from Doug on the couch and lifted her head so she could look into his eyes. "I'm scared, Doug. Every time you or Samantha leaves the house, I worry about you until you're home again."

Doug pressed his lips to her forehead. "I know. And when we find the bastard who's behind this, I'll make him pay for that."

44

*K*endall introduced Stephen to some show riders who were having cocktails on the hillside next to the polo arena, and as they chatted about Aiken and people they might know in common, her thoughts drifted to Jake. She'd run into him a couple of times during the day at Fox Run, and it hadn't been as uncomfortable as she'd thought it would be.

"Come on," Stephen said, reaching for her hand and slipping his fingers through hers. "Let's go get something to drink."

Stephen wasn't using his crutches, and the walking cast made his gait deliberate and slightly uneven, so Kendall slowed her pace to match his. She tried to pull her hand away, but that made him tighten his grasp even more, so she gave up, not knowing how to extricate herself without making a big deal out of it.

There was a crush of people by the Gazebo, in line for the bar, and Stephen's brow puckered in a look of annoyance. "This tournament has been going on all week, right? Plus, they have weekly Saturday-night matches? You'd think they'd be able to anticipate the number of people by now and set up more than one bar."

Kendall gave him a small smile. "You don't have to stand in line on my account. I can get by without a drink."

Stephen shrugged nonchalantly. "I'll fight the crowd."

"Okay." Kendall looked towards the arena. "Why don't I find a place for us to sit? It's filling up fast."

He frowned as he scanned the crowded hillside. "All right. What would you like to drink?"

Kendall took a step away from him. "White wine, please."

Stephen gave her hand a squeeze before letting go. "I'll see you in a minute."

Kendall turned to make her way down the slope, and she heard a woman's voice call out her name. She stopped and looked around, uncertain where it had come from.

The voice called out again. "Kendall, over here."

She realized the voice came from the throng of people to her left, and she turned, to see Helen Dunning waving furiously at her.

"Oh shit," Kendall muttered. Helen was the last person she wanted to talk to. She started to wave and keep on walking, but then she realized that Margaret was standing beside Helen, so she eased her way in their direction. She could see the arm and shoulder of a man who stood next to Margaret, but she couldn't see his face through the crowd.

"Hi, Margaret, I didn't expect to see you here," Kendall said, leaning forward to give her a hug. She pulled back from Margaret's embrace and glanced towards the man standing next to her.

Kendall drew a sharp breath. "*Jake.* What are you doing here?"

Jake gave her a long, steady gaze. "Watching polo. What about you?"

She forced a smile. "Watching polo."

"Who's that man you were with?" Helen asked.

Kendall stole a look at Jake. *Had Jake seen Stephen holding her hand?* Jake regarded her with a level look but raised an eyebrow slightly.

She felt her face grow hot. "Nobody."

Helen laughed. "'Nobody'? Does Mr. Nobody have a name?"

"That's Stephen Lloyd," Margaret said. "He's a polo player from Aiken, and he's considering moving his horses up here. When he gets his cast off, that is."

"A polo player?" Helen regarded Kendall thoughtfully. "That sounds like a good match for you, Kendall. He must be rich, and he's awfully good-looking."

"He's just a friend, Helen. I'm trying to introduce him to some people in the community."

"Oh, of course he is, Kendall. That's just how it looked to me." Helen gave her a knowing smile. "Oh, look, here he comes now."

Kendall turned, to see Stephen slowly making his way towards her, a drink in each hand. He smiled and handed a clear plastic cup of wine to her. "Whew, they really make you earn your drinks around here."

Kendall gave him a tense smile. "Stephen, you know Margaret, of course, and Jake. And this is Helen Dunning. Helen, Stephen Lloyd."

Helen held her hand out. "It's a delight to meet you, Stephen. I understand you play polo. When are we going to see you down in the arena?"

Stephen gestured at his cast. "Just as soon as I get this off, I'll be putting my breeches on. I hope I'll get to play before the season is over."

"Oh, I hope so, too. Are you any good?"

Stephen smiled broadly at her. "I do all right."

"What's your handicap?" Margaret asked.

Stephen hesitated for an instant. "Three goals."

"Really?" Margaret raised an eyebrow. "Is that your arena handicap, or grass?"

"Arena."

"That's quite impressive."

"Thanks."

"I should get your phone number," Helen said, taking a pen out of her purse. "I know some gentlemen who would be thrilled to have you play on their team. Here, you can write your number on my napkin."

Stephen took the pen and napkin from her. "Sure, no problem."

Margaret watched him write. "You're left-handed and you're a three-goal player?"

Stephen shrugged as he handed the pen and napkin back to Helen. "It's no big deal. It's just like swinging from the other side of the plate in baseball. In fact, I think it works to my advantage. It tends to throw the other players off."

Margaret regarded Stephen thoughtfully over the rim of her glass as she took a long sip of her drink. "What's your grass handicap?"

"I don't play on grass."

Margaret gave him a quizzical smile. "That's interesting."

Stephen nodded dismissively at Margaret and slipped his arm around Kendall's waist. "Want to go closer to the arena and look for a place to sit?"

Kendall stiffened against Stephen's touch, but he acted as if he didn't notice and drew her closer, tilting his head towards the arena. "Come on, it looks like they're getting ready to start the match."

"I'd better get back to my box before my guests wonder what happened to me," Helen said, rushing off with a smile and a wave. "Nice to meet you, Stephen."

Stephen lifted his hand and waved at Helen with his drink, then tugged at Kendall's waist. "Kendall, let's go." There was an edge to his voice.

The warmth of Stephen's hand radiated through Kendall's linen blouse and she resisted the urge to shove his hand away. She cast a glance in Jake's direction. "Sure."

"Do you mind if we join you?" Margaret asked. "I enticed Jake to come here tonight by telling him I'd do my best to explain the rules of the game to him, and I might be able to use a little help from you, Stephen."

Before Stephen could respond, Jake spoke up. "Thanks anyway, Mrs. Southwell. I'm feeling a little *off my feed* all of a sudden. I think I'll be heading on back, if you can find another ride home."

Margaret gazed intently at him. "Don't you worry about me; I'll find my own way home. But I'm sorry you're not feeling well, Jake. Can I do something to help you?"

Jake shook his head. "It's nothing time won't cure." His eyes locked with Kendall's for an instant. "Good-bye, Kendall."

Kendall placed her hand on his arm. "Jake, wait."

He turned away.

"*Jake.*"

Stephen tugged on her again. "Come on, Kendall, are we going to watch the match or not?"

Kendall watched Jake disappear into the crowd and she shook her head, barely bothering to look at Stephen. "You and Margaret go ahead. I have to talk to Jake about something."

Stephen groaned and dropped his hand from her waist. "I don't believe this."

Kendall ignored him and took off after Jake. She worked her way through the crowd, mumbling "Excuse me" as she pushed past them, zigzagging amid the maze of picnic blankets spread out on the hillside. By the time she caught sight of Jake again, he was almost to the parking area.

"Jake!"

He half turned and looked back at her, slowing his pace, and she hurried down the drive after him.

"Jake, please stop. I want to talk to you."

He took a few more steps forward, then stopped abruptly and spun to face her, his hands on his hips. The arena lights cast a soft glow over him, and Kendall could tell from the way he clenched his jaw that he was angry.

She stopped a few feet from him, suddenly unsure what to say. The drawl of the announcer's voice boomed over the sound system above their heads, announcing the start of the first chukker.

"You said you wanted to talk, so talk," he said.

"I . . ." She drew in a breath to slow her pounding heart. "I just wanted to say I'm sorry."

"Sorry for what?"

"Sorry for tonight." Kendall gestured towards the polo arena. "For Stephen."

"You're apologizing for Stephen?"

Kendall felt her face redden. "I mean, I apologize for being with Stephen. For your having to see me with him."

Jake's expression was unreadable. "No need to apologize, Kendall. You're free to date whomever you want to."

"It wasn't a date. Not really."

"Not really?"

She shook her head. "No, not really. At least I didn't think it was. I told Stephen I wasn't ready to date yet, and I thought we were just coming here as friends."

Jake's mouth curved into a cool smile. "He was sure being mighty friendly."

"I know. It took me by surprise, and I didn't know what to do about it."

"How about telling him to take his goddamned hands off you?"

Kendall flinched at his tone. "It's not like Stephen was molesting me, Jake. I didn't want to make a big deal about it."

"You didn't want to make a big deal about it?" Jake narrowed his eyes at her and slowly shook his head. "Back where I come from, it's a big deal if a guy touches a woman when she doesn't want him to, and if she has any self-respect, she tells him so."

Kendall stiffened and looked away. *That's the problem, Jake. Peter stole my self-respect.*

Jake studied her for a moment, then exhaled loudly and shook his head. "I don't know what I was thinking last night, Kendall. I'll never fit into your world."

He stepped towards her and ran the back of his fingers across her cheek. "You take care of yourself," he said softly, then turned and walked away.

Kendall felt her throat close up. "*Jake!*"

But he just raised his hand in a backwards wave and kept on walking.

*Z*elda flopped down in the motel room chair by the air conditioner, furious with Earl for wanting the three of them to go over the plans one more time. Zach knew she was pissed, and he'd retreated to the bed farthest away from her. She turned her face towards the window unit and closed her eyes, letting the icy air blast her face.

"Are you paying attention, babe?" Earl asked.

She ignored him for a minute, then nodded, keeping her eyes closed. "Um-hmm."

"Then would you mind doing me a favor and looking at me when I'm talking to you? Timing is key to pulling this off tomorrow." Earl's tone was as frigid as the blast from the air conditioner.

Zelda rolled her head in his direction and opened her eyes. God, he was so damned hot-looking; it was hard to stay mad at him. "I'm listening," she said, arching her back against the armrest of the chair to show off her chest.

"The field trip is scheduled for nine o'clock, so make sure you don't show up at the barn until a few minutes before that. We don't want to give them enough time to check on the driver substitution. Zach will be at the barn, and he'll create a distraction if they start asking you too many questions."

Zelda tugged her shirt tight. "I know. We've already been over this a hundred times. We'll leave here at seven and get to where the bus is kept at by seven-thirty, in plenty of time to ambush the driver, who usually gets there around eight. I'll drive the bus to the barn, but I'll make sure I don't get there too early."

Earl nodded at her. "Right. And after you hit the road with the bus, I'll take care of the bus driver. Once you leave the barn with the kids, I'll meet up with you and we'll deal with the guard; you know that drill."

There was something about the way he said "take care of the bus driver" that caught Zelda's attention. "You ain't getting any crazy ideas about the bus driver, are you?" she asked.

"That's my department, babe. You don't need to worry yourself about that."

Zelda sat upright in the chair. "Tell me what you're going to do to the bus driver."

"You're better off not knowing." Earl glanced at Zach and held out his hand. "Give me that knife you're wearing."

Zach looked down at the knife on his belt. "What for?"

Earl didn't answer. He wiggled his fingers. "Come on. Hand it over."

"What do you need it for? You got your own damned knife," Zach muttered. But he unclipped the knife from his belt and tossed it to Earl.

Zelda narrowed her eyes at Earl. "What's going on with you? We're partners in this gig. You can't be calling all the shots and keeping Zach and me in the dark about everything."

Earl's mouth twisted into a sneer. "Sure, babe. Whatever you say."

Zelda felt blood rush to her face and she jumped up out of the chair. "This is bullshit!"

Earl's hand shot out and grabbed her arm. "Don't push me, babe."

The look in his eyes sent a chill through Zelda, and she bit back a retort. She knew she had gone too far. "Sorry."

"That's better." Earl relaxed his grip, pulling her into a long kiss, and Zelda crawled onto the bed.

"Zach, that's your clue to get out of here," she said, closing her eyes and parting Earl's lips with her tongue.

"Suits me just fine," Zach said, slamming the motel room door as he left. Zelda felt a twinge of guilt about Zach, but she rolled Earl onto his back and slid on top of him. "Show me how much you missed me."

His hands slid down to her buttocks and pulled her close to him, but she didn't feel the familiar bulge in his pants. Zelda began to rub against him in the slow, rhythmic motion that usually drove him crazy, then pulled back and frowned.

"What's the matter? Ain't you happy to see me?"

Earl turned his head to the side and closed his eyes. "I'm just exhausted, babe."

Zelda felt a flicker of panic. Earl had never been too tired before. "Oh yeah? Let's just see if we can't change that," she said, unbuckling his belt.

46

$\mathcal{K}$endall had a pounding headache, probably because she hadn't slept well the night before, and she had to bite her tongue to keep from yelling at the girls for being too loud as they jumped over the fences in the indoor arena, pretending to be horses. She leaned against the railing and glanced at her watch. *Where was Elizabeth?*

Todd passed in the aisle with a wheelbarrow full of fresh shavings. "Everything okay, Miss Waters?"

"Good morning, Todd. You wouldn't happen to know why Elizabeth is late today, would you?"

Before he could answer, the door to the office opened and Margaret stuck her head out. "Kendall, you have a phone call."

Kendall sighed. "Thank God. I hope that's Elizabeth. I left a message on her cell a few minutes ago. Would you do me a favor and watch the kids for a minute while I get the phone?"

"Sure, no problem." Todd lowered the handles of the wheelbarrow and walked to the arena gate.

Kendall hurried to the office and picked up the receiver on the desk. "Hello."

"Good morning, Kendall; it's Anne."

"Anne, hi. Is Samantha on her way? We need to leave in about ten minutes."

"No, that's why I'm calling. Samantha woke up with a sore throat and a fever, so she won't be going on the field trip today."

Kendall heard Samantha wailing in the background. "I don't feel sick, Mommy. I really want to go to the Land of Little Horses."

"Poor Samantha," Kendall said. "I'm so sorry she's sick. I know how much she was looking forward to the field trip. Tell her I'll bring her a special souvenir."

"Thank you, Kendall. I'll tell her."

"Okay, and give her a hug for me. I'll call you later to see how she's doing."

Kendall hung up and turned to Margaret. "As you probably heard, Samantha's sick and won't be coming along on the field trip today."

"That's too bad. I'm sure she's disappointed."

"She is, and we're going to have seven more disappointed children if Elizabeth doesn't show up soon."

"Have you tried to call her?"

"Yes. There's no answer at her house or on her cell."

"She's been on time all week, hasn't she?"

Kendall nodded. "Yes, she's been very reliable. I just can't understand why she hasn't at least called. Anyway, if she doesn't show up soon, I don't know what I'm going to do. Unless you're willing to bend the rules and let me take the kids on the field trip without an assistant."

Margaret pursed her lips and shook her head. "I can't, Kendall. Our insurance company requires that two chaperones accompany the children on all outings."

"I don't suppose there's any way you could come along, is there?"

"Unfortunately, I can't. I've got customers coming to look at a horse this afternoon. I need to be here for that."

Kendall tried to think of an alternative. "Does it have to be an employee, or could I see if I can get one of the parents to come along?"

"As I recall, I think insurance dictates that it be an employee." Margaret looked at her watch. "I can call my insurance agent and confirm that with her, but I doubt she'd be in the office yet."

Kendall closed her eyes and rubbed her throbbing temples. "Never mind. By the time you reach her, and I try to get a parent to join us, it will put us too far behind schedule. If we're not at the Land of Little Horses by eleven-thirty, we'll lose our spot."

Margaret held her finger to her lips. "I'm just trying to think whether I have someone from the barn staff I could spare for the day."

"What about Todd? He knows the kids, and he was really good with them when he came along on our field trip to the kennels."

Margaret hesitated. "I don't know. He's mighty young."

"He's about the same age as Elizabeth. Besides, that's probably one of the reasons the kids like him."

Margaret nodded. "All right. If you're comfortable with having Todd as your assistant, that's fine with me."

Kendall reached for the doorknob. "Thank you, Margaret."

"Kendall, please wait a moment."

She turned around.

"Something has been bothering me since last evening, and I want to get it off my chest."

"What's that?"

Margaret drew Kendall to the couch. "I know your love life isn't any of my business, but I feel the need to speak my mind."

"Okay." Kendall's stomach cramped into a knot as she sat down. *Was this about Jake?*

"I don't trust Stephen Lloyd, Kendall," Margaret said in a tight tone. "I'm sorry I encouraged you to go out with him."

Kendall's breath escaped in a rush. "Margaret, I have no romantic interest in Stephen. It was a mistake for me to go to the polo match with him last night."

"Oh, thank goodness." Margaret held her hand to her chest. "He was so obviously smitten with you last evening, I feared the feeling was mutual."

"Hardly. There's definitely no attraction there. At least not on my part." Kendall shuddered at the memory of Stephen's arm around her waist.

"Good," Margaret said. "Because I think he's a phony."

"A phony? In what way?"

"Well, first of all, I don't believe he's from Aiken, but if he is, I don't think he plays polo there."

Kendall frowned at her. "Really? Why?"

"I first became suspicious when Stephen said he has a three handicap. If he's that good, why would he want to board his polo ponies at my barn? That would be like you boarding Wellington at a polo barn. That's why I asked him whether his handicap was on grass or in the arena. Remember? And he told me he only played arena polo?"

"Yes."

"Well, I've never heard of anyone playing arena polo in Aiken."

"Why would he lie about that?"

Margaret raised an eyebrow. "Who knows? Maybe he's just trying to make an impression. But I wouldn't be surprised if, when Stephen's cast comes off, we learn he can't play polo worth a lick."

Kendall laughed. "Maybe Stephen did exaggerate his handicap, but I thought he seemed pretty knowledgeable about the sport."

"I disagree. Remember when Stephen said as soon as he got his cast off he'd be putting his breeches on? *Polo players don't wear breeches.* They wear white jeans. And they refer to them as whites." She shook her head. "Then there was that baloney about being a left-handed player."

Kendall remembered Stephen bragging about playing left-handed. "I've never seen anyone play left-handed. Is it extremely difficult?"

"Difficult? You've never seen anyone play left-handed because it's strictly prohibited under the rules."

elda took a deep breath as she steered the bus through the gates of Fox Run Farm.

"This is it," she said, exhaling slowly.

She was relieved to see that everything looked just as Zach had described it, and her racing heart began to slow as she braked to a stop across the parking lot from the office door. She didn't see signs of a guard around, but she figured he was in the barn watching over the Cummings kid. In fact, no one was outside, but she opened the bus door anyway, just like Zach had told her to.

As she waited, Zelda's eyes roamed the farm, taking in the beige wood-and-stone buildings surrounded by neatly trimmed grass; the horses grazing behind black wooden fencing; and the dozen or so expensive-looking cars and SUVs in the parking lot. A manure spreader hooked up to a John Deere tractor was parked in front of the nearby entrance to the barn.

A breeze kicked up a whirlwind of dust in the gravel drive, sending a strong whiff of fresh manure and urine-soaked bedding through the open door of the bus, and Zelda was flooded with memories of the summer she'd spent mucking stalls at Charles Town Racetrack. Even now, sixteen years later, she felt sick to her stomach just thinking back to what had started out as the best, and ended up as the worst, summer of her life.

Earl had taken a job driving for a truck transport company that summer and was on the road all the time, so when she'd heard they were looking for workers at the racetrack, no experience required, she had decided to give it a try. She figured anything would be better than staying at home without Earl and working the shitty job she had waitressing at Moe's Diner.

She'd found out quick enough that mucking stalls was backbreaking work, and she hadn't been crazy about getting up before the crack of dawn every day, but the pay was good, and she liked hanging out at the backside and going drinking at the Winner's Circle lounge after work with the other stable hands. She especially liked hanging out there on race days, when the trainers came in. It had been a race day when she'd met Gatsby.

Zelda closed her eyes for an instant and pictured the way Gatsby had looked the first night she'd seen him at the lounge. She had noticed him talking with some other trainers near the bar, and she could tell right off he'd been partying for a while. His blond hair was all mussed up, his necktie was cockeyed, and half of his shirttail was untucked from his khaki pants. His face was too thin to be called handsome, but there was something sexy about him. It was his eyes, she decided. All blue and shimmering, like those pictures she'd seen of the ocean in Hawaii.

She asked a friend who knew him to introduce her, and when Gatsby had learned her name, he'd held both hands over his heart and said that at last fate had delivered his true love. She hadn't understood what he was talking about, but he had laughed and told her Gatsby wasn't his real name, just a nickname based on some famous novel written by a guy whose wife was named Zelda.

Zelda had gone home with Gatsby that night, and most every night after that for the next couple of weeks. Then one day he'd come to the track half-drunk and all pissed off, and told her he had to ship his horses back home for a while. Something about his mother pulling the plug on his bank account. He told her he'd stay in touch, but he never did, and by the time Zelda found out she was pregnant with Zach, Gatsby was nowhere to be found.

The office door opened and Zelda shook her head to clear her thoughts. There was no sense in thinking back to that summer. She was with Earl again now, and that was all that mattered.

elda watched a group of young girls burst out of the office, carrying lunch boxes and backpacks. They were followed by a tall brown-haired woman, wearing khaki shorts, a black polo shirt, and sneakers, who carried an armful of blankets and a picnic basket. Zelda figured the woman was the camp counselor, Kendall. She wasn't bad-looking, if you went for the too thin, flat-chested model look.

The woman left the office door open, and a minute later Zach appeared in the doorway, shouldering a large ice chest. He turned to wave at someone inside, then closed the door and followed the woman and girls towards the bus.

"So far, so good," Zelda said.

The little girls arrived first, and Zelda counted heads as they climbed aboard the bus, trying to single out Samantha Cummings. There was one blond girl wearing a pink T-shirt who might be her, but Zelda couldn't tell for certain. She hadn't seen the kid in over three months, and at that age they grew like weeds.

Zelda frowned as the last kid walked down the aisle, and she turned to count them again quickly. *There were only seven kids on the bus.* There were supposed to be eight.

She whipped her head back around and searched the parking lot, but there wasn't another kid in sight. Just Zach and the woman. The woman reached for the railing and raised her eyes to Zelda as she stepped into the bus.

"Hello," she said, frowning slightly. "Where's Mrs. Parker?"

Zelda flashed a smile. "I'm substituting for her today."

"No one told me about that," the woman said, a tight-lipped look of annoyance clouding her face.

"It was last-minute. She took sick overnight. She called me all frantic this morning, asking if I'd substitute drive for her. I'm Connie, by the way. Connie White."

"Hi, Connie, I'm Kendall. I'm the camp counselor." She half turned and motioned behind her towards Zach. "And this is Todd. He's going to be my assistant today."

"Nice to meet you both," Zelda said. "We better get on the road if we want to keep to the schedule. I don't go over the speed limit, so if we're behind schedule, we're just going to get there late."

Kendall studied her for a moment. "You know, I think I should just go check with the farm's owner to make sure she's all right with the substitution."

Zelda's heart raced, but she forced her voice to be cool. "You suit yourself on that one. You're the one knows when you have to be there. I'm happy to show you my driver's license, if that would make you feel better."

Kendall glanced at her watch. "Sure, I guess that would be okay."

Zelda reached above the visor for her fake driver's license and handed it to Kendall. "Mrs. Parker told me I was supposed to drive eight kids today. I only see seven."

"One of the girls is sick today," Kendall replied, studying the license.

"That's too bad." Zelda shot a questioning look at Zach. "Wonder if it's the same bug that Mrs. Parker has."

Kendall handed the license back to her. "I don't know, but something must be going around, because my regular assistant didn't show up today, either. Thankfully, Todd agreed to come along."

Kendall looked at Zach, who gave her a shy smile and said, "I'm honored you asked me, Miss Waters."

Oh please, Zelda thought. *Where had the kid learned to act like that?*

Kendall moved past Zelda and headed down the aisle, taking a seat in the fourth row, right in front of the kids. She placed the picnic basket on the seat in front of her. As Zach drew close to Zelda, he leaned down and said, "The Cummings kid is the one missing."

Zelda stared wide-eyed at him. "Now what?"

Zach shrugged and followed Kendall down the aisle.

Shit! With or without Samantha Cummings, they couldn't turn back now.

Zelda pulled the lever that closed the bus door and put the bus in drive.

"I've got a couple of rules that I want everybody to listen up to," she said as she eased up on the brake and headed slowly out the drive, working hard to imitate what a bus driver would say. "I want everybody to have fun today, but I don't tolerate no screaming and hollering on my bus. So you just keep your voices down, and we'll do just fine together. Everybody understand?"

"Can you tell Mrs. White you understand the bus rules?" Kendall asked, facing backwards in her seat towards the kids.

"Yes, Mrs. White," the girls said in harmony.

"All right, then." Zelda turned the bus onto the road.

They hadn't traveled more than a mile when Zelda thought she heard the shrill ring of a telephone. *Ring-ring.* There it was again.

She glanced in the rearview mirror and saw Kendall put a cell phone to her ear.

"Hello."

Damn it. She should have figured the camp counselor would have a cell phone.

"Hi, Kevin," Kendall said. "No, I just left Fox Run to take the girls on a field trip, and I won't be back until late this afternoon, but the shoe is hanging on Wellington's door."

Kendall listened and nodded. "That's wonderful. Thanks so much. He took a big chunk out of his hoof when he pulled the shoe off, so I hope you have enough hoof left to nail the shoe to."

She nodded some more, frowning. "How expensive are glue-on shoes?"

More nodding. "Okay, just do whatever you need to. And thanks so much for calling me back so quickly. I really appreciate it."

Kendall lowered the cell phone from her ear and punched a button, then looked up and caught Zelda's eyes in the mirror.

"I don't tolerate no cell phone conversations on my bus," Zelda said. "I guess I forgot to mention that earlier."

"I'm sorry," Kendall replied. "I was just talking to my blacksmith."

"I don't care who you was talking to, honey. The call was distracting to me, and I take my driving responsibility seriously." Zelda took her right hand off the steering wheel and held it out. "Why don't you leave that phone up here with me for the drive? I'll give it back to you when we get there."

"You don't have to take the phone away from me, Connie. If you don't want me to use it on the bus, I won't."

Zelda set her mouth grimly and shook her head. "Nope. I want it up here. I know a driver who got in an awful wreck because someone's cell phone kept distracting her."

Kendall's expression tightened. "I need to have my cell phone with me when I'm chaperoning the kids, in case something happens. It's part of my job."

"It'll be right up here if you need it." Zelda wiggled her hand in an impatient motion.

Kendall sighed loudly and rose from her seat. "*Fine.*"

Zelda took the phone from her hand and deposited it in the cup holder on the dash. "You can have it back when we get to Gettysburg." She shifted her gaze in the mirror to the back of the bus. "None of those kids have cell phones, do they?"

"They're five and six years old," Kendall said with a laugh.

"I didn't ask you how old they was," Zelda snapped. "I asked you if any of them had a cell phone."

Kendall flinched and took a step backwards. "No, they don't."

Zelda flashed Zach a look of triumph in the mirror as Kendall walked back to her seat. She'd shown that bitch who was boss.

"I wish I could go with you when you pick up Chancellor," Anne said as she watched Doug lean down and run a rag over his paddock boots.

Doug looked up at her. "I do, too. Are you sure you're okay with me doing this today? I can put it off until tomorrow if you want me to take Sam to the doctor."

"Don't be silly. Of course I want you to get Chancellor today. I'll take Samantha to see Dr. Russell and, depending on how she's feeling afterwards, maybe we'll stop by Richard's and see Chancellor. It would probably cheer Samantha up. She's so disappointed about missing the field trip."

Doug straightened up and tossed the rag on the boot rack.

"You look like you're feeling better today," Anne said.

"Much better." He leaned towards her for a kiss. "Give me a call when you leave Dr. Russell's. I'm going to drive to Richard's now and ride in the van with him to the EMC."

"Did you decide to take Jake up on his offer to help?"

"I called Fox Run a little while ago, but Margaret hasn't seen Jake yet this morning. Maybe I'll swing by on my way to Richard's and see if he's around and wants to come along."

Anne studied Doug for a moment, then slipped her arms around his waist and rested her head on his chest. "Every time you leave, I can't help but remember the day of your accident. Samantha and I waved good-bye as you left for the trail ride that morning, totally unaware of what was about to happen to you."

Doug wrapped his arms around her, but his embrace was stiff. "Anne, you can't worry every time I walk out the door. We have to get on with our lives."

She nodded. "I know."

He pulled back and leaned down to look her in the eyes. "Hey, speaking of getting on with our lives, two weeks from today we're going to have a baby."

Anne gave a small shake of her head. "I don't know about that. When I saw Dr. Sommers yesterday, he said I'm not starting to dilate at all. Besides, first babies are usually late."

Doug grinned and placed one hand on her belly. "Not ours. We're both lawyers. Our baby will understand the importance of a deadline."

The baby kicked against his hand and Anne smiled at the look on Doug's face.

"What's so funny?" he asked.

"I was just thinking how much you've changed in the last nine months."

He raised an eyebrow. "Really? Tell me how I've changed."

"You were a carefree playboy when I met you. Hardly the daddy type. Now look at you. You get all misty-eyed just feeling your baby kick." She fingered his wedding ring.

Doug smiled. "The reason I was a playboy was that I hadn't met you yet." He lowered his lips to hers for a long kiss.

"Umm," he mumbled against her lips. "Maybe I should forget about picking up Chancellor and we should go back upstairs."

Anne laughed and pulled away. "Hold that thought."

"I was afraid you'd say that." Doug grabbed her hand as he walked towards the door. "Give Sam a kiss for me when she wakes up from her nap."

"I will."

He gestured towards the empty puppy crate next to the door. "Is Rascal upstairs, sleeping with Sam?"

She nodded and held her hand up. "Don't say it. I know. The puppy's a great baby-sitter."

Doug chuckled, then paused with his hand on the doorknob. "I want Ben to ride in the car with you and Sam today, not follow behind like he has been."

Anne's smile faded. "Okay."

He kissed her one more time. "I love you."

She nodded and squeezed his hand, resisting the urge to caution him to be careful.

50

The girls were entertaining themselves, playing cheerfully with their Breyer horses, and Kendall leaned her head against the window and closed her eyes. The faint vibration from the glass was hypnotic, and as the bus rolled smoothly along James Monroe Highway, Kendall began to settle down from the frenzy of the morning. Her thoughts drifted to Jake, and she wondered for the hundredth time why she had let Stephen touch her so possessively at the polo match, especially in front of Jake.

She had planned on stopping by Jake's cottage to talk to him when she'd driven Margaret home after the match, but the cottage lights were off and his truck wasn't there. And she'd arrived at the farm early that morning, hoping to catch him then, but there was still no sign of his truck. She'd even knocked on the cottage door, but there was no answer.

Kendall felt the bus make a sharp left-hand turn, and she opened her eyes in time to see the driver turn off the highway and onto Harmony Church Road.

"Excuse me, why are you turning here?" Kendall asked, sitting up straight in her seat.

"I'm taking a shortcut," Connie replied, straightening through the turn and stepping on the accelerator.

"To Gettysburg?"

"That's right."

Kendall frowned. "I don't think so. James Monroe Highway is Route Fifteen, which is a straight shot north to Gettysburg."

"I'll hook back up with Route Fifteen later," Connie said. "I'm just avoiding the traffic around Leesburg."

Kendall frowned at her in the mirror. "I'd prefer it if you'd keep to the main road."

"Honey, why don't you concentrate on your job and let me do mine, okay?"

Kendall bit back a retort. Connie obviously felt the need to run things her way, and there was no sense getting into a power struggle with her. On the other hand, they couldn't afford to take some detour that might cause them to arrive late.

"Do you mind telling me what route you're taking?"

Connie didn't answer her.

"Miss Waters, are we lost?" Emma Horton asked.

Kendall looked back at her. "No, sweetie. Mrs. White is just going a different way from the one I'm used to."

"How much longer until we get there?" Emma asked.

"It will be a little while yet."

Harmony Church Road was hilly and full of turns, and the spongy suspension of the bus bounced the girls off their seats as they crested a hill and leaned into a twisty curve.

"Whee, that was a pee-pee hole bump." Caitlin Dunning giggled, sending the rest of the girls into peals of laughter.

Kendall smiled at them and winked at Todd.

"Miss Waters, my tummy hurts," Emma said, holding her hand over her mouth. "I think I'm going to throw up."

Kendall took a deep breath. *Oh great, that was just what she needed to top the morning off.* "Are you carsick, sweetie?" Kendall asked, putting her hand on Emma's arm.

"Uh-huh."

Kendall grabbed a picnic blanket off the seat next to her and held it in front of Emma. "If you have to throw up, do it in here."

She looked at Todd. "Do you mind sitting here and holding this for Emma? I'm going to talk to the driver about going back to the main road. This is ridiculous."

Todd's lip curled in distaste, but he moved over and held the blanket gingerly. "Sure."

"Thanks." Kendall stood and started up the aisle.

"Take your seat, hon. I don't want nobody walking around when the bus is moving," Connie called.

Kendall ignored her and continued walking towards the front of the bus.

"Look, Connie, the girls are getting carsick on this curvy road. Besides, I know this area very well, and I'm quite certain you're not saving time by going this way. I'd prefer it if you'd turn around and go back to James Monroe Highway."

Connie took her eyes off the road and glared at Kendall. "I told you to sit down."

"This is crazy!" Kendall reached for her cell phone. "I'm going to call Margaret at the farm and have you speak with her."

Connie's hand shot out and grabbed Kendall's arm. "I wouldn't do that if I was you."

Kendall jerked her arm back and snatched the phone from the cup holder.

The bus leaned precariously into a sharp curve and Connie grabbed the wheel with both hands and shouted, "Zach."

Kendall sensed a movement and spun around. Todd stood right behind her, so close that she could feel his breath on her face.

He spoke in a low voice. "Just do what we say and none of you is going to get hurt."

Kendall frowned. "What's going on?"

Todd shoved a hard object into her side and motioned down with his eyes. "I don't want to use this, but I will if I have to."

Kendall lowered her eyes and saw the gray metal barrel of a gun. "Oh, my God."

"Hand over the phone."

"Miss Waters, Emma threw up," a small voice called from the back of the bus.

Kendall swallowed. "I'll be right there."

Todd held out his hand. "Give me the phone and you can get back to the kids."

Kendall handed him the phone and held her hands up in a gesture of surrender. "My God, Todd, what are you doing?"

"Zach, get her back there with the kids," Connie ordered.

Todd tossed the phone to Connie and grabbed Kendall by the arm, pulling her past him in the aisle. He shoved her towards the back of the bus, walking behind her with the barrel of the gun pressed against the small of her back.

Kendall turned her head towards him. "Why is she calling you Zach?"

His breath was hot on her cheek. "Because that's my real name. Want to know my real last name?"

Why was he asking her that? Why did it matter what his last name was?

"It's McGraw," he said, not waiting for her answer.

Kendall's stomach tightened. "As in Zeb McGraw?" Her mouth was so dry, she could barely get the words out.

Zach shoved her into the seat in front of the girls and sat down next to her. "Bingo."

*K*endall wiped the vomit off Emma with napkins from the picnic basket. "There, that will have to do for now," she said, cleaning Emma's mouth with a wet wipe she found in her purse.

"Are you cold, Miss Waters?" Emma asked.

"No."

"Then why are your hands shaking?"

Kendall attempted a smile. "I don't know, Emma. I guess maybe I am a little cold."

Zach let out a laugh.

"What's so funny, Todd?" Emma asked.

He lifted the gun as if to show it to Emma.

"Don't," Kendall pleaded softly, shaking her head at him.

Zach narrowed his eyes. "Are you telling me what to do?"

"No. I'm sorry. Just *please* don't frighten the kids."

He shot a glance at the girls but kept his hand down.

The bus slowed and Kendall looked out the window. A light blue car was parked by the side of the road with its hood raised, and she could see the figure of a man wearing blue jeans bent over, looking under the hood. Connie turned on the emergency flashers and pulled behind the parked car.

Connie stood and motioned towards Kendall. "You watch her," she said to Zach, opening the bus door and disappearing down the steps.

Kendall watched her walk to the front of the car and saw the man straighten as she approached. The man was partially hidden behind the raised hood, and Kendall couldn't see his face. Connie stood close to him, talking animatedly and using lots of hand gestures.

"Are we there?" Emma asked.

Kendall shook her head. "No, sweetie."

"I have to go to the bathroom," Caitlin said.

"There's no place to go here, Caitlin." Kendall turned to face her. "You'll have to wait a little longer."

"But I *really* have to go."

Kendall looked imploringly at Zach, who shrugged and said, "She'll just have to hold it."

"Where are we going?" Kendall asked, keeping her voice low.

Zach looked towards the front of the bus. "You'll recognize it when we get there."

Kendall followed his gaze and saw Connie climb back aboard the bus and take the driver's seat, her eyes narrowed into a dark scowl. She closed the door and shoved the gearshift into drive, punching down the accelerator and causing the bus to skid on the gravel as she pulled onto the road.

"What's the matter?" Zach asked.

Zelda looked at him in the mirror. "Earl's pissed about the Cummings kid, as if that was my fault."

Kendall drew a sharp breath. *Is that what this was about? Had they been trying to kidnap Samantha?* She glanced out the window as they passed the blue car and saw that the hood was down and the man was in the driver's seat. She caught a glimpse of his arm and shoulder as they passed, but she still couldn't see his face.

"He'll get over it," Zach said. "Hey, Ma, you left the emergency flashers on."

Ma? Kendall turned back to Zach. "Is Connie your mother?"

"Yeah, but she ain't Connie."

"What's her name?"

"Zelda."

Kendall closed her eyes and shook her head. "Let me guess. Her last name's McGraw."

"You got it."

"Is Zeb McGraw your father?"

Zach stared at her for a minute. "You know what? You ask too many questions."

"Miss Waters, I can't hold it much longer," Caitlin said.

Kendall looked at Zach. "You heard her, Todd. What are we going to do?"

"My name ain't Todd."

"Sorry. *Zach.*"

"We ain't stopping for her to pee."

Kendall stared tight-lipped at him. "I have plastic bowls in the picnic basket. At least let me get one so she can go to the bathroom in that."

"Fine. Get it and let her pee. But no funny business." He waved the gun. "I'll have this aimed at you and the kid the whole time."

Kendall reached over the seat in front of her and opened the lid to the picnic basket.

"Hey, what's she doing back there?" Zelda shouted.

"One of the kids has to pee; she's getting a bowl for her to go in," Zach said.

Zelda moaned. "Jesus Christ."

Kendall expected Zelda to tell her to forget it, but Zelda turned her concentration back to the road, so Kendall took the potato chip bowl out of the picnic basket. "Come on, Caitlin. Let's go up to another row of seats. You can go to the bathroom in this bowl."

Kendall didn't want to get any closer to Zelda McGraw than she had to, so she led Caitlin to the second row, right in front of the picnic basket, and placed the bowl on the seat.

"Okay, Caitlin," she said, standing her on the seat and helping her pull her shorts down. "You get to be the first one to use our special bus potty."

The bus lurched around a corner and Kendall grabbed the seat back and held on to Caitlin. She caught a smirk on Zelda's face and figured she must have made the sudden movement on purpose. Kendall gritted her teeth and braced herself against the seat back in front of her, in case the bus took another unexpected turn. She placed Caitlin on the bowl and held her securely while the little girl emptied her bladder.

"Thank you, Miss Waters," Caitlin said when she had finished.

"No problem, sweetie." Kendall zipped her shorts for her and helped her step down off the seat.

"Does anyone else have to go?" Kendall asked, looking at the rest of the girls.

Zach shook his head. "That wasn't part of the deal. I said one kid could pee. That's it."

"You heard him. Get on back there and sit down," Zelda ordered.

"What would you like me to do with this?" Kendall asked, holding up the bowl.

Zelda scowled at her. "Dump it out the window."

"Okay," Kendall replied. "Would you mind slowing down, so I can empty it without it blowing back in the bus?"

"Yes, I would mind," Zelda said. "Just do it."

Kendall struggled with the window locks and slid the window down. She was barely able to fit the large bowl through the opening, but finally she managed to do so without spilling the urine. She held her breath and leaned away from the window as she dumped the contents, watching the urine spray along the side of the bus.

Zach turned in his seat and looked out the rear window. "It sprayed all over Earl's windshield," he said with a snort.

Kendall followed Zach's gaze towards the back of the bus and saw that the blue car was following them.

"Hey! Shut that window, now, and get back to your seat," Zelda shouted.

Kendall closed the window and placed the bowl on the floor. As she walked towards the back of the bus, she ducked her head and looked through the rear window towards the blue car, trying to get a look at the driver's face.

*Z*elda pulled to a stop in front of a set of black iron gates with redbrick pillars on both sides and a sign that read HIGH MEADOW.

"Pull up to that box with the buttons on it," Zach said.

Zelda eased up on the brake and let the bus roll forward until she was even with the box.

"All right, what do I do now?" She looked at Zach in the mirror as she lowered the driver's side window.

"Tell her the code to open the gate," Zach said to Kendall.

Kendall stared openmouthed at him. "What's going on here, Zach?"

"Just tell her the code."

"It's one, two, three, four, plus the pound sign," Kendall said.

Zelda snorted as she reached out to punch the buttons. "As if we couldn't have figured that out for ourselves."

The gates opened and Zelda drove the bus through, watching in the exterior mirror to make sure Earl got through before the gates closed.

"Okay, now where do I go?" she asked Zach.

"Just keep on going down this road, past the humongous mansion."

Ring-ring. Zelda jerked her head towards Kendall's cell phone, which she'd put back in the cup holder.

"Shit! Who's that calling you?"

Kendall shook her head. "I don't know. It might be Margaret at the farm, checking to see if the field trip is going all right."

"Get up here and answer it," Zelda snapped, holding the phone out towards her. "But don't you say nothing to tip nobody off. You tell them that everything's going just fine."

Zach stood up and shoved Kendall towards the front of the bus. "Hurry, before they hang up."

Kendall stumbled to the front and took the phone. Zelda could see her hand shaking as she flipped the phone open and held it to her ear. "Hello?"

She listened for a minute. "We're fine."

"Make sure you talk normal," Zelda said in a loud whisper.

Kendall frowned. "No, nothing's wrong. Emma just got carsick, that's all, but she's fine now."

She listened again. "Yes, we're making good time."

Another pause. "Okay, I'll call you when we get there. Bye."

Kendall flipped the phone shut and Zelda grabbed it out of her hand. "You did real good there. You keep cooperating like that and you won't have no problem."

Zelda put the bus in gear and followed the drive as it wound past a huge redbrick house. She pulled to a stop in front of a large aluminum-sided building with a garage door in the center.

"This is it," Zach said. "Let me out and I'll open the door so you can drive in. The control button is right by the door."

Zelda put her arm out to stop him. "Hold on. Get Earl on the bus first. I don't trust her not to try something." She cocked her head at Kendall, who still stood in the aisle.

Zach nodded. "I'll go get him."

Zelda pushed the button to open the bus door and tapped her fingers impatiently on the dash while she waited for Zach to get Earl. She'd feel a whole lot better once they had the bus out of sight.

Earl appeared in the door and Zach gave her a thumbs-up as he ran past the bus towards the garage.

"Hey, babe, ain't this some kind of place?" Earl said as he climbed the steps.

Zelda heard a gasp. She turned and saw Kendall, white as a sheet, gawking at Earl.

Kendall watched Stephen Lloyd move briskly up the stairs onto the bus. *He no longer had a cast on his leg.* Stephen barely glanced at Kendall as he grabbed her by the arm, shoved her onto the front seat, and sat down beside her.

She slid as far away from him as she could. "Stephen, what's going on?"

He snorted "Come on, Kendall. You're a smart girl. You must have figured it out by now. Does the word *kidnapping* mean anything to you?"

"But why?"

Stephen rubbed his fingers together in front of her face. "Dough, babe. Why else?"

"But why you? Why are you involved in this?"

Stephen cocked his head to the side and flashed a smug smile. "Why not? Because you thought I was one of your rich polo friends?"

Kendall took a deep breath and turned away as the bus began to move forward towards the garage. *Margaret had been right about Stephen being a phony. Too bad she hadn't figured it out earlier.*

"Hey!" Stephen grabbed her chin roughly and forced her to look at him. "You blew me off last night, but you're not going to get away with it today. You look at me when I'm talking to you."

The bitter taste of bile rose in Kendall's throat, but she looked him in the eye.

Stephen smirked. "That's better." He loosened his grasp and caressed her cheek before releasing his hold on her.

Kendall flinched and he gave a low laugh. "What's the matter, you don't like it when I touch you? You better get used to it, because you and I are going to be spending some time together."

"Earl!" Zelda yelled, slamming on the brakes and bringing the bus to a sudden halt.

Stephen turned slowly towards Zelda. "What?"

Zelda scowled at him in the mirror. "I was talking to you."

"Sorry, babe. I was busy with Kendall."

Zelda opened her mouth as if to respond, then closed it and gave him an icy stare. "When you have time to focus back on *business,* just let me know."

Stephen snickered and glanced out the window. "Zach's got the door closed," he said, rising and springing towards the steps. "Get the kids off the bus and into the storage room."

Zelda jumped up from her seat and waved her arm at Kendall. "You heard Earl. Get the kids off the bus."

Kendall stared at Stephen's retreating back. *Earl.* So Stephen Lloyd wasn't his real name. She wondered if he was a McGraw, too. She rose slowly and turned towards the back of the bus. "Come on, girls. We're going to get off the bus for a little while."

"Are we at the Land of Little Horses?" Caitlin asked.

Kendall shook her head. "No."

"Should I bring my backpack and my lunch box?" Emma asked.

"No, just leave everything on the bus," Kendall said, ushering the girls up the aisle.

Zelda stood at the front of the bus, waving her arm impatiently. "Come on, get them moving."

Kendall followed the girls off the bus, with Zelda right on her heels. She reached for the girls, gathering them around her. "Stay right here with me."

Zelda snapped her fingers at Zach. "Earl wants them in the storage room."

Zach steered Kendall towards an open doorway in the corner of the large garage. "Over there."

When they reached the doorway, Kendall motioned for the kids to go in. "Come on, let's go in here, like Mrs. White said." Several of the girls walked into the room, but Emma and Caitlin held back.

"I don't want to," Emma said. "It's dark in there."

"I don't, either. I want to go see the little horses," Caitlin said.

"We can't see the horses right now," Kendall said, giving them a gentle push on their backs. "Go on."

Emma planted her feet and didn't move. "But why, Miss Waters?"

Kendall saw Zach raise the gun and take a step towards them, and she grabbed Emma's hand and dragged her though the door. "Emma, just do as I say!"

"Stop. You're hurting me," Emma cried.

The light from the garage spilled into the long closetlike room, and Kendall could make out piles of winter horse blankets folded neatly on shelves along one wall. The opposite side was lined with foldout chrome blanket racks, and a bandage box was attached to the end wall.

Kendall sat on the floor beneath the blanket racks and pulled Emma onto her lap. She gestured to the other girls to sit next to her. "Come on, everyone, sit close to me."

Zach closed the door behind them with a loud thunk, plunging them into darkness.

mma threw her arms around Kendall's neck. "I'm scared," she whispered.

Kendall felt several small hands grab her arms.

"What's that spooky noise?" Caitlin asked. "It sounds like a ghost."

Kendall stroked Emma's hair. "Shhh, it's okay. Don't be scared. The sound you hear is just pigeons cooing. There is a big pigeon house at the back of this building."

"Why did they make us come in here?" Emma asked, sniffling.

Kendall hesitated. *What should she tell the kids?* "I think they are playing some kind of game with us."

"I don't like this game," Emma said.

"Me neither," several other voices chimed in.

Neither do I, Kendall thought grimly.

"I don't like Mrs. White," Caitlin said. "I think she's mean."

"Listen, I have an idea," Kendall said, struggling to keep the tremor out of her voice. "Why don't we tell stories? Does anyone know a good one?"

"You tell us one, Miss Waters," Emma said.

"All right. Let me see; how about the story of the Midnight Pony? Come on, everyone snuggle close."

Kendall embellished the story and tried to drag it out as long as she could, but after awhile the girls started to get restless.

"I'm hungry," Emma said. "Is it lunchtime yet?"

Kendall raised her wrist to within a few inches of her face and peered at the dial of her Rolex. She was surprised to see the faint glow of the hands reveal that it was only ten-thirty. It seemed as if they had been locked in the closet for hours, but in reality it probably hadn't been more than thirty minutes.

"It's not quite time for lunch yet, Emma," she said.

Emma squirmed on her lap. "I don't want to be on the field trip anymore, Miss Waters. I want to go home now."

Kendall heard the sound of raised voices outside the doorway. She stretched her arms out in the darkness and drew the girls closer to her. "Come on, everyone, let's hold hands."

The door burst open and Zach appeared. He motioned towards Kendall. "Come on."

"Let's go, girls," Kendall said.

Zach shook his head. "Not the kids. Just you."

Kendall tightened her embrace around the girls. "I'm not leaving them alone here in the dark."

"Oh yeah?" Zach put his hand on the gun that was tucked into the waist-band of his jeans.

"All right," Kendall said, quickly removing Emma from her lap and ris-ing to her feet. "But please turn a light on. Or at least give them a flashlight."

Zach glared at her, but he flipped a switch outside the door, which illuminated a fluorescent light in the center of the room.

"Thank you," Kendall said, stepping around the girls and walking towards him. "Girls, I'll be back soon."

Emma reached her hand out. "Miss Waters, please don't leave us all alone."

But before Kendall could respond, Zach pulled her through the doorway and slammed the door shut. Kendall glared at him. "Zach, the kids are terrified. Why are you doing this?"

"Stop dicking around, Zach, and get on over here with her," Zelda bellowed from somewhere across the room.

Zach pushed Kendall ahead of him towards where the bus and blue car were parked in the center of the garage. "Get moving."

The garage appeared to be deserted, but Kendall quickly scanned the area, trying to determine where Zelda was. They rounded the front end of the bus, and Kendall saw Zelda standing before a man who lay on the floor with his hands tied behind his back. The man was facing away from Kendall, but she was pretty sure, even from the back, that he was Albert, the Worthingtons' farm manager.

Zelda's arms were folded across her chest and her mouth was twisted into an ugly scowl. "There are two ways we can do this, mister. You can go ahead and cooperate, and things'll be easy for you, or you can give us a hard time, and Zach here will have to do some convincing."

The man didn't respond, and as Zach and Kendall drew close, Zelda looked at Kendall and shook her head. "This man here don't seem so smart about cooperating with us like you've been doing, camp counselor. I'll give you one minute here to try to talk some sense into him."

Zelda grabbed Kendall's arm and thrust her to the ground in front of the man.

Kendall gasped. It was Albert all right. One of his eyes was swollen shut, and blood oozed from both nostrils. She placed a hand on his shoulder. "Albert, are you all right?"

Albert rolled his head back slightly so he could see her out of his good eye. "I'm doing about as well as you could expect, considering these thugs here think they can just waltz in and make themselves at home at High Meadow."

"See what I mean?" Zelda snapped. "I don't think Albert here understands the seriousness of the situation. Zach, go ahead and show him we mean business."

"Wait." Kendall held her hand up. "Don't hurt him again. Let me talk to him."

Zach looked at Zelda, who nodded, and Kendall let out a sigh of relief. "Tell me what you want from Albert."

"For starters, we need to know what vehicles are on the farm and where the keys are at," Zelda said.

Albert simply grunted in response and Kendall leaned closer to him. "Albert, I know you want to do your job to protect High Meadow, but there's more at risk here than just property. There are seven little girls locked up in the storage room, and you and I need to do whatever we can to make sure they get back home safely to their parents."

"That's right. You listen up to what she says," Zelda said.

Albert glared at Zelda, then focused on Kendall. "What's the guarantee they're going to release the kids?"

There is no guarantee, she thought. But the alternative was unthinkable. Kendall swallowed hard and looked at Zelda. "Will you let us go if Albert tells you about the vehicles?"

Zelda's lip curled into a snide smile. "I ain't promising that, but it'd be a good start. If you both play this right, you and the kids will get out of here just fine. We don't want to hurt nobody, do we, Zach?"

Zach shrugged. "Not unless we have to."

Kendall squeezed Albert's shoulder. "Please, Albert, tell them."

Albert wet his lips with the tip of his tongue. "There's the farm truck. It's parked behind the barn. And I have an old Toyota Camry. It's got some miles on it, but it runs good. If you need transportation, take it."

"Where's it at?" Zelda asked.

"My house," Albert said. "Farther down the drive, past the equipment shed."

Zelda nodded at Zach. "Go check both of them out. Earl's outside. He'll go with you."

"Where are the keys at?" Zach asked.

Albert lowered his gaze towards the jumble of keys dangling from his belt.

"I'll get it," Kendall said quickly, unsnapping the key ring.

Zach snatched it from her hand. "See you in a few," he said to Zelda.

55

elda had untied Albert's hands and begrudgingly agreed to let Kendall wash off Albert's face, but she was perched on a nearby tack trunk, smoking a cigarette, with her gun pointed at them.

"Do you know what they're after?" Albert asked in a low voice, standing tall as Kendall wet a rub rag in the sink and dabbed at his nose.

"No, but I know who they are, and they're not people we want to mess with," she said quietly.

Kendall wiped harder and winced as Albert's nose made a crunching sound. "I'm sorry."

Albert flinched but squared his shoulders and didn't say anything.

"Did Zach do this to you?" she asked.

"No, it was the big guy. I think they called him Earl."

Kendall shuddered. *Earl.* She had to stop thinking of him as Stephen Lloyd.

Albert squinted at her. "Did they hurt you or any of the kids?"

"No, and I hope they won't harm us as long as we comply with their demands."

Albert set his jaw and looked at Zelda out of the corner of his good eye. "Until they don't need us no more. Then what will they do with us?"

Kendall didn't answer. She rinsed the rag in clean water and handed it to him, then turned to Zelda. "There's ice in the cooler on the bus. Can I get some to put on his eye to take the swelling down?"

"I ain't worried about his eye," Zelda said, exhaling a cloud of smoke as she stood and pushed the button to raise the garage door.

Kendall heard the sound of tires on the gravel drive, and a moment later

Earl drove a green truck through the open door, followed by a brown Toyota Camry with Zach at the wheel. Both vehicles rolled to a stop beside the blue car and Earl and Zach climbed out.

Zelda pointed to the words *High Meadow* written in white on the side of the truck and snorted. "Ain't it kind of like advertising where we're at if you take that?"

Earl slammed the door and nodded. "Yeah, it's a problem. So we'll use your car for the accident and the Toyota for the getaway car." He turned to Zach. "Zach, go put a new set of plates on the Toyota."

"Why's it have to be *my* car in the accident?" Zelda demanded.

"You won't need that old rust bucket after this," Earl said. "You'll have enough money to buy yourself any damn car you want to."

Zelda's frown slid into a grin. "Yeah, I will, won't I? I think I'll buy me a red Corvette."

"Sounds good, babe." Earl jerked his head towards Albert. "Lock the old man up with the kids, so Zach and me can hit the road."

Zelda waved her gun at Albert. "Get going, old man."

Albert scowled at her but moved towards the storage room door.

Earl grabbed Kendall by the arm. "Come on. We're going for a ride."

Kendall strained to turn towards the storage room. "What about the kids? They don't know Albert. You're going to scare them to death if you put a stranger in there."

Zelda glanced over her shoulder. "Honey, we don't really give a shit."

Earl laughed and shoved Kendall towards the cars. "Hey, Zach, find something to tie her hands with."

Zach retrieved a loop of rope from the trunk of the blue car and tossed it to Earl, who caught it with his free hand.

"Put your hands behind your back," Earl ordered.

Kendall shook her head but did as he said. "You don't have to tie me up. I'm not going to do anything."

Earl pulled the rope tight and spun her around, his face only inches from hers. "That's right, Kendall, you're not going to do anything stupid, because if you do, the kids are going to pay the price. You know that, don't you?"

Kendall swallowed hard and nodded.

Earl twisted her hair in his hand and yanked her head back. "I didn't hear you."

His grip pulled at Kendall's scalp and tears started to fill her eyes, but she managed to keep her voice steady. "Yes, I know that."

Zelda appeared at Earl's side. "The old guy's locked up."

Earl gave Kendall a hard look and let go of her hair. "Tell Kendall what you're going to do to the kids if she tries any funny business."

Zelda held up her gun. "You stop cooperating, I'll use this."

Kendall stared her in the eye. "Could you really shoot an innocent child?"

Zelda gave her a twisted smile. "Trust me; you don't want to test me."

Earl opened the driver's door. "Put her in the trunk."

*K*endall concentrated on memorizing the turns Earl made after leaving High Meadow, and when the car pulled off the gravel road onto asphalt, she was pretty certain they were headed north towards Leesburg on James Monroe Highway. They traveled straight for a while, but then Earl took a series of sharp right and left turns on paved roads, which left her totally disoriented.

She could tell from the traffic noise and the stopping and starting that they must be on a heavily traveled road, but she had no idea where they were. And no clue as to where they might be headed.

After a few minutes, the road became bumpy, and it sounded as if they were on gravel again. The roughness of the road increased, but Earl didn't slow down, and Kendall was thrown repeatedly against the trunk lid as the wheels dipped into holes and ruts. The rugged road continued for several minutes, and then the ride became smooth, and it felt as if they were back on asphalt. Kendall tried to think of a road that changed from asphalt to gravel and back again, but she couldn't come up with one.

The car jerked to a stop and Kendall heard a car door slam, and then the sound of another, more distant, car door slamming. She heard footsteps approaching; then the lid of the trunk popped open and bright sunlight streamed in.

Earl reached in and grabbed her roughly by her arm, pulling her to a sitting position. "Get out."

Kendall's muscles were cramped from being confined in the small space, and she looked around as she stretched her legs slowly, trying to get her circulation going. She heard the distant noise of speeding traffic and then realized they were on Sycolin Road, just beyond the overpass to the Toll Road. *Where in the world were they taking her?*

"Come on, we don't have all day," Earl said, yanking her to her feet.

Her legs were asleep and she stumbled and would have fallen to the ground if Zach hadn't reached out and steadied her.

Earl slammed the trunk lid down. "Get her in the backseat before someone sees her."

Kendall heard an approaching car, and Zach must have heard it, too, because he dragged her to the rear door and yanked it open. "Hurry up and get inside," he said, pushing her onto the backseat. "And stay down."

Zach slammed the door closed, and before Kendall lay flat on the seat she saw a car round the bend in the road and come towards them. Zach leaned against the car so his body blocked the view into the rear window. Kendall could see Earl standing a few feet from him.

The other vehicle stopped next to them, and Kendall heard a man's voice say, "You guys all right? You got car problems or something?"

"No, we're just chatting. Thanks for stopping, though. That's very kind of you," Earl said in his smooth Stephen Lloyd voice.

"All right. Take care," the man said, and Kendall heard the sound of the car accelerating.

Once the sound had faded, Earl said, "Let's get moving before another car comes by."

The back door opened and Earl pushed Kendall's legs to the floor and slid onto the seat. "Sit up."

Kendall struggled to a sitting position in time to see Earl pull a knife out of his back pocket and flip it open. He held the blade in front of her face.

"You see this? If I have to use it on you, it won't be pretty." He pressed the blade against her cheek, just hard enough for her to feel its sharpness. "You understand?"

"Yes."

"Good. Now turn around."

He withdrew the blade from her face and pushed her upper body away from him. "Hold out your hands."

Kendall's hand were tied so tightly behind her that she could barely move them, but she did her best to inch them in Earl's direction. She felt him slide the knife blade between her wrists, and a moment later her hands were free.

Earl gripped her by the chin and brought her face close to his. "Now you listen to me and you listen good, Kendall. What's about to happen, we've planned a long time, and it's all going to work just fine unless you decide to do something dumb and try to screw things up."

"I won't."

Earl nodded. "That's right, you won't. You know why? Because if you do, Zelda is going to kill those kids, one by one, while the others watch. And the old man, too. Understand?"

Kendall closed her eyes.

"Look at me!"

She opened her eyes, and tears slid down her cheeks.

"Don't go crying, Kendall. I don't got time for that," Earl said, jerking her chin.

"I just don't want anything to happen to the girls." Her voice was a whisper.

"It won't if you go along with the plan." Earl let go of her face. "Here's the way it's going to play out. There's going to be a car accident, and there will be lots of rescue workers and cops around. But you're not going to try to talk to one of them, are you?"

Kendall shook her head and Earl smirked. "That's right. You're going to follow my lead and act however I tell you to, okay?"

She nodded.

"All right. You're going to keep your eyes on me, and when I signal you to move, that's what you're going to do, right?"

"Right."

"And if you don't do what I say, what's going to happen?"

She took a deep breath. "You're going to call Zelda."

"That's right," he said. "And what's Zelda going to do?"

Kendall stared at him and shook her head.

Earl raised the knife blade and ran it along her neck. "Come on, Kendall, I want to hear you say it."

She clenched her teeth. "She's going to shoot the kids."

"That's right, Kendall. Zelda's going to shoot the kids, and she's going to kill them. *One by one.* I want you to remember that."

57

endall watched from the backseat as Earl turned on his emergency flashers and followed Zach's car off the highway. Zach got out of the Toyota, raised the hood, and tied a white rag to the radio antenna, then walked back to the blue car and opened the front passenger door.

"Where are the keys?" Earl asked him.

"Right here." Zach dangled the key chain from his finger as he dropped into the passenger seat.

Earl nodded towards the Toyota. "Put them under the floor mat on the driver's side."

"Why?"

"In case we don't all make it out, I want the keys in the car."

Zach stared at him. "You mean in case I don't make it out, don't you?"

Earl gave him a steely-eyed gaze. "Put the keys under the mat, Zach. And leave your wallet there, too."

"Son of a bitch," Zach muttered, jumping out of the car.

He stormed up to the Toyota and tossed the keys under the mat, then returned to the car, slamming the door after he got in.

"Thanks," Earl said with a sarcastic smile. He handed a navy windbreaker to Zach. "Here, put this on."

Zach scowled. "Are you nuts? It's like ninety degrees out there."

Earl picked up another windbreaker from the front seat and shrugged into it. "It ain't for warmth; it's so no one will see your gun."

Zach didn't respond, but he slid the jacket on.

Earl eased the car into the lane of traffic headed westbound on Route 7 and maneuvered the car into the far left lane of three lanes of traffic. He put his left-turn signal on as they neared the intersection with Belmont Ridge Road, then pulled to a stop at the red light.

"Figures Zelda would have a car with a clock that don't work," Earl said, pounding the dashboard with his fist. "What time is it?"

Zach lifted the sleeve of the windbreaker and looked at his watch. "We're okay. It's eleven-forty-five."

Earl nodded as he got a green arrow and began the turn. "Right on schedule."

He made a U-turn, heading east on Route 7. Traffic was light for the normally busy highway, and Earl stayed in the left lane, keeping his speed steady at fifty miles per hour.

They had traveled about a hundred yards when Zach jerked around in his seat and peered out the back window. "Do you hear that?"

Earl frowned. "What?"

"A siren. Is that him already?" Zach's blue eyes darted wildly between Earl and the view through the back window.

"Gwen hasn't called yet. It can't be him." Earl slowed the car and looked in the rearview mirror. "Besides, there's a hospital up ahead. It's probably another ambulance."

"What if it isn't?" Zach asked, breathing heavily.

"Then I'll pull in front of it."

Zach waved his arm frantically towards where they had left the Toyota. "But we're too far from the car."

"Calm down and shut the fuck up, Zach," Earl yelled, keeping his eyes focused on the rearview mirror.

The sound of the siren grew louder and Earl pulled halfway onto the center median of grass but kept driving. "It's not him."

"How do you know?" Zach asked, still peering out the back window.

"There's no cop car behind it."

There was a loud whoop of the siren as the ambulance passed them, and Earl pulled back onto the highway.

Zach faced forward and settled down in his seat. "That freaked me out."

"Yeah, I noticed." Earl flipped on his left-turn signal and moved into the turning lane at the intersection with Lansdowne Boulevard.

Earl turned left and drove past the hospital. As he made a U-turn at a four-way stop sign, his cell phone rang. He pressed the call button and held it to his ear. "Hello?"

He grunted in satisfaction as he listened, then ended the call and looked at Zach. "That was Gwen. The ambulance is on its way."

Zach let out a whoop and made a fist in the air.

"What's going to happen?" Kendall asked.

"Fireworks," Earl replied, pulling to a stop at the light.

"Want me to pop the hood?" Zach asked.

"Wait until the cars in front of us go, so I'm first in line."

They waited in silence until the light turned green and the cars in front of them began to move. Earl eased up on the gas and moved forward until he was first at the light, then put the car in park and turned on the flashers.

"Now?"

Earl nodded. "Yeah, then stand out there and wave the cars around us. When I give you the signal, drop the hood and get your ass back in here."

When Zach was out of the car, Earl looked over his shoulder at Kendall. "Move over behind my seat and fasten your seat belt."

"Why?" she asked, doing as he said.

"You'll see." Earl stared at the highway, drumming his fingers restlessly on the steering wheel.

Zach's face appeared from behind the hood. "I hear a siren," he shouted, pointing towards the west.

Earl nodded at him and straightened in his seat.

Kendall's mouth grew dry as she scanned the road, waiting for the ambulance to come into view. As the seconds ticked away, she realized she was holding her breath, and she wiped her sweaty palms on her shorts and forced herself to breathe.

Earl gave a short blast on the horn. "That's it!"

Zach dropped the hood and dashed back to the passenger seat.

Kendall watched an ambulance with its flashers on roll along Route 7, followed by a sheriff's car. The ambulance slowed to allow a car in front of it to pull over, then moved on, gaining speed until it was at the intersection, where it hovered briefly before accelerating into the turn.

"Hold on!" Earl yelled as he punched the accelerator, steering the car directly into the path of the ambulance.

"Oh my God," Kendall screamed, gripping the door armrest with one hand and bracing herself against the back of the driver's seat with the other.

Earl continued on a steady course, gunning the car headfirst towards the ambulance, and then, just before the moment of impact, he turned the wheel hard to the left, directing the brunt of the force towards Zach's door.

*K*endall heard a man's voice in the distance, faintly calling her name, but she was too dazed to figure out where it came from. She heard the voice again. Then someone shook her shoulder, causing a throbbing pain to shoot down her arm.

"No," she moaned, trying to pull away from the person's grip.

"Kendall, come on, get out of the car."

Kendall forced her eyes open and saw Stephen Lloyd leaning over her, tugging at the seat belt buckle. She tried to speak, to ask him where they were and what had happened, but she couldn't get her lips to move.

He released the buckle and yanked the seat belt off her chest. "Come on," he said, grabbing her arm and trying to pull her from the car.

The pain that shot through her was unbearable. Kendall groaned and tried to lean away from him. "Stop. That hurts."

"All right, settle down." He let go of her arm and grabbed her around the waist. "Let's go."

Kendall leaned against him and let him lift her from the car. "What happened?"

"Can you stand up?"

"I think so." She frowned at him as he dropped his arm and let her feet fall to the ground. "Where are we?"

He tightened his hold on her waist and drew her with him towards the back of the car. "Come on, there's no time for this shit."

Kendall stared at him. *Why was Stephen talking to her like that? And where were they?* There were people shouting behind her and she struggled out of his grasp and turned around.

"Oh my God," she said, staggering backwards. The right side of the car she had been sitting in was crushed, and a group of rescue workers were huddled around the front passenger door. An ambulance with a dented front end was parked a few yards away.

She felt Stephen's arms encircle her middle and almost lift her off her feet. "Get moving, damn it, or I'll make a call to Zelda."

Zelda. Suddenly, it all came back to her. *He wasn't Stephen Lloyd.* His name was Earl. And he and Zelda McGraw had kidnapped her and the girls.

Kendall heard a whistle and saw a sheriff's deputy standing near the front of the car. He waved his arms at them. "Move back. Clear the way for the rescue squad."

Kendall turned to Earl. "Is Zach still in the car?"

"Yeah." He dragged her towards the rear of the nearby ambulance.

"Aren't you going to try to help him?"

"Forget about Zach. There's nothing I can do for him now." Earl continued towards the ambulance, without even so much as a glance towards the car.

"Okay, this is it." He paused and gave her a hard stare. "Remember, Kendall, those kids'll die if you don't do what I say. Got it?"

She nodded.

"Good." Earl pulled her towards a sheriff's deputy who stood by the back doors of the ambulance. He looked young, probably in his early thirties. He was a good six inches shorter than Earl and had a much slighter build.

"Deputy, I need your help. My wife was in the car accident and she's hurt. She hit her head, and I think she broke her arm. Can she lie down in the ambulance?"

The deputy looked at Kendall and shook his head. "I'm sorry, ma'am. They're transporting an inmate in this ambulance. The rescue workers from this ambulance are busy with the injured passenger right now. There's another ambulance on the way. It should be here in a few minutes."

Earl stepped to the side, turning his head so the deputy couldn't see his expression, and glared at Kendall. "Do something," he mouthed.

Kendall put a shaky hand to her forehead. "I'm feeling faint. Is there someplace I can sit down?"

The deputy reached out to steady her, and Earl whipped out his gun and hit the deputy hard across the side of his head, catching him under the arms as he slumped towards the ground.

"Open the ambulance doors," Earl ordered.

Kendall couldn't raise her left arm, and her right hand was shaking so hard that she could barely grasp the handle.

"I said open it!"

She tried, but her hand slipped off the handle.

"Worthless bitch." Earl supported the deputy with one arm and yanked the door open with his free hand.

He aimed his gun inside and took a quick look, then grabbed the deputy under both arms again. He nudged Kendall with his shoulder. "Get on in there."

Kendall climbed into the ambulance and hesitated in the doorway. There were no rescue personnel in the ambulance, just a man lying on the stretcher, clad in orange-and-white-striped clothing.

Earl shoved her towards the foot of the stretcher and hoisted the deputy into the ambulance. "Move over." He hopped up after the deputy and slammed the door closed.

"Hey, man, get these cuffs off me," the man on the stretcher said, sitting up as far as he was able with his hands secured to the bar of the stretcher. "The key's on the cop's belt."

Earl searched the deputy's belt and removed the key for the handcuffs. "Long time no see, Zeb," he said, leaning over the stretcher and unlocking the handcuffs.

Kendall shrank closer to the door. *The man on the stretcher was Zeb McGraw.*

McGraw sat upright and rubbed his wrists. "Everything going the way we planned it?"

"Like clockwork." Earl squatted down next to the deputy. "Help me get his uniform off."

McGraw and Earl removed the deputy's uniform down to his T-shirt, boxers, and brown socks, then handcuffed him to the stretcher.

"All right, man, get the uniform on and we're ready to roll."

McGraw eyed Kendall as he stripped off his prison clothing. "Who's she?"

"The kids' camp counselor," Earl said, checking the ammunition in the deputy's gun.

"So you know my little friend, Samantha." McGraw sneered at her, revealing a set of stained, crooked teeth. "I can't wait to see her again."

Kendall lowered her eyes and didn't respond.

McGraw stepped into the deputy's trousers, swearing as he tugged at them. "These pants are too fucking small."

The whoop of a siren sounded nearby and Earl peered out the window. "Shit. The other ambulance is here. Forget about putting the uniform on; we've got to make a run for it."

McGraw pulled his prison pants back on and Earl grabbed Kendall by the arm. "As soon as I open the door, we're making a run for it. Remember, I'll have a gun to your back. If you try anything funny or hold me back, I'll shoot you. You understand?"

Kendall nodded.

Earl tightened his grip and eased the door open a crack. "We're heading for a brown Toyota parked across the highway with its hood raised," he said over his shoulder to McGraw.

"I'll be right behind you."

Earl drew a deep breath. "It's show time." He flung open the door and thrust Kendall out first, then jumped out behind her.

He poked her in the back with the gun, propelling her forward. "All right, get moving." Earl walked briskly as he steered her around the back of the sheriff's car and headed for the grass median.

"Hey, wait a minute," someone behind them shouted, and Earl pushed her into a run. They sprinted across the wide grass strip and into the lane of westbound traffic, causing tires to screech as drivers slammed on their brakes to avoid hitting them. Kendall heard the sound of pounding footsteps behind them, but she had no idea whether they came from McGraw or from someone who was pursuing them.

"Stop or I'll shoot," a voice bellowed behind them.

Earl stopped and swung Kendall around, his gun pointed at her head. "Drop your gun or she's dead," Earl shouted, continuing to move sideways towards the car.

The deputy who had waved them away from the rescue squad was approaching them from the median, his gun drawn.

"I mean it!" Earl thrust the barrel of his gun against Kendall's temple. "Drop the gun."

The deputy hesitated for an instant, then slowly placed his weapon on the ground.

"Get behind me," Earl said in a loud hiss to McGraw. "We'll get in the car from the passenger side. I'll drive and you sit in the back with your gun on her."

McGraw ignored him, leveling his gun at the deputy. "I'm gonna take him out."

Earl gave a quick sideways glance and shook his head. "Forget about him. Close the hood and open the doors. *Now*."

CHAPTER

59

nne had just finished giving Samantha her medicine and tucking her
back into bed when she heard the front doorbell ring. "I'll be back up in a
minute," she said, kissing Samantha on the forehead. "You try to get some sleep."

"Okay, Mommy. I'm really tired." Samantha rolled onto her side and
closed her eyes.

The doorbell sounded again, and, as Anne hurried downstairs to answer
it, the phone began to ring. She grabbed the cordless phone off the hall table
as she passed by on her way to the front door.

"Hello?" She held the phone to her ear as she turned the handle to open
the door.

"Good afternoon, Anne; it's Patrick Talbot."

"Hello, Patrick." Anne opened the door. Samantha's guard, Ben, stood
outside, along with a woman, and Anne pointed apologetically towards the
phone and motioned for them to step inside.

"Do you know where I can reach Doug?" Patrick asked.

"He's transporting a horse; you can try him on his cell."

"I already tried that, but I didn't get an answer."

"I spoke with him about an hour ago and he was getting ready to leave
the Equine Medical Center and head for Richard Evan Clarke's farm. The
cell service isn't the best in that area. He was probably out of range when you
tried him. Do you want me to give him a message when he gets home?"

There was a long pause. Patrick cleared his throat. "I'm afraid I have
some bad news. I had hoped to speak with Doug."

Anne frowned and perched on the edge of one of the hall chairs. "What's
the news?"

Another pause. "I just learned that Zeb McGraw has escaped from jail."

Anne gasped. "*What?*"

"I'm sorry to have to tell you over the phone, Anne. I've assigned Ben and another guard to stay with you in the house. They should be there any moment."

Anne glanced at Ben and the woman. "They just arrived. Tell me what you know. When did this happen?"

"The details are sketchy at this point. The only information I have is that McGraw escaped sometime this morning and is on the loose."

"Oh my God." Anne sank back in the chair.

"Anne, I'm concerned that I haven't been able to get in touch with Doug. I've also tried to reach Mike, the guard who's with him, but I haven't been able to get him on his cell."

Anne clutched the arm of the chair. "Do you think something's happened to Doug?"

"No, I'm not saying that. I just want Doug to know about this as soon as possible."

"Me, too." The phone shook in Anne's hand and she paused and took a deep breath. "I'll call Richard's farm right now and see if Doug's there."

"Great. If you reach him before I do, would you ask him to have Mike call me?" Patrick asked.

"Sure."

"All right. And, Anne, there's something else you and Doug should know."

She gripped the phone tighter. "What?"

"McGraw is armed."

Anne ended the call and turned to Ben. "That was Patrick Talbot on the phone. He told me about Zeb McGraw."

Ben stepped forward. "Mrs. Cummings, I'm sure the news of McGraw's escape comes as quite a shock to you, but I want to assure you that we'll do all we can to keep you and your family safe. Zeb McGraw is probably miles away by now, but even if he were to make his way here, there are plenty of guards patrolling the farm. And Charly and I will be stationed here in the house."

The woman gave a quick nod. "Hello, Mrs. Cummings. I'm Charly."

"Nice to meet you, Charly." Anne turned to Ben. "Do you need me to show you around the house?"

Ben gestured towards the phone in her hand. "It sounds like you need to call Mr. Cummings. We're fine on our own, if that's all right with you."

Anne nodded. "Samantha's in bed upstairs. Her room is the second door on the right. Would you mind keeping an eye on her until I get up there? I know her room is on the second floor, but still. . . ."

"Of course, I understand," Ben said. "I'll stay with Samantha, since she knows me, and Charly will be down here."

Anne nodded. "I'll be in the study, if you need me."

She found Richard Evan Clarke's barn phone number in Doug's Rolodex and pressed the numbers on the cordless phone.

It rang six times and then a breathless voice with a British accent said, "Hello, Old Mill Farm. This is Sara speaking."

"Hello, Sara. This is Anne Cummings. I'm looking for my husband. Is he there?"

"He sure is. Mr. Cummings arrived here just a little while ago with Chancellor. Would you like to speak with him?"

Anne let out a sigh of relief and sank into Doug's desk chair. "Yes, please, Sara."

"Okay, hold on a moment while I fetch him. He's outside grazing Chancellor."

The line was silent for several moments, except for an occasional whinny, and then Anne heard the sound of footsteps on the brick aisle.

"You're not in labor, are you?"

Anne breathed a sigh of relief at the sound of Doug's voice. "No, I'm not in labor."

"Okay, good. You had me scared for a minute. What's up?"

Anne hesitated. *How should she tell him?*

"Anne?"

She drew in a sharp breath. "Doug, I have to tell you something."

"Are you crying?"

"No," she said, lying.

"Hey, what's wrong?"

Then, before she could respond, he said, "Oh God, is it Samantha?"

"No, she's fine," she said quickly.

"Then what is it?"

Anne leaned her head back against the chair and closed her eyes. "Zeb McGraw escaped from jail this morning."

"That can't be!"

"I wish you were right, but Patrick Talbot just called here and gave me the news."

"*Holy Christ.* I don't believe it. How did he escape?"

"I don't know. Patrick didn't have any details, just that McGraw escaped and he's armed."

There was a long pause. "Are you and Sam at home?"

"Yes."

"Is there a guard in the house with you?"

"Two. And Patrick wants you to tell Mike to call him."

"All right. I'm on my way home."

CHAPTER

61

*K*endall succumbed to the numbness that crept through her body and wondered fleetingly if she were going into shock.

"Hey, I asked you for the gate code," Earl shouted.

She was lying on the floor in the back of a painting contractor's van, the third vehicle Earl had carjacked since leaving the accident scene.

Kendall didn't bother to raise her head. "One, two, three, four, pound."

McGraw snorted. "That's a stupid security code."

"No shit," Earl replied.

Kendall closed her eyes and concentrated on the rhythmic crunching sound of the tires on the gravel drive.

"Look at that motherfucker of a house," McGraw said.

"Yeah, these people are rolling in dough. Too bad we don't got one of their kids."

McGraw laughed. "Maybe we can kidnap one of their horses."

"This is it," Earl said, bringing the van to a stop. "Keep an eye on her. I'm going to go push the button to raise the door."

"She don't look like she's going nowhere."

"Don't underestimate her."

Kendall opened her eyes and the interior of the van seemed to swim around her in a circular motion, triggering a surge of nausea. She forced herself to focus on a spot on the dashboard until the rotation stopped and her stomach settled.

"Well, well, look who's awake," McGraw said.

Without moving her head, Kendall shifted her gaze to Zeb McGraw, who was leering at her from the passenger seat. His pale green eyes protruded from sunken eye sockets, and as he winked at her, Kendall closed her eyes again.

She heard Earl climb back into the car, and McGraw said, "Sleeping Beauty's awake. I think she and I may have some fun together later."

Earl grunted in response and drove the van into the garage.

They both got out of the vehicle and Kendall heard McGraw say, "Hey, sis, you're looking good."

Zelda laughed. "You could use a little sunshine, bro."

So, Zelda was Zeb McGraw's sister, not his wife, Kendall thought. That meant Zach was McGraw's nephew.

"Hey, babe, everything go okay here?" Earl asked.

"Her damned cell phone rang a couple of times," Zelda said. "But other than that, things have been quiet."

"That's good," Earl said. "They must have figured out the bus never arrived."

"Are we going to call them?"

"Not yet. We'll let them sweat for a couple of hours first; then Zeb'll make the call."

Kendall heard the back doors of the van open and light streamed across the floor.

"Come on, time to get up," Earl said, grabbing Kendall's leg.

She turned towards Earl and sat up slowly, seeing two images of Earl float dizzily before her as she inched her way to the door.

He tugged on her leg. "Come on, we don't got all day."

"I'm dizzy," Kendall said, slowly lowering her feet to the ground.

Earl pulled her from the van and gripped her by the elbow. "You'll get over it."

"Hey, where's Zach?" Zelda asked, sticking her head inside the van.

Earl steered Kendall towards the storage room. "Zach stayed in the car and faked being hurt so we could get away."

Kendall stared openmouthed at Earl and he jerked her arm and muttered, "Keep your mouth shut."

Zelda whirled towards McGraw. "Zeb, you son of a bitch, you left my kid behind?"

"Chill out, sis. I didn't even know Zach was in the fucking car."

"It was Zach's idea," Earl said over his shoulder. "He's going to make a run for it from the hospital."

"That wasn't our plan," Zelda called after him.

Earl opened the door to the storage room. "Well, babe, the plan changed."

he phone rang while Anne was warming soup for Samantha, but it stopped after the second ring, so she assumed that Doug had answered it. A moment later, he appeared in the kitchen, holding the cordless phone.

"Anne, it's Margaret on the phone. She wants to know if you've heard from Kendall this morning."

"Not since I called her to tell her that Samantha was sick. Why?"

Doug raised the phone to his ear. "Anne hasn't heard from her, Margaret."

He nodded, his mouth set in a firm line. "Yes, I think you should call the Sheriff's Office."

Anne stopped stirring the soup and walked over to Doug.

"All right, Margaret. Please keep us informed. And call us if there is anything we can do." Doug pushed the button to end the call and set the phone on the kitchen table.

"What's wrong?" Anne asked.

He shifted her, so she stood in front of him, and put both hands on her shoulders. "The bus for the field trip never arrived in Gettysburg, and Margaret can't reach Kendall on her cell phone. Margaret heard Kendall tell you this morning that she would call to check up on Samantha, so she was calling to see if you had heard from her."

Anne felt as if someone had knocked the wind out of her. "*The whole busload of kids is missing?*"

He nodded grimly. "Or at least out of contact."

She covered her mouth with her hands. "Samantha was supposed to be on that bus."

"I know."

"Do you think this has anything to do with . . . "

"McGraw? Let's not jump to conclusions, Anne. I hope there's a simple explanation, like the bus just broke down somewhere and Kendall's out of cell phone range."

Doug's tone was reassuring, but one look at him told Anne he, too, was fighting back panic.

63

*K*endall knelt down next to the kids, who were huddled beside Albert on a pile of horse blankets. "Are you girls okay?"

"Yes, except we're starving," Caitlin said.

Kendall sighed deeply and sat on a blanket. "I'm hungry, too," she said, leaning her head against the wall.

"You look a little peaked. Are you all right?" Albert asked.

Kendall glanced at the girls. "I'm okay. I hurt my arm."

"Is it this arm?" Caitlin asked, placing her hand on Kendall's left arm.

Kendall jumped. "Ow! Yes. That's the one."

"It's all purple."

"And you have a big bump on your head," Emma said, pointing to the left side of Kendall's forehead.

Albert leaned towards her. ""I don't know if your arm's broke, but you sure banged it up good. Does it hurt bad?"

The room was spinning and Kendall closed her eyes until it quieted. "Only when I move it."

Albert stood and took a polo wrap from the bandage box. "Let me make a sling for you."

He knotted the ends together and looped it around her neck, gently helping her ease her arm into it. "Does that feel better?"

She nodded, then instantly regretted it as the spinning began again. "Yes, thank you."

Albert studied her for a moment. "You need a painkiller."

"There's no chance of getting that."

Albert stood and pounded on the door. "Hey, open up."

"Albert, what are you doing?"

"Open the door!" Albert pounded with both fists.

A moment later the door swung outward and Earl and Zelda stood in the doorway. Earl waved his gun at them. "What's going on in here?"

"Kendall needs some pain medicine," Albert said. "There's aspirin in the cabinet by the sink."

Earl narrowed his eyes. "You disturbed me to ask for a bottle of aspirin?"

Albert nodded. "Yeah, and she could use something to eat. The kids could, too. Their lunch is on the bus."

Earl kicked the door. "What do you think this is, a fucking hotel?"

"What the hell, Earl, it don't hurt none to give them something to eat," Zelda said, grabbing the door as it swung closed.

Earl lowered the gun and walked away. "Feed them if you want to. I don't give a shit."

Zelda stared after Earl for a moment, then motioned to Albert. "Come on, old man."

C H A P T E R

64

*L*ieutenant Mallory was the deputy in charge of the investigation into McGraw's escape, and Anne gripped Doug's hand as they sat in the study with Patrick, listening to the lieutenant fill them in on the details of the getaway. The lieutenant had a deep voice and a commanding manner about him, and Anne figured he'd been with the department for a while. He looked to be in his mid-fifties—graying at the temples and sporting the hint of a paunch.

When he finished speaking, Anne asked, "Do you think McGraw was actually injured in the jail fight?"

The lieutenant shook his head. "No. At this point, I've got to believe Zeb McGraw staged the fight and had the whole escape plot preplanned."

Anne frowned. "But wouldn't he have to be injured in order to be transported to the hospital?"

"He could fake it. Apparently, he was complaining of chest pain and shortness of breath after the altercation with the other inmate, and that pretty much guaranteed him a ride to the hospital to be checked out."

"Do you have any leads on the identity of the man who helped McGraw escape from the accident scene?" Doug asked.

"Not yet," the lieutenant said. "But we have several eyewitnesses who got a good look at him. We have an artist working on a sketch right now."

"What about the woman hostage?" Anne asked.

"Same thing there. No ID as of yet, but good eyewitness descriptions."

"And you don't know whether the victim in the car was another hostage or an accomplice?" Doug asked.

"No, we don't. His face is pretty banged up, so it may be hard to identify

249

him. He's a young male, probably in his mid-teens, with blond hair and blue eyes. That's about all we have to go on. I think I mentioned earlier that he had no wallet or any form of ID on him."

"What's his condition?" Anne asked.

"Critical."

"What about the car that was used in the accident? Have you found out whom it was registered to?" Doug asked.

The lieutenant nodded. "It was registered to Zelda McGraw."

"Zeb McGraw's sister," Anne murmured. "Do you think she was the woman with them?"

Lieutenant Mallory raised his shoulders. "We don't know. By all accounts, it sure looked like the woman was a hostage, but that could have just been a ploy to help them get away. It's possible the woman was Zelda McGraw and that she was in on it all along."

"Have you tried to locate Zelda McGraw?"

The lieutenant nodded. "Unsuccessfully, but we have an APB out on her."

They were silent for a moment; then Patrick asked, "Which direction was McGraw headed in when he fled?"

"West. They fled the scene headed westbound on Route Seven in an old-model brown Toyota Camry with West Virginia tags. We ran the tags, but they're registered to another vehicle. There were a couple of other vehicles reported stolen in the vicinity this morning, immediately following the escape. We don't have enough information yet to determine if those incidents are linked to this case, but we're on the lookout for those vehicles as well as the Toyota."

The Nextel radio clipped to Lieutenant Mallory's belt beeped twice, and he removed it and looked at the display. "Excuse me," he said, holding the radio to his ear.

"Lieutenant Mallory." He gave a quick nod. "Terrific. Hold on, let me see if there's a fax machine here."

He lowered the phone and looked at Doug. "The artist has finished the sketches of the driver and the woman. If you have a fax machine, I'll have them sent over."

"Sure." Doug recited the fax number to the lieutenant.

Lieutenant Mallory repeated the number into the phone. "Please make sure those are sent right way."

The fax machine on Doug's desk rang almost immediately, and Doug rose and held his hand out to Anne. They gathered by the fax machine, and Anne felt her chest tighten as she saw the paper begin to emerge from the front of the machine. The fax machine groaned as it spit out the page, and Anne saw the sketched image of a woman's hair and forehead slowly appear; then there was a brief pause, and the full sketch shot out of the machine.

The lieutenant retrieved the page and turned it around.

Anne clutched Doug's arm. "That's Kendall!"

"Oh Christ," Doug muttered through clenched teeth. "That means McGraw has the kids."

Lieutenant Mallory frowned as he looked from Anne to Doug. "What kids?"

CHAPTER

65

$\mathcal{L}$ ieutenant Mallory sent a car to pick up Margaret, and twenty minutes later she was seated on the couch next to Anne. Doug shifted restlessly by the fireplace.

The lieutenant opened a folder and handed Margaret a sheet of paper. "Do you recognize this woman?"

"Of course," Margaret said. "That's Kendall."

"Kendall Waters?"

"Yes."

"You're sure?"

"Absolutely."

"And she accompanied the kids on the field trip today?"

"Yes."

The lieutenant nodded and handed her another sheet of paper. "What about this man, do you recognize him?"

"That looks like Stephen Lloyd."

"Are you acquainted with him?"

Margaret nodded. "Yes, he talked to me about boarding his horses with me."

"Stephen Lloyd?" Anne repeated. "Didn't Kendall go out with him?"

"Yes, she did," Margaret replied.

Lieutenant Mallory hunched forward in his chair. "Miss Waters is dating this man?"

"No, they're not dating," Margaret replied. "In fact, I spoke with Kendall about Stephen just this morning, and she made it clear that she has no romantic interest in him. But she did go out with him once or twice. In fact, she went to the polo match with him last evening. What does he have to do with this?"

The lieutenant let out a heavy sigh. "This sketch is of the man who helped Zeb McGraw escape from jail this morning."

"Oh my Lord." Margaret's hand flew to her chest. "I knew there was something that didn't ring true about him."

Lieutenant Mallory pointed to the sketch of Kendall on Margaret's lap. "And that sketch is of the woman at the scene of McGraw's escape, who appeared to be a hostage."

Margaret's mouth dropped open. "Are you saying that Zeb McGraw has something to do with the disappearance of Kendall and the children?"

"I'm afraid it looks that way, Mrs. Southwell. I need to get as much information as possible from you about the children, the vehicle they were riding in, and who might be involved in their disappearance. You need to tell me everything you can think of, even if you don't think it's relevant to the children going missing. All right?"

Margaret raised a shaky hand to her forehead and closed her eyes. Her lips moved slightly, as if she were speaking, but no sound came out.

Anne reached for her arm. "Are you okay, Margaret? Would you like a glass of water?"

Margaret's eyes opened. She took Anne's hand in hers. "I just had to say a prayer." Her voice quivered. "Lieutenant, proceed with your questions."

He nodded. "Okay, let's start with the bus the children were riding on."

"It's from the Greenfield Academy."

"Do you use the same bus for all your field trips?"

"Yes, for the last couple of years, anyway. A friend of mine runs the Greenfield Academy, and they let me use their bus for my camp field trips, since school's not in session."

"Do you use their driver as well?"

"Yes, Louise Parker."

"And she drives for all your field trips?"

"Yes."

Lieutenant Mallory took a moment to write on his notepad. "Okay, what time did the bus arrive today?"

Margaret paused for a moment. "I guess it was a couple of minutes before nine. I didn't really notice when it drove in, because things were a bit hectic in the barn."

"Why was that?"

"The assistant camp counselor, Elizabeth, didn't show up like she was supposed to this morning. My insurance doesn't allow for the kids to go on the field trip without two employees present, so Kendall was in a frenzy, calling all over trying to find Elizabeth. When she couldn't reach her, Kendall talked to me about who else might be able to substitute for Elizabeth."

"And what did you tell her?"

"We finally settled on letting Todd, one of the stable hands, go along. He's a nice boy and the kids like him, so he seemed like the best choice under the circumstances."

"Okay, let's stop here for a moment. Tell me more about Elizabeth. What's her full name?"

"Elizabeth Carey. Her father's a vet at the Equine Medical Center."

The lieutenant wrote on his pad. "And you said she's the assistant camp counselor. Has she worked for you long?"

"No. She just started this week. We made a deal to trade board and training for Elizabeth's horse in exchange for her helping out at camp."

"And had she been reliable up until today?"

"She sure had. Elizabeth was a great help all week. It was a shock when she didn't show up for work today."

"And you still haven't heard from her?"

Margaret shook her head.

Lieutenant Mallory signaled to a deputy who was standing nearby. "Get Dr. Carey at the Equine Medical Center on the phone for me."

"Yes, sir."

The lieutenant turned his attention back to Margaret. "Tell me about the boy who substituted for Elizabeth." He looked at his notes. "Todd."

"Todd Rucker. He's a nice boy who's worked for me for a couple of weeks, maybe a month. He mucks stalls, mostly."

"And was he agreeable to accompanying the children on the field trip this morning?"

"Yes, he was. He said he felt bad that Elizabeth hadn't shown up for work and that he'd be happy to help us out." Margaret frowned. "He and Elizabeth had become rather close, and I think maybe Todd felt like he was helping Elizabeth out by going along on the field trip."

"Can you describe him for me?"

"He's tall—not quite six feet, but he probably will be when he finishes growing. He has blond hair, kind of on the longish side. And striking blue eyes." Margaret pursed her lips and gave a small shake of her head. "I think it's his eyes that captivated Elizabeth."

"When we're finished talking, can you call your farm and get his employment information for me?" the lieutenant asked.

"Of course."

"All right. What happened after you and Kendall agreed to have Todd substitute for Elizabeth?"

"Kendall rounded up the kids and they got on the bus and left."

"Did you go out to the bus with them?"

Margaret shook her head. "No."

"Did you have any contact with anyone on the bus after they left your farm?"

"Yes. I called Kendall about an hour or so later to see how it was going. I had an appointment to show a horse to a customer and was going to be busy for a while, so I thought I'd call and check in before I got all involved."

"And did you reach her?"

"Yes. Kendall said that everything was fine except that one of the girls had been carsick."

"And was that the last time you spoke with her?"

Margaret frowned. "Yes. Then a little after noon, I received a call from the Land of Little Horses inquiring why they hadn't arrived at their reserved time. So I tried to reach Kendall on her cell phone several times, but I didn't get an answer."

Lieutenant Mallory paused and read over the notes on his pad. "Okay, can you think of anyone who was at the farm today who was not ordinarily there? Or anyone who was normally there who did not show up today? Other than Elizabeth, that is."

Margaret thought for a moment. "I haven't seen Jake yet today, but he doesn't really have any set work hours."

"Who's Jake?"

"He's been riding some horses for me."

"What's his last name?"

"Dawson. Jake Dawson."

Lieutenant Mallory wrote on his notepad. "How long has he been employed by you?"

"About a week."

The lieutenant regarded her thoughtfully. "That's interesting. None of these people, Jake Dawson, Todd Rucker, or Elizabeth Carey, has worked for you very long."

Margaret shrugged. "That's not unusual. The horse business has a very high turnover rate. I've resigned myself to it after all these years."

"True. Still, it's worth noting," Lieutenant Mallory replied. "How did you meet Mr. Dawson?"

"I met him through Kendall."

Doug spoke up. "He saved my horse's life, Lieutenant. Jake was driving by when I had the car accident we told you about. He stopped and helped with my horse. Jake met Kendall afterwards, at the Equine Medical Center."

Lieutenant Mallory tapped his pen against the pad. "Very interesting."

"What are you thinking?" Anne asked.

"I just think it's an odd coincidence that Mr. Dawson showed up, essentially out of nowhere, and now Miss Waters appears to have been taken hostage, Miss Carey is missing, and Mr. Dawson didn't show up for work today."

Patrick leaned forward in his chair. "I'm on the same wavelength as you with that line of thinking, Lieutenant Mallory. In fact, I ran a background check on Jake Dawson just a couple of days ago, because I thought his sudden appearance in the area when these incidents started happening to Doug and Anne seemed suspicious."

"Did you find anything?"

Patrick shook his head. "The preliminary results came up clean, but I went ahead and requested documentation, which I haven't received yet."

"Sounds like we need to check him out." The lieutenant turned back to Margaret. "Can you think of anything else, Mrs. Southwell?"

"No, sir, I can't."

Lieutenant Mallory stood up. "All right. We need to contact the children's parents, and then I'm going to request that an Amber Alert be issued."

𝒵elda handed Zeb the pair of jeans and T-shirt she'd packed for him. "Here. I brought these for you."

Zeb took the jeans, but made a face at the black T-shirt. "What's with the Goth shirt? They have a special on these down at Wal-Mart or something?"

Zelda scowled. "Just be happy you don't have to wear stripes no more."

Zeb grumbled as he changed into the jeans and T-shirt, then announced he was going outside to scout around. Zelda closed the door behind him and climbed aboard the bus, where Earl sat in the driver's seat. She pressed her chest against Earl's shoulder and slid her arms around him as he twirled the radio dial.

"Not now," he said, pushing her hands away.

"Aw, come on, Earl." She ran her tongue slowly down the side of his neck until she reached the hollow spot at the base of his throat. "Let's have some fun."

"I want to hear the news first." He continued to fiddle with the dial, but he didn't make any attempt to stop her from sucking on his neck.

The crackly voice of the deejay announced that the news was next, and Earl turned up the volume.

Earl pulled her around so she was sitting on his lap. "Listen to this, babe. You might hear your name on the radio."

A male voice boomed over the radio. "We have breaking news to report from Loudoun County, Virginia. This just in: A prisoner has escaped from the Loudoun County Jail. The Sheriff's Office has confirmed that inmate Zeb McGraw, awaiting trial on murder and kidnapping charges, escaped shortly before noon today. We have a live report now from Joan LeGraff, who's on the scene in Leesburg. Joan, what can you tell us?"

"Hello, Brian. I'm live at the Loudoun County Sheriff's Office in Leesburg, where Sheriff Fred Boling just issued a statement telling us that Zeb McGraw managed to escape from custody today while being transported by ambulance to the Loudoun Hospital Center. The ambulance McGraw was riding in was involved in what is assumed to have been a staged car accident. During the aftermath of the collision, a sheriff's deputy was overpowered by a man who is thought to be an accomplice of McGraw's, and McGraw was able to escape."

"Any word on the identity of the accomplice?"

"Yes, Brian. An identification has been made from a police sketch, and the accomplice is believed to be a man by the name of Stephen Lloyd."

Zelda stared at Earl. "*Who?*"

"That's my fake name."

She scowled. "Now you're screwed. You need to get new fake ID."

Earl held his hand up to silence her. "Shhh. I've already got another one. Now listen up."

The woman reporter was talking. "Authorities are advising local residents to be on the lookout for McGraw and Lloyd, who were last seen in a late-model brown Toyota Camry. Both men are considered armed and dangerous."

"Joan, if a listener thinks he or she has seen these men, is there a number to call?"

"Yes. People should call the Loudoun County Sheriff's Office with any information. Also, Brian, the Sheriff's Office is seeking information regarding two other individuals who were at the scene of the accident. An unidentified woman was seen fleeing the scene with the prisoner, and although the Sheriff's Office is not commenting on who she might be or what role she may have played in the escape, they have confirmed that the vehicle used in the crash was registered to Zeb McGraw's sister, Zelda McGraw. There was also a young male in the crash vehicle—"

Earl punched the power button and turned off the radio. "You're famous, babe."

"Hey, why'd you turn it off?" Zelda reached for the dial. "She was getting ready to say something about Zach."

She turned the radio back on in time to hear the woman say, "—critical condition."

"Thank you, Joan, for that report. We will keep our listeners informed as details become available on this important local story. Now, coming up, traffic and weather on the nines."

Zelda felt blood rush to her face and she punched the power button on the radio. "She said *critical condition*! Was she talking about Zach? You told me he wasn't hurt."

"He wasn't," Earl said, sliding his hand up under her T-shirt. "He's faking it, just like Zeb did at the jail."

"Hey." She pushed his hand away. "Are you lying to me?"

Earl put his hand back and covered her mouth with his. "I wouldn't lie to you, babe. You know that."

CHAPTER

67

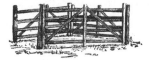

A loud pounding echoed through the garage and Earl jumped up and grabbed his gun off the dashboard.

"What the hell is that?" he asked, zipping his pants.

"It's probably Zeb." Zelda tugged her denim skirt down and retrieved her underwear from the aisle. "I locked the door after he went out."

Earl ran to the door and peered through the glass panel. "Damn it, Zeb, you're lucky I didn't blow your brains out," he said, yanking open the door.

"What the fuck did you lock me out for?" Zeb asked, slightly out of breath.

Earl didn't answer him. "Where've you been?"

"I was scouting the farm out. There's a power line that runs behind the back of the farm, and there's a gate leading to it from the horse pasture. I think we should leave a vehicle back there, just in case we need to make a run for it."

Earl stared at him thoughtfully. "Yeah, that's not a bad idea." He pointed to the green truck in the center of the garage. "Let's stash the truck in the back of the farm. That way, if someone sees it, they won't think nothing about it being there."

He opened the driver's door on the truck and turned to Zelda. "Open the door, babe."

Zeb headed for the bus and Earl scowled at him. "Hey, Zeb, you think I'm going to walk back? Get in the car and follow me."

Zeb snorted. "What, is it too much for you? I just ran there and back."

"Yeah, well, I haven't spent the last nine months locked up with nothing to do but work out all day," Earl replied, climbing into the truck and slamming the door.

Zeb didn't make a move towards the car. He eyed Zelda. "Fucking asshole. Who put him in charge?"

"Cut him some slack, Zeb. Earl's been working real hard planning all this. He got you out of jail, didn't he?"

Zeb gave her a cold stare. "I planned the jail break. All Earl did was help me out. And don't you forget that, little sister. I'm the one calling the shots around here."

Zelda rolled her eyes. "Okay, Zeb. Whatever. Just go follow Earl, so he can drop the truck off like you said he should."

Zeb moved towards the car. "Yeah, you got it. Like *I* said he should."

Once both vehicles were out, Zelda closed the garage door and grabbed a can of soda and a bag of chips from the bus, then stood by the door, chewing thoughtfully on the chips as she watched for them to return. It wasn't a good sign that Zeb and Earl were already going at each other.

She saw a cloud of dust in the drive as the car sped towards her, and she pushed the button to raise the garage door. Zeb was at the wheel, and Zelda could tell from his pissed-off expression that things still weren't going real great between him and Earl.

Both men climbed out of the car without speaking, and Zelda held the bag of chips out. "Hey, I got some of the kids' food. Want something?"

Earl walked right past her and snatched Kendall's cell phone off the dash of the bus. "It's time for Zeb to make the call."

Zeb's face reddened and contorted into a scowl. "*It's time for Zeb to make the call,*" he mimicked.

Earl snorted. "What's your problem?"

"What's my problem? What's my fucking problem? I'll tell you what my problem is. *You.* You're my problem. Because somewhere along the way you got confused, and now you think you're running things." Zeb kicked a soda can towards the back of the garage. "And if those pigeons don't shut the fuck up, I'm going to blow them away."

Earl flashed a look at Zelda and held his hands up. "Hey, Zeb, chill. You're still the man. I'm just trying to help you out here."

"Yeah, uh-huh." Zeb swaggered towards Earl. "You're trying to help me out."

Earl held the phone out. "Here you go. You decide when you want to make the call."

Zeb grabbed the phone. "You got that right. I'll make the call when *I* decide it's time to make the call."

He stared back and forth from Earl to Zelda for a few moments, breathing heavily. Finally, he looked at the phone. "What's the fucking phone number?"

Earl gave him a superior smile. "It's on speed dial. Oh, by the way, Zeb, there's one bit of info you should know before you call Cummings."

"Yeah, what's that?" Zeb scrolled through the stored numbers on the cell.

"We don't have his kid."

CHAPTER

68

he girls' parents were assembled in the living room, waiting to hear from Lieutenant Mallory, but when the lieutenant arrived, he drew Doug aside.

"I'd like to speak with you and Mrs. Cummings privately first, if I may."

"Sure, let's go to the study."

Once they were seated, the lieutenant said, "I'm afraid I have bad news. The body of the bus driver, Louise Parker, was found just about an hour ago, behind a storage shed at the Greenfield Academy."

Anne buried her face against Doug's shoulder. "Oh my God."

"How did she die?" Doug asked, putting his arms around Anne.

"She had a single gunshot wound to the head." The lieutenant glanced at Anne. "And she had a note stabbed to her chest with a Buck knife. It read, 'Don't fuck with us.'"

"Jesus, they killed her as a warning."

The lieutenant nodded and gestured in the direction of the living room. "I'm sure they are going to be even more terrified for their daughters' safety when I tell them about Mrs. Parker's death. I've already told Dr. Carcy, and he took it real hard."

"Do you have any leads on Elizabeth?"

"Yes. Dr. Carey told us that Elizabeth left home around seven o'clock this morning to go to the farm and prepare for the field trip. He said she received a ride from a young man she worked with, named Todd."

Anne frowned. "But didn't Margaret tell us Todd agreed to go on the field trip because he felt so badly about Elizabeth not showing up for work?"

Lieutenant Mallory gave a grim nod. "That's right."

"So, Todd was in on this," Doug said.

"It certainly looks that way."

"Do you think Todd is the boy in the car who was injured?" Anne asked.

"Quite possibly. We still have no ID on the young man. We ran his prints, but we came up blank. And he doesn't appear to have had any dental work done, so we can't get an ID from that. I'm going to ask Mrs. Southwell to pay a visit to the hospital and see if she can identify him. I'm also trying to track down a photo of Zelda McGraw's son, Zach."

"Is he still in critical condition?"

The lieutenant nodded.

There was a knock on the door and a deputy stuck his head in. "Excuse me, Lieutenant Mallory, but some information just came in that I thought you'd want to know about right away."

"Come on in. What do you have?"

The deputy handed him a sheet of paper. "This is a copy of Jake Dawson's birth certificate. Look at who's listed as his father."

Lieutenant Mallory studied the paper for a moment, then closed his eyes and shook his head. "Patrick Talbot was right."

"Whose name is listed?" Doug asked.

The lieutenant handed the sheet of paper to Doug. "Zebulon McGraw."

Doug narrowed his eyes as he studied the birth certificate. "*Jake is Zeb McGraw's son?*"

"I can't believe that Jake is part of this." Anne held Doug's arm and looked at the paper.

Lieutenant Mallory turned to the deputy. "Let's get an APB out on Dawson."

"Yes, sir, right away. Also, sir, we got positive ID on the fingerprints from the accident car and the ambulance. The man previously identified as Stephen Lloyd is Earl Davis. Davis was released from jail last winter after serving time for embezzlement and grand theft." The deputy handed another sheet of paper to Lieutenant Mallory.

The lieutenant read the document. "I see Davis served time in D.C., so that doesn't explain his connection to McGraw."

Anne sat forward. "Maybe it does."

"How so?"

"That's where Zeb McGraw's brother, Zeke, was in prison."

The lieutenant looked at the deputy. "See if Davis and Zeke McGraw served time together."

"Yes, sir." The deputy walked briskly towards the door.

The lieutenant turned back to Anne and Doug. "There's one more bit of information I want to pass on. Mrs. Southwell checked out the cottage Jake Dawson had been staying in and found that he had cleared out all his belongings. The only thing he left behind was a man's shirt with a note on it that read, 'Thanks. It's time for me to move on.'"

Anne looked at Doug. "That's probably the shirt you gave Jake to wear the night of the fire."

Doug nodded.

She thought it over. "If Jake is involved with McGraw, why would he bother to write a note like that?"

Doug shook his head and sighed deeply. "I don't know, Anne."

"By the way," Lieutenant Mallory said, "I understand Chester Rawls is the FBI agent who handled the McGraw case last time. I received word a little while ago that he's going to be heading up the FBI team on this investigation."

"That's good news," Doug said. "Will he be here for the meeting?"

The lieutenant shook his head. "No, they're pulling him in from the West Coast, so he's taking the red-eye tonight. He'll be here tomorrow morning."

Lieutenant Mallory stood up. "I dread doing it, but I'd better get out there and brief the parents."

*Z*eb narrowed his eyes at Earl. "What do you mean, you don't have the Cummings kid?"

"She didn't show up for camp today."

"Why the fuck didn't you tell me before?"

Earl shrugged. "What difference does it make? It don't really change anything. We've got the rest of the kids. We'll still get the money."

"The hell it don't change nothing! What about Cummings?"

"What about him?"

"We was supposed to make Cummings pay."

"Who gives a shit where the money comes from?"

"I'm not talking about the money." Spit flew from Zeb's mouth. "I'm talking about making Cummings suffer."

"That's your problem. I came on board to help spring you from jail and wind up with some dough. I don't give a shit about Cummings or whether he suffers."

"Well I do!"

Zelda placed herself between the two of them, warding off a fight. "Hey, Earl, what about everything Zach did to scare Cummings so he'd cooperate with us? What's the payoff for that now?"

Earl stared thoughtfully at her. "How about if Zeb tells Cummings *he* has to be the one to deliver the ransom money? Zeb can do whatever he wants with Cummings after we get the dough."

"Why would Cummings agree to that?" Zelda asked.

Earl smirked. "Because Cummings is such a fine, upstanding citizen, he'll probably feel guilty that the kids got kidnapped because of him, even though he's happy that his kid is safe at home. I bet he'll do whatever Zeb tells him to, to save the rest of the kids."

Zelda looked at Zeb. "What do you think, bro?"

Zeb's mouth twisted into a grin and he pressed the speed-dial button on the cell phone.

he spacious living room was packed with family members and personnel from the Sheriff's Office and the FBI. The buzz of conversation made Anne slightly claustrophobic, so she chose a chair by the door, rather than following Doug and the lieutenant to the far side of the room.

Lieutenant Mallory held up his hand to quiet the conversation. "Good afternoon. For those of you whom I have not yet met in person, I'm Lieutenant Mallory, and I am heading up the investigation for the Sheriff's Office."

He paused and took a deep breath. "I know this is a very trying time for you, and I will answer your questions. But first, let me bring you up to speed on where we stand in the investigation so far."

Anne heard the distant ringing of the phone, and she slipped out of the room and picked up the cordless phone in the hallway.

"Hello?"

No one responded.

Anne pulled the phone away from her ear and glanced at the caller-ID display on the handset. "Waters, Kendall" was illuminated on the screen, followed by Kendall's cell phone number. Anne rushed back into the living room.

"Hello? Kendall?"

She heard a man's low laugh. "This ain't Kendall."

"Who is it?" She hurried across the room towards Doug and waved her hand to get his attention.

"You know who it is." His tone sent a chill through her. "You've got five seconds to put Cummings on the phone."

"Don't hang up. He's right here." Anne handed the phone to Doug.

"It's him," she whispered.

"Hello?" Doug held the phone slightly away from his ear so Anne could hear what McGraw was saying.

"Hey, Cummings, have you missed me?"

Doug clenched his jaw. "What do you want from us, McGraw?"

McGraw laughed. "I always knew you was a smart guy, Cummings. See, you already figured out I want something."

Doug didn't respond.

"Fucking cell phone." McGraw's voice grew faint, as if he had moved the phone away from his mouth. "I think I lost him."

There was a murmur of muffled voices in the background; then McGraw's voice was loud again. "Are you there, Cummings?"

"Yes, I'm here."

"You answer me when I talk to you or I'll blow a fucking kid's head off, you understand?"

Doug stiffened and Anne saw bright spots of color rise in his cheeks, but he kept his tone even. "Yes, I understand."

"Yeah, you understand, because you're a smart guy and you know I mean business, don't you?"

"Yes, I know you mean business. We'll do whatever you want." Doug glanced at the roomful of parents. "Just don't harm the kids."

A gun shot rang out from the phone and Anne gripped Doug's arm.

"McGraw?" Doug shouted. "*McGraw!*"

The phone line was silent for a moment; then they heard McGraw's cackling laughter. "Scared you, huh? Don't worry, Cummings, that wasn't aimed at a kid. The fucking pigeons just pissed me off."

Doug exhaled loudly. "What do you want, McGraw?"

"A million bucks, for starters," McGraw replied, the laughter gone from his voice.

"A million dollars?"

"That's what I said; you hard of hearing or something?"

"No, I heard you. It'll take some time to get that kind of money."

"You've got twenty-four hours. After that, I'll kill a kid an hour."

"It's Saturday afternoon, McGraw. The banks aren't even open. How do you expect us to get that kind of money in twenty-four hours?"

"You got connections. And these cute little girls all have rich daddies. You figure it out."

Doug paused. "How do we know the kids are all right?"

"I guess you'll just have to trust me."

"You know I'm not going to do that. Can I talk to Kendall?"

"Why, you got the hots for her?" McGraw laughed. "She's a looker, that's for sure. I'm thinking of having some of her later myself."

Doug closed his eyes and took a deep breath. "Assuming we can get the money, what do you want us to do with it?"

McGraw snorted. "You think I'm stupid enough to tell you that now? Better stop stalling, Cummings, and start figuring out how to get the money, 'cause the clock's ticking away. Hear it? Tick-tock, tick-tock. Bye-bye."

"*Wait*. When will I hear from you again?"

"When I call you. And, Cummings"—McGraw made a kissing noise—"tell Samantha I miss her."

The line went dead.

*K*endall heard the shot in the garage and she scooted over closer to Albert. "Albert, did you hear that?"

He nodded.

"We've got to figure out a way to get out of here before they start shooting at one of us." She kept her voice low so the children couldn't hear her.

"The only way out of this room is through that door." Albert pointed towards the locked door at the front of the small room.

Kendall nodded. "I figured that. But what if we talk them into letting you or me out of this room again, like you did earlier when you asked to get the food. Is there a way we could escape and run for help?"

"I don't know how we'd get out without them seeing us. The only way out of here is through the garage door or the people doors in front and in the back. All of those are in the wide open."

"Are there any windows?"

Albert shook his head. "Nope. Just the glass in the doors."

Kendall thought for a moment. "I saw a staircase at the back of the garage. Where does that lead?"

"It just goes up to the clean-out for the pigeon roost."

"Can you get through it to the outside?"

"You'd have to crawl through the pigeon roost on your belly."

Kendall's pulse quickened. "But there's an opening to the outside?"

"Yeah, but it's a good twenty-foot drop to the ground. There's a wooden ladder on the outside wall that runs to the clean-out, but the top rung is a good ways below the opening. It's not meant to be used to climb into the roost, just so someone can stand on the top rung and reach into the opening. There's no way either of us could safely lower ourselves from the opening to the ladder, especially you with your arm banged up like it is. And sure not the kids."

Kendall massaged one temple as she considered other options. "Is there an alarm we could set off?"

Albert thought for a moment. "There's a fire alarm."

Kendall felt her chest tighten with a glimmer of hope. "Is there an alarm panel?"

He shook his head. "No. The alarm systems for all the outbuildings are monitored from the alarm panel in the stable."

She sat forward and stretched her neck to get a good look at the ceiling. "Is there a smoke detector in this room we could set off?"

"No, the fire detectors are only in the garage area. Besides, they're not smoke detectors. There's too much dust out here; smoke detectors would be sending off false alarms all the time."

"What kind of fire detectors are they?"

"Heat detectors. And I don't know of a way to make one of them go off, other than holding a match up to it."

Kendall slumped back against the wall. "What else could we do?"

Albert's face wrinkled into a frown and he stared thoughtfully at her.

"There's the drainage pipe."

"Tell me."

"The Worthingtons are having a drainage system put in that goes from all the barns to a big culvert that flows into a collection pond in the back pasture. You see, the way these buildings sit down in the hollow like this, when we get a real gully-washer, all the water comes down the hill and washes away the drive and just makes a hell of a mess. Then I have to grade the drive and rake all the gravel out of the grass—"

Kendall gave his arm a small shake. "Just tell me about the drainage pipe."

"The drainage pipe running to the pond has been put in, but they're waiting until the winter to do the digging around the stable area, so it won't look all tore up this summer and all. Right now the opening to the culvert is still exposed. If you could get to it, you could go all the way to the pond. Hell, we could all go. Once we were inside the pipe, they'd have no idea where we were."

"How far away is the pond?"

"A good half mile. And it's close to where the power line runs behind the farm. So, if we could make it that far, we'd have pretty easy going following the power line to the main road."

Kendall frowned. "A half mile's pretty long. I don't think the kids could make it that far crawling through a pipe."

"It's a three-foot drainage pipe. The kids could probably stand in it, as tiny as they are. I'd be more worried about you making it through."

"Don't worry about me. I'll go through anything to get out of here." She thought it over for a minute. "What about where the pipe ends at the pond? If we all go, is there a way to get out of the pipe without having to take the kids through the water?"

"The pond's so low, as dry as it's been, we could probably crawl right out of the pipe onto the dry bank."

Kendall's heart quickened. "How would we get to the pipe?"

"It's right across the drive from the back door."

"Wouldn't that be the first place they'd look?"

He shook his head. "The Worthingtons landscaped in front of the opening, so you can't see it. If you weren't looking real hard, you'd never know it was there."

Kendall felt almost giddy. *It just might work.* "Okay. Now we just have to figure out a way to talk them into letting one of us, or all of us, go outside."

arl hunched forward in the front seat of the bus, his arms draped over the metal divider, and Zelda stood in front of him on the bus steps. Their attention was focused on Zeb, who sat in the driver's seat, twirling the radio dial.

"This is a special report from Prime News Network. Glenn Garrison reporting live from Middleburg, Virginia." Zeb let go of the tuning dial and turned up the volume. "The investigation in the case of the missing busload of campers has escalated in recent hours with the discovery of the body of a woman identified by police as Louise Parker. Authorities tell us that Ms. Parker was the driver of the bus in which the children went missing."

Zelda turned and scowled at Earl. "Goddamn it, Earl. I said I didn't want no killing."

"I didn't have a choice, babe. I had to send them a message, or they would have tried to screw around with us."

"But now we're wanted for murder. They're never going to stop looking for us."

Earl gave a dismissive shrug. "Zeb's already wanted for murder. Now shut up and let me listen. Turn up the volume, Zeb."

"To recap, an Amber Alert has been issued for seven young girls who went missing this morning while on a field trip from their horseback-riding camp. The children were last seen in a white Ford F-450 bus with *Greenfield Academy* written on the side in green lettering. The vehicle has Virginia tags, JLK-4395, and was last seen at nine o'clock this morning, heading east on John Mosby Highway, near Middleburg, Virginia. The Sheriff's Office has confirmed that they have received a call from someone claiming to be holding the children in captivity, but they did not release any details of the call, or reveal whether a ransom demand had been made."

Zeb reached his hand out and flicked the power button. "They didn't say nothing about the other girl."

Earl shrugged. "They must not have found her yet."

"What other girl?" Zelda asked.

"The assistant to the camp counselor," Earl replied, shooting Zeb a look of irritation.

"What about her?"

Earl hesitated. "Zach took care of her."

Zelda's eyes widened. "Did he kill her?"

"Don't worry about it."

"Answer me! Did you get my boy mixed up in murder?"

"Don't get so hot about it, babe. Did you think we was just going to walk in and ask for a million bucks? Zach knew what he had to do to get their attention."

She glared at him. "What's going on with Zach, anyway? It's been five hours since you ditched him at the accident."

Earl looked away.

"Answer me!"

$\mathcal{L}$ ieutenant Mallory allowed the uproar to take over the room for a few moments, then held his hand up. "May I have your attention, please."

The buzz of conversation slowly faded. "Thank you. I know you have a great number of questions, but we won't get anywhere with everyone talking all at once. First of all, let's address the ransom demand."

Bob Horton, Emma's dad, leaned forward in his chair. "There's no question we'll pay the ransom."

The lieutenant hesitated. "Let's talk about that for a minute."

"There's nothing to talk about," Ed Dunning said. "You can't put a price tag on our children's lives. I'll sacrifice everything I own to get Caitlin home safely."

"Of course. We all will," Deb Horton said, her voice rising to a shrill pitch. "But how will we get that kind of money by tomorrow?"

Her husband reached for her hand. "Don't worry, honey. It's just a question of logistics—"

"Not for us, it isn't." A tall, thin man on the far side of the room stood. "We don't have anywhere near the kind of money to pay our share. I guess we don't come from the same means as some of the rest of you do. My wife has taken to baby-sitting for the neighborhood kids this summer, just to scrape together enough money for our Brittany to go to riding camp."

The man's voice cracked, and he closed his eyes and pinched his thumb and forefinger against the bridge of his nose. The petite blond woman next to him rose and wrapped her arms around him. After a moment he lowered his hand and drew a ragged breath. "We'll pay as much as we have now. And we're good for the rest of our share. If I have to work two jobs for the rest of my life to pay it back, I will."

Anne choked back a sob and gripped Doug's knee. He cleared his throat. "We'll take care of the ransom."

The man stared at him. "But your daughter's not even involved."

"Only because she stayed home sick today." Doug covered Anne's hand with his. "We're all in this together."

"All right," Lieutenant Mallory said. "Let's talk logistics."

Anne squeezed Doug's hand and whispered, "I'm going upstairs to check on Samantha. I'll be right back."

As she left the room, a young man followed her into the hallway.

"Mrs. Cummings, can I talk to you for a minute?"

Anne stopped and turned back towards him. "Yes?"

"Hi. I'm Steve. I drive the horse ambulance for the Equine Medical Center. I'm a good friend of Doc Carey and Elizabeth."

"Nice to meet you, Steve."

"Can I ask you a question?"

"Of course."

"It's about something Lieutenant Mallory said earlier. About the bus driver who was killed." He hesitated. "He said that she had a note stuck to her chest with a knife."

Anne shuddered. "That's right."

"Well, the lieutenant mentioned that the knife was a Buck knife, and I couldn't help thinking that I'd seen someone use a Buck knife. Just about a week ago. When we were rescuing Mr. Cummings's horse after the accident." He shifted uneasily.

"Go on." She felt the hair stand up on the back of her neck.

"It was the cowboy who stopped and offered his help. Jake was his name. He had a real nice Buck knife that I was admiring." Steve squinted at her. "Do you think I should mention something about it to Lieutenant Mallory?"

*I*t was almost an hour later when Anne finally made her way up to Samantha's room. She found Samantha sitting up in bed, playing cards with Ben.

"What are the two of you up to?" Anne asked as she sat down on the edge of the bed.

"I taught Ben how to play Go Fish."

Ben held up his handful of cards and frowned. "Yeah, and she keeps beating me."

Samantha drew a card from the deck, then grinned as she placed the remaining cards from her hand on the bed.

"See what I mean?" Ben said.

Anne placed her hand on Samantha's forehead. "You don't feel warm anymore. Are you feeling better?"

Samantha nodded, then giggled. "Rascal, stop it! That tickles."

Anne looked around the bed, but the puppy was nowhere in sight. "Where is Rascal?"

Samantha pulled the covers back and revealed the puppy snuggled up next to her. "He was licking my arm," Samantha said, petting him gently on the head.

"What's Rascal doing under the covers?"

"He was cold, so I let him snuggle up with me."

"I don't think that's a good idea, Samantha. Beds are for people to sleep in, not dogs."

"Daddy let me put Rascal under the covers yesterday."

Anne gave her a weary smile. "He did, did he?"

"Uh-huh. You're not mad at Daddy, are you?"

"No, honey, I'm not mad at Daddy." She gathered Samantha in her arms and rested her cheek against the top of Samantha's head. "Mommy and Daddy love you so much. You know that, don't you, sweetheart?"

"Um-hmm." Samantha lifted her head and pulled back so she could see Anne's face. "Why are you crying, Mommy?"

Anne ran her fingertips across her cheeks. "Because I'm so happy that I'm your mommy."

Samantha threw her arms around Anne's neck. "I think it's silly that grown-ups cry when they're happy."

Anne smiled and kissed her. "Me, too. Say, you know what? I'll bet Rascal needs to go outside. Why don't I take him downstairs, and he can come back up when I bring your dinner."

"Okay. Can I have chicken noodle soup again?"

"Sure, if you want to."

"And raspberry Jell-O?"

"Of course." Anne picked Rascal up. "Ben, can I bring you anything?"

"You can have chicken noodle soup and Jell-O, too," Samantha said.

Ben smiled at her. "That sounds great."

"All right. I'll be back in a little while."

When Anne descended the stairs, the front hall was empty, but she heard voices coming from the kitchen. She found Doug and Ned Carey sitting at the kitchen table. Charly, the bodyguard, stood by the back door.

"Has everyone gone?"

Doug nodded. "The meeting ended a few minutes ago, and Lieutenant Mallory just left with Steve. They went to see if Steve can identify the knife from the bus driver's murder as the one he saw Jake use. And a deputy took Margaret to the hospital to see if she can identify the injured boy." He stood and reached for the puppy. "Does Rascal need to go out?"

Charly stepped forward. "I'll take him out, Mr. Cummings."

"Thanks, Charly." Anne handed Rascal to her and turned to Ned. "I was just getting ready to make dinner for Samantha. Can I talk you into staying and having a bite to eat with us?"

A vibrating sound came from Ned's cell phone and he held his finger up. "Sorry, Anne. Let me answer this." He unclipped his cell phone from his belt and held it to his ear. "Ned Carey."

He bolted forward in his chair. "*Elizabeth.*"

Ned paled. "Calm down, honey. Try not to cry. Just tell me if you're okay."

Anne couldn't make out what Elizabeth was saying, but her voice shrieked over the phone. It sounded like she was talking a million miles a minute.

"Don't worry about that right now, honey," Ned said. "The important thing is that you're all right. Tell me where you are."

Ned listened for a long moment. "Is someone with you?" He nodded. "Great. Can I speak with Mrs. Strump?"

Ned turned the phone slightly away from his mouth. "Elizabeth's safe."

"Where is she?" Anne asked.

"The beagle kennels."

He brought the phone back to his mouth. "Hi, I'm Ned Carey, Elizabeth's dad. Tell me what happened."

Ned eyed Doug and Anne as he listened. "Are you sure Todd's no longer around?"

He nodded. "Keeping a rifle handy sounds like a good idea. I'll call the Sheriff's Office and then I'm on my way. Tell Elizabeth just to sit tight. I'll be there as fast as I can."

Ned stood and his hands trembled as he clipped the phone back to his belt. "Thank God Elizabeth's alive and unharmed!"

"Did she tell you what happened to her?" Doug asked.

Ned reached in his pocket and pulled out his car keys. "She was crying and talking so fast, I could hardly understand her, but from what I gathered, Todd took her to the beagle kennels, tied her up, and left her in a stall. He must have said something to her about kidnapping the kids, because Elizabeth sounded hysterical when she asked if the kids and Kendall are all right."

Doug rose. "Do you know how to get to the kennels?"

Ned shook his head.

"Come on, I'll drive you there."

Anne stiffened and Ned glanced at her. "No, Doug, you stay here with your family. Just give me directions."

*A*nne was sound asleep in Doug's arms when the phone rang. She glanced at the digital reading on the bedside clock. Five-eighteen A.M.

Doug reached out and grabbed the phone. "Hello." His voice was thick with sleep.

"Hello, Lieutenant. What's happened?" He propped himself up on his elbow. "Where did you find him?"

He nodded. "All right, yes, I'd like to be there."

Anne put her hand on his arm. "What's going on?"

"Can you hold on for a moment, Lieutenant?" He covered the mouthpiece with his hand. "They found Jake and they're bringing him in for questioning."

Anne threw the covers back. "I want to be there when they question him."

Doug hesitated. "It's early Anne. Why don't you try to go back to sleep?"

"No. I want to be there."

He lifted his hand off the mouthpiece. "Lieutenant, Anne and I would both like to be present when you question Jake. Would it be possible to bring him here?"

Doug listened for a moment and nodded. "Great. We'll see you shortly."

"They're bringing Jake here," he said, placing the phone back on the cradle.

"Thank you."

"Lieutenant Mallory actually thought it was a good idea, so I won't be away from the phone if McGraw calls."

Anne nodded and stepped out of bed.

"Anne."

"Yes?"

"I know you like Jake and feel indebted to him for what he's done to help us, but don't lose sight of the fact that he's Zeb McGraw's son. And that last night Steve positively identified that knife as Jake's."

"I'm a criminal defense lawyer, Doug. I know how to keep my emotions out of it." She smiled tensely. "I also know that things aren't always as they seem. Jake deserves a chance to tell his side of the story, just like you did when you were falsely accused of murder."

Doug sighed. "It's not the same, Anne."

She pulled on her robe. "I'm going to get dressed; then I'll put on some coffee."

When Anne carried the coffee into the study, Jake was seated in a straight-backed chair that had been placed in front of the fireplace. Lieutenant Mallory sat in a leather armchair and Doug was seated on the couch. A deputy stood to the side of the hearth, and another deputy stood by the door to the hall. The deputy who was monitoring the phone line was seated at Doug's desk.

Anne set the tray down on the coffee table in front of the couch and sat down next to Doug.

"Hello, Jake."

He hesitated, then said, "Good morning, ma'am."

"Would you like coffee?"

Jake shook his head. "I'm afraid I'd have a hard time drinking a cup of coffee right now." He twisted slightly to the side so she could see his arms were handcuffed behind him.

Anne looked at Lieutenant Mallory. "Why the handcuffs, Lieutenant?"

"It's just a precaution. Mr. Dawson gave the deputy who picked him up a hard time."

She motioned towards the deputies in the room. "Given the situation, I don't believe the handcuffs are necessary."

Lieutenant Mallory gave her a long look, then gestured to the deputy by the fireplace to remove the handcuffs.

Anne gave him a brief smile. "Thank you, Lieutenant. Now, Jake, would you like some coffee?"

"Yes, ma'am." Jake stretched his arms in front of him and rubbed his wrists.

Anne handed a cup of coffee to Jake and poured cups for Doug and the lieutenant.

Lieutenant Mallory sat forward in his chair. "Mr. Dawson, our main priority is to find the children and Miss Waters and to bring them home safely. Any help you give us in that regard will be taken into consideration."

Jake stared at him. "Is that what this is all about? You think that I had something to do with the disappearance of Kendall and the kids?"

Anne broke in. "Jake, we saw a copy of your birth certificate. We know that Zeb McGraw is your father."

Jake's face colored and he lowered his gaze towards the floor, shaking his head slowly.

"Talk to us, Jake," Anne said. "Tell us what's going on."

The room was quiet for a long moment. Jake cleared his throat. "I don't blame you for thinking the worst of me. I should have told you everything right off the bat."

"Tell us now," Anne said.

Jake sighed and leaned back in the chair. "Zeb McGraw is my father, but I haven't had any contact with him in almost sixteen years."

"Why haven't you had any contact with him?"

"Because my mother and I ran away from him."

"Why did you run away?"

Jake raised his eyes to hers. "He beat us. My mother, mostly. And I figured that if I didn't take her away from him, he'd kill her."

"Where did you go?"

"Oklahoma."

"Why did you go there?"

Jake gave her a wry smile. "I bought us Greyhound tickets to the farthest destination we could afford."

"When did you see Zeb McGraw again?"

"I haven't."

Anne studied him for a moment. "What brought you to Virginia?"

Jake took a deep breath and let it out slowly. "My mother passed away a few months ago, and I decided to go back to West Virginia and look up my father."

"Why?"

"I wanted to confront him about what he had done to us."

She raised an eyebrow. "How were you going to confront him?"

"I hadn't decided yet."

"Were you angry with him?"

His expression hardened. "That's an understatement."

"Were you looking for revenge?"

"Maybe."

Anne paused and studied Jake for a moment. Either he deserved an Academy Award or his hatred for Zeb McGraw was genuine. "So, did you confront your father?"

"No. I snooped around town and learned that he was in jail."

"What did you do then?"

"I didn't know what to do. I was all fired up to confront him, and it was a big letdown." Jake shrugged. "I thought about going to see him in jail."

"Did you?"

He shook his head. "I headed in that direction, but I never made it."

"Why not?"

"I came upon Mr. Cummings's accident. You know the rest."

"How did you know that Doug was the person involved in the accident?"

"I didn't until I was at the Equine Medical Center watching Chancellor's surgery. Then Kendall mentioned Mr. Cummings's name."

"Did you know Doug was the person your father had gone to jail for?"

Jake nodded.

"You must have been surprised."

"That's putting it mildly."

Anne paused for a moment. "Why didn't you say something to Kendall?"

"I don't know. I guess I just didn't want to tell anyone that Zeb McGraw was my father. It's not a fact I'm proud of."

"Did you feel like you were keeping something from us?"

He looked away. "Of course I did."

Anne waited until he made eye contact with her again. "Why did you stay in town after you helped rescue Chancellor?"

"I don't know." He ran his hand through his hair. "I felt sorry for you and Mr. Cummings and all you were going through. I thought I might be able to help out with Chancellor."

"Is that the only reason?"

Jake gave her a long look. "No."

"What's the other reason?"

"Kendall."

"What about Kendall?"

He shifted uncomfortably. "I enjoy spending time with her."

"I think she enjoys being around you, too," Anne said quietly.

Jake's face reddened and he raised his coffee cup to his mouth.

"Why did you leave town?"

"Kendall and I had a fight, and I realized I would never fit into her world." Jake gestured around the study. *"This world.* So I decided it was time to quit living a fantasy and go back home to Oklahoma."

"What did you and Kendall fight about?"

He didn't answer.

"Jake? What was your fight with Kendall about?"

He sighed. "I ran into her at the polo match. She was with another guy."

"Who was she with?"

"Stephen Lloyd."

"Do you know Stephen Lloyd?"

Jake shook his head. "I didn't really know him, but I'd met him at Fox Run."

Lieutenant Mallory sat forward in his chair. "Do you know Earl Davis?"

Jake shifted his gaze to the lieutenant. "No, sir, I don't recognize the name."

"What about Zelda McGraw?"

"Yes, I know Zelda."

"How do you know her?"

"She's my father's sister."

"Your aunt."

He shrugged. "In terms of blood relations, that's what she is. But I always thought of her more as my cousin. She's much younger than my father."

"Do you know her son, Zach?"

Jake shook his head. "No. The last time I saw Zelda, she didn't have any kids."

Lieutenant Mallory sank back in his chair and nodded at Anne.

"You said you decided to go back to Oklahoma. Is that what you did?" she asked.

"I headed in that direction."

"What's in Oklahoma?"

"I have a little spread there."

"A ranch?"

"Yes, ma'am."

"Where is it?"

"Just outside Tulsa."

Anne eyed Jake curiously. The fact that he had a ranch came as a surprise. Kendall had given her the impression that Jake was a drifter.

"So you were going back to your ranch?" she asked.

Jake nodded.

"When did you leave?"

"Friday night."

Lieutenant Mallory interrupted. "Mrs. Cummings, a sheriff's deputy spotted Mr. Dawson at a gas station near Lucketts, Virginia, this morning."

Anne frowned at Jake. "How is it that you were still in Virginia if you left for Oklahoma on Friday night?"

"I heard the Amber Alert on the radio, and I was headed back here to offer my help." Jake looked at Doug and then back at Anne. "I'm sorry about Samantha. I know it must be real hard for the both of you right now."

Anne exchanged glances with Doug. "Samantha wasn't on the bus, Jake. She was sick yesterday morning, so we kept her home from the field trip."

Jake exhaled. "Thank God."

Anne slid her hand into Doug's. "You said you heard the Amber Alert and you headed back here to offer your help. Why didn't you call someone?"

"I don't know. It just seemed like the best thing to do was to hightail it back here."

Anne studied him for a moment. "All right. Where were you when you heard the Amber Alert on the radio?"

Jake thought for a minute. "I was just east of Terre Haute."

"Indiana?"

"Yes, ma'am."

"What road were you on?"

"I-Seventy."

"Had you driven straight through since you left here on Friday night?"

Jake shook his head. "No. I drove as far as Columbus, Ohio, and then stopped to get some rest."

"Did you go to a motel?"

"Yes, ma'am."

Anne's eyes darted to the lieutenant and back. "Which motel?"

"It was a Holiday Inn Express."

"Do you have a receipt from the hotel?"

"Yes, ma'am. Back in my truck."

"Where's your truck?"

Jake looked at Lieutenant Mallory. "I don't know. Last time I saw it was at the gas station in Lucketts."

Lieutenant Mallory snapped his fingers at the deputy. "Have someone check the truck for the receipt."

"So you stopped in Columbus," Anne went on. "What time was that?"

Jake thought for a moment. "Probably around four o'clock."

"In the morning?"

"Yes, ma'am."

"How long were you there?"

"I sacked out for a few hours and was on the road again by noon."

"And you headed west towards Oklahoma?"

He nodded.

"Tell me how you heard the Amber Alert."

"I was just driving along on the highway, listening to the radio, and I heard it."

"Were you surprised to hear it?"

"Of course."

"What did you think?"

Jake's eyes flickered. "Honestly?"

Anne nodded.

"My first thought was that I was a fool to have left Kendall."

Anne gave him a small smile. "Did you think your father might have been involved?"

"No, not at that time. But when I got back closer to Virginia, I heard the news on the radio about my father's escape from jail. Then I feared the worst."

Lieutenant Mallory cleared his throat and Jake looked in his direction. "Mr. Dawson, do you own a Buck hunting knife?"

Jake hesitated. "Yes, sir."

"Do you have it with you?"

He shook his head slowly. "No, sir. I lent it to someone, and I left town without getting it back from him."

The lieutenant's eyebrows shot up. "Whom did you lend it to?"

"Todd."

"Todd Rucker?"

Jake nodded.

"How do you know him?"

"Just from working at Fox Run."

"Tell me what you know about him."

"Todd's a nice kid, but he seems pretty troubled. It sounds like he didn't have a very stable upbringing. His mom raised him and he says he never knew his dad. He has a bit of a chip on his shoulder about folks with money."

The lieutenant pulled a photograph out of a file on the coffee table and showed it to Jake. "Do you recognize this boy?"

Jake studied it for a moment. "That sure looks like Todd. His hair's just a little shorter, that's all."

Lieutenant Mallory flipped the photo over and handed it to Anne. The name *Zach McGraw* was written on the back in black marker.

*T*he hands on the mantel clock ticked slowly towards three o'clock without a phone call from McGraw.

"Jake, you're going to wear a path in the floor if you keep pacing like that," Anne said.

"Sorry, ma'am." Jake dropped onto a chair. "This waiting around doing nothing is driving me nuts."

The motel receipt had been recovered from Jake's truck, clearing him of suspicion in the kidnapping, but Anne could tell by the way Jake regarded Lieutenant Mallory that he harbored some resentment over his arrest.

Doug, seated beside Anne on the couch, glanced again at his watch. "We should have heard from McGraw by now."

As if on cue, the phone rang and the deputy monitoring the phone raised his hand. "It's him."

Doug sprang from the couch and grabbed the phone. "Hello."

He nodded, the receiver clenched against his ear. "Yes, I have the money."

Anne noticed Jake hunch forward in the easy chair, his fists clenched, his elbows resting on his knees. She shifted her gaze back to Doug.

"All right. But first I want to speak with Kendall," Doug said. "I need some proof that the girls are okay."

McGraw must have refused, because Doug shook his head. "That's no good, McGraw. I have the money and I'll agree to your demands, but first I need to know that everyone's all right."

Anne could tell from the way Doug clenched his jaw that McGraw was giving him a hard time. "No, don't hang up," he said quickly. "I'm not trying to run the show. I just need proof." He frowned. "All right. Let's start with that."

Doug covered the mouthpiece with his hand. "McGraw won't let me talk to Kendall, but he's going to let me talk to one of the kids."

He stared grimly at Anne as he waited for someone to come on the line; then his expression softened. "Hi, this is Samantha's daddy. Who is this?" He listened for a moment. "Hi, Emma. Are you okay?"

Doug gave Anne a slight nod and a thumbs-up. "Is Miss Waters with you?" His eyes narrowed as he listened. "How did Miss Waters hurt her arm?"

Doug frowned. "Emma?" He swore under his breath and held the phone away from his mouth. "McGraw took the phone away from her."

He quickly moved the phone back to his mouth. "Yeah, McGraw, I'm still here."

Doug looked at his watch. "All right. Six o'clock. Yes, that's my cell phone number." He took a deep breath. "I promise I'll be alone. What's my guarantee that you'll release Kendall and the children when I deliver the money?"

He listened for a moment. "McGraw? Are you still there? Damn it!" He looked at Lieutenant Mallory. "I lost him."

The deputy monitoring the call said, "He hung up, but it looks like we got a cell tower location."

"Good, try to pin it down." Lieutenant Mallory looked at Doug. "Fill us in."

Doug set the cordless phone on the coffee table. "Emma said she's hungry and wants to come home but that all the kids are okay."

"What did she say about Kendall?" Jake asked.

Doug frowned. "She said something about Kendall having hurt her arm, but McGraw grabbed the phone away from her before I could ask her anything else."

"What does he want from you?" Lieutenant Mallory asked.

Doug gave Anne a quick glance. "McGraw wants me to take the money to the ransom drop, but he didn't answer when I asked for a guarantee that he was going to release the kids. I'm supposed to leave here in my car at six o'clock and head west on Route Fifty. He said I'm to keep driving until he calls me on my cell and tells me what to do next."

Anne swallowed hard and looked away. She knew Doug would do as

McGraw said. There was no way he'd risk having McGraw harm the kids.

"We've got the location, Lieutenant," the deputy called.

The lieutenant hurried towards the deputy, and Doug walked over and held his hand out to help Anne up from the couch. Jake followed them to the desk.

"The cell tower the call came from is located right about here." The deputy placed his finger on the Loudoun County map that was spread out on the desk.

Doug squinted and leaned closer. "That's between Philomont and Hamilton. There's nothing in that area but farms and a few new subdivisions."

Lieutenant Mallory nodded. "I expected them to be much farther away by now. They're hiding right under our noses."

"They could be holed up in a house under construction in one of the subdivisions," Doug suggested. "It's the weekend, so it would be a safe bet that no one would be there before tomorrow morning."

"But they've got to be someplace where they could hide the bus without having anyone see it," Anne said.

Right." The lieutenant frowned. "Which means they're probably not at a construction site, because the bus would stick out like a sore thumb. Unless there is a structure large enough to drive the bus inside."

Doug stared at the map. "They have to be someplace that's unoccupied, or they would have been spotted by now. I'm trying to think of a farm in this area that's not currently in operation, or one with an abandoned storage barn or some other remote building they could hide the bus in."

Lieutenant Mallory turned to one of the deputies. "Send some manpower out door-to-door along Harmony Church Road, asking if anyone's spotted the bus."

"Yes, sir."

Jake took a step towards the map. "Did you say Harmony Church Road?"

The lieutenant nodded. "Why?"

"Can I take a look at the map?"

Doug shifted to the side to make room for Jake.

"Where's the cell tower?"

"Right here." Lieutenant Mallory stabbed at the map with his finger.

Jake ran his finger along the map from the area of the cell tower to

Harmony Church Road. "I think I know where they are."

"Where?"

"A farm named High Meadow."

Doug frowned. "That's George and Dana Worthington's farm."

"Right. I went there with Kendall to pick up a horse for Mrs. Southwell. There's a big storage garage for their horse van, which the bus would easily fit in."

"I know the building you're talking about," Doug said. "But it's right behind the stable. There's no way that they could be hiding there without being seen."

Jake nodded. "I think there is. The Worthingtons' farm manger, Albert, told us that the Worthingtons take all the horses and the staff and leave town for the month of August. The only person left on the property is Albert."

Lieutenant Mallory stared thoughtfully at Jake. "How would McGraw know about the garage, or the fact that the farm was going to be vacated in August?"

"Because Todd was with us. Or I guess I should say Zach. And now that I think about it, Kendall took us to see the Worthingtons' horse van, and Zach seemed much more interested in the layout of the garage than he did in the van."

Doug looked up from the map. "Wait a minute. I seem to recall hearing George say something about building a pigeon roost at High Meadow. Did you see one when you were there?"

Jake nodded. "There's a pigeon roost under the eaves at the back of the garage."

The lieutenant looked at Doug. "Why do you ask?"

"When McGraw was on the phone yesterday, he shot the gun off and said something about being pissed off at the pigeons."

Lieutenant Mallory slapped his palm against the desk. "Okay, I think we've got them." He turned to Jake. "How well do you remember the layout of the farm and the garage?"

"Pretty well."

He picked a legal pad off Doug's desk and handed it to Jake. "Draw me a map of the farm, and as detailed a diagram of the garage as you can."

"What's our next step?" Doug asked.

"I'll call Chester Rawls to assemble his FBI team, and we'll bring in a SERT team and surround the garage."

"What's a SERT team? Is that like a SWAT team?" Anne asked.

The lieutenant nodded. "Same thing. It stands for Sheriff's Emergency Response Team."

She frowned. "But you can't predict how McGraw will react to that. He might go crazy and hurt the kids. Shouldn't you comply with his ransom demand first and see if he releases the children, before sending in the troops?"

"We can't take that risk. Realistically, the odds are against us that McGraw will release the children as promised. If we can zero in on their location and surround them, we'll have the upper hand."

"What do you want me to do?" Doug asked.

"I'd like you and Mr. Dawson with me at the scene."

Anne looked at her watch. "It's three-forty-five now. What time do you want to leave?"

"As soon as possible," the lieutenant said.

"In that case, let me go say good-bye to Samantha and tell Ben we're going to be leaving."

"Anne."

She stopped and looked at Doug. "What?"

He glanced at Lieutenant Mallory.

"Mrs. Cummings, I don't want any nonessential people there. Just Mr. Cummings and Mr. Dawson."

"I'm a *nonessential person*, Lieutenant? It's all right for my husband to risk his life, being bait for Zeb McGraw, but I can't be there?"

Doug sighed. "Anne, please."

The lieutenant gave her a reassuring nod. "Mrs. Cummings, I promise you, I won't risk your husband's safety. I need him as the go-between with McGraw, but I will not put him in harm's way."

Anne folded her arms across her chest. "You obviously don't know my husband very well, Lieutenant. He'll do whatever it takes to save those kids."

"And I'll do whatever it takes to keep him safe."

She looked away and Doug put his arms around her. "It's going to be all right," he whispered, pressing his lips to her forehead. "I promise."

C H A P T E R

78

*K*endall stiffened at the sound of the door unlocking. "Follow my lead," she whispered, squeezing Albert's hand.

The door swung open and Zelda stepped into sight. "Come on, camp counselor."

"Before I go anywhere, can I take the girls to the bathroom?" Kendall asked, rising stiffly to her feet.

Zelda snorted "There you go again. Acting like this is some kind of hotel."

Kendall forced a smile. "We've been using a bucket for the kids to pee in, but now a couple of them have to do number two, and it's really going to smell in here if they use the bucket."

Zelda shrugged. "Let it smell."

Kendall stepped closer to her. "You're a mother, Zelda. You understand how it is with kids. What can it hurt to let them use the toilet?"

"There ain't no toilet here anyway."

"What about going outside?" Kendall struggled to keep her tone casual. "They can go in the bushes."

Zelda regarded her for a moment.

"Hey, Zelda, what's taking so long?" McGraw shouted.

"Come on." Zelda slammed the door closed and grabbed Kendall by the arm, pulling her towards the bus.

Kendall heard the sound of raised voices, and as she climbed the steps into the bus, she saw McGraw jump out of his seat.

"I ain't going to argue with you about which vehicle to take," McGraw shouted. "The truck stays where it is. We're going to meet Cummings with the van."

Earl shrugged and stayed seated. "Suit yourself. But I still think it's a stupid shit idea to take a van that the cops are probably already looking for."

"So change the damn plates. We need the van so Cummings will think the kids are in the back," McGraw said.

"Go ahead." Earl made a sweeping gesture towards the bus door.

McGraw spun around and pushed Kendall towards the door. "Come on, move it."

Zelda stepped out of the way, and McGraw shoved Kendall ahead of him down the bus steps.

"Open the garage door," McGraw ordered Zelda as he stormed past her.

"Ain't you going to wait for Earl?" Zelda asked.

McGraw didn't respond, and when he was off the bus, he muttered under his breath, "Fuck Earl."

Zelda followed them off the bus. "Zeb!"

"Open the door," he yelled, not turning to look at her.

"Fine." She stormed to the front of the garage and slapped her hand at the green button that opened the door.

The mammoth door had begun to creak towards the ceiling, when Earl screamed, "*Shut the door!* Someone's out there."

Kendall strained to look out the door, but McGraw drew his gun and ran towards the other side of the van, dragging her in front of him like a shield. Through the van window, Kendall could see Zelda repeatedly hitting the red button, even though the door was already sliding back towards the floor.

Earl, with his gun aimed towards the door, sprinted across the garage and took refuge with them behind the van.

"What'd you see out there?" McGraw asked.

"I saw someone move in the bushes on the other side of the driveway."

McGraw narrowed his eyes. "You sure it wasn't the wind blowing the bushes around?"

"It wasn't the wind," Earl replied, glaring at him. "I saw someone out there."

The door clunked to a stop as it met the concrete floor and Zelda removed her hand from the button and ran to join them.

She grabbed Earl's arm. "What's going on?"

"Earl thinks he saw somebody outside," McGraw said.

Earl scowled. "I did see someone outside. I ain't imagining things."

"Who was it?" Zelda asked.

"I don't know; I didn't get that good a look." His eyes darted towards the door, and he gestured with his gun towards the narrow line of windows that ran about chest high across the garage door. "I'm going to take a look."

As Earl approached the door, Kendall crossed her fingers and silently prayed. *Please let it be the police out there.*

Earl poked his head into the opening and stood watchfully for a moment. "Shit!"

"Who is it?" McGraw demanded, tightening his grip on Kendall.

"It's the cops. I see two of them in the bushes across the drive."

McGraw pulled the cell phone out of his pocket. "Cummings is going to pay for this."

*D*oug flipped open his cell phone. "Hello?"

"You just gave those kids a fucking *death sentence,* Cummings."

The muscles in Doug's chest tightened and he felt sweat bead on his forehead. He drew a deep breath. "Calm down, McGraw."

McGraw's voice bellowed over the phone, and Doug eased the cell away from his ear. "Don't you tell me to calm down. I told you no cops, and now we're surrounded by them."

Doug stared at the garage through the trees. "I have the money, McGraw. Let's just make the trade. You release the kids, and you'll get the money."

McGraw let out a laugh. "What good does the money do me if I go back to the slammer?"

Doug said nothing.

"Where the fuck are you, anyway?" McGraw asked. "You out there with them?"

"Yes."

It sounded as if McGraw had covered the phone, and Doug could hear muffled voices; then McGraw's voice hissed in his ear. "I'll give you one last chance to save the kids."

Doug swallowed. "Okay."

"You bring the money in here. Then I'll let the kids go."

Doug closed his eyes and felt a knot form in the pit of his stomach. "You know I won't do that, McGraw. You can have the money, but first I need to know the girls are safe."

"Cut the crap, Cummings. You already talked to one of the kids."

"That was hours ago. I—"

Two rapid-fire gunshots rang from the building and a woman's scream drifted over the cell phone.

"Oh Jesus." Doug gripped the phone tighter. "McGraw!"

"See what happens when you piss me off, Cummings?" McGraw spoke in a low voice, his tone chillingly emotionless.

Doug's breath escaped in a rush. "I'm not trying to piss you off."

"Too late, Cummings. You already did."

The sound of another shot exploded in Doug's ear.

"All right, McGraw, stop!" Doug took a step towards the building. "I'll do whatever you want. *Just stop shooting.*"

"I'll stop shooting when I have the money."

"It's in my car," Doug said, lying. "By the front gate. I need time to get it."

"You got five minutes."

"All right. Just don't hurt Kendall or the kids."

Silence.

"McGraw?" Doug saw from the display on his cell phone that the call was no longer connected, and he let his hand drop to his side as he turned to Lieutenant Mallory.

"What'd he say?" the lieutenant demanded.

"I told McGraw the money was in my car. He said I have five minutes to get it or he'll start shooting again."

"What does he want you to do with the money?"

"He said if I bring it inside, he'll let the kids go."

The lieutenant stared grimly at him. "Yeah, I'll just bet he will."

Neither spoke for a moment.

Doug drew in a deep breath. "I've got to give it a try."

Lieutenant Mallory shook his head. "That's out of the question."

Jake stood off to the side. "Let me take the money in," he said, stepping towards them.

"This isn't just about the money," Doug said. "McGraw's looking for revenge. That's why he wants me in there."

Jake nodded. "Yeah, I know. But I'll bet his vendetta against you pales in comparison to the way he feels about me."

Lieutenant Mallory held his hand up. "Let's dispense with this kind of talk right here. If anyone goes in there, it will be one of my men. Someone trained for this."

"McGraw will never go for that," Doug said.

The lieutenant's face creased into a frown. "Then we need to try to buy some time to get the SERT team in place and see if we can penetrate the building. I've got a chopper on the way. Do you think you can stall him?"

"No." Doug gave a quick shake of his head. "McGraw sounds like he's ready to blow. If I'm not ready with the money when he calls back, God only knows what he'll do. We can't take that risk."

Lieutenant Mallory's jaw muscles worked as he studied Doug. "Then you've got to talk him into a compromise, because going inside that building would be suicide."

Doug's cell phone rang and his heart skipped a beat as he pressed the button to answer the call.

80

$\mathcal{M}$cGraw flexed his muscle and the crook of his arm tightened against Kendall's throat.

She clawed at his arm. "I can't breathe."

"Shut up."

Kendall's head was pinned tight against McGraw's chest, straining her neck muscles, and a piercing pain shot through her left shoulder and down her arm.

"You try anything funny and I'll choke you. I'll break your neck. Understand?"

Black dots danced before Kendall's eyes. "Yes," she whispered.

He eased up slightly and held the barrel of his gun to her temple. "And if you don't make the kids do what I say, I'll blow their fucking brains out."

Kendall gulped a deep breath. "I know."

McGraw's arm and chest muscles twitched against Kendall's back, and she could almost feel the energy that surged through him.

"Zelda, get the kids and the old man over here," McGraw shouted.

"Get going," Zelda said, and Kendall heard a chorus of sneakers padding towards them across the cement floor.

"Stop right there." McGraw spun Kendall around to face the girls.

"Tell them what to do," McGraw said.

Kendall's throat closed up as she looked at the tear-streaked faces, and she drew a shaky breath. "You get to go home to your mommies and daddies in just a minute. You just have to do exactly what I tell you when we go outside, okay?"

The girls nodded. "Okay." Kendall attempted a smile. "Now, when we go outside, you have to stay right in front of me. Samantha's daddy is going to be there, and he'll take us home. But you can't run up to him when you see him. You have to wait for me to tell you what to do. Just like when you're in a horse show and you don't walk or trot until the judge tells you to. Everybody understand?"

The girls nodded again and McGraw turned Kendall back towards the garage door. "Tell them to get in front of you." He clamped his arm tighter around her neck.

"Come on, girls," Kendall said, reaching her arm out. "Get right here in front of me."

McGraw whipped his head towards Zelda. "Make sure you keep the old man in the doorway, where they can see him."

"I know, Zeb," Zelda snapped. "I ain't stupid."

Earl stood by the door control, a rifle cradled in his arm and a handgun tucked into his belt. "I still think this is a dumb-ass idea. You never should have agreed to open the door."

McGraw jerked the gun away from Kendall's head and pointed it at Earl. "You shut the fuck up. I know what I'm doing. I'll get the money, and Cummings, too." He snorted. "With the cops watching."

Earl's lips twitched, but he just shrugged. "Okay. It's your ass out there." He pressed the green button, and as the expansive door began to crank methodically upwards, a blast of late-day August heat wrapped around Kendall.

"Get moving, real slow like," McGraw said in her ear.

"Come on, girls." Kendall touched those closest to her on their shoulders. "Start walking forward, really slowly."

They stepped through the vast opening, and Kendall was blinded for an instant by the setting sun. She squinted and looked away from the blaze of pinks and oranges that layered the western sky.

"Tell them to stop," McGraw ordered.

"Stop walking," Kendall said.

The girls stopped and Kendall's eyes focused on the other side of the drive. Doug stood directly in front of them, not more than forty feet away, and farther behind him, partially hidden by the bushes, was a cluster of men. Sheriff's deputies, most of them. A couple of men in dark clothing. *And Jake.*

Kendall's heart leapt as she focused on Jake. He was staring directly at her, and he gave her a grim nod when she made eye contact with him, then folded his arms across his chest.

"Where's the money?" McGraw yelled.

Doug gestured towards two large duffel bags on the ground by his feet. "It's right here."

"Throw it over here."

Doug shook his head. "That's not our deal, McGraw. I'll hand you the money when you release Kendall and the girls."

"I ain't taking another step." McGraw jerked the gun against Kendall's temple as he spoke. "You want the kids, you come get them."

Doug hesitated, then stooped and picked up the bags.

Kendall held her breath and looked at Jake, who raised his hand and ran his fingers feverishly through his hair.

"Get moving," McGraw said.

Doug took a step towards them. "All right, McGraw. Now release Kendall."

"What do you think I am, *a fucking idiot*? I'll let go of her when I have the money in my hand."

Doug's eyes met Kendall's and she saw a flicker of a question. *Should he give McGraw the money?* Oh God. She didn't know. Should he?

McGraw put his mouth to her ear. "*Tell him.*" His breath was moist and a foul smell drifted to her nostrils.

Kendall shuddered and lowered her eyes. "Give him the money."

McGraw let out a laugh. "See, she's smarter than you, Cummings. She knows I ain't letting no one go until I get the money."

"All right," Doug said. "When the kids are safely behind me, I'll hand you the money."

"Give me the money now," McGraw screamed, jamming the gun against Kendall's head.

"Okay, McGraw. Calm down." Doug held the duffel bags out towards McGraw.

"Throw them over here!"

Doug stepped forward and tossed the bags towards McGraw.

McGraw kept the gun to Kendall's head, but he released his hold on her neck and bent down, as if reaching towards one of the bags. In a swift motion, he flung his arm around her chest, whipped the gun away from her head, and fired.

Kendall heard herself scream, "*Oh my God.*" The blast knocked Doug to the ground, and as McGraw pinned her to his chest and dragged her back towards the garage, she shouted, "Run, girls."

"Grab the money and shut the door," McGraw yelled as he pulled her inside the building.

The door began to clank and grind overhead and Earl leapt forward and grabbed the duffel bags.

Kendall caught a glimpse of Doug lying motionless on the ground as half a dozen deputies encircled the girls. Her eyes darted to the bushes, searching for Jake, but she couldn't spot him. Then, just as the barrier lowered to cut off her view of the outside, she caught sight of Jake dashing towards the side of the building.

eb leaned against the dashboard of the bus, watching Zelda and Earl paw through the money.

Zelda grinned as she held a handful of bills to her face and took a deep whiff. "I can't believe we actually pulled it off."

"We ain't home free yet," Zeb said.

"Aw, come on, Zeb. Why are you always such a spoilsport? You're out of jail, ain't you? And we're sitting here looking at a million bucks, ain't we?"

Zeb's lip curled in disgust. His sister had a one-track mind. Money. No, make that a two-track mind. *Money and sex.* He snorted. "Ain't you overlooking the fact that we still need to get out of here?"

Zelda's smile faded. "We'll figure out a way. We still got hostages."

He looked at the camp counselor and the old man, huddled together like scared rabbits in the backseat of the bus. Yeah, they still had hostages. That was their ticket out of there. But first, he needed to know that Cummings was dead.

Zeb dropped into the driver's seat and pushed the power button on the radio, twirling the dial past snippets of songs until he found a news broadcast. A man's voice predicted a fifty percent chance of overnight thunderstorms, some possibly severe in nature. Then a woman's voice announced breaking news in the disappearance of seven young girls who had gone missing while on a camp field trip. Zeb turned up the volume.

"For the latest developments in this tense situation, let's go to Glenn Garrison, who is on location in Leesburg, Virginia. Glenn."

A man's voice played over the radio. "I'm at the Loudoun County Sheriff's Office in Leesburg, Virginia, where we have just learned that the seven girls have been released from captivity and are on their way here to be reunited with their parents."

"That's great news, Glenn. What can you tell us about their release?" the woman said.

"The details are sketchy at this time. We haven't yet learned whether the kidnappers released the girls voluntarily or if they escaped. But we do know that the girls' camp counselor is still being held hostage, as is at least one adult male."

"Do you know where they are being held?" the woman asked.

"The authorities are referring to it as an undisclosed location in rural Loudoun County."

"Thank you, Glenn," the woman said. "We'll come back to you as the story develops."

Zeb raised his arms and flipped both middle fingers towards the radio. "Why don't you tell us what happened to Cummings, you dickhead?"

"Calm down, Zeb," Zelda said. "If Cummings is dead, they can't say nothing until they notify his next of kin."

Next of kin. Zeb spun in his seat and stared at her for a moment. "You know what, sis? You're fucking brilliant."

Zelda frowned. "What do you mean?"

Before Zeb could respond, Earl shushed her and put his hand to his ear. "*Listen.* What's that?"

Zeb punched the power button on the radio and heard a loud flapping of wings from the pigeons, followed by the sound of an engine whirring overhead.

"They've got a chopper up there!" Earl said.

Zelda frowned. "Maybe they called one of them medevac helicopters to take Cummings to the hospital."

Zeb snatched the cell off the dash and pressed the speed-dial button for Cummings's cell phone.

"Hello."

It wasn't Cummings. It was a man's voice he didn't recognize. "Who the fuck is this?" Zeb demanded.

"Lieutenant Mallory."

Zeb could barely hear him above the sound of the chopper, and he held the cell phone to his ear so hard, his hand began to cramp. "Call off the chopper, Mallory, or I'll kill the counselor and the old man."

Mallory hesitated. "It's not our chopper. It's the media."

"I don't give a shit if it's the media! You got two minutes to get them the hell out of here."

Almost immediately, the sound of the engines began to fade away, and Zeb let out a breath and relaxed his grip on the cell. "You're a fast learner, mister lieutenant. Now, you listen to this. I don't want no choppers for Cummings. And no ambulance, neither."

"All right."

"And don't think you can fuck with me on that just because I'm inside. I know what's going on out there."

"You have my word. I won't call an ambulance. There's no need for one."

"Why not?" Zeb demanded. "Because Cummings is dead?"

There was a long pause. "No."

Zeb jumped up from the seat. "No? What do you mean, no? I saw Cummings go down with my own two eyes."

"He was wearing body armor. The blast knocked him out. That's all. The body armor protected him." Mallory spoke slowly, like he was talking to a child.

"Don't talk to me like I'm an idiot," Zeb shouted. "I know what the fuck body armor does."

He pulled the cell phone away from his ear and stared at it for a minute. *Goddamned cop.* Fucking talking down to him. He'd show him who the smart one was. Zeb pushed the power button and slammed the cell onto the dash.

"What's the matter?" Zelda asked.

Zeb threw his hands up and kicked the seat. "Cummings was wearing a fucking bulletproof vest."

Earl snickered and Zelda glared at him. "But we all saw Cummings go down," she said.

"The cop said it just knocked him out."

No one spoke for a moment. Then Zelda said, "Maybe the cop was lying."

Zeb glared at her. "Why would he do that?"

She raised a shoulder. "I don't know. Maybe he wants you to think Cummings is alive so they have something to bargain with."

He gave her a long stare and slowly nodded his head. "You know, sis, you might be right. If Cummings is still alive, why didn't he answer his phone?"

"Maybe he was still knocked out," Earl said.

Zeb shook his head. "No. The cop said Cummings didn't need an ambulance. If he was knocked out, he'd need an ambulance, wouldn't he?"

Earl shrugged. "Yeah, it sounds like the cop is lying about something."

"So, what are you going to do?" Zelda asked.

"I don't know. I ain't figured it out yet." Zeb turned towards the bus door. "I need to take a piss."

CHAPTER

82

$\mathcal{A}$nne snatched the phone off the hook in the middle of the second ring. "Hello?"

"Hi."

It was Doug. Anne closed her eyes and breathed a sigh of relief. "I can barely hear you. Are you all right? Tell me what's happening."

"The kids are out and they're okay."

"Oh, thank God. What about Kendall?"

"McGraw's still got her and the Worthingtons' farm manager. But the sheriff's deputies and the FBI have the building surrounded."

"Have you seen her? Do you know if she's all right?"

"Yeah, I saw her for a couple of minutes. She seemed okay." He paused and Anne heard him draw a deep breath. "Look, I better go. I just wanted to call and let you know that the kids are okay."

Anne frowned. Doug sounded beat. "Doug, are you all right? You sound out of breath."

"I'm fine."

She fingered the handset for a moment. "When are you coming home?"

Doug hesitated. "I'm not sure. I'd like to stay until they get Kendall out of there."

"Promise you'll stay safe?"

There was a brief pause. "I promise."

Anne's heart quickened. "Doug, what's going on?"

"Nothing." His voice sounded strained.

She took a deep breath. Something was bothering him, but he obviously wasn't going to tell her what it was. "Okay. Will you call me as soon as you know something?"

"I will, but don't wait up, Anne. We might be here all night. I'm in no danger, and you and Sam are safe now that they have McGraw surrounded, so try to get some rest."

"Okay."

As Anne hung up, she heard footsteps in the hallway, and a moment later Ben walked into the kitchen, carrying Samantha in one arm and Rascal in the other. Charly was right behind them.

"What are you doing up, sweetie?" Anne asked, holding her arms out to Samantha.

"She's not feeling well," Ben said.

Anne put her hand on Samantha's forehead. "I think your fever's back again. Let me get you some Tylenol."

She set Samantha on the table and picked up the bottle of Tylenol from the counter. The bottle felt light in her hand, and she frowned as she held it up and peered at the red liquid inside.

"What's the matter, Mommy?"

"I'm not sure there's enough Tylenol left for a full dose," Anne said, taking a medicine spoon out of the drawer. She poured the cherry liquid into the spoon, but it only reached halfway to the dosage line. "Nope."

"Don't we have another bottle?" Samantha asked.

Anne frowned. "No. It's on my shopping list, but I haven't made it to Safeway."

"I can run into town and buy some for you, if you'd like me to," Charly said.

Anne turned to her. "Charly, that would be wonderful. I hate to have Samantha go through the night without it."

"No problem." Charly looked at her watch. "Is there a store in Middleburg open this late on a Sunday night?"

"Safeway's open until ten."

Ben shook his head. "I don't like that idea, Charly. Patrick wants two of us in the house at all times."

"No, it's okay," Charly replied. "I just spoke with Patrick. Everything's under control. They have the subject surrounded." She glanced at Samantha. "I'll tell you about it in a minute."

Ben turned to Anne.

She nodded. "Doug just called and told me the same thing."

"What's Charly talking about?" Samantha asked.

Anne lifted her from the table. "I'll explain it to you later. Right now, I want to get you back up to bed."

Ben looked down at the squirming puppy. "Mrs. Cummings, I should probably take Rascal out for a walk."

"That's fine. I'll be upstairs with Samantha."

CHAPTER

83

*K*endall strained to hear what Zelda and Earl were saying about an escape plan.

"Maybe we should split up from Zeb," Earl said. "We've got two hostages. We'll take Kendall and let Zeb have the old man."

"Why would we want to do that?" Zelda asked.

"We have a better chance of getting away. The cops are more interested in Zeb. We can make a break with the money and hook up with Zeb later."

Zelda frowned. "I don't like that idea. I think we should stick together."

"We will be together. But first we need to get out of here with the money." Earl stroked her arm. "I'm just trying to look out for you, babe."

Zelda's face flushed with pleasure and Kendall held back a smirk. *Come on, Zelda. Can't you see what he's doing? Earl wants to sacrifice Zeb, just like he did Zach.*

"Where will we meet up?" Zelda asked.

"We'll figure out a place."

Zelda hesitated. "What about Zach?"

"We'll hook up with Zach, too." Earl lowered his mouth and nuzzled Zelda's neck, and Kendall could tell from Zelda's dreamy expression that Earl had won her over.

Damn it. Kendall felt like she'd made a connection with Zelda, and had held a glimmer of hope that Zelda might convince Earl and McGraw to release Albert and her, now that they had the money. But that was wishful thinking. It was obvious that Zelda would go along with whatever plan Earl cooked up.

Kendall turned away and looked out the rear window to see if McGraw

312

was on his way back. A movement on the stairway near the pigeon roost caught her eye, and she looked more closely. A man was crouched near the top landing!

The man raised himself slightly to peer through the slats of the railing and Kendall caught her breath. *It was Jake.*

Kendall shifted in the seat and rested her back against the side window so she could see out the back without making it obvious to Zelda and Earl. Her heart raced as she watched Jake cautiously make his way down the stairs. *Where was McGraw?* Her eyes darted around the garage. Jake was only a few steps from the bottom when she saw McGraw step out from behind some garbage cans in the opposite corner of the garage and zip up his fly.

She gripped the seat, praying that Jake would see McGraw before McGraw spotted him. McGraw started back towards the bus, then stopped and headed towards the back door, with Jake directly in his line of sight. Kendall exhaled slowly as she saw Jake freeze and flatten himself against the wall.

McGraw stopped at the door and peered through the narrow glass pane, looking first towards the left, in Jake's direction, and then shifting his gaze to the right. Something seemed to catch McGraw's attention, because he pressed his face to the glass and turned his body towards the right, facing away from Jake.

Jake quickly descended the last few stairs and grabbed a shovel that hung next to a broom and a rake on the wall. Staying close to the wall, Jake stole swiftly towards McGraw, gripping the shovel with both hands and holding it high over his shoulder. He was almost within striking distance when McGraw suddenly pulled back from the window and turned towards Jake.

Jake leapt towards him and McGraw opened his mouth, but before any sound came out, the shovel hit McGraw's head with a thud and he slumped to the floor. Jake stooped down and snatched McGraw's gun.

"What was that?" Earl asked, raising his head from Zelda's neck.

"It's probably Zeb, getting after them pigeons again," Zelda said.

"Where the hell is he, anyway? It don't take that long to take a leak." Earl pried Zelda's arms from around his neck and rose from the seat.

Zelda reached out and grabbed his hand. "Aw, come on, Earl. Don't go getting into it with Zeb again. Just let him be. He'll come back in a minute."

Kendall saw a shadowy movement outside the window, behind Zelda and Earl, and she held her breath as she saw Jake creep towards the front of the bus. *She had to do something to keep them from seeing him.*

"Zelda! Earl lied to you about Zach," she blurted out.

Both Earl and Zelda turned towards her.

Kendall's mouth felt like it was lined with cotton and she ran her tongue over her lips. "Zach was hurt in the accident, Zelda. Badly hurt. Earl planned it so the ambulance would hit Zach's side of the car. He used Zach as a distraction so he could get away."

Earl's face contorted in a look of rage. "You fucking bitch." He moved down the aisle in two swift steps and backhanded Kendall across the face.

The blow was so hard, Kendall's teeth snapped together, and a stinging pain shot along her right cheekbone. Her eyes filled with tears, but she stared defiantly into Earl's gaze. "It's true, Zelda. Earl sacrificed your son."

Earl lunged at her, and as his hands closed around her neck, Kendall saw Jake step aboard the bus.

*J*ake rushed down the aisle and wrapped his left arm around Earl's neck. He held McGraw's gun to Earl's head as he dragged him away from Kendall. "Get your hands off her, you son of a bitch."

"What the hell?" Earl clawed at Jake's arm.

Jake jammed the gun against Earl's temple. "Raise your hands in the air!"

Earl slowly raised both arms and Jake gave Zelda a quick glance. "Don't make a move, Zelda, or I'll shoot him."

She gawked at him. "How do you know my name?"

Jake didn't respond. Keeping the gun to Earl's head, he slid his other hand along Earl's waist until he felt the handle of a gun. As he lifted the gun from Earl's belt, his eyes settled on Kendall.

"Are you all right, Kendall?"

She nodded, placing a hand to her throat as she drew a raspy breath. Jake saw an angry purple welt on her right cheek, and he shoved the gun hard against Earl's head, fighting back an overwhelming urge to pull the trigger. He grabbed Earl's shoulder and gave him a rough yank. "Turn around."

Earl turned slowly towards him, and Jake lowered the gun to Earl's chest.

"Well, well, if it ain't Jake the cowboy," Earl sneered.

Out of the corner of his eye, Jake saw Zelda lean forward and peer at him. "*Jake?*" She raised her hand to her mouth. "Oh my God. Jake Dawson?"

Jake ignored Zelda, but he noticed Kendall stiffen and saw confusion cloud her eyes. Or was it distrust? He gave her a reassuring nod, but her frown only deepened. He took a deep breath. *Come on, Kendall. Have some faith in me.*

He held Earl's gun out towards Albert. "Here. Keep this on Zelda."

Albert stood, but as he stepped forward and reached for the gun, Earl kicked backwards, knocking Albert off balance. The gun clanked into the aisle and Zelda dove for it, aiming it at Jake as she scrambled to her feet. "You get that gun off Earl right now, Jake!"

"Not a chance." Jake's eyes slid towards Zelda. "Go on. Make a move with that gun, Zelda. Give me an excuse to shoot him."

He could see Zelda's hands shaking, but she didn't lower the gun. Her eyes darted wildly between Earl and him. "Just let Earl go, Jake. We don't want to kill nobody else; we just want to take the money and start a new life somewhere."

Jake's finger tightened on the trigger. "I'm going to count to three, Zelda. And if you haven't dropped that gun by then, I'm going to shoot him."

Earl shook his head. "He's bluffing, babe. Don't drop the gun."

Jake gave him a cold stare. "One."

Sweat rolled down Earl's forehead. "What are you waiting for, Zelda? Shoot the bastard. Zeb will be here any minute to back you up."

Kendall leaned forward. "Don't let Earl talk you into murder, Zelda. He's not worth it. Remember what he did to Zach."

Zelda glanced towards Kendall, but she held the gun steady.

Jake shoved the revolver against Earl's chest. "Two."

"Jake, *please*." Zelda's voice trembled. "Just let us go."

He gave her a thin smile as he looked her in the eye. "Three."

"No!" Zelda lowered the gun.

CHAPTER

85

Doug paced restlessly in the darkening woods across from the garage. With each passing minute, his sense of dread deepened. When McGraw had turned off the cell phone, cutting off their only line of communication, Doug had known the hope of getting Kendall and Albert out alive was greatly diminished. *If only he'd insisted on keeping the phone with him when he'd gone to the ambulance to let the rescue squad check him over. If he'd been the one to answer the call, rather than Lieutenant Mallory, he might have been able to make some kind of deal with McGraw.*

He glanced at the lieutenant, who stood a few yards in front of him, talking on his radio. The sound of a low voice crackling over the radio was almost drowned out by the noisy chorus of cricket frogs, katydids, and whip-poorwills that signified the approach of nightfall. A screech owl sang from somewhere across the woods, its cry like the sound of a woman calling for help.

Doug looked around the group again for Jake, but he was nowhere to be seen. The lieutenant told him he hadn't seen Jake since the chaos following the shooting. Doug wondered if Jake had gone off on his own, trying to find a way to rescue Kendall.

The shrill ring of his cell made him jump and his fingers trembled as he fumbled to flip it open. "Hello?"

"It's Kendall, Doug." Her voice was shaky. "Send the police inside. Hurry."

"Hold on." He turned to Lieutenant Mallory, who had rushed to his side at the sound of the ring. "It's Kendall. She says to send your men in."

The lieutenant took off at a jog, talking into his radio, and Doug lifted the phone back to his mouth. "Are you all right?"

"Yes, we're okay. Jake's in here. He has a gun on them." Her voice broke.

"Okay, Kendall. Just hold tight. The police are on the way in."

He flipped the phone shut and caught up with the lieutenant, who motioned him back as the SERT team broke through the door to the garage and stormed into the building. Lieutenant Mallory kept his radio to his ear and after a few moments nodded at Doug and waved him forward. Once inside, Doug stood for an instant, allowing his eyes to adjust to the bright lights.

The SERT team had the bus surrounded and Doug could see several armed men aboard the bus. Doug waited with Lieutenant Mallory as a tall, angry-looking man in handcuffs was led down the stairs.

"That's Earl Davis," the lieutenant said to Doug, stepping towards the man.

A blond woman with a tear-streaked face followed him out, flanked by two deputies. Zelda, Doug presumed. He felt himself tense, expecting McGraw to be next.

But it wasn't McGraw.

Kendall appeared in the doorway, with Jake right behind her. As they stepped off the bus, Jake spoke close to her ear and wrapped his arms protectively around her.

Doug walked forward to meet them and Kendall gave him a weak smile. "Hi."

He returned her smile. "You okay?"

She nodded and rested her head against Jake's shoulder. "What about you? I saw you go down when McGraw fired."

Doug instinctively raised a hand to the painful spot in the center of his chest. "I'm okay."

He looked at the bus again and saw an elderly man with a swollen eye descend the stairs, followed by a couple of deputies. No one else. Doug craned his neck to see through the bus window. The bus appeared to be empty.

He frowned and turned to Jake. "Where's McGraw?"

Jake gave a backward glance towards the other side of the garage. "Over there."

"Is he . . ."

"Alive?" Jake finished the question for him. "I'm not sure. I didn't hang around to find out. I hit him over the head with a shovel and he went down like a rock."

Doug heard the sound of running footsteps. A deputy rounded the corner of the bus and rushed towards them, his weapon drawn.

"*Lieutenant*," the deputy said, breathlessly. "McGraw's gone."

86

*Z*eb flattened himself against the exterior wall of the garage and watched from the shadows as a cop passed by on the gravel drive. The cop stopped beneath the floodlight at the end of the building and lit a cigarette, then turned and headed back towards Zeb.

Full darkness had settled over the farm, giving Zeb the advantage. All he had to do was make it across the drive to the drainage pipe he had spotted when he'd scouted out the farm. Then he'd be home free. From there, he could crawl through the pipe to the back pasture, where the truck was waiting. *He just had to make it to the pipe.*

The cop neared the edge of the arc from the floodlight and reached for the flashlight attached to his belt. He turned it on, aiming the beam in front of him.

Zeb sucked in a short breath. *Shit.* The cop was no more than thirty feet away. Any minute now, the beam from the flashlight would reach where he was standing. Zeb dropped swiftly to his knees and quietly stretched out on his belly along the edge of the building, thankful that Zelda had bought him the black Goth shirt. As the cop neared, Zeb closed his eyes and turned his face into the grass.

Gravel crunched under the cop's feet. *Crunch. Crunch.* His steps were slow. Steady. *Crunch. Crunch.* Louder then. Almost even with him. *Crunch. Crunch.* The cop was right next to him. Zeb held his breath. Waiting for the cop to pass. *The footsteps stopped.*

Zeb tensed, ready to roll over and kick as soon as he sensed the cop was close enough. He waited. The cop didn't move. Zeb was forced to take a shallow breath, and the smell of cigarette smoke hung in the air. He heard the cop exhale loudly, and then the footsteps sounded again. Slowly. *Crunch.* *Crunch.* Going away from him.

Zeb waited and counted ten steps before he lifted his head. The cop was halfway to the end of the building. He rolled onto his side and crept slowly to his knees. As soon as the cop rounded the corner, he'd make a run for it. *Just a few more steps.*

The cop's radio squawked, and the cop stopped and put his hand on the radio. A man's voice laced with static screeched over the radio. Zeb couldn't make out what the voice was saying, but the cop drew his gun from the holster. He looked in Zeb's direction, then turned back and jogged around the corner of the garage.

Zeb leapt to his feet and sprinted across the drive, diving into the bushes just as he heard the pounding of footsteps on the gravel drive. He crawled towards the opening to the drainpipe and crept inside, cringing as his shoes made a clanging noise against the corrugated metal. He inched his way along the pipe at first, careful not to make too much noise. But once he figured he was far enough from the entrance for anyone to hear him, he raised himself on all fours and scrambled towards the truck.

*H*nne closed her eyes and bent her head forward, stretching her neck from side to side to let the jet of warm water massage her tight muscles. After a moment, she reached for the shampoo bottle, squeezed the thick liquid onto her hair, and worked it into a lather. The soothing aroma of green tea and ginger drifted over her, and she inhaled deeply, feeling some of her tension ease.

It's almost over, she told herself. *Doug's okay, and the children are safe.* They only had to rescue Kendall and Albert and the nightmare would be over.

She ducked her head under the stream of water and rinsed her hair until it squeaked, then reached for the tube of conditioner and squeezed until a small glob squirted into her hand. Anne slowly massaged the conditioner into her scalp and ran her fingers through her hair to untangle the snarls.

The phone rang just as she finished rinsing off. *Maybe that was Doug with news about Kendall.* She quickly turned off the water and reached out for a towel. As she wrapped the towel around her, she stepped from the shower and grabbed the cordless handset she'd left on the vanity.

"Hello?" She grabbed another towel and pressed it to her hair.

"I was beginning to get worried. What took you so long to answer?" Doug asked.

"I was in the shower. Is there any news about Kendall?"

"She's safe."

"Thank God." Anne felt a flood of relief. "What about McGraw and the rest of them?"

Doug paused. "McGraw got away."

Anne sank onto the vanity bench. "What happened?"

"Jake knocked McGraw out, but by the time the authorities got inside, McGraw had regained consciousness and escaped."

"How far could he have gone? Didn't they have the place surrounded?"

"Yes, but there's a large drainage pipe right next to the garage. They think McGraw crawled through that and escaped through the back of the farm."

"Have they gone door-to-door and alerted the neighboring farm owners?" Anne asked.

"They're doing that now. But they doubt McGraw's still in the area. Apparently, he had a truck parked in the field at the back of the farm, and they think he escaped in that."

Anne clasped the towel tighter to her chest. "Where are you right now?"

"I'm getting in the car to drive home."

"Don't stop anywhere, Doug. Come right home. Please."

"I'm not stopping."

"Okay, please hurry. I love you."

"I love you, too. I'll see you in a few minutes."

Anne placed the phone on the vanity and could hear the Disney Channel blaring from their bedroom, where Samantha was watching TV in bed. She dressed quickly and ran a brush through her hair, then headed to her bedroom closet for a pair of shoes.

When Anne entered the bedroom, she walked to the television set and lowered the volume. "Honey, that's way too loud."

She turned towards Samantha, but the bed was empty.

Anne looked around the room. "Samantha?"

No answer.

"Samantha?" She flung open the bedroom door and crossed the hallway to Samantha's room.

Samantha wasn't there.

"Samantha! Where are you?" she shouted, descending the stairs and racing to the kitchen.

Silence.

The kitchen was deserted and Anne ran back down the hall towards the front of the house. She rushed past Doug's study to the parlor, where Samantha loved to play with her toy horses in the cabinet under the front window. The room was dark, and Anne's hand trembled as she fumbled along the wall for the light switch.

Light flooded the empty room.

"Oh God, Samantha, where are you?" she whispered, backing into the hall and turning towards Doug's study.

"Mommy?"

Anne whirled around and saw Samantha standing in the darkened doorway of the living room, her stuffed pony in her arms. Anne stumbled across the hall and dropped to her knees, throwing her arms around Samantha.

"What are you doing down here?"

"I couldn't find Blackie and then I remembered that I left him down here this afternoon when Ben was reading me a book. So I came down to get him." Samantha struggled to get out of Anne's arms. "Ow, Mommy, you're hurting me."

Anne released her grasp on Samantha and sat back on her heels. "Samantha, you scared me because I didn't know where you were. *Don't ever do that to Mommy again.* When I'm in the shower and I ask you to stay someplace, I don't want you to go somewhere else. Okay?"

"Okay," Samantha said quietly. "Please don't be mad at me."

"I'm not mad at you, honey. I was just scared." Anne struggled to her feet and held out her hand. "Come on. Let's take Blackie upstairs."

Samantha slid her hand into Anne's. As they reached the staircase, Anne heard the distant sound of Rascal barking. She stopped and frowned. "I wonder what Rascal's barking at?"

Samantha shrugged. "I don't know, Mommy. Ben said that when he walked Rascal earlier today, all Rascal wanted to do was chase squirrels and wasn't very interested in pooping."

Anne smiled tensely. "He must be barking at a squirrel, then."

They climbed the stairs and Anne tucked Samantha back in bed. "Daddy's on his way home, so you can stay in our bed until he gets here."

Samantha yawned. "Okay, Mommy. I sure hope Charly gets home soon with the Tylenol. My head hurts."

The alarm panel on the bedroom wall emitted a series of three beeps, indicating a door opening, followed by another series of beeps as the door closed.

Anne kissed Samantha on the forehead. "That's probably Charly now. I'll be right back."

CHAPTER

88

The kitchen was empty when Anne entered. She stopped in her tracks and looked around. "Charly?"

No response.

The door to the hall creaked behind her and she whirled around as Zeb McGraw stepped from behind the door. He raised his hand and flashed a butcher knife in front of her face, tilting it so the ceiling light reflected off the gleaming blade. "Hey there, lawyer bitch. Look what I have for you."

A voice in her head told her to turn and flee towards the back door, but she didn't move. *She couldn't leave him in the house with Samantha.*

McGraw's hand flew out and snatched Anne by the hair, slamming her against his chest. He held the tip of the knife to her throat and stuck his face inches from hers.

"Tell me what those beeps from the alarm were when I came in."

His breath was sour and Anne gagged reflexively. She swallowed and forced herself to breathe through her mouth. "When the door opens, I need to punch in a code that tells the alarm company everything's all right," she said, lying. "Otherwise, they send someone out."

"Do it, then." McGraw released his grasp on her hair and shoved her towards the back door, waving the knife towards the alarm.

Anne's eyes darted towards the window as she stumbled to the alarm panel. *Where were Ben and Charly?* She groped for the cover over the keypad, but it slipped out of her shaking hand. She fumbled for it again, and raised it, then hesitated. *Should she press the panic button?*

McGraw jabbed the knife against the small of her back. "Don't go doing anything dumb like pushing a button to call the cops. I ain't stupid. I'm watching you."

Anne's fingers hovered over the keys, trembling.

"Do it!" McGraw shouted.

It was too risky to try the panic button. Her fingers felt numb, and she clumsily entered the code to disable the door chime. If an exterior door opened, at least McGraw wouldn't be alerted.

McGraw yanked her by her hair. "Now get away from there."

She backed away.

"Where's pretty little Samantha?"

Anne hesitated. "She's at a friend's house."

"Don't you fucking lie to me." McGraw thrust the knife at her throat. "I saw her through the window five minutes ago. Now where is she?"

Tears welled in Anne's eyes. "She's upstairs. In her room," she whispered.

"Get going. We're going to go upstairs and get her." McGraw shoved her towards the door to the hall.

McGraw's thrust caught Anne off balance and she grabbed the edge of the table to keep from falling. *She had to stall him.* She could not let him get near Samantha.

"Doug will be here any minute," she said, turning to face him. "And there are guards outside. If you harm Samantha or me, you'll never get out of here alive."

McGraw snorted. "Your asshole husband ain't coming to rescue you."

"Yes, he is. I just spoke with him. Doug's on his way home."

Rage flared in McGraw's eyes. "Are you lying to me?"

"No."

"When did you talk to him?"

"Just a few minutes ago."

"How long?" he demanded.

Anne didn't answer and McGraw poked the knife at her chest. "Answer me when I talk to you!"

"Ten minutes. Maybe fifteen."

His face twisted into a scowl. "So, the fucking cop wasn't lying."

Out of the corner of her eye, Anne saw a shadowy movement through the window in the back door. She resisted looking in that direction, and took a step backwards, drawing McGraw away from the door.

The corner of McGraw's lip lifted into a sneer and he twirled the knife. "Where do you think you're going?"

Anne saw the door ease open and she took another backward step.

"Hey! Answer me. Where do you think you're going?"

"Nowhere." She took another step and felt the edge of the counter against her back.

"Nowhere is right." McGraw let out a laugh. "You ain't dumb enough to think you can run away from me."

Anne saw Doug slip through the doorway, but she kept her eyes on McGraw.

"No. I don't think I can run away." A cramping pain gripped her abdomen and she lowered her hands to her belly.

McGraw cocked his head and his eyes focused on her hands. "Maybe I'll let Cummings see his baby before he dies."

He ran his tongue over his bottom lip as he brought the knife down and touched the tip to her belly. "I might just slice you open and let Cummings catch a peek, so he knows what he's going to be missing."

Anne's pulse pounded as she saw Doug lift his hunt whip off the hook by the door and move towards them. *Oh God. Doug was going to come after McGraw armed only with his hunt whip. Couldn't he see that McGraw had the butcher knife? She had to keep McGraw talking. She couldn't let him turn around.*

"Why didn't you just keep running after you escaped from jail?" she asked, panting as the cramp intensified, taking her breath away. "You could be a thousand miles away from here by now."

He snorted. "I had unfinished business to take care of."

Doug stole swiftly towards them, holding the hunt whip near the thong and raising it over his head like an ax.

Anne forced herself to stay focused on McGraw. "Unfinished business?" Her voice quivered. "What was that?"

McGraw brought the knife back to her throat. "You know the fucking answer to that—"

Doug grunted and heaved the whip downward, driving the sharp point of the horn handle deep into McGraw's skull.

89

The door to Anne's hospital room was partially closed. Kendall shifted the package in her arm and knocked lightly.

"Come in."

Anne reclined in the bed, with the baby in her arms.

Kendall smiled. "Hi. I just passed Doug and Samantha on their way to the cafeteria. Doug's certainly looking every bit the proud papa." She placed the baby gift on the bed and leaned down to give Anne a hug.

"Doug didn't try to give you a cigar, did he?" Anne asked.

"No, thank goodness." Kendall laughed and perched gingerly on the edge of the bed. "How are you feeling?"

Anne's face was pale and drawn and she had dark circles under her eyes, but her face lit up with a smile. "Like I'm the luckiest woman in the world," she said, kissing the dark curls on top of the baby's head.

Kendall reached out and tentatively touched the baby's tiny hand with her finger. "He's beautiful. Have you decided on a name yet?"

"No. We're still tossing a few around." A smile tugged at her lips. "Samantha wants to call him Ben."

"After her bodyguard?"

Anne nodded. "Ben is Samantha's hero now. She found out that he spent half an hour chasing Rascal around the farm when the puppy took off after the rabbit."

Kendall's mouth dropped open. "But that's how McGraw was able to get into the house."

"Well, Samantha doesn't know that," Anne replied. "Besides, Ben wasn't really neglecting his duties. As far as he knew, McGraw was at High Meadow, surrounded by police. He didn't think we were in danger any longer."

Kendall nodded. "That's true."

Anne was quiet for a moment, then gestured towards the Hermès scarf Kendall had tied around her neck as a sling. "How are you doing?"

"It's a clean break, and I don't need surgery, thank God." Kendall fingered the soft cast on her arm. "Dr. Gannon is waiting for the swelling to go down before he sets it."

Anne studied her for a moment. "I wasn't just asking about your arm, Kendall. You've been through a lot. How are *you* doing?"

"I'm okay. The girls and I had a session with a therapist this morning at Margaret's, and I think it was helpful for all of us. We'll continue to meet regularly with him." She hesitated. "And I have Jake. He's been my rock."

"So you and Jake are together?"

Kendall felt herself blush. "Yes."

Anne smiled. "Congratulations. Does that mean Jake will be staying in the area?"

"At least for a while. I found out Jake has a ranch in Oklahoma, and he wants me to spend some time there with him. But he says he's not in a hurry to head out there. He's taken an interest in Zach, so that's another reason for him to stay here for now."

Anne frowned. "What do you mean?"

"Zach came out of the coma last night and the doctor wanted a family member to talk to him. Since Zelda's in jail, Jake agreed to see Zach. I think Jake feels a sense of responsibility, since Zach's his cousin."

"How did that go?"

"Jake said it was tough. He said Zach looked so vulnerable hooked up to all those machines." Kendall sighed. "Jake was just about Zach's age when he and his mom ran away from McGraw. I think maybe Jake hopes he can help give Zach the same opportunity that he had to start a new life. But it's hard for Jake to come to terms with Zach's involvement in the kidnapping."

Anne's expression hardened and Kendall regretted mentioning Zeb McGraw. She reached for Anne's hand and squeezed it. "I'm sorry. I shouldn't have brought that up."

Anne shook her head, nestling the baby closer to her chest. "It's okay. It's over now. McGraw was the one behind it all, and he'll never harm anyone again. Doug saw to that."

Kendall nodded and gave her a hug. "I'd better go. Jake's meeting me downstairs. We're having dinner with my parents tonight."

Anne's eyes widened. "When did they arrive in town?"

"This morning. Elizabeth Carey called my father and told him about the kidnapping, and he and my mother flew out on the red-eye. I didn't know anything about it until Elizabeth and Ned brought them to my door."

"What was your reaction?"

"Shock. Joy. Apprehension." She smiled. "But it's been good. It will take some time, but I think my father and I will be able to bury our past differences."

"That's wonderful. I'm so happy for you, Kendall."

"Thanks. I'll see you later. Tell Doug to call me if I can do anything to help."

Kendall had the elevator to herself on the ride down, and the lobby was empty, except for a man standing by the front door. The man's back was to her, but there was something familiar about his stance, and as she neared him, he turned and smiled at her.

"Jake! I didn't recognize you dressed like that." He was wearing a navy blazer and khakis, with a button-down blue oxford-cloth shirt and a blue striped tie. His cowboy boots had been replaced by tassel loafers.

"Did you think I was going to go to dinner with your parents wearing blue jeans and cowboy boots?" Jake leaned down and kissed her and she caught a subtle whiff of coconut.

Kendall smiled and slipped her arm through his. "Mm, you smell good."

Color rose in his cheeks. "It's some fancy shampoo they used at the hair place."

She noticed his neatly trimmed sideburns. "You got a haircut."

"Yeah, I decided to go all out." Jake gave her a lopsided grin. "I want to make a good impression on my future in-laws."